Their paths co… undercover. So… different sides of the law.

A top operative at the CIA, Ryan Quinn is used to hunting down the worst of the worst. Manipulation is the game. And he is exceptionally good at the game. His latest case involves him playing the role of a wealthy and bored businessman as he sneaks into the inner circle of some very dangerous individuals. The tool he uses to get into that circle? The lovely and innocent Simone Sailor.

Fun fact...She's using him. Men always underestimate her...Too bad. That's their mistake.

Simone has a job to do, and nothing will stop her from achieving her goal. She has some trinkets to retrieve for a very upset family. *Retrieval specialist*–yep, that's her. She thinks that title sounds so much better than say...thief. So she lies, she pretends, and she gets the job done. *One hundred percent success rate.* Playing innocent and fooling her marks? Please. That's something that she can do in her sleep. Except this time, she finds herself getting a little too close to one of her targets...the gorgeous and seemingly clueless Ryan. A bored but way too sexy billionaire. A man who has a touch that sends wildfire racing through her veins.

She's distracted during her heist. He distracts her, and she gets caught in the act of *retrieving* property. And death is the punishment. For her...and for Ryan.

Uh, oh. Simone *may* have underestimated the danger in her latest job. When she and Ryan are suddenly kidnapped, she realizes that, for the first time in her life, she could seriously use a hero...and turns out, Ryan is not the useless rich boy that she assumed. He's smart, he's incredibly dangerous... and Ryan just killed someone without blinking in order to save her life. Oh, and also...he's saying that she's under arrest. That he has to keep her close, twenty-four, seven, and that there is now an exceedingly large bounty on her head.

She's his prisoner. His leverage. And...his absolute obsession.

Simone is not innocent. She is not sweet. She is going to drive Ryan absolutely and utterly insane. He crossed lines with her–so many complicated lines. He's killed for her, and he will do whatever it takes to keep her alive. She's now a very important witness, and the CIA intends to leverage her knowledge of the international crime world. But...Ryan just wants her. And the longer they are together, the hotter the desire between them blazes.

But liars aren't supposed to fall in love.

Too bad because Ryan is pretty sure that he's falling hard for gorgeous Simone. Now, if he can just keep her alive, if he can capture all the bad guys who want her dead, and if he can prove to her that, for the first time in her life, she's finally found someone that she can truly trust...then maybe this spy will have a chance at a happy ending with the pretty thief who may have stolen his heart.

Author's note: Simone never thought that she'd need a protector, but now, her life is on the line, and a *good guy* is the only one who can keep her alive. On the run, thrown together in close confines and chaos, with their enemies fast on their trail...she has no choice but to rely on Ryan. As for Ryan, he's about to prove to Simone that this good guy knows all about playing dirty, fighting hard, and burning down the world in order to protect the woman who was meant to be his.

Author's note: Simone never thought that she'd need a protector, but now, her life is on the line, and a good guy is the only one who can keep her alive. On the run, thrown together in close confines and chaos, with their enemies fast on their trail, she has no choice but to rely on Ryan. As for Ryan, he's about to prove to Simone that this good guy knows all about playing dirty, fighting hard, and burning down the world in order to protect the woman who was meant to be his.

When He Lies

A Protector And Defender Romance
Book 7

Cynthia Eden

This book is a work of fiction. Any similarities to real people, places, or events are not intentional and are purely the result of coincidence. The characters, places, and events in this story are fictional.

Published by Hocus Pocus Publishing, Inc.

If you have any problems, comments, or questions about this publication, please contact info@hocuspocuspublishing.com.

For the readers who enjoy any (or all) of the following:

1. *A dress with pockets.*
2. *Really good bread.*
3. *A tattooed hero.*

Happy reading!

Chapter One

Prey or predator?

Early in life, Simone Sailor had realized that most people had two options in this world. They could be the prey. The victims who were hurt. Used. Or they could be the predators. The big, bad sharks swimming through life and taking whatever the hell they wanted as they opened their mouths wide and enjoyed a giant bite.

She'd chosen to be a predator...

Disguised as prey.

It worked for her.

"You look stunning," her date told her. The tall, dark, *billionaire* Ryan Quinn stared at her with his intense brown eyes and truly looked as if he were the one who wanted to take a bite. Too bad for him, she wasn't on the menu. No snacking allowed.

Simone batted her lashes. Fake lashes because she was going all in for this event. Fake lashes. Carefully applied makeup. Bold red lipstick. A red dress to perfectly match her lipstick. A strapless dress, with a tight bodice that shoved up her breasts in the best possible way. The dress hugged her waist, but the layered skirt flared and swirled around her. When she turned, it would spin out in the loveliest way. Yes, she'd spun a few times in her bedroom. A woman had to enjoy herself when she could.

Though, truth be told, it was a little hard to breathe in the damn dress. The bodice was seriously *tight*.

Her red heels and her tiny red bag also matched the dress and the lipstick. Her heels were high and sexy, and her hair had been swept up into a twist that had taken her an hour to achieve. But the end result had been worth the effort and the curses.

Predator. She was the predator. Meanwhile, her handsome date looked at her with lust in his eyes. He stood close to her. His hand lingered near her waist. He escorted her easily through the crowd and into the VIP event and, to the whole world, it looked as if she belonged there.

Ha. Never in a million years would a girl who'd spent too much time bouncing around the foster care system actually belong with these people. She didn't *want* to belong. There were dukes at the party. Maybe an earl or two. She'd caught a whisper that said some Middle Eastern prince might even be in attendance. They were in the English countryside, at a sprawling residence that looked more like a castle than anything else. Champagne flowed heavily. Diamonds dripped from every woman's hand and ears, and oh, but it would be so easy to rob them all blind. The drunker people became, the easier prey they were. Most of them would probably not even realize they'd been robbed until they sobered up the next day. Such tempting pickings. Right in front of her.

"Simone?"

But she had her standards. And some heists were just too easy. She liked a challenge. After all, what was life without a few interesting obstacles? The best things required effort. Also, her date had said she looked stunning, and she needed to focus on him and not the diamonds she would *not* be stealing. Not like she was some petty thief. "Thank you so much for the compliment." Her hand rose to press to his chest. Right over his heart. "You look quite handsome yourself."

He smiled at her, and *her* heart gave a little kick that she couldn't control. Unfortunately, her words were not a lie. Ryan Quinn was ridiculously handsome. The kind of handsome that should have only existed in movies or on TV. The kind that came from good camera angles and the right lighting.

The lighting around them was currently shit, but the man was *gorgeous*. Thick, dark hair. Tousled as if he didn't care. As if he had not spent *forever* getting it to appear just right. Probably because he hadn't. No doubt, he'd just hopped out of the shower and looked awesome.

A faint covering of stubble grazed his powerful jaw. Ryan had the kind of strong jaw that just made a woman want to nibble on it for a bit.

Down, girl. No snacking for her on this case, either.

Ryan's features were not perfect. Truly, they were not. He had a *slightly* crooked nose. The bridge was a bit off. Only instead of that tiny flaw making him less attractive, the little crook somehow made him even more handsome. Which should have been impossible.

He was tall, probably around six-foot-three or four, with broad shoulders that filled out his tux perfectly. He towered over her smaller frame, even though Simone wore her highest heels. He had a Rolex around one wrist, but no other adornments showed on his body. She was pretty sure that Rolex of his was worth an easy hundred grand.

She knew her watches. She'd lifted a few back in the early days. Yes, her past was checkered. *She* was checkered.

"Thanks for agreeing to come to this little event with me tonight," he said, his voice rolling through her. He was an American, like her. His voice was warm. Deep. She couldn't quite pinpoint which area of the US he'd grown up in, though. But, fair enough, it wasn't as if she had a Midwestern accent or a Southern drawl, either. At least, not if she didn't want one. If she wanted, Simone could adopt an accent as easily as she applied her fake lashes. For this particular case, she didn't want an accent.

Simone Sailor had no accent. Simone Sailor was a hard-working administrative assistant who'd been transferred to the London branch of her employer's office three weeks ago. She was diligent. She was quiet. She got the job done.

Planning and logistics.

Oh, yes, those were her specialties.

"I hope your boss didn't mind that I stole you away from him." Ryan had carefully guided them through the dancers in the ballroom and toward the double doors that led to the gallery area. She wanted inside of that gallery. Badly. So she'd eagerly followed him across the ballroom and toward those coveted doors.

But at his words, her head turned, and her gaze swept through the crowd. Most of those glamorous dresses had to cost thousands of dollars, she knew that. Her own gown had been borrowed from a costume shop. And by borrowed, ahem, yeah, she *would* be returning it before the owner realized it was gone.

But beyond those high-end, designer gowns and the glittering jewelry, her gaze did not find Frederick Bradwin, her current employer. A silver-spoon baby who'd recently taken over his father's company—a company that had been in the Bradwin family for generations. Textiles had been the cash cow that kept the family loaded in wealth. But textiles had taken a downturn under the leadership of Frederick's father, and, in order to save the business, Frederick was now branching into electronics. Surveillance equipment. As Frederick had told her on more than one occasion, surveillance was the future. Security was the goal.

"I think your boss might be a bit...enamored by you," Ryan said.

Laughter spilled from her. Simone couldn't help it. She didn't remember the last time someone had used the word "enamored" around her. Her stare cut back to Ryan, and she caught him staring at her. No humor appeared on his face.

"Enamored?" Simone tested the word. "I don't think so."

"Fine." Ryan's stare did not waver. It was a very intense and focused stare. Such a deep, dark brown. "He wants to fuck you."

She sucked in a sharp breath. Her hand jerked away from his chest and fell to her side because, surely, a shocked and appalled reaction was what she should give him? "You are mistaken." *Nah, you're not. The jerk has been putting the moves on me since I came to London.* "We have a very professional relationship." Frederick was getting on her nerves, and his focused attention had made her speed up her game plan. Luckily for her, Ryan Quinn had strolled through the office doors just in time. Almost like a prince charming. While coming for an appointment with Frederick, Ryan had spotted her, and he'd paused immediately by her desk. Ryan had gazed at her as if truly smitten and immediately asked her out, in front of Frederick.

Since she'd declined Frederick's multiple offers for an, um, *outing* under the guise of being his employee and not mixing her personal and professional life, Frederick had been pretty pissed by Ryan's bold action.

He'd been even more furious when she accepted Ryan's offer. Again, right in front of him.

That brought her to this location. The big party. Her boss's family home. And being just steps away from her goal. So close that Simone could taste success. It tasted like the champagne she'd sipped moments before.

"*You* might be professional," Ryan returned, his voice a little on the growly side.

How odd. He wasn't normally growly. This was, in fact, their third date, and he'd been an absolute gentleman on their previous outings. Voice incredibly polite. Not growling. Not with just the faintest hint of savagery lurking beneath his words.

"But the man wants to fuck you," he finished.

Her shoulders rolled back. A deliberate move in the strapless dress. One designed to try and shift his attention. "I am not interested in fucking him, I assure you." She gave a little sniff. "I don't fuck my employers."

"Are you interested in fucking me?"

Her jaw dropped. "I—" *Yes.* Her immediate thought. But...*No.* No, no, she was not. Because she truly did not mix her personal and her professional worlds and getting involved with Ryan, even if it was just for one hot, sweaty, passionate night...

Oh, the temptation.

Maybe she'd had a few fantasies about him. Maybe she'd wondered what he'd look like all naked and sweaty. Maybe she'd woken up one night, with his name on her lips, and her body aching.

But she was in too deep on her current mission. She couldn't afford to screw anything up. Lust was not worth failure. Pleasure was not worth pain.

"Because I would very much like to fuck you, Simone," Ryan told her. Calm. Easy. "Just getting that out there for the record." His head inclined toward her. "But how about we settle for a tour of the gallery right now? I've heard that Frederick has quite the impressive collection."

A squeak escaped her. Not quite faked. He'd thrown her off-balance. A hard thing to do. She'd pegged him as the perfect gentleman. Eminently controllable. Except there was something about his expression...The flare of heat in his eyes warned her that she might have missed a few layers when she'd analyzed him before.

Bored billionaire. He was supposed to be another one of those. She'd carefully checked his background. He'd inherited money, just like Frederick had. Only Ryan invested his money in other people's companies. His investments had allowed Ryan to double, then triple his own wealth. Frederick currently wanted a considerable investment from him. That was why Ryan was there that night. Why he'd been invited to the London office in the first place. Frederick wanted his money.

"Simone?" Ryan quirked a dark eyebrow at her. "Would you like to tour the gallery with me?"

Her gaze darted to the gallery doors. Doors that were blocked by two of the security staff members. "Guests aren't permitted inside the gallery." Her stare slid back to Ryan.

"But you're not just a typical guest, are you?" A playful wink. "You're the boss's trusted administrative assistant. And I bet you know those guards or they know *you*, at least. Surely you can get us a quick glimpse inside? A special privilege?"

Ah, she *surely* hoped that she could get them inside the gallery. Talk about a perfect opportunity. She'd hoped to be able to sneak into the gallery. She'd just thought that she'd have to convince Ryan to enter with her. That she'd have to work really hard to stir the man's interest in exploring with her. Instead, he was taking her straight to her goal. Honestly, Simone could have kissed him right then and there.

Instead, she gave Ryan what she hoped looked like an uncertain smile. "We can try, but I, uh, might have to tell a little white lie." Her speech was halting, deliberately so.

"I don't mind white lies."

Good to know. Especially since she told them all the time.

Nodding, Simone headed directly for the gallery doors. She did, indeed, know the guards. Simone had made a point to know them. So there was no particular surprise from her when Hugo Thomas stepped into her path.

"I'm sorry, but the gallery is off-limits to guests, Simone," Hugo reminded her. He sent her a warm smile. "You know that." The overhead lights hit his dark hair.

The second guard, Alexei Morozov, didn't speak. Just watched them with his narrowed, light green eyes. Alexei made her nervous. There was something about him that seemed dangerous.

A vibe. Instinct. She never ignored her instincts. There was no world where she ever wanted to be alone with Alexei and his big, scarred fists. The Russian barely spoke to anyone, but he was always around at important events. Always close and at the ready for Frederick.

But she knew how to put on a show, so Simone plastered a broad smile on her face. "I'm not a guest. I'm an employee.

You know that, Hugo." A light, tinkling laugh. "Frederick asked me to give his dear friend and business associate a private tour." That would be the white lie part. Frederick would never allow her into his gallery. Employees truly were not permitted. Guests, in general, were not, either but...

Bigwigs who were potentially giving the company billions of dollars? The guards wouldn't know to stop someone like Ryan. Not when she was at his side, vouching for him.

"I wasn't informed of the tour," Hugo replied, appearing uncertain. "I need to check with Frederick." He reached for his tux pocket. Probably going for a phone so he could call or text Frederick.

Such a bad plan. Her heart sank. "Um..."

"Forget it," Ryan announced, sounding bored and arrogant all at once. "I told you, Simone, I have no interest in the gallery."

He had *not* told her those words. Quite the opposite, in fact. *Now who is telling white lies?* She gaped at him.

"My interest in the entire business is waning," Ryan continued with a sardonic twist of his lips. "Perhaps I should reevaluate all my plans."

"No!" Her sharp cry. Her frantic gaze whipped back to Hugo. "We need to tour the gallery. A quick tour." She swallowed. "Now."

Hugo tensed, but he clearly did not want to be the reason why a major deal fell through for his boss. "Five minutes," he said.

Right. Yes. Brilliant. She could do so very much with five minutes.

Hugo unlocked and opened the doors. "Five," he repeated.

"*Not* a good idea," Alexei rumbled, his Russian accent hitting hard on *not*. "They should not enter."

Yes, well, she didn't care about his opinion.

"Don't touch anything," Hugo warned her. "Everything has an alarm trigger."

Great fact to know. "Look but don't touch," she replied. "Understood." Grabbing Ryan's hand, Simone hurried inside the gallery. The doors shut behind them, and the sounds of the party were immediately muted. Her breath whispered out as her gaze darted around the gallery. Finally, she was inside. Now, if she could just find her prize, she could proceed to step two.

"Well, color me impressed. I'd heard the collection was good, but this goes beyond my expectations." Ryan began to amble around the space. "I think I recognize a Monet, and that sketch is a Rembrandt."

She crept away from him because she had zero interest in the fine art that hung on the walls. Though she *was* interested in the two security cameras she'd just spotted. Being careful, she made sure to stay out of their range. "Frederick fancies himself as a collector. He believes that he has an eye for beauty."

Ryan's dark gaze darted toward her. "Does he?"

She could see the jewelry at the back of the gallery. A crown that had once belonged to a French queen. A bracelet that had adorned the wrist of a pharaoh's favored wife. Ryan was also making his way toward the jewelry, and that was unfortunate. Simone needed space to work. Why couldn't he go stare at the Monet or something?

She'd gone through the gallery's logs at the London office. She knew the items that were *supposed* to be there, the ones that had been heavily insured. But she wasn't looking for the listed items. She was looking for the ones that Frederick had deliberately kept off any official record.

"Nice statue," Ryan mused. He'd stopped nearby. "Heavy emotional intensity. Pretty sure that's a Camille Claudel."

Simone's gaze had just landed on her target. A shiver skated over her body. "Sounds to me like you're quite the expert on beautiful things, too."

"I try," he allowed. His voice drifted behind her. Had he stopped to view the Claudel work? Maybe it would keep him busy for a bit.

"Claudel is a favorite of mine," Ryan continued, voice musing. "I had no idea this one was even in a private collection."

"You should try offering to buy it from Frederick," she said. A quick glance over her shoulder showed her that he was about five feet away, seemingly fixated on the small bronze piece. "Make the right offer, and you never know what you'll get." Her fingers were practically itching as she darted her hand into the tiny, red bag that hung over one shoulder. She'd been given the option of checking her bag when she arrived at the estate. How adorable. Why would she check something that would be needed later?

She'd have to be careful with her next movements. But she had not come completely unprepared. She'd suspected that even a slight touch would set off all the alarms in the gallery. It had certainly been helpful of Hugo to confirm that suspicion for her. She'd be fast, she'd be accurate, and if she played this scene just right—

An alarm blasted, the shrill cry ear-piercing. Her bag fell to the floor as a startled scream tore from her. Immediately, she whirled, her gaze searching for Ryan.

The alarm blasted—endlessly. The shriek made her ears

hurt as her heart threatened to jump right out of her chest. This was bad. This was...

Ryan grabbed her. His hands closed around her shoulders, and he hauled her against him. She caught sight of the gallery doors flying open. Hugo and Alexei bounded inside, and they both had their guns drawn.

Bad. So bad. This is—

Ryan's mouth crashed down onto hers.

Chapter Two

He had not intended for this to be their first kiss.

A first kiss should be special. Romantic. It should be about passion. Lust. Need. It shouldn't be used as a distraction technique because he'd screwed up and two guards were running toward him with their guns drawn.

But...it was what it was.

And he believed in making the best of a bad situation so...

Ryan Quinn took a moment to enjoy the kiss. To thoroughly enjoy the softness of Simone's plump lips. To find her seductive taste to be utterly intoxicating. Her mouth was open, and it was just too easy to slip his tongue inside. To feel lust burn sharp and hot within him.

He pulled her tightly against him, curling his body around hers. Both to shield her completely from the jerks with the guns and to have the added bonus of feeling all of her lush curves against him.

Wanting Simone so badly had never been part of his

original plan. He did not mix business and pleasure. And yet...

And *yet*...

She shivered against him.

"Get the hell away from her! And both of you—put your hands up!"

The alarm was still blasting, and Ryan was very much enjoying the feel of Simone in his arms, but duty called. Duty, work, whatever. Slowly, he eased away from her and turned toward the two guards. Guards who struck him as entirely too eager to point a gun at an unarmed man and woman. Ryan made sure to blink a few times, as if utterly confused, then he winced. "Can someone please turn off that horrible noise? Pretty sure it's splitting my ear drums."

"Put your hands up!" Ah. That would be the Russian barking that particular order. Alexei Morozov. A mercenary for hire who had left far too many bodies across Europe.

Ryan lifted his hands. He also made sure to keep his body in front of Simone's. Her getting shot was not on the agenda. "I fear we set off your alarms," he said. Because... obviously that screeching was from one of the many alarms in the gallery.

And, finally, the screeching ended. It ended as Frederick came running through the open gallery doors. Frederick gripped a small remote in his hand, and he pushed a button that sent blessed silence into the cavernous space. "No one else gets in," Frederick barked behind him.

Someone—more guards or mercenaries—immediately shut the doors behind him.

Frederick's face was twisted in rage. His tux coat flapped open as he rushed toward Ryan. "What in the hell is happening?" Frederick thundered.

"We caught them stealing," Alexei announced.

"Oh, for shit's sake." Ryan rolled his eyes. "You caught me making out with a beautiful woman. Potentially stealing her heart? Sure, trying to do that. Definitely stealing a kiss. *Not* stealing Frederick's art."

Frederick came to a shuddering stop about three feet away. "Ryan?" He craned his head to look beyond Ryan's body. "Simone?"

"Um, hello, Frederick," Simone returned after a delicate clearing of her throat.

Frederick's face flushed dark red. "What the fuck are you two even doing in here?"

Hugo glanced at Alexei, then at Ryan, his confusion plain to see. "I...I thought you wanted—"

"I wanted a tour," Ryan cut through the man's words to say. Not like he wanted Hugo to out him in a lie then and there. Things were certainly awkward enough without that admission. Hugo Thomas was a relatively new hire, Ryan's intel had told him that. Former British Special Forces. He might look nice enough with his round face and friendly eyes, but Hugo could be just as dangerous as Alexei. Maybe even more so.

"A *tour?*" Frederick huffed. "No one gets a tour without my express—"

"You caught me. I'm a liar." Ryan nodded.

"Oh, no," Simone whispered behind him. "Do not...oh, *don't...*"

Oh, but yes. Yes, he was. Because he knew how to play this scene to save his ass. And, unfortunately, he was going to have to use the lovely Simone in order to make things work out. Sadly, that was what he'd been doing since the day they'd met. He'd taken one look at her big, blue eyes...at her gorgeous body, at the elegant lines of her face and thought...

I can totally use her to accomplish my mission.

Did that make him an asshole? Absolutely. *Was* he an asshole? *Absolutely.* But he was an asshole who would make sure that Simone didn't get hurt, so, there was that element to perhaps even out his karma. "I didn't really give a damn about the gallery." This declaration was for Frederick and his trigger-happy guards. "I just wanted somewhere I could be alone with Simone. I told the guards I had permission to come in."

"Uh—" Hugo began.

"I got carried away in here," Ryan continued determinedly. "I was kissing Simone, and I must have bumped up against something that set off an alarm. My apologies." So, right then, he really needed for Simone to stay quiet. Because if she said the wrong thing, if she admitted that the alarm had sounded *before* Ryan kissed her, then he'd be screwed.

He held his breath. If she contradicted him, this scene was about to get a whole lot messier. And a whole lot bloodier.

Frederick glared at him.

Ryan had made sure he did not get caught on the two mounted cameras that he'd spotted. It had been easy enough to time his steps so that he'd stay out of sight as the cameras rotated. Child's play, really. Frederick should step up his system in the gallery. The man was supposedly working *in* the surveillance field now, so the lax camera situation in his own home was almost an embarrassment.

A useful embarrassment, but, still, an embarrassment.

"Oh, come on," Ryan muttered as the tension in the gallery stretched. "Like you wouldn't have done the same thing." He really had seen the way the dick looked at Simone. *You want her. Too bad, you aren't having her.*

Whoa. Whoa. Whoa. Ryan had to blink at his own possessive thoughts. Simone was a convenient cover. This was not personal. They were not real. They were not an actual couple.

"It's my fault," Simone confessed, sounding miserable behind him. "I...forgot myself."

Now Ryan whipped around to face her because no way could he quite control his shock.

She batted her long lashes at him. Then she hurriedly scooped up the little bag that she'd dropped.

Ryan's head cocked as he studied her. Interesting...Had she truly *forgotten* herself when they kissed? Was that what she'd meant? He would love to explore that intriguing development with her, but he had men with weapons waiting so Ryan turned back toward them. "Could we lower the guns?"

Jaw tight, Frederick motioned for the men to lower their guns. He also tucked his small remote back into his tux pocket. Inside pocket. Left side.

"Simone, we *will* be talking about this situation," Frederick assured her. "I thought you understood your role at my company. Now I'll have to reevaluate your worth to me."

Oh, was the prick seriously saying that he was going to fire Simone? Nope. Not happening. "I want to buy the Claudel," Ryan announced. He pointed toward the piece. "Name your price." For the stolen artwork. That onc was stolen, and so was the Monet. Frederick had been very, very naughty. "I also think I've made my decision about investing in your company." He reached back and caught Simone's hand. Now that the guns weren't directed at him, he pulled her to his side. He also brought her hand to his mouth so that he could press a tender kiss to her knuckles. "Thanks to Simone," he murmured, "I've seen the value in assisting with your expansion plans."

Her eyes widened as she stared at him.

Ryan lowered her hand but didn't let go. "I need to take Simone home." The sooner he got her out of there, the better. His head angled toward Frederick. "But let's plan for a Monday morning meeting, shall we?" Nah. They wouldn't. By Monday, Frederick would be locked away, and Ryan would be in the wind.

But Frederick was eagerly swallowing his lies. A broad smile curved Frederick's lips. "Excellent! I knew you'd see the benefit of working with me." A pause. "But why rush off? The party is just getting started. In fact, many of my guests are staying the night."

Nope, Ryan would not be staying. Or rather, Simone would not be because he was not about to put her at greater risk.

Before he could reply, Frederick advanced a step toward him and Simone. "It's a long drive back to town. I do believe the weather is taking a bad turn, as well," Frederick mused. "Far better for you both to stay here than to try and make it back to London in a dangerous storm. I have ample guest quarters. There is plenty of room for you both."

"Thanks, but no thanks." Ryan kept his voice polite. "Let's just plan for that Monday meeting." A dip of his head toward Frederick, and then, "Simone, let's go, shall we?" He tugged her forward with his grip on her hand.

Or, he attempted to tug her.

Only to discover that her feet seemed to have become rooted to the spot. "I would *love* to stay the night, Frederick. Thank you." A shudder slid over her shoulders.

"I hate storms. Have ever since I was a child and my family was in a car accident during one of the worst thunderstorms I'd ever seen." Another little shudder wracked her.

Well, damn. He didn't want the woman terrified on the road, but staying in the lion's den wasn't exactly an optimum situation. "I bet we can beat the worst of the weather."

Her head jerked toward him. Her horrified eyes locked on his. "I...would prefer to stay."

"*You* can stay, Simone." Frederick's voice had softened considerably. "Don't you worry at all on that score. I'll get the best room we have available for you."

Oh, sure he would. Probably the room right next door to Frederick's own bedroom. *Nice try, prick.* "I'll stay, too." Brisk. "If the weather is as you predict, then travel might not be wise." As if he'd leave Simone unprotected. She was a pawn in his game, but the woman was not going to be a victim. Not on his watch. He'd never been a fan of collateral damage.

Simone flashed him a warm, gorgeous smile. It was a slow smile, one that started at the edges of her mouth and ended with her blue eyes flashing at him. Her bright blue eyes and her dark, sleek hair were such a contrast. Beautiful.

"Will you be wanting one bedroom..." Frederick asked, body tense, "or two?"

"One," Ryan fired.

"*Two,*" Simone announced at the same time.

Their heads whipped toward each other again.

One of her dark eyebrows quirked. "Two," she repeated with a shake of her head. "Ryan, I hardly know you well enough to share a room with you. Three dates do not equal one bed."

Dammit. His back teeth snapped together. He'd wanted one bedroom to better protect her.

And to increase your odds of fucking her. Don't even lie to yourself.

No, no—he was *not* going to fuck Simone. That had not been on the to-do list. Or, maybe it hadn't been until he'd kissed her, and his whole body had surged with the strongest lust he'd felt in years. Or, maybe, ever.

No. You do not fuck women when you are lying to them. That shit is not cool. You do not do that. You're an asshole, but you are not a total bastard. At least, not yet.

"Two rooms." Frederick tapped his chin. "Done. All guest rooms here are fully stocked with necessary toiletry items and bathrobes."

Wasn't that convenient? Ryan rolled back his shoulders and focused on his host once more. "The rooms will need to be next to each other."

Looking smug, Frederick nodded. "Sure. I can make that happen."

Outside the third-floor window, a flash of lightning blazed across the dark night.

No thunder rumbled. Not yet. Ryan found himself waiting for the sound. Maybe the storm wasn't as close as old Freddie was trying to predict.

Thunder boomed.

Simone sucked in a sharp breath. Her hand rose to linger over her chest.

That sexy, sexy chest...her gorgeous breasts pushed hard against the dipping top of her red gown.

Be a gentleman, asshole. Stop staring at her breasts.

His gaze whipped up. For just a moment, he could have sworn that he caught...amusement...in her stare. But, no, surely not? Because this was not some fun scene. Men had just pointed guns at her.

Simone's long lashes swept down, and when she stared at him again a moment later, her expression showed her fear. Her worry.

He found himself easing ever closer to her. Wanting to protect Simone. She was in way over her head. The woman had no clue that she was swimming with sharks. "It is unacceptable," he bit out as one hand closed around her shoulder, "that your men pulled guns on Simone tonight. She must be terrified."

She wet her lips. "I've never...never had guns aimed at me before."

He glared at Frederick. "And your guards are *still* here, hulking about. Don't you think it's time you sent them away?" He especially didn't like the way Alexei was eyeing Simone.

"Their job isn't complete yet," Frederick told him. "You both have to be searched before you are allowed to leave the gallery."

What the fuck? Now he wasn't just holding Simone's shoulder. He'd launched his body right in front of hers. "Any man who tries to search her will find his fingers immediately broken."

Frederick laughed. "Such a bold claim."

Yeah, shit. It had been bold. He'd meant the words, but he'd dropped character for a moment when the visual of Alexei or Frederick putting hands on Simone flashed through his mind. He was supposed to be the billionaire who did not get *his* hands dirty. He certainly didn't engage in fistfights in the middle of posh, private galleries. So, different tactic time. Though he had, one hundred percent, been truthful about his intent to break fingers. If one of those bastards tried to frisk Simone, fingers *would* be broken. "How is this for a bold claim?" He sent a smile straight at Frederick. "Forget my offer of an investment. If you can't trust me to stroll into your precious gallery and not steal from you, then clearly you cannot trust me in a business deal."

There it was. A break in Frederick's mask. Desperation. The man wanted money. Badly. So badly that he'd been willing to work with some extremely dirty international players. The kind of players that routinely dumped bodies and made their enemies disappear.

Frederick was getting pulled into that dark world, and he needed a lifeline.

Unfortunately for Frederick, Ryan wasn't so much a lifeline as he was...*the man who is going to send you to prison.* So, surprise.

"Fine," Frederick bit out. "No physical searches of your bodies."

Damn straight there would not be any of those.

"I think..." Simone's low voice. "I think I've had more than enough excitement for one night. This is, uh, a lot for me."

Yes, he was sure it was. Having guns shoved at her. Having a prick boss who wanted to *search* her.

"I'd love to just go to an available guest room," Simone continued in her soft, husky tone.

"We'll *both* go to our rooms." Ryan maintained his protective position near her. "The rooms that will be right next to each other."

Nostrils flaring, Frederick nodded. "Of course."

No doubt, Frederick Bradwin hated him, but he needed Ryan's money. When you needed billions of dollars, you tended to be accommodating.

Twining his fingers with Simone's, Ryan headed for the doors. They'd almost reached the doors when...

"Simone!" Frederick had followed them. "Simone, I need to look in your bag."

"The fuck he does," Ryan gritted back.

But Simone had pulled away. "He's my boss," she whispered. She opened her bag and hurried toward Frederick. "Here. Not much is inside." Right when she reached him, she stumbled, one of her ankles seeming to twist in those sexy high heels that she wore. Even as Ryan reached for her, she was colliding with Frederick. Her hands slammed into Frederick's chest. She fumbled, righting herself, and, of course, Frederick tried to grab hold of her, too.

Ryan pulled her back, his brows lowering in concern. "You okay?"

Frederick had snagged her small bag. Of course, the prick was looking into it and not checking on Simone. Typical.

"I...my ankle just twisted. I'm fine, really, I—*Ryan!*"

He scooped her into his arms. The better to get her the hell out of there, fast, and...hell. The better to hide the small item he'd stolen. The item currently inside one of the interior pockets in his tux.

He was such an asshole sometimes.

But an asshole who would protect her.

"This is unnecessary." One of her arms had curled behind his neck. "It was just me being clumsy. I'm fine."

Their eyes were inches apart. That tempting mouth of hers was so close. Sadly, their audience was close, too. Time to ditch the jerks. "Her bag," he demanded imperiously.

Frederick shoved the bag toward them.

Simone snagged it. "This is so embarrassing."

Probably not her best date ever. Jeez. He could do fabulous dates. Really, he could wine, and he could dine. Alas, that was not in the cards for them. At least, not that night, and, sadly, probably never. He'd be completely gone from her life soon.

She clutched the bag with her left hand while her right arm still curled around his neck. Satisfied that she had her belongings and that it was definitely time to go, he strode for the doors.

"You *can't* actually take me out into the crowd this way," she muttered. "We will draw far too much attention."

He didn't particularly care about attention. He did care about getting her away from the goons with guns.

Frederick beat him to the doors. "I'll escort you to the guest rooms," he said. "Personally."

Figured that would be the case.

"What else could I do for my future business partner?" Frederick offered him a smile that didn't reach his eyes.

It was cute that the man actually seemed to believe they would be partners. Not gonna happen. Within the next twenty-four hours, Ryan intended to arrest the creep.

Fun point to know, Ryan wasn't a billionaire looking to invest wads of cash. He wasn't some bored trust fund brat who had money to burn. He was a CIA operative, working undercover. His mission was to find evidence to tie Frederick Bradwin to one of the deadliest criminal masterminds in Europe, and, thanks to his little side quest in the gallery, he now had that evidence tucked in his pocket.

The alarm had sounded when Ryan stole his prize and replaced it with a fake. A fake that would not be discovered until it was much, much too late. But now, he had to protect his pawn. Had to make sure that Simone was sheltered from the coming storm. Not just the rain and the lightning, but the absolute chaos that would come when the CIA swarmed and Frederick's world crashed down around him.

* * *

He carried her to the bed. A big, antique brass bed on the second floor of the house. Based on Ryan's calculations, Simone's guest room was directly beneath the gallery. So was his, considering that he'd be taking the room right next door.

"I take it that this room is acceptable?" Frederick inquired from the doorway.

"Perfect." Simone's soft reply as her arm slid away from Ryan. "Thank you."

"You're next door," Frederick informed Ryan. "Now, if you'll both excuse me, I have other guests waiting."

He had a non-stop party, check. Not like Frederick would want to miss that fun.

"I will look forward to our upcoming talk, Ryan," Frederick added. "I think our partnership will be very beneficial for us both." A moment later, the door clicked closed.

Simone released a slow breath. Ryan realized that he was still looming over the bed. Still looming over her. He should step back. Probably offer an apology for the kiss in the gallery. Probably attempt some serious damage control with her.

But when he started to step back, her hand flew out and curled around his arm. Staring straight into his eyes, and with a small smile playing at her red lips, Simone said, "Ryan Quinn, you are a liar."

Yep, guilty as charged. Straight to his soul. "I can

explain," he began. Because he could. He could spin a bullshit story in an instant.

Except he didn't get a chance to explain because sweet Simone pulled him toward her, and her mouth pressed to his.

So, yeah, screw explanations.

Lust surged through his veins.

Chapter Three

He'd carried her poor, injured self out of the gallery, through the ballroom, down the stairs and then along a very twisting corridor until they'd reached their rooms. The man hadn't even strained with the effort while she'd just hung out all comfortable in his arms and made occasional soft and despondent sighs. She'd worried the sighs might have been too much, but, nope, they seemed to have done the trick.

She was the poor, stressed, incredibly vulnerable personal assistant who'd almost lost her job. She couldn't handle going out into a terrible storm. Men had pointed guns at her.

Seriously, the part with the guns *had* been stressful and not on her bingo card. If given the option, Simone would have preferred to avoid a gun scene. Violence was not her drug of choice. But that was over, and time to move on to bigger and better things.

Ryan Quinn was a stellar kisser. New point to know about him. As her hands fisted around the lapels of his tux coat and her lips parted beneath his wonderfully plundering mouth, Simone took a moment to savor the feel of his wicked tongue and to enjoy the sensual promise of his kiss.

She was a firm believer in pausing to appreciate the small things in life. Though, honestly, the way he was making her feel did not exactly qualify as a *small thing*. Desire whipped through her blood and had her heartbeat racing in her chest even as parts of her seemed to melt for him.

So unexpected.

Almost as unexpected as him being a stone, cold...*liar*. Which brought her back to the present moment and her predicament. Sadly. She stopped tugging those lapels of his, and she eased back. *Maybe* her tongue licked over his slightly cruel but oddly sexy lips one more time because she just couldn't help herself, but then Simone had to accuse, "Liar" yet again because she truly did call them as she saw them.

Besides, it was fun to find a man who shared one of her vices.

She adored a good lie, too.

His eyes opened. His breath had gone ragged, and there was no missing the lust staring back at her. Whatever else he might be fibbing about, the desire he felt for her was real. Excellent. She hadn't wanted him to just be kissing her purely as a distraction in the gallery. And she knew that was what he'd done.

But he blinked those deep, dark eyes of his at her, and a little furrow appeared between his brows. "What have I lied about?"

Her own lips thinned. Was he going to stop being fun? Now? And go back to being boring? That would be a disappointment. "You set off the alarm in the gallery." She shifted around on the bed, bringing her legs to the side and sitting ramrod straight. Simone would have gotten off the bed, but Ryan's rather large form was in her way.

He bent more toward her. His hands pressed to the bedding on either side of her body. "I don't know what you mean."

She rolled her eyes. Did it look as if she had the patience for this? "I didn't set off the alarm." Her stare went right back to him. To that handsome, charming, *lying* face. "That means you did."

No confirmation. No denial.

"You told the guards the alarm went off while we were kissing." She could still taste him. She very much liked his taste. Simone swallowed. "Not true. You only kissed me *after* the alarm sounded. That means you lied to the guards."

"And yet you did not call me on the lie. Not to the guards. Not to your boss." He was so close to her.

Her nostrils flared a tiny bit as she pulled in his sensual scent. Masculine. Woodsy. Sandalwood? Whatever it was, the scent beckoned her forward. She was sure that if she just nestled her nose right there in the crook of his neck, kinda like a kitten, she'd find more of that delicious scent. She even started to lean forward.

Then caught herself. This was not the time for games. She had things to do.

Lightning flashed beyond the window in her room. Seconds later, thunder boomed. She jerked at the sound. Deliberately so. She'd long ago learned to stop flinching at thunder. Reacting now was simply to set the stage.

The story about her parents had been true. There had been a terrible storm. A storm that had wrecked her life. A storm that had sent the car her parents drove careening off the road, into a tree, and then down into a steep ditch. Her parents had died in the crash, while she'd been trapped inside the wreckage and the water had begun to rise and rise as her young voice shouted frantically for help.

"Why didn't you tell them I was lying, Simone?" His hand rose, and he caught a lock of hair that had escaped her twist. So much for the perfect twist. He gently tucked that lock behind her left ear.

"I didn't want to get you in trouble," she returned. A partial truth. "As you said, they had guns. I thought it would be better to keep quiet and get out of there."

His fingers lingered against her cheek. Slightly callused fingertips, something she had not expected from a man with so much money and power. Most men like him had baby soft skin. Buffed nails. Annoyingly arrogant lives.

But those men were controllable. Predictable.

Something about Ryan was just...off. She'd noticed that *off* bit when he surged in front of her, immediately shielding her from the men with the guns in the gallery. Nice of him to be a physical barrier for her. Points for him. But...off. Not what she would have expected.

And when he'd threatened to *break* any fingers that were going to search her, she'd actually believed his words.

In light of those little *off* issues, Simone felt it necessary to perform a test on him. That was why she had kissed him again. To see how he would respond. His lust had been real enough. So now it was time for an interrogation. One done in her own, careful way. "What did you steal?"

Okay, perhaps that had not been so careful. It had been blunt and to the point.

In response, he laughed. Hard. He had a wonderful laugh. Deep, rich, and warm. His eyes crinkled at the edges, and his white teeth flashed with his grin. *Killer.* So very dangerous. A man with a gorgeous grin was someone who could disarm people far too easily.

Her stomach seemed to twist.

"I was hoping to steal your heart," he replied, voice all rumbly and deep and sliding over her skin like the best caress ever. "Guess I didn't succeed, if you think I'm a liar?"

Oh, so dangerous. And so delightful. She caught herself before she smiled at him. "Why did the alarm sound in the gallery?"

"I got too close to the Claudel. I was one hundred percent serious when I said I was a fan of her work." His hand slid under her chin, cupping her jaw. "I've found that I get far too close to the things I covet. A character flaw that I possess."

Was he saying he coveted her? Sure seemed that way. Simone didn't think she'd ever been *coveted* before. "You touched the statue?"

"I might have not-so-accidentally skimmed my fingers over it." His stare did not waver. "But do I look like a thief to you?"

She didn't reply. In her experience, anyone could look like a thief.

More of his warm laughter. "I offered to buy the work from him. If I wanted to steal it, why would I pay for it?"

"You could have just said that you touched the piece. Kissing me was not necessary."

The darkness of his eyes heated. "Believe me, it was one hundred percent necessary."

Her toes almost curled. "You're more than I expected."

His hand slipped away. Almost immediately, Simone missed the warmth of his touch. How strange was that? She never missed anything. Or anyone. She had no attachments. Attachments led to pain. They led to you screaming in a storm for people who were gone while the water rose and rose...

More lightning flashed beyond her window.

Okay, the current bad weather was getting to her. Stirring up painful memories that were better forgotten.

"One," Ryan said as his gaze remained on her. "Two, three..."

The thunder cracked.

She'd been so focused on him that the sudden, sharp sound gave her a real flinch. Simone hadn't realized that he was counting the time between the lightning flash and the thunder's rumble, not just that loud crack.

"I can stay with you tonight," Ryan offered. He straightened to his full height and stared down at her with a considering gaze. "If you're afraid, I can sleep right here."

She rose, too. Her full height which was not nearly as tall and intimidating as his. "If you stay, you'll want to share my bed."

"I already want to share your bed." An instant retort. "But we're on date three, and I distinctly recall you saying that three dates do not equal one bed so..." He glanced at the floor. "I can bunk down on the carpet."

It was her turn to laugh.

His head snapped up at the sound, and his wide eyes locked on her face.

She enjoyed the mirth, letting it roll through her because her real laughs were few and far between. When the humor finally settled, she had to swipe away a tear from her left eye.

"I've amused you?" he asked, crossing his arms over his broad chest.

"Yes. I'm not used to billionaires offering to sleep on the floor for me. Quite the novel experience."

His lips pressed together.

"We both know it's an offer you didn't mean. The lights will go out, and then you'll be kissing me again. But, nice try. Points for the attempt."

"You don't trust me." His brow furrowed.

"It's not just you. I don't trust most people." The true statement just slid out. Something she probably should not have confessed, but it was too late to pull the words back. Whoops. Definitely time to end this date. "I'm tired. It's certainly been an...interesting evening with you."

He stared back at her. All intense. Handsome. Sexy.

And not moving.

Since Ryan was not taking her very obvious hint, she darted around him and made her way to the closed bedroom door. Pasting a bright smile on her face, Simone said, "Thank you. I will not forget this night anytime soon." Now, time for him to exit. She opened the door. Wide.

He slowly stalked toward her. Slow, steady steps. He didn't go through the open doorway. No, that would have been too easy. Of course, he stopped right in front of her. "I certainly hope you don't forget me. I'll be seeing you soon."

She widened her eyes. "You will?"

"Um. Knowing your boss, I'm sure there is some massive breakfast that Frederick will offer his guests. I'll see you then."

Nah. He wouldn't. She'd be long gone by dawn. "I'm not much for breakfast."

"I was your ride here, Simone. I will safely take you home."

"Aren't you the gentleman?"

"Not really." He sucked in a breath. As if his own admission had caught him by surprise.

At least she wasn't the only one sharing things that she shouldn't be saying.

Still, he lingered. Even as she kept the door open. "Is there something else?" Simone finally asked because, honestly, as devilishly handsome as the man was, she had things to do. A gallery that she had to sneak back into. A particular item that she needed to retrieve.

Simone had never liked to think of her work as *stealing*. The items she collected had already been stolen from their rightful owners. Others had taken them. *Stolen them.* They were the thieves, not her. She was simply retrieving the stolen property and taking the material back where it belonged. That was like, doing community service. Goodwill.

"Why did you kiss me?" He waved back toward the bed. "Here?"

"Well, it certainly wasn't to distract guards." An edge of annoyance underscored her words. When a man kissed her, she wanted him to do it because he was desperate to taste her. Was that too much to ask? Simone certainly didn't think so. No one should kiss her as a distraction. Talk about insulting. "I wanted to see if the kiss would be as good when you weren't faking things."

"Faking. Things." A muscle flexed along his ever-so-kissable jaw. "What is it that you think I faked?"

Almost everything. Her inner alarms were just too loud with him.

"My desire for you is quite real," he assured her.

Was it? "You've kept your hands carefully *off* me for each of our previous dates."

"I was being a *gentleman*."

"Yet you just said you were not a gentleman."

They stared at each other.

"Let me get this straight." He seemed to speak through clenched teeth. "You're mad because I was a gentleman?"

"I'm not mad." A few fast blinks. Technically, she did feel annoyed. "I just think that if a man truly wanted a woman, then he would not wait and kiss her only as a distraction when guards were swarming." There. "He would kiss her on one of their dates. Not hold himself back so carefully."

"Gentleman," he gritted again. Those teeth seemed to have clenched harder. "I thought I was being a good guy."

Since when did she want one of those? She'd never found good guys to be particularly useful in any way. They were annoyingly focused on rules. On things like obeying the law. Following orders. Coloring in the lines. They tended to see the world in black and white, and since she primarily operated in a lovely shade of gray, the good guys out there did not understand her.

"Simone?"

She summoned another smile. A big, bright one. "Thank you for being a gentleman. It was very gentlemanly and *good* of you to put yourself between me and the guns."

The furrow between his brows deepened.

Uh, oh. She was really not playing this scene right. Maybe the smile had been too bright. "I'm tired." She let her shoulders slump. A hint of fear entered her voice as she explained, "And I'm still shaken. I've never had guns pointed at me before." She had. So many times. "I-I fear I'll have nightmares tonight." If she slept, she probably would have nightmares, but Simone did not intend to rest anytime soon.

Concern flashed on his face. "I'll be right next door. If you get frightened, call for me. I can come right over." His gaze darted toward the bed. "Or, if you want me to stay, the offer to sleep on the floor still stands," he muttered.

Nope. She needed him out of the room. How in the world was she supposed to slip away in the darkness if she had a sleeping *good guy* between her bed and the door? Her hand rose and curled around his arm. "I appreciate the offer." A little squeeze of her fingers. "Thank you, but I need to be alone now." So she could put her plans in motion.

Staying the night at the estate had not been on her agenda. She'd fully intended to get her prize—um, *retrieve the stolen property*—while the bash had been in full swing. And if Ryan hadn't screwed up and set off the alarm, she would have succeeded. Luckily, Frederick had offered her a second chance with the offered guest room, and she was snatching that chance while she had it.

Plus, she'd snagged the remote for the alarm system from Frederick's pocket back when they'd been in the gallery. Talk about being too tempting to pass up. The remote was currently hidden inside her dress, in one of the gown's amazing hidden pockets. Oh, but Simone did love a dress with pockets. What woman didn't?

If Ryan would just get moving, she could get busy. Very, very quickly.

Lightning flashed again. The lightning and the thunder were coming almost constantly now.

"I understand," Ryan finally said, voice lower. "I will see you again soon."

And yet, the man kept lingering.

Her hand pulled back. It took all of her considerable self-control not to make a shooing motion toward the door for him. Seriously, what was it going to take?

He turned away. Moved for the open door.

Her breath shuddered out.

He looked back at her. "Just so we are clear, I will stand between you and any threat."

That was something new. No man had ever said those words to her before.

"You will be safe with me, always."

Again, brand new words. And they made her feel all funny inside. Not that she needed his protection. She was more than capable of looking out for herself. But it was nice of him to say. So she should respond appropriately.

Ah, what *was* the appropriate way to respond? After swiping her tongue across her lower lip, Simone said, "Thank you. I'll remember that."

His eyebrows shot up.

Dammit. That had probably not been appropriate.

But he had moved forward a bit more, actually stepped into the hallway, and she started swinging that door closed. "Good night." The door was nearly shut—

He spun back around. His hand slapped against the wood of the door before it could close fully.

What is it going to take with this man?

"I wanted to kiss you on our first date. I wanted to kiss you on the second date. I wanted to kiss you tonight, as soon as I picked you up."

Simone sucked in a breath.

"If you want the full truth..."

She would love it, yes.

"I wanted to kiss you the very first moment I saw you. I've wanted to kiss you every moment that we've been together."

His words sounded truthful.

"Now that I have kissed you..." Deeper, a little darker.

"I will never forget how good you taste. I'll never forget the little moan you make when my lips take yours."

She did not remember moaning. Not that she had not potentially done so. Simone just did not recall a moan.

"I want your mouth against mine even more than I did before because, Simone Sailor, you are one hell of a fucking fine kisser." With that, he let go of the door and walked away.

She shut the door. Then her fingers rose to her mouth. Her index finger slid along her upper lip. *You are one hell of a fucking fine kisser, too, Ryan Quinn.* It was really too bad that she would never have the chance to kiss him again. But some things were simply not meant to be.

She and Ryan were one of those not-meant-to-be things.

A thief—no, no, a *retrieval specialist*—did not belong with a billionaire. Not even for one amazing, sweaty, heart-stopping night.

Her hand fell. Her fingers darted into one of the hidden pockets of her gown, and Simone pulled out the remote control for the gallery's alarm. Time to get to work.

* * *

"Mission accomplished, Jez," Ryan said as he paced the guest room to the left of Simone's room. His right hand gripped his phone, holding it against his ear, while the other hand shoved into his inner tux coat pocket and pulled out his prize. An egg. Not just any egg, of course. A Fabergé egg that had been created for the Russian Imperial family all the way back in 1897. Very distinct. Made of gold, diamonds, designed to match the coronation gown of—

"You found the egg?" Jezebel Jenkins demanded. "You

waltzed into the party and just *found* a thirty-million-dollar egg?"

"You seem surprised." He lifted up the egg, squinting at it. "Come on," he chided her. "First, it's me. So why was there ever any doubt that I could do the job? And do it in record time?"

His boss's sigh traveled straight to his ear. Jezebel was in the top echelons at the CIA. The woman normally tolerated zero bullshit, but, since he happened to know for a fact that he was her favorite agent, he was allowed to tease her a bit. Carefully, of course.

"I didn't expect you to succeed quite so quickly," Jez muttered. "I also expected Frederick Bradwin to not be such a colossal dumbass and to make this so very easy for you."

The light hit the egg. "I think you're underestimating the value of my prize," he told her. "We both know some estimates have this baby as high as one hundred million—" Ryan broke off.

Had he just heard a creak from the hallway? He shoved the egg back into his tux pocket.

"You *are* being extremely careful with the egg, aren't you?" Jez asked.

"Absolutely." He cracked open the bedroom door and caught sight of a distinct figure in a glorious red dress darting down the hallway. *What in the hell?*

"That egg is key for our investigation," Jezebel said. "We can prove Frederick's involvement with Konstantin Volkov because that egg is the link between them."

Konstantin Volkov. Otherwise known as the Russian Wolf. A seriously dangerous international criminal who had been at the top of the CIA's apprehension list for years. Finally, *finally,* they were going to take down the bastard.

It wasn't that the egg was just payment for services rendered. Oh, no. The web was far more complicated than that.

"Konstantin intends to access the supply lines that Frederick's family once used for their textile business. Only instead of shipping and sending out textiles, they plan to funnel drugs and weapons around the world. This is going to be a big break for the Agency." There was no missing the satisfaction in Jezebel's voice. "We'll bring Frederick in, question him, make him turn on Konstantin and—uh, Ryan? Ryan, are you listening to me?"

He was still peering down the hallway. Simone had vanished. Where had she gone? And why? *Why did you haul ass out of that room when you just told me that you needed to be alone?* "Something has come up. I have to go."

"Uh, no, no you do not. You have the egg. You need to give me a full update. Is anyone aware of the switch?"

He'd left an exceptionally good forgery in the gallery. A fake that had come courtesy of the CIA. "Of course not. I'm a professional." *Where was Simone going?*

"And you're away from the scene?"

"Uh..." Not quite.

"You have left the property and are returning to London, yes?"

He had to go find Simone. "About that..."

"*What* about that?"

"There's a storm."

"So? I've literally seen you drive through hurricanes."

Guilty. "My date doesn't like storms. So we're staying overnight at the country estate."

Silence. The ominous kind.

"Your...date? You mean the woman you were using as a cover?"

"I don't love the word 'using'," he mumbled back. "Makes me feel less than noble."

"*Ryan.*"

"She's on the move, something I find concerning since she said she wanted to be alone, so I have to go stalk her and find out what the hell is happening."

Jezebel seemed to choke. "Excuse me? You're going to *stalk* your date?"

He was already doing just that. He'd slipped out of the guest room and was heading for the staircase.

"*Where is the egg?*" Jezebel's voice rose in his ear. "The egg is the priority! It is a *stolen* egg."

Yes, and not just because he'd stolen it. The egg should have been in a Russian museum, but Konstantin and his crew had taken it years ago. Getting it back into the proper hands was a major deal for the CIA. "It's safe. Got it close to my heart." Truly, he did.

"*Ryan.*" She did not seem reassured. "I want the egg, and I want what is *inside of it.*"

He was aware.

"You know the contents within the egg are of vital importance to me."

Yes. That was why he'd taken the damn thing. Because the material *inside* the egg was of extreme importance to the CIA. It wasn't simply about acquiring a fancy trinket. He'd already glanced inside the egg to make sure the real prize was in place.

"You need to get the hell away from that location and meet the team at the rendezvous as we agreed! Ryan, Ryan, are you listening to me?"

"I always listen," he assured her. Did he always follow directions? Nope. Because sometimes, you had to do your own thing in this world.

"Forget your date! Get away from that estate before you get burned. Stay mission-focused."

"Mission-focused, check. On it. I am locked and loaded. Goodbye, Jez."

"Ryan!"

He glanced down the staircase. Then up. Which way had Simone gone? Up would lead back to the party, one that was still in full swing. The party—and the big gallery with all of the stolen art. Down would lead to the estate's main exit, a route that Simone would have taken if she was intent on dashing off into the night.

Choices, choices.

Ryan rolled back his shoulders, then he began to descend the staircase.

Chapter Four

She'd disengaged the alarm. The guards at the gallery door had been distracted, thanks to some very flirtatious catering staff members that Simone had paid handsomely. She'd bribed them long before arriving at the event. It paid to plot in advance.

Slipping inside the ballroom once again was a piece of cake, particularly since Hugo and Alexei were no longer the guards on duty. They'd been replaced by fresh guards, and *those* guards were way easier to distract.

One of the new guards was currently making out with a blonde while the second guard had been lured to the side by a redhead. Seriously, Frederick should look into better personnel. These men were practically amateurs.

But the poorly trained guards were good for her. Her win. Frederick's mistake.

She picked the lock in a blink, hiding the action behind the voluminous skirt she wore, and then she slipped in and, because of her handy-dandy stolen remote, she didn't have to worry about shrieking alarms interrupting her work.

And, bonus, she'd made a pitstop on her way to the

gallery. The two video cameras in the gallery had gotten their power cut. Yes, she knew how to avoid the cameras, and she could have done so, but she'd had the time, so why not just be extra safe and guarantee zero footage of her little adventure?

Simone went straight to her prize. The pearl and ruby broach and matching earrings were hardly the most valuable items in the collection. But they were her goals. A certain individual would be very, very grateful to receive them back.

She owed that individual a great deal, and the return of these pieces would go a long way toward paying the debt.

Her gaze darted around the gallery. So many wonderful works of art. So many tempting treasures. Not for her, though. Only the broach and the earrings were for her. Her hand reached for the waiting broach. Time for these jewels to return home.

"You should stop, now." A low, gravelly voice. One with a heavy Russian accent. A voice that came from the right. From behind the long, billowing curtains that lined the floor-to-ceiling windows.

Her head had snapped toward those curtains as soon as she heard the distinct voice.

And, sure enough, Alexei shoved the curtains aside as he stepped forward, with a gun gripped in his hand. For the second time that night, Alexei advanced and pointed a gun right at her.

The man was such a pain in her ass.

Since her head was turned toward him, she angled her body in his direction, too, and when she made that angle, Simone happened to pick up the broach and the earrings. Her hand dipped into one of the many pockets of her dress. The delightful pockets in the gown's skirt were the sole reason she'd been drawn to the costume dress in the first place.

Simone adored a dress with pockets. So useful.

"Hands up!" Alexei barked.

She lifted her hands up. Both hands were now empty, so why not lift them up? "I think there is some sort of mistake here."

"*Your mistake.*" Spittle flew from his mouth as he snarled those words. Then he was lurching forward.

She tensed.

The gun shoved into her face. That was not a very polite response.

Simone shifted one of her hands, and she pressed her index finger to the barrel of the gun as she carefully pointed it a few inches *away* from her face. Not like she wanted a blast between her eyes. Or, anywhere on her, actually. "I can explain."

The gun immediately aimed between her eyes again.

"Get Frederick!" she urged him. "He's the one who told me to come back inside. We were supposed to meet here. Frederick is—"

"The one who told me to wait when he realized his alarm control had been stolen."

Oh, damn. She'd truly thought it would take him longer to notice that bit of theft.

"But Frederick thought Ryan Quinn would be the one to sneak in here like a rat." More spittle. Especially on the *rat* part of the sentence.

Her shoulders stiffened. "I do not like having a gun shoved in my face."

"Then you should not be a *dirty* thief." His accent hit hard on *dirty*.

Her eyes narrowed. "I work for Frederick. I am

following *his* commands. If you don't believe me, get him in here." Anything to buy her some time to figure a way out of this mess.

"The boss doesn't want dead bodies near his guests."

Well, that was something. Especially since she did not want to become a dead body.

"You're coming with me," Alexei ordered.

"What? Like, now?"

He reached out and grabbed her wrist. That grip of his *hurt.* She could feel her bones grinding together as he yanked her in front of him. The jerk actually moved pretty fast. One moment, the gun was in her face, and in the next instant, she was positioned in front of him, with the gun shoved against her back and him looming behind her.

"Yes, like *now!*" Rage poured in his voice.

She did not like the muzzle of the gun cutting into her back. The cold metal of the gun pressed directly to her skin since the back of her gown did a daring plunge. "This is such a mistake."

"A fatal mistake that you have made."

"I'm Frederick's *personal assistant!* I'm assisting him!"

"He was suspicious when we found you and Ryan Quinn in this gallery."

Her heart slammed into her chest. Hard.

"Frederick wanted eyes in here. He sent me to wait. To watch. I caught you. Like a rat in my trap."

Again with the rat comparisons. "So insulting," she muttered.

"You *will* tell the boss everything."

She didn't have much to tell. "I'll tell him what an asshole you are and that he should fire you immediately! Seriously, threatening me with a gun? Twice in one night? I don't know what kind of jobs you usually do..." Though she had plenty of suspicions. He was a scary man, and her instincts were usually not wrong about people. "But this is not how one handles typical business."

"It is how I handle my business." He moved the gun long enough to yank open the gallery doors. Alexei blasted orders at the guards who were still, ah, distracted by the catering staff. Then Alexei was pushing her through the sprawling manor. He repositioned the gun behind her and kept her tucked closely against him, so none of the drunk guests probably even realized that she was a woman fighting for her life.

She considered crying out desperately for help, but...

That gun was pressed against her spine. If she screamed, Alexei could just fire. He was too unpredictable for her. So she had to play along. For now.

He didn't take her out the front of the house. Sent them straight out into the storm that instantly soaked her skin and had her hair falling out of the twist she'd worked on so long. The heavy locks clung to her shoulders. Not some gentle shower of rain, either. The downpour felt more like hard, pounding nails biting into her flesh. He shoved her through the rain and toward an ominous, black van.

"Get into the van!" Alexei shouted at her.

Sure, why not? She'd just jump into the van and go meekly to her death. *Nope.* This was the instant where she was going to make her escape. If she acted as if she was going to climb into the back of the waiting vehicle, Alexei would have to move the gun away from her. She'd get free for a few, precious moments and...

"Simone!"

Her head jerked to the right. Blinking against the rain, she saw a big, dark figure running toward her.

No, no way.

She even shook her head in denial.

"*Simone!*" But that big, hulking figure in a *tux* was not stopping. It was Ryan Quinn, and he was heading straight toward her. "Simone, what in the hell are you doing out here?"

She could use him. He could be a distraction to help her flee. But, if she did that, then Ryan...he could get hurt. Alexei was already swinging the gun toward him, and she feared that he would shoot Ryan at any moment.

I can't use him. I can't risk him. "Ryan, *run!*" Simone screamed.

And he did run—right for her. He hurtled fast toward her even as Alexei pointed his weapon at Ryan.

"No!" Simone threw her body against Alexei.

The gun fired, and the eruption of the bullet sounded just like thunder.

She drove her fist into Alexei's stomach. Then into his face. In response, he threw her against the side of the van.

There was a loud roar. She was pretty sure it came from Ryan.

Alexei was preparing to fire again. She surged from the van and jumped on his back. Her wet dress whipped around them both. He struggled, trying to throw her off, but she just clung tighter.

Ryan ripped the gun out of Alexei's hand. Simone actually thought that might be the moment when they won the fight. Maybe they could even race away to safety.

But then the other guards swarmed. At least ten other guards. And Simone realized that they were not, in fact, getting away.

Five minutes later, she and Ryan had been tied up, gagged, and tossed into the back of the waiting van.

Ten minutes later, she'd managed to yank her hands out

of the ropes and free her ankles. Simone bounded toward the rear of the van. Unfortunately, about *twenty seconds* after her scramble for freedom, Alexei caught her. He shoved a foul-smelling cloth over her face, the world spun, her body went limp, and her mind went absolutely dark.

The blast of thunder—or of a gunshot—was the last sound she heard.

* * *

"OHMYGOD." Simone gagged. "What is that awful smell?" Because she could smell before she could see. It was the terrible stench that had her jolting to wakefulness. Her eyes flew open and—

Ryan sat across from her. As in, about five feet away from her. He was in a wooden chair, with ropes around his body. His chest. His upper arms. His hands appeared tied behind his back. His ankles were tied to the chair legs.

And he had a strip of duct tape over his mouth.

She lunged toward him.

Only to realize that she was tied up, too. Not her chest and upper arms. But her hands were tied behind her back as thick rope bit into her wrists. Her ankles were tied to the chair legs, too, just like Ryan's. Luckily, she didn't have duct tape over her mouth. "You're alive!" Simone frowned, remembering a blast. "I was afraid that Alexei had shot you!"

He said something. Ryan's face twisted with fury as he fired off *something*, but all she heard were grunts and mumbles.

"Huh. Yeah. Not getting that." Her head turned to the right. She sniffed again. "I swear, I smell shit."

More grunts and mumbles. But she didn't look back at

him, not yet. Simone was too busy surveying the area and being glad that they were both still alive. She was super glad to be breathing. Super glad he was breathing, too.

Light trickled through the wooden slats around them. Slats on the walls to the left and right of them. Slats above them. And... "Straw on the ground." Great. She had allergies. She'd probably start sneezing any moment.

In fact—

Something neighed.

Her head turned toward the sound. A series of stalls waited to the right. "Horses." A nod. "Right. That would explain the straw and the shit. We're in a barn. No, wait, stables? We're in stables?" Now she looked back at Ryan.

He glared at her.

"Uh, oh." Focused now, she studied him a little more closely. "That is one killer black eye you have going on there. Want to tell me who gave it to you?"

Grunts. Snarls.

She nodded. "Alexei. Figures."

Surprise had Ryan's dark eyes widening.

"Yeah, no." She rocked forward, testing her chair because she had an idea. "I didn't actually understand your words. I just made a wild guess." She pulled in a deep breath. "That guy always gave me the creeps. Got the instinct that he was bad. My instincts are usually dead-on target." She tightened her arms around the back of the chair, or, tried to tighten them. "Okay, I'm coming toward you." Maybe.

He grunted.

She...hopped. Sort of. She'd lifted the chair and hopped forward with her desperate movement. Simone tried a second time. A third. And, yes, she was actually moving her chair. A bit. Slowly. Forward, toward him. It was just hard as hell. Panting, she shook hair out of her eyes and told him, "You could help, you know. Did you even *try* hopping toward me?" Why was she having to do all the work? She'd been the one who was unconscious.

He blinked.

"I'll get the tape off your mouth. It will be my first to-do, right after we get together. So let's eliminate this distance and make some magic happen, shall we?" She hopped again. Went forward a bit more. Yes!

His gaze sharpened on her. She could practically see the wheels turning in his mind and then...he started lurching forward in his chair. Not hopping as she had been doing. More like jerking one side of his body, then the other. Left. Right. Left. Right again. His technique was a lot more powerful than hers, and he eliminated the distance between them in moments with those hard, yanking heaves of his body.

Impressive.

Their knees collided. His gaze pinned her, and his expression seemed to say...*Now what?*

She wet her dry lips. "Lean toward me. As much as you can."

He stretched toward her.

"Down more," she urged him. "Slouch and stretch. Come on, make this happen!"

More grunts from Ryan.

She leaned toward him. As far as she could.

His eyes narrowed to slits as he stared back at her. A growl rumbled in his throat.

She put her mouth on him—

He whipped back.

"Seriously!" Simone caught herself and lowered her voice. "Do not be a baby about this! What did you think I was going to use in order to get the tape off you? My eyes?" Which, by the way...her fake lashes were gone. Dammit. Another sin to put on Alexei's shoulders. Maybe the lashes had come off in the rain or during her struggle in the van—whatever. Alexei's fault. "I only have my mouth free. So I'm going to use my lips and my teeth and I'm going to tug the tape off you. The edge is loose, I can see it. If you will just come toward me..."

He did. Watching her very, very closely.

"Good." Soft. "Now, give me a second..." She stretched and craned her head. Her lips brushed over his skin, and then her teeth delicately caught the loose edge of the tape. She bit it and started to tug it free. Slowly, slowly, and then she...

Spat out the tape. "Yes!"

"*Keep your voice down,*" he rasped back at her.

"Don't be grumpy with me! I just helped you!"

"*You got us kidnapped.*"

She opened her mouth, then snapped it closed. Her head swirled with options and lies. "I...did not." She fluttered her lashes. Not nearly as effective when she didn't have on her gorgeous falsies, but she had to work with what she had. "Alexei has obviously gone crazy."

A muscle flexed along Ryan's clenched jaw.

"He put a gun to my back." Oh, the tremble in her voice had been an excellent touch. It had also been real. She'd been quite terrified that a bullet could sever her spine during that forced walk through the country house. "He forced me outside. Into the rain. Into the van. That's, um, you know, around the time you appeared."

His nostrils flared.

"I remember fighting." Of course, she remembered that.

She'd fight, always. "I think he drugged me?" That was the hazy part for her.

"He slapped a rag over your mouth. Probably was chloroform," Ryan said, voice low. "Or something like it."

Chloroform? Simone swallowed. "Did you stay conscious the whole time?" Her stare darted toward the bruise near his eye. "Quite the shiner you have, by the way."

"Got that when I rammed the bastard after he slapped the cloth over your face. When you first collapsed, I didn't know if you were unconscious or dead. Either way," he gritted, "I was not happy."

She smiled at him. "You tried to save me. That was incredibly kind of you."

"Who the hell are you?"

Wow. That had been angry. She sniffed. "Um, I get that we are in a stressful situation."

"We have been kidnapped."

"So it would seem." Her gaze left him and darted around the stables. Just horses were in there with them. No people, not yet. Which meant they had time to escape. She began yanking hard at her ropes even as her gaze darted upwards.

"Who the hell are you?" he repeated.

Her gaze jumped from the rafters back to his face. "Did you hit your head after you got punched? Like, did the blow take you down?" She frowned at him in worry. "I'm Simone. Simone Sailor. We've known each other for a few weeks."

Another growl from him.

"Did that help?" she asked sweetly. "Remember me, now?"

That muscle in his jaw flexed again.

"How about you and I concentrate on escaping, shall we?"

Apparently, she needed to keep the man focused. "You wouldn't happen to have a knife hidden on your person, would you? Because a hidden knife would be awesome right now."

He stared back at her.

She took his silence to mean...no knife. "Next option..." He wasn't throwing out options. Why did all the work have to be on her? "Is this your first kidnapping?" she muttered. "Because I believe it is, and it shows."

"What?"

"We have to escape. Bad things are going to happen when Alexei returns." Simone nibbled on her lower lip. "Did he happen to say anything to you after he dumped us in here?"

"Yeah."

She waited.

Nothing.

Once more, she looked toward the rafters. This time, she was desperately trying to find patience. Unfortunately, Simone discovered none. "*What* did he tell you?" Why did she have to pry everything out of this man?

"Said that when he came back, he'd force us to answer all of his questions. *His* questions. And Frederick's questions. Told me that he couldn't wait to see how much pain we could take before we broke."

Oh, no. Her horrified stare bounced down to Ryan once more.

"He predicted you couldn't handle a lot of pain."

Goosebumps rose on her skin. "I handle pain just fine, for the record." Her wrists twisted, hard, against the ropes. She could feel the rough hemp biting into her skin. "I just don't particularly like pain. That's a normal response, by the way. Most people do not go through life just loving pain."

"He's coming back to *torture* us, Simone."

"Yes, I heard you, Ryan!" More hair fell into her face. She tossed her head, trying to knock it back out of the way. "Look, I'm really sorry that you got dragged into this mess. Not like I intended for it to happen."

"What did you do?"

She huffed out a breath. "Are you even trying to get out of the ropes? Because it doesn't look like you are."

"Appearances are deceiving."

"What?"

A loud squeak. And a creak. And...

Her head snapped to the right.

The stable doors were opening. She was not free. Not. Good. Because time appeared to have run out. Alexei stormed forward, a smug smile on his face. A smile that vanished when he realized just how close Simone and Ryan were sitting to one another. Snarling, Alexei lunged forward. He grabbed the back of her chair. Simone screamed.

And Ryan bellowed, "Hurt her and I will fucking *kill* you!"

Chapter Five

Alexei laughed. Hard. Deep guffaws of laughter that just annoyed the ever-loving-hell out of Simone as he ignored Ryan's threat and hauled her—and her attached chair—a good three feet away from Ryan.

And then...

Alexei put a knife to her throat, even as the jerk kept laughing.

"Don't," Ryan warned him.

"What are you going to do, rich boy? You think you can stop me?" Alexei's accent slid hard into the words. "You're weak. Pathetic."

"That's..." Simone licked her lips. "Really unnecessary." She craned her head back, trying to get away from the knife. "No need to insult people. Isn't it enough that you kidnapped us? Do you have to be rude on top of things?"

Ryan stared at her as if she'd lost her mind. She had not. She was simply trying to buy time. She also wanted to get the knife away from her throat. "Can't we all be civilized? Is it such a crime to be polite?"

The knife left her throat.

Yes! She pulled in a deep breath.

Only for Alexei to tell her, "I'm going to ask you questions, and when you lie to me, I'll respond by cutting off a finger. One finger for each lie."

"What?" A screech from Simone as terror squeezed her heart. She happened to have a deep attachment to all of her fingers. And they clearly had a deep attachment to *her*. "In what world is that *polite?* You can't just go around cutting off—"

He went behind her. She felt the press of the knife against her left pinky finger.

"Fingers," Simone whispered, finishing. She had to swallow down bile. "Okay, I think we should all calm down. Clearly, this situation has accelerated. We should de-escalate."

"Get the fuck away from her!" Ryan roared. "You want to target someone, then target me! Come at me with your knife!"

She literally almost said...*Yes, go threaten his fingers.* But she didn't. Because this mess was hers, and she didn't want an innocent man getting hurt for her crimes. "The broach and the earrings are in one of my dress pockets." She still had on the dress. Slightly wet. Definitely clinging itchily to her skin. Her eyes squeezed closed. "And you should let Ryan go. He had nothing at all to do with the theft." There. Full confession. No need for anyone to lose fingers.

"Simone?" Ryan seemed to be choking on her name.

Grimacing, she opened her eyes and peeked at him. "Hi."

"Theft?" he repeated.

"Um, so, I *may* have misled you a bit about who I really am." Then, duty bound, she added, "It was also more about retrieving stolen property than outright thievery. *I* was not the original thief. That would be Frederick. He seems to enjoy taking things that belong to others." She made a show of looking around. "Alexei, where is your boss? And does he *always* have you do the dirty work for him?"

"Yes. Always," Alexei returned without any hesitation. "Because it's my favorite type of work to do."

"You don't say. Never would have guessed." A mutter. Like she hadn't figured that out with his knife play. The man liked pain and blood. Terrible to know because it meant her current situation was about to get a whole lot worse. "Will Frederick be making an appearance soon?" She found him far easier to manipulate than Alexei. She also wanted to know how many enemies she'd be facing. Right now, it was just her against Alexei. Well, her and Ryan against Alexei, but Ryan was zero help so...

It was her against Alexei.

"He's coming," Alexei assured her. "Had to get the last of those big-money guests out of the way. Should be arriving with the team soon."

Did that mean it was morning? Sunlight had been streaking through the slats in the stable, so, yes, definitely morning. She'd been unconscious for quite a while. Bad. But no time to dwell on that bit of news. "I don't suppose you'd define 'soon' for me, would you? Is it like...an hour from now? Ten minutes? Is it—*ow!*" The jerk had just grabbed her hair and yanked her head back. The knife was at her throat. *Again.* Fear poured through her veins, completely chilling her, but she would be damned if she showed that fear to Alexei. She blinked quickly, refusing to let any tears fall as he yanked *harder*.

"I don't care about the broach! Or any stupid earrings! I took those from you hours ago!" Thundering words that blasted at her. "Where is the egg?"

"What?"

"The egg!"

"I heard you!" She had. "I just have zero clue what you're talking about!" Why in the world would she have some egg?

The knife cut her skin. She felt the trickle of blood on her neck.

"*Stop.*" Low. Chilling. From Ryan. "Stop *now.* Or you're a dead man."

What a bold and meaningless threat. Her gaze caught his. "Look away," she told Ryan. Because this was about to get bad. She'd just managed to work her right hand free. She would have to move quickly. Alexei had a major size and strength advantage on her. Given his passion for dirty, bloody work, Simone suspected that Alexei had a whole lot more killing experience than she did. But Simone would have the element of surprise on her side, and she would not be hesitating.

Still, Ryan did not need to see this attack. Especially if, say, something went wrong and she wound up getting her throat slashed open from ear to ear. Not the last visual she wanted him to have of her. "I really enjoyed our kisses, by the way." Zero clue why she said those words. Or why she added, "I wish our time could have been different."

A deep furrow cut between Ryan's eyes.

"*Where is the egg?*" Alexei snapped at her as spittle flew from his mouth.

"Look away," she told Ryan again.

Alexei thundered, "The egg—"

"Go find a damn chicken! Because I don't know where your egg is!"

The knife pressed harder.

And her left hand was free now, too. *Yes!* She'd just managed to wrench it out of the ropes.

"You have stumbled into the worst nightmare of your life," Alexei promised her. "They know what you did."

Great. Fabulous. Her head turned. "Come closer," she whispered to Alexei as she let her shoulders sag. "I'll tell you everything." No, she would not.

But he leaned in toward her, and with that lean, he also lifted the knife a wee bit. Sort of an instinctive response. One part of the body moved, and another did, too. She'd been hoping for that response.

If only my feet were free. Then I could really have a fighting chance. But at least her hands were going to be in this battle. Alexei had been so intent on his threats that he hadn't even heard the faint slither of the ropes falling from her wrists. She sucked in a breath and prepared for the worst. Because she'd had too many *worsts* in her life.

"Leave her alone!" Ryan yelled. "I have the egg!"

What?

Both Simone and Alexei craned their heads toward Ryan.

"Me!" Ryan shouted. "I took it. Not her. *Me.*"

He'd stolen an egg? What was happening?

"I've got the thirty-million-dollar trinket in my tux pocket right now. You searched her, but you didn't search me because you are such a dumbass."

Had he just said...*thirty-million-dollar trinket?*

"Come and get it!" Ryan taunted.

And Alexei was going. He was surging toward Ryan. Slashing out with his knife even as she screamed.

But...

Ryan was on his feet. In a blink, he was on his feet. No ropes on his ankles. No ropes around his wrists. The ropes around his chest and upper arms had fallen away because he was not bound to the chair any longer. He was up. Ready.

She was screaming at the top of her lungs. Horses were neighing nearby. Ryan caught Alexei's forearm, stopping the downward slice of the knife before it could make contact with him. Stopping it in one serious, badass motion.

"You should never threaten a woman," Ryan growled. "Bastard." Then he attacked.

Fists flew. Bodies collided. Alexei's knife was swinging, and she was still screaming. Screaming and clawing at the ropes around her ankles because she needed to get out of that chair and help Ryan. The man could not be killed right in front of her.

But even as the last rope finally gave way beneath her twisting, shaking fingers and Simone leapt to her feet, a body was falling.

Right. In. Front. Of. Her.

Alexei hit the floor of the stables with a resounding *thump*. Her breath heaved. Her hands fisted.

Ryan stepped over the fallen man. Technically, Ryan kicked him first, then stepped over Alexei's body. Ryan reached out to her. With a careful grip, he caught her chin and tipped back her head. "The bastard cut you." Low, lethal words.

A shiver skated over her at the murderous look in his eyes. Um, where had the playboy billionaire gone? "Barely feel it," she mumbled. Her gaze dropped to the floor. To Alexei. Just as he swung out with his knife toward Ryan because Alexei was *not* unconscious. He was slicing right toward Ryan's Achilles tendon. "No!" Simone bellowed even as she grabbed for Ryan and attempted to toss him to the side.

Her toss didn't happen. She was the one who got thrown. Ryan threw her even as he avoided the slice from Alexei. She hit the stable floor—which kinda felt rubbery beneath the spread straw—and shoved up to her knees even as Alexei leapt at Ryan in a brutal attack. The two men collided. Fists—and the blade of that knife—went flying. Terrified that Ryan was about to get his ass kicked, she lunged up and scrambled to find a weapon so she could help him.

Except she didn't get far. Alexei had broken free of Ryan and surged toward her. Alexei's beefy fingers curled around her ankle, and he brought her down, hard. All of the air left her in a whoosh even as he was flipping her over and bringing that knife of his swinging toward her face.

"No!" Ryan ripped the knife from Alexei's fingers. In a lightning-fast move.

Alexei turned toward Ryan.

"Come at *me,* you prick! Me, not her!" Then Ryan kicked Alexei in the face.

Oh, that brutal kick had to hurt. She shot away from the men. *Weapon, weapon, weapon.* She needed a weapon so that she could help Ryan. What kind of weapon could she find in the stables? Where and what kind and—*there.* A pitchfork. Against a stall with a terrified horse.

"Nice horse. Nice," she soothed as she grabbed the pitchfork. "Do not stampede at me." The pitchfork was heavier than she expected because this was the first time in her entire life that she'd ever held an actual pitchfork. She spun back around and hurried toward the fighting men.

Only they weren't fighting any longer.

Alexei was down. Flat on his back. Blood poured from his neck and a knife hilt protruded from his chest. Sure looked to her like that knife blade had been buried *in* his heart.

Ryan glared down at the fallen figure. "You really thought you'd cut her fingers off? Slice her throat? While I was right *here?*"

She squeaked. Then clamped her lips shut when Ryan's head turned and his gaze immediately pinned her.

Nausea rolled in her stomach. There was an awful lot of blood on Alexei's body. And around his body. And on Ryan.

Blood and gore had never been her scene.

Meanwhile Ryan was staring at her like...like...

Ice cold eyes. Handsome face locked in lines of savage intent. Hands fisted.

So. Much. Blood. That blood had sprayed across his tux coat. "Um, you've got a little..." A really hard swallow. "Something on you."

His gaze went even colder. He ripped off the coat and tossed it onto the floor, next to Alexei. An unmoving Alexei.

Now would he just toss away the tux coat if it truly had a thirty-million-dollar egg in one of its pockets? She did not think so. But she did think he had the egg. Somewhere on him.

She'd get back to the egg in a bit. For the moment, she should probably do something to address the man with the knife in his chest.

"We should help him," Simone decided. Why was her voice so squeaky? She was never ever squeaky.

"He's past the point of help."

Was he? Probably. But maybe they should still try?

"Are you going to stab me with that thing, Simone?"

His sharp voice had her glancing at her weapon and realizing that she did have it pointed at him. She immediately tossed down the pitchfork. "I was coming to save you with it."

"I don't need saving."

"I did not know that at the time." She should reevaluate. They were free. Alexei was dead. Reinforcements were coming, and she needed to get the hell out of there. "We should run. You go that way." She pointed vaguely to the right. "And I'll go this way." To the left. "Stay safe. And let's never speak of this again." With those words, Simone took off.

Except she did not get far because strong arms wrapped around her and yanked her back against Ryan's powerful body. Her hands flew down, darting over his hips. The top of his thighs. "Let me go!"

He didn't. He did spin her around. "We are not separating."

One of Simone's hands shoved into one of the hidden pockets in her dress. Immediately, she realized that Alexei had not been bluffing. The broach and earrings were gone, dammit. Her gaze darted to his fallen body. Did she dare search through those blood-drenched clothes of his? Were the items she needed still on Alexei? Oh, but she bet they were.

"It will be better if we separate," she tried to reassure Ryan. "They are going to search for us. If we split up, the odds will be higher."

"Higher for what, Simone? Higher odds that they'll find me and not you?"

"I was talking about the odds of our survival!" Simone sucked in a dramatic gasp of air. "I'm trying to save you!" And herself.

He leaned in closer. "You are not getting away from me."

Had he experienced some sort of mental break? His grip was way too strong. Not painful. Just strong. "You just killed a man."

He grunted.

"That's probably stressful for you." *Probably?* It should have been extremely stressful, but there Ryan was, acting like he had ice pumping through his veins. His voice didn't even tremble. His hands were rock steady. "You aren't thinking clearly. So I will spell things out for you." With all of her might, she tried to keep her voice calm. "Bad guys are coming. Bad guys who will hurt us. The fact that you are richer than sin is not going to help you right now. You just killed Frederick's number one goon. We are in a boat load of trouble. We have to run."

He...shook his head.

"Ryan?"

He leaned in closer to her. "You're not getting away from me."

"Fine." If he was going to be difficult about things. "Then we will run together. I, just, um, have to check the dead man. Or, the maybe not-so-dead man."

"What?"

"I can't leave without making sure he's actually dead! Let me check and then we're out of here. Done."

His hold loosened. She darted toward Alexei. Choked down more nausea. "What did you do? Slit his throat first?" Simone risked a glance at Ryan. She needed him to be staring at her, making eye contact, while her hands were busy. At thirteen, she'd mastered the art of misdirection.

Nothing was more useful to her in this world than a skillful bit of misdirection.

She gave a pronounced heave. Such a hard, long, and despondent sigh.

A hint of worry darkened Ryan's expression. Finally.

"You slit his throat," she repeated. "Then you...stabbed him in the heart?"

No response.

Her fingers flew over Alexei. As if she was looking for a pulse. "I don't want to tell you how to handle your affairs," she mumbled, "but I think that was overkill."

Wait—had Alexei just *gurgled?*

Her fingers whipped back. She jumped to her feet. "He's still alive!" Very, very dramatic.

Ryan immediately surged down toward her. His hands went toward the knife still in Alexei's chest.

She used that prime opportunity to scuttle back, to shoot to her feet, to leap around Ryan, and try to flee. Yet, once again, Simone got dragged back against Ryan's chest.

"Simone." A bit impatient. A bit sighy. "I know when I've killed someone and when I haven't. That man is dead."

Okay, there was a *lot* to unpack in that statement of his.

"I also know that you just swiped the broach and the earrings from his dead body, didn't you?"

This did not feel like the moment to announce that she was *guilty.* "Let me go!" Then, to be polite, "Pretty please?" She'd try being polite first. If that didn't work, she'd have to get physical.

Except she'd just seen him get physical with Alexei, and the end result of that very physical confrontation had been a dead Russian guard.

"I'm not letting you go." And, again, Ryan whipped her around.

Whipped her around even as she was pretty sure that she could hear the distant growl of an engine. Was a car approaching? Frederick and more goons?

Ryan stared down into her face with his deep, dark, intense eyes, and he told her, "I'm arresting you."

Chapter Six

She looked so beautiful and so confused and, yes, dammit, so scared. Ryan wanted to haul Simone into his arms and promise her that everything would be okay but...

Dead body.

Bad guys closing in.

Time was running out.

Things were *not* okay.

Simone sent him an uncertain smile. "I think I misheard."

He was quite sure she had not.

"Did you just say that you were going to arrest me?"

He nodded. He also could hear the sound of an approaching vehicle, so they had to get moving, stat. It had taken him too long to break out of the ropes. Honestly, Simone's idea of him *hopping* toward her had helped enormously. Once he'd started jerking and heaving his chair toward hers, the ropes around him had begun to loosen. They'd loosened enough that when the sonofabitch Alexei had been threatening her with his knife, Ryan had been able to break free.

Speaking of that knife...

Alexei could still see the faint line of blood on her neck. "He was dead the minute he put the knife against your skin."

"Okay." A brisk nod. Followed by a deep inhale. "There is a lot happening here. I strongly suspect that you might be disassociating. Is that what's happening? Granted, I'm certainly no mental health expert, but you have been through a highly traumatic situation. I'm betting this was your first kidnapping."

She'd said something before about it being his first kidnapping. Time to disabuse her of that notion. "It wasn't." His head angled to the left. To the upset horses. He began pulling her toward them.

"It...*wasn't* your first kidnapping?" Surprise had her words rising. "Just how many times have you been kidnapped?"

He thought about her question even as he tried to find the calmest horse. The calmest one was actually the big, black stallion with the white spots who waited in the rear stall. "Four. No...Five times?" His hand moved down to her wrist.

She hissed out a breath. One that sounded painful. Just like that, his gaze was back on her face.

"What hurts?" Ryan demanded.

"I...nothing. I was just surprised that you had been kidnapped four—sorry, *five*—times. That's quite a lot of kidnappings. A high, shocking number, in fact. I'm pretty certain that most people go through life and aren't even kidnapped once, much less *five times*."

"I'm not most people."

"Obviously." A disgruntled mutter. "Is that like, a

billionaire thing? Have you been snatched and held for ransom again and again?"

Nope. He'd usually been taken by enemies who thought they could torture intel out of him. They'd been mistaken. Eventually, his abductors had also been dead. "I'm not a billionaire."

Her shoulders slumped. "I was afraid you would say that." A faint click as she swallowed. "Just what are you?"

"I'm the man who just killed to save your life." He turned back for the horse. Opened the stall.

She dug in her heels as he tried to pull her forward.

Sighing, Ryan asked, "Is there a problem?" Besides the many obvious ones. *A kidnapping. A dead mercenary. Bad guys closing in.*

"Yes. I don't think we should go toward the big, angry stallion."

The stallion stared back at Ryan. Unblinking. Not moving. The horse didn't strike him as being particularly angry. Big, sure. But angry? Not so much. "I don't have time to find his saddle. We are going to have to do this bareback."

"Do *what* bareback?"

"What do you think?" He freed her wrist, but only so his hands could close around her waist. He lifted her up and tossed her onto the horse. Right before he hauled ass up after her.

Simone had slammed her hands down on the horse in order to try and balance herself, but when Ryan eased in front of her, she immediately wrapped her arms around him. "This can't be happening," she said. Ryan felt Simone press her head to his back. "Cannot be happening."

Oh, it was happening. "Good boy," Ryan praised the horse as he gave him a rub. This idea could be dumb as hell.

He and Simone could both get their asses thrown by the stallion or they might get lucky and escape before the bad guys could kill them. "Let's get the hell out of here."

"Um, are you talking to me or the horse?" Simone asked.

He directed the stallion. The mighty horse took off. As if he had been *waiting* for his shot at freedom, the stallion bolted from the open stall. Shot past the dead body. Erupted into the daylight beyond the stables.

Simone let out a little shriek, and her hold tightened even more around Ryan.

"Trust me," he told her even as he urged the horse onward and Simone's red gown billowed up and down around them. "I've got you."

And he had no intention of letting her go.

As far as Ryan was concerned, when you killed for a woman, you should get to keep her.

* * *

Frederick Bradwin slammed the door to his Rolls Royce and glared at the stables. He could not believe the fuckery that had happened at his country estate.

Simone stole from me? What. The. Bloody. Hell? When he got his hands on the woman, she would pay. And to think, she'd denied all his most gracious invitations for dinner. She'd spouted that prim BS about not mixing business with pleasure when all along, she'd been planning to steal him blind.

The lying vixen.

She would pay.

He began marching for the stables.

"Boss!" Hugo grabbed his arm.

Frederick whirled on the guy.

"Easy!" Hugo threw up his hands. Sweat beaded his forehead. It wasn't even that hot yet. Why was the man sweating so profusely?

"Before we go in there..." Hugo squared his shoulders. "What are we going to do about Ryan Quinn?"

Ryan Quinn. Talk about a clusterfuck. Alexei had actually kidnapped his would-be investor. *Of course,* Ryan would have interrupted when Alexei was trying to shove Simone into the back of a van. The fool had been just as taken in by Simone as Frederick had been.

But abducting Ryan had been a major mistake. Alexei had informed Frederick all about that unfortunate situation. Ryan had tried to play hero, and, in return, Alexei and the men under his command had wound up practically kidnapping Ryan. *There is no practically about it.* "I'm going to kill him," Frederick promised, voice seething with rage.

Hugo's eyes widened. Shock had his round face going slack. "You're going to *kill* your new investor? I am new to this private sector stuff, but boss, isn't that, like, really, really bad for business?"

He needed to be saved from idiots. "Not him. I'm going to kill Alexei! Alexei should *never* have dragged Ryan into his mess. He should have handled Simone far more discreetly." But the big Russian knew zero about being discreet. Truth be told, Frederick hated working with the guy, but he didn't exactly have a choice in the matter. In order to keep his current lifestyle—Frederick really, really liked his lifestyle—he'd recently had to make some unfortunate business deals with some shady people.

Or, specifically, with one very, very dangerous individual in particular. That person controlled Alexei.

And, for the moment, that person also controlled Frederick's life. *For the moment.*

But... "I'm going to kill him," Frederick vowed again. Because Alexei had just cost him billions, and he had no idea how he was going to smooth this shit over with Ryan Quinn. Not like he could just waltz into the stables and be all like...*Sorry, chum. My guard mistakenly kidnapped you. Still ready to give me billions of dollars?*

No, that ship had long since sailed. Perhaps, though...

Hell, if he's already kidnapped, maybe I can work this... someway. Maybe I can still get a payday.

No, dammit to hell and back. This whole situation was a mess. Breath heaving, he stormed toward the stables. He'd been so close to having everything he wanted. Then Simone had truly screwed his plans. This was all her fault, and he would be sure that she suffered.

As he drew nearer, he realized that one of the large, wooden doors to the stables hung open. Squaring his shoulders, he entered, shouting, "Alexei, how dare you drag my good associate Ryan into this—"

But then his words stopped. He stopped. Because Frederick had just caught sight of Alexei. A very bloody, unmoving Alexei. A knife appeared to be lodged in the man's chest.

Frederick gaped. And gagged. Because...

First dead body.

He yanked a handkerchief from his pocket and pressed it over his mouth and nose even as Hugo shoved past him. Hugo crouched next to the body. He...

"Are you *touching* him?" Frederick demanded as disgust and nausea rolled through him.

"Yes, that's how I determine if he is alive or dead!"

"He's in a pool of blood!" His other guards rushed

inside. "There is a knife in Alexei's chest, and I can see the inside of his throat. He is *dead*."

Hugo yanked the knife out of Alexei's chest.

"What are you doing?" Frederick stumbled forward. "Now your prints are on it!"

Hugo squinted at him. "We're calling the cops? That's what you want to do here, boss? Call in police officers to handle this scene? Because I'm pretty sure only the authorities will care about prints. Though I have to tell you, calling them in will just raise a whole lot of questions that I don't think you want to answer."

No, he did not want to answer *any* questions that the authorities might have.

Hugo grunted. "Thought so. And if we aren't going to let the police investigate the scene, then who cares if my prints are on the knife? We'll just make all of this vanish."

"I've never made a body vanish before." He'd been thinking of killing Alexei moments before, but that had just been...anger. A temporary rage. He had never actually murdered anyone.

"Sir." Hugo inhaled. "Do you *see* the ropes near his body?"

Yes, he saw the damn ropes. "What of them?"

"Simone Sailor and Ryan Quinn were no doubt tied to those empty chairs. They are gone. They are *kidnap* victims. If we call the authorities, we'll have to explain how and why two people were kidnapped."

Okay, Hugo could stop it already. His case had been made. "We aren't getting the authorities out here. We'll have to handle things ourselves." While he might not know how to make Alexei's body vanish, Frederick did know someone who had experience in that area. His gaze darted around the area. Was that a discarded, bloody tux coat? Oh, no. If Ryan had been hurt by Alexei...*fuck me. This could be disastrous.* "We have to find Simone. And Ryan." This was going from bad to worse. "They can't get to the police!" If Simone and Ryan reached the authorities, if the police came out to the stables and discovered Alexei...

Frederick's breath heaved in and out. "Clean the scene. We have to clean the scene first." No way could any police arrive to find blood and ropes and a dead man. He whipped out his phone and called the person he really, really did not want to call.

Alexei's boss.

And...*the man currently in charge of my life.* Konstantin Volkov.

The phone rang in his ear.

"Boss." Hugo stood right in front of him. "Boss, we have a big problem."

He was aware. He'd seen the body. "Trying to deal with the problem."

"Boss, who killed Alexei?"

"Hello?" A low, rumbly voice in his ear.

Frederick blinked at Hugo.

"*Hello?*" The voice in his ear had sharpened.

"Who did it?" Hugo wet his lips. "Because Alexei was one tough bastard. *Who did that to him?* You think it was that silver-spoon guy, Ryan? You think it was Simone? She's *tiny.*"

Yes, Simone was physically delicate. He never would have thought she could be capable of murder. Then again, he hadn't thought she was a thief, either.

"This was a vicious kill," Hugo muttered. "It was brutal. And..." An exhale as his words just drifted to a stop.

Alexei's killer had to be one of them. Either Ryan or Simone.

"Frederick, I know it's you." The voice wasn't just disgruntled. It was pissed. Coldly furious. "Don't ever fucking call me and just leave me hanging. You got something to say, then you say—"

"Alexei is dead." His voice cracked. "And I have a big problem on my hands."

"What?"

"S-Simone Sailor." She was the problem.

Hugo was shaking his head. Over and over.

Frederick ignored him.

"Who the hell is Simone Sailor? And why should I care about her?" Konstantin demanded.

"Simone Sailor was, um, my personal assistant. Or I thought she was...and she stole from me." This made him look incompetent, and he hated that. His rage seethed as he added, "Alexei found out. She must have killed Alexei." He didn't mention Ryan Quinn. Maybe if he didn't mention Ryan, then the billionaire would stay alive. Frederick could fix the mess with him. Still get Ryan's money. Somehow. "She killed Alexei, and now she's vanished."

"That sounds like a fucking *you* problem."

What? "What does that even mean?"

"It means...*you* solve this problem. You find the bitch. You bring me her heart. *Alexei was my cousin.* My favorite one."

All of the blood seemed to drain from his head. Frederick felt his body sway. He'd known Alexei worked for the other man, but he'd had no idea at all that they were related. Could this situation get any worse?

And so much for getting Konstantin to help him make the body vanish. This did not seem like the right time to ask for that particular favor.

"You make her pay," Konstantin raged, "or I destroy you. That's why it's a fucking *you* problem."

He lowered the phone. Swallowed three times. Then rasped to Hugo, "She has to be on foot." Right? She must have run? On foot. "Find her. Search for her. *Now*."

"What about Ryan?" Hugo whispered.

He muted the phone. No sense in putting Ryan Quinn on a death list, too. At least, not until he had Ryan's money. "He lives. She dies." His breath panted out. "Understand? Spread the word. Pull in any help that you need to get this done."

"But..." Hugo glanced back at the body, then his stare returned to Frederick. "What about the egg?"

Simone—Simone had stolen the egg during her trip to the gallery. Either on the first trip or on the second damn one. She'd left a fake one in place of the real egg. He'd known it was a forgery the minute he touched the thing. *Thirty million dollars feels different.*

That bitch. She did deserve to die.

But he would let someone else do the dirty work. Not like he wanted to get bloody.

As far as the egg was concerned, he was not mentioning it to the man on the phone. *The egg came from him. He will lose his mind if he finds out it was taken.* Wasn't it enough that Konstantin already lost his cousin? No sense informing him that the egg Frederick had been supposed to protect for him was in the wind.

"Simone must still have it." She'd better have it. "Bring it to me. Bring her to me. *Then* she's dead. Happy now?"

Hugo did not look happy. But he said, "Deliriously so," as he turned and stalked toward the body.

"We have to get rid of his body ourselves," Frederick choked out.

Hugo glanced back at him.

"Do you think we need to dismember him?" Frederick asked. No, time to rephrase. "Are *you* going to dismember him?"

"Fuck," Hugo said.

Indeed.

Chapter Seven

Ryan lifted her off the horse. All gallant and careful and as if he did not still have blood drops on the fancy white shirt he wore. His hands lingered against her waist, and Simone tried to figure out just what her next move should be.

Then the stallion *ran away*.

She gaped after the horse, expecting Ryan to give chase or *something*. He did not. He just kept right on holding her. "What are you doing?" she demanded.

"Making sure you don't fall. I got the impression you'd never ridden a horse before."

Her chin notched up. "Whatever gave you that impression?"

"The way you clung to me with a death grip."

Sure, why not just drop *death* between them? "I'm fine." A sniff. She was not. That stallion had gone helluva fast. She'd been bouncing like crazy during the frantic ride. There had been no saddle. And her thighs hurt. "You can release me."

He did. She nearly crumbled so her hands flew out and grabbed onto him so she could stay upright.

"Another death grip," he rasped.

She glared at him. "The horse is getting away."

"I am aware."

"He's our *ride*."

"Correction, he was our ride. Now he's heading back to the stables so he can rest."

She kept holding him because her legs were still feeling jiggly. The only way to describe them. "How on earth do you know that he's heading to the stables?"

"Because he's brilliant, and I trust him."

Sure. Why not? "You get that the bad guys can just follow his hoof prints and come find us, right?" Due to the powerful storms that had swept through the night before, the ground was a muddy mess. Her bare feet were currently sinking into the mud. It felt squishy and cold between her toes, and she'd only realized that she'd lost her fancy heels when they'd been galloping across the English countryside.

"They can follow his hoof prints, but they will not find us. We'll be long gone before they get here." His head tilted to the right. "Want me to just carry you?"

"No, I do not." Truthfully, though, yes, that might be a great idea. "Carry me where?"

"To our next ride."

Her heart raced a little faster. "You have a next ride waiting, already? Do not tease me on this."

He smiled at her.

And her heartbeat pounded *faster*.

Ryan winked. "They didn't search me, remember?"

No, she did not remember that. "I was drugged, *remember*? Let's act like things are blurry for me."

His smile dimmed. "Are things blurry for you?"

Um... "Yes." Husky. Weak. A little trembly. "Blurry. And my heart is racing." True story. "I...I feel a little faint." When she thought of the dead body they'd left behind, she *did* feel faint. Look at her being all truthful.

He swung her into his arms. Her muddy feet kicked in the air, and her soggy dress trailed down his arm.

"We are heading to a little cottage around the bend," Ryan informed her as his worried gaze swept over her face.

How on earth did he know a little cottage waited around the bend?

"An extraction team will be arriving within the half hour," he added as his hold tightened on her.

An extraction team sounded incredibly official. "How, exactly, does this team know where to go?"

"Because I texted them."

"*When?*"

"When we were riding on the horse."

A dull throbbing began at her right temple. "Bullshit."

He kept walking while carrying her, as if it was the easiest thing to do in the world. Spoiler, it was not. No way it could be easy. Not with her and her soggy dress.

"Not bullshit," he promised. "They're coming."

"Why would an *extraction* team be coming?"

He looked down at her. "Because I'm CIA."

She wanted to laugh. Instead, she came pretty close to sobbing. "I am not in the mood for this." Fear pumped through her. He had mentioned before...she distinctly remembered him saying...

She was under arrest.

"I am definitely feeling dizzy." Simone closed her eyes. "So weak. Nauseous. It was all I could do to hold on to you when we were riding that horse." Her body went limp.

"Oh, yeah, that grip of yours was helluva weak. It's

amazing you didn't fall off the horse's back during the ride. Don't know how you managed to keep that death grip going."

Not funny. She kept her eyes closed. CIA. *CIA*. Ryan was CIA, and this was going to be so bad for her. "Why couldn't you just be a billionaire?" Would that have been too much to ask?

"Because a billionaire wouldn't have been able to save your ass."

Her eyes cracked open.

"But a CIA operative knew how to kill to protect you."

Well, there was that.

Now, she just needed to figure out a way to escape from her CIA guy before his extraction team arrived, and they all proceeded to arrest her ass. Because maybe, okay, definitely...she was a wanted international criminal.

* * *

Ryan kicked the door shut and strode inside the old, abandoned cottage.

"Tell me how you even knew this place was here," Simone said, suspicion heavy in her voice.

"I didn't know it." Not like he'd had some clue the place was out there when they'd been abducted and dragged off into the stormy night. "But one of my contacts told me it was a safe place to hide."

"Your contacts." A nod. "Someone you *texted* while riding the horse? How was there even service out here?"

"At first, there wasn't any service. But when we rose up that first hill, I was able to get a signal." Like texting and controlling the stallion—without a saddle—had been an easy feat to accomplish. Why did Simone not seem impressed? Just what did it take to impress the woman? "He pinged me the location."

"So you weren't just riding blindly on that horse? You were coming *here*?"

Yeah, he had been. He'd also learned an important lesson. *Don't ride a stallion and text.* Ryan had feared they'd be flying off the horse at any moment. Especially since he'd quickly realized Simone had never ridden a horse before. Or, if she had ridden one, it had been a very, very long time ago.

"You can just put me down," Simone instructed in her husky, sexy voice. "Anytime at all is good."

He didn't put her down. He kept holding her. No furniture was inside the cottage. The place sported some busted windows. Glass littered the floor. There were also definite signs that some very large critters had taken up residence inside the place. "I can keep carrying you." Not a problem. What *was* a problem? The fear and the absolute rage that still pumped in his veins when he thought about what could have happened to her.

When her body had collapsed in the van, when he hadn't been sure if she was alive or dead...

"Put me down." A definite order from Simone.

His grip tightened.

When that sonofabitch Alexei threatened to torture her, to cut off her beautiful fingers, when he put his knife to her neck...my whole world ignited in red.

Blood red. Alexei had been a dead man from that point forward.

"Yo, down!" She struggled in his grip. "Because I think I deserve answers."

His jaw locked, even harder than it had been locked already. Super slowly, he lowered her. Not all the way down. Her toes hovered over the ground about three inches because… "Your feet are bare." He didn't want her getting cut on the glass.

"They are currently covered in layers of mud so it's like I'm wearing my own magical, muddy shoes. Just drop me, would you?"

He didn't *drop* her. He gently let her feet touch down. Away from the glass shards. And still his hands lingered around her waist. "Are you okay?"

Simone's expression showed that she doubted his sanity for even asking the question. "No." A hard, negative shake of her head that sent her heavy, dark locks flying over her shoulders. "I am far from okay. I was kidnapped. I was threatened with torture. I was physically attacked. *I am not okay.*" She stepped back, and the heavy red folds of her dress slid over the dirty floor of the cottage. "I need rest. I need safety."

He could give her safety.

"I need a man…" Her eyes narrowed to chips of blue fury. "I need a man who is *not* threatening to arrest me after the horrifying ordeal that I have just endured."

Yeah, as to that… "Sorry, but you're not getting away from me."

"Why on earth would you want to arrest me? Did you miss the whole dramatic part where *I* am the kidnap victim? Me?" Simone touched her chest. Right between her truly glorious breasts.

He swallowed. Time to get down to business and not focus on her truly glorious breasts. "Why were you kidnapped?"

She took two more steps back as her hand fell to her side. "Are you victim blaming right now?"

"Simone..." He paused. "Don't go back another step. There is glass behind you."

She looked behind her, then scooted to the right.

He nodded. "Good." He rolled back his shoulders. "Now answer my question."

"What question?"

Oh, she knew what question, but he'd repeat it for her. "Why were you kidnapped?"

Her eyes went very wide. "How can I explain the actions of a madman? How can anyone?"

Alexei had been fucking crazy, no doubt. And way too excited about giving pain. *You should never have tried to hurt Simone.* Ryan realized that his hands had clenched into fists. Normally, he had no problem maintaining control on his cases. No matter what sort of hellhole situations he found himself facing, he dealt with the matter. He eliminated threats. He kicked ass. He moved on.

He...

Edged closer to Simone. Worry whispered in his voice as he asked her, "Do you need medical treatment?" He'd needed to get her away from those stables, so he hadn't been able to check and assess her injuries.

Her plump lips parted. No longer a slick red but instead a soft pink. Beautiful. Full.

All of her makeup was gone. Her hair was a tangled darkness around her face. Her eyes glinting. Her cheeks too pale.

Yet to him, she appeared even more gorgeous than when she'd been so carefully styled at the party.

He might have some problems.

"Yes, yes, I need medical treatment!" Simone declared, voice passionate. "I was drugged! Who knows what was in that smelly cloth?" Her hand flew in the air. Did a little spin. Then dropped back to her side.

Based on the reaction she'd had to the cloth, he strongly suspected she'd been chloroformed, and Ryan was sure he'd mentioned that fact to her before. "Do you have other injuries? You, ah, fought Alexei pretty hard in the van."

Now her hands went to her hips and balled into little fists. "Of course, I fought him hard. What was I supposed to do? Go meekly along with my own kidnapping?" She spun, giving him her back, as she began to pace the length of the abandoned cottage.

He stalked after her. "You told *me* to run."

Her head turned. Her gaze cut over her shoulder. "Did I?"

"Yes, you did. When I first saw you, when Alexei had you at the van, you said for me to run." Talk about something that had pissed him off to his core. "Why the hell would you do that?"

"Uh, to save your life?" She squinted at him. "To keep you out of trouble? To be a good person?"

He really wanted to touch her. He *needed* to touch her.

Ryan closed the last bit of distance between them, and his hand extended. Carefully, almost hesitantly, his fingers curled around her shoulder. Her bare, delicate shoulder.

A shudder worked over him.

"What are you doing?" Simone turned to fully face him. "Are you having some kind of medical episode? Maybe you're the one who needs medical treatment?"

No, dammit, he was not. He just *needed to touch her*.

Because he'd been terrified that Alexei would kill her, right in front of him. The stark terror was new for Ryan. He never became afraid on missions. He rode adrenaline highs. He kicked ass. He...dammit, his muscles were still twisted with tension at the thought of anyone hurting Simone.

"I have no idea what happened to you while I was unconscious." Now she edged closer, and her left hand rose to press to his cheek. Worry darted over her pretty face. "That is one hell of a black eye."

"Got it when you collapsed in the van. Had to get to you." And he had. "I picked you up. I held you on the drive. They *weren't* touching you."

Her lashes—normal lashes, not the longer, thicker, fake ones that she'd had before—flickered. He liked her normal lashes. They made her eyes seem bigger. Softer. More innocent. "You held me?" Simone seemed surprised.

"Yeah, I did." And Alexei had held a gun to Ryan's head the whole time, but that didn't seem like a point to share at that particular moment. "Until we got to the stables, yeah. I kept you in my arms." He'd been reassured by her steady breaths as he cradled her in the back of that damn van. "Then they pulled you away from me." It had taken five of them to do the job. "They tied me in one chair. Put you in the other. Then they left us." He'd watched her, struggling to see in the dark. Straining to speak behind the duct tape. He'd been so sure she would be terrified when she woke. And instead, when the sun had finally started to send streaks of light through the wooden slats of the stables, Simone had opened her eyes and shown zero fear.

"I'm sorry that you were hurt trying to help me." She rose onto her toes, and her lips brushed lightly over the skin around his left eye. "You really should have ran."

"Screw that." His hands locked around her waist. He lifted her up, wanting to make sure she avoided the glass shards that he'd just spotted near her. He took three steps, and he had her caged between his body and the wall.

"There's something you need to understand about me right now." He released her waist, but then his fingers immediately moved to curl around her wrists. With his grip, he lifted her hands and held them against the wall.

"Is it that you're big and bad and a super dangerous spy? Because you already made that shocking reveal to me."

She was *stunning* to him. A faint smile on her lips. Zero fear in her eyes. Trying to quip with him when she should have been shaking in her shoes. *She isn't wearing shoes.* "I will not abandon you," he growled.

And...

Fear.

It came fast. Blooming in her eyes right before she blinked. "Yes, you will." A smile curved her lips. "I think you're planning to arrest me for some made-up crime and then toss me into a cell someplace while you go about your merry way." She licked her lips. Cocked her head to the side. "Tell me, how does an American spy even have the legal authority to arrest someone here in the UK? I mean, *do* you have the authority or were you just threatening me for fun?"

"I'm working with MI6."

She absorbed that info with a slight nod. "The Secret Intelligence Service. Sure, why not be working with them? Because my day and night had not been bad enough before." She did not try to break out of his grasp. And his gaze just dropped to her mouth.

He loved her mouth. The shape of it. The feel of it beneath his. The way her lips would part, and she moaned ever so softly when he kissed her.

Ryan swallowed. "It's for your protection," he muttered.

"What is?"

He wanted her mouth. He wanted *her*.

She pulled her lower lip between her teeth. Nibbled a bit. Then let go. "See something you like, Mr. Spy?"

His gaze flew up to catch her gaze. "Don't play with me."

"Sorry. Is that what I'm doing?"

He was quite sure it was.

"Let's blame it on the adrenaline, shall we? My emotions are out of control. *I'm* not quite in control." A deliberate pause from Simone. "Are you?"

"Am I what?" His body pressed to hers, and, even through that billowing skirt of hers, she probably felt his dick shoving against her. He eased back, a little, but didn't let her go.

"Are you in control?" Simone asked him.

"*I'm always in control.*"

Her brows climbed. "You don't sound that way. You sound like adrenaline might be pushing you to the edge, too."

Adrenaline. Fury. Desire. The remnants of fear that he never, ever should have felt.

"Do it," she dared.

He sucked in a breath. "Do what?"

"Kiss me. You know you want to do it. I want you to do it. What will one tiny kiss hurt?"

There was not going to be anything *tiny* about their kiss, dammit. That was insulting.

She rolled one shoulder. "Not like we're going to kiss and then frantically rip each other's clothes off, am I right?"

She should not tempt him that way. Ripping off her clothes seemed like a fabulous idea to him.

"I'm filthy." Her nose scrunched in a way that he found too adorable. "Your fancy extraction team is coming any minute, and I'm thinking that when you valiantly came to the rescue last night, you didn't stop to grab a condom so..." An exhale. "A kiss is all we get. A real kiss. No pretending this time. Just you and me. Just the two of us actually kissing. Actually letting go and seeing what the desire between us is really like before, well, before your associates *try* to arrest me for some crime that I don't even remember committing."

She needed to stop fascinating him. "I'm pretty sure you're a thief."

Her lips parted. "That is insulting." Yet, somehow, her words came out like a sensual temptation.

"You're definitely a liar." His head was lowering toward hers because there was no way he could hold himself back. He was going to kiss Simone.

"Me? I think *you're* the liar. I believe that lying is the way of life for a spy."

He was a breath away from her mouth.

"Also, should you just be confessing that you're CIA?" She made a little tut-tut click with her tongue. "Your spy status doesn't feel like something you should tell the world."

"You're not the world."

"No."

"You're mine."

"What?"

He took her mouth.

Chapter Eight

He didn't kiss with restraint. With gentleness. Didn't kiss with seduction and careful skill. Ryan was way past the point of all that. Instead, he kissed Simone with near desperation. With a desire and dark lust that made his entire body ache. With complete intent and consuming focus.

With possession.

You're mine.

He felt that way about her, even though it was not rational. Maybe it was due to the adrenaline or the fact that he'd killed a man in order to protect her. Not his first kill. In his line of work, he'd had to face evil and fight to survive too many times before.

But this time, it had been different.

This time, he'd been fighting for her. Because if he had not stopped Alexei, Ryan knew what the bastard would have done to Simone.

He was going to take her fingers. Going to make her beg and plead. Going to slit her throat and the blood would have poured down her neck and blended with the red of her dress.

His Simone. Dead?

No fucking way.

His hands tightened around her wrists. Her mouth opened wider for him, and she met him eagerly. Her kiss was as frantic and wild as his. As hungry. As filled with lust and a desire that would not be denied.

A moan built in her throat. He *loved* that little moan.

A growl broke from him.

Her taste enflamed him. Made him want to take and take and take.

He'd come too close to losing her. In one night, she could have been stolen from him. If he hadn't gone down the stairs at that country estate, if he hadn't been driven to walk out into the storm, she could have vanished.

No fucking way would she get away from him again.

The rumble of an approaching engine had his body stiffening. Then his head lifting. Reluctantly.

Her lips were red from his mouth. So very tempting.

She pressed her lips together, then Simone said, "You kissed me like you meant it."

"I *did* mean it."

"So it was just pretend before? You were using me all along? I was just the cover for some secret spy work so that you could get close to your target?"

The rumble of the approaching engine was getting louder. "It started with me using you." A painful truth.

"Asshole."

"Yeah, I am." A nod. "I'm a brutal and controlling bastard. Probably something important for you to know about me."

"What other important things should I know?"

"I killed to keep you safe once, and I would do it again with no hesitation."

Simone sucked in a sharp breath.

"I also think that you were using me, weren't you, sweetheart?"

She didn't respond.

The rumble of the engine was practically on top of them. Time to move. "I want you to hide while I check to see who is approaching." He let go of her wrists.

Simone's stare was very watchful. And wary. "You were using me so that you could get your all-access pass into Frederick's life."

"And you were using me so that you could steal from him."

"Please. I could do that on my own."

"Then why go out with me three times?" Why was he asking? Why did he want to know so badly? "Why did you go out with me if you weren't using me?"

"Is it so crazy to think I might have liked you?"

Liked the billionaire he pretended to be, check. She did not know the real him. At all. Ryan put more distance between them. "I need you to stay out of sight."

"I'm sure I can somehow manage that feat." She made a show of straightening the long, loose, and muddy folds of her dress. "So much for taking this back without anyone noticing it was gone."

Wait...had she *stolen* the dress, too?

"This is going to cost me a fortune."

So now she was going to pay for her stolen dress? "You confuse me."

"I get that a lot." She plucked at the dress. "It was such a pretty gown. And it had pockets. Do you know how amazing it is when a gown like this has pockets?" Her shoulders slumped. "I freaking love pockets."

"I'll make a mental note of that." Then, gruff, "I'll get

the damn dress professionally cleaned for you. It will be fine." Time was up. He'd spotted a door to the right. He yanked it open and found a cobweb-filled closet space. "Get in here."

She crept closer and poked her head into the dark space. Then her head swung back toward him. "You are not serious."

Sadly, he was. His hands wrapped around her waist. He lifted her up and put her inside.

But her hands flew out to curve around the doorframe. "No! Dammit, it's *dark* in there!"

"Light will spill in under the bottom of the door." Maybe. The only light in the cottage had come from the sunlight that trickled in through the boarded-up windows. There were very high odds that she'd be in total darkness inside the closet. "It will only be for a few moments."

"There are spiders and creepers and who knows what else in there!" She kept clinging to the doorframe.

What in the hell was a creeper? Never mind. He shook off the question. "You weren't afraid of a Russian mercenary who wanted to slice off your fingers, but you're afraid of spiders?"

Her chin notched up. "I was terrified of Alexei. I just don't typically like to let people see my fear."

"Seems like I'm seeing it right now."

Instantly, she released the doorframe. She sniffed even as her chin notched up. With a glare, Simone snapped, "Fine. Lock me in the dark closet."

Now he felt like an extra bastard, but that rumbling engine was right outside of the cottage. "I'm not locking you in," he rasped. "I'm protecting you."

"You're kissing me, then shoving me in a spider-filled

closet. Doesn't feel like protecting me." She crept back a bit. "Shut the door. Do it. Go ahead."

Fuck, fuck, fuck. Guilt ate at him. "I will be right here. Guarding you."

"With what?"

He blinked.

"Do you happen to have a weapon hidden on you? Because I'm pretty sure you left the knife *in* Alexei."

He had.

Her arms crossed over her chest. "Try not to die while I'm hiding in the closet, will you? Because if I get stuck in here, I will be pissed."

"I'm not going to die." A disgruntled mutter. "And you are not going to get stuck." He shut the door. Slowly.

It clicked.

He was not going to die. He could handle the enemy even without a weapon. Had she meant to insult him? He *had* just pushed her into a cobweb-filled closet right after they'd made out. And, yes, he should have probably not kissed her. Not then. But he had. There was no going back from that particular choice.

He slipped toward one of the boarded-up windows near the front of the cottage. He peeked through the slat of boards and saw the black Range Rover slide to a fast stop. The driver's side door swung open, and relief filled Ryan as he saw the blond hair of his MI6 counterpart, Harry Wilson. Harry wore a pair of sunglasses to shield his gaze, and as the MI6 agent bounded forward, his dark coat flapped open a bit. No noticeable weapon on him.

Ryan opened the front door before Harry could reach it.

"We've got a five-minute lead on them," Harry snapped out.

Ryan did not question how Harry knew this fact.

"Let's go," Harry urged.

Right, so...Ryan hadn't exactly had time to explain in his text that he had a companion with him. Companion, witness, criminal—all of the above in one tempting package. "I'm not alone."

"What?" Harry's brows shot up over his sunglasses.

"She's coming, too. Hold on." Ryan spun and bounded back to the closet.

"Mate, we have got to *go!*"

"Understood." He yanked open the closet door.

Harry's steps rushed behind him.

Only, the closet was empty. There was no gorgeous woman in a soggy and damaged red gown waiting inside.

"What is happening here?" Harry demanded. "Are you, uh, having some sort of episode?"

Ryan whirled back toward him. "I barely left her for a minute!"

"Left *who?*" Harry yanked off his glasses. His golden stare raked Ryan. "Did you hit your head? Your eye looks like hell, by the way. That's a serious shiner."

He shoved Harry out of his way. Ryan had just caught sight of the small, muddy footprints on the floor. They snaked to the left, around a crumbling wall that had half of a fireplace still clinging to it.

"Time to leave! We've got to go!" Harry's voice cracked around the edges.

"Not without her!" Ryan kept following those muddy prints and realized he was in the remains of a kitchen. His head whipped up as he found his target. Simone. A Simone frantically struggling to open what appeared to be the cottage's back door. "*Sweetheart.*"

She paused mid-struggle. "Was it the good guys outside?" A peek over her shoulder. "Or the bad?"

He closed in.

She let go of the doorknob and turned to face him. "I didn't like the closet, so I thought I'd hide in here."

Cute. "You were running away from me."

"More like...I was running away from MI6 *and* the CIA."

Harry rushed into the old kitchen. "Who are you talking—wow. *Who is she?*"

Simone flashed him a bright, sunny smile. "Hi."

Not happening. She was not going to charm the MI6 agent. Sighing, Ryan leaned forward and tossed Simone over his shoulder. Immediately, a ton of muddy skirt ruffles hit him in the face. He shoved them out of the way, but as he shoved them, Ryan felt a distinct...clink.

Simone had been struggling in his arms, but at that *clink*—a sound they both had to hear—she stilled. Momentarily. Only to rally instantly and renew her struggles with even more force.

He tightened his grip on her. "Don't test me right now."

"Why not?" Her perky retort. "Will there be a better time for me to test you later?"

Harry cleared his throat. Loudly. "In case you missed it before..."

Ryan strode toward the agent, with Simone over his left shoulder.

"I had a five-minute lead on our enemy. That lead is down to like, three minutes now. Either we get the hell out or we will probably all die."

"Does it look like I'm dying?" Ryan snapped back.

Harry pursed his lips. "It looks like you're kidnapping that woman. I...don't think that's approved CIA behavior."

His jaw locked harder. Ryan gritted, "Get the fucking ride moving."

Harry scrambled out to get the fucking ride moving. Ryan kept his prey, and he hurried outside on Harry's heels. The sun beat down on him, the streaks of light slipping through the drifting clouds. Harry jumped in the front of the vehicle, and Ryan surged into the back with Simone.

Surprising no one, she tried to immediately open the door near her and jump from the vehicle. Sighing, Ryan hauled her closer. "I do not want to have to cuff you." But she was about to give him no choice.

"Oh, please." She tossed her hair over her shoulder. "You don't even have cuffs on you."

Granted, he did not. "Harry!"

Harry slammed on the gas. The vehicle lurched forward, taking them away from the cottage and rushing onto a stone-covered road.

"Harry, do you have cuffs on you?" Ryan demanded.

Simone glared at Ryan. "The vehicle is moving now. I'm not going to toss myself onto the road while we're driving this fast. Not like I have a death wish." She straightened her shoulders. "For the record, I wasn't running before."

"The hell you weren't."

"I didn't like being shoved in a dark closet! Sue me, but I can't stand the dark!"

Her words almost held a ring of truth, but he'd come to realize she could lie incredibly well. "Who are you?" He needed answers. He would get them.

"Simone Sailor."

He growled.

Her head turned toward the front of the vehicle. "I'm Simone." She cleared her throat and leaned toward the driver. Her hand reached out to touch his shoulder. "I did not catch your name."

"Harry," he replied. His accent had thickened, making the name sound more like "Air-ree" as the H dropped.

"Just fucking *drive,*" Ryan blasted at him. He caught Simone's hand and pulled it off Harry. Did he like her touching the MI6 agent? No, he did not.

What is my deal?

"That is so rude," Simone told him. She huffed out a breath. "I apologize, Harry, for Ryan's tone and for his language."

His language?

"Thank you so much for coming to our assistance," she continued in a honey-sweet voice. "It's been a very trying twenty-four hours for me, and I am grateful to you."

Seriously? Seriously?

Ryan caught the straightening of Harry's shoulders. Saw the guy adjust his rearview mirror so he could get a better view of Simone. "Simone, I will keep you safe," Harry promised her.

The hell he would. "I'm on it," Ryan growled. Then he grabbed the fluffy red material of her skirt and shoved it up.

Simone immediately shoved it back down, but not before he'd gotten a truly glorious view of her legs. *Killer* legs. Insanely attractive. Legs that he could all too easily imagine wrapped around him and holding tight.

"What in the world are you doing?" Simone cried.

Harry nearly drove them off the road.

"Focus, Harry!" Ryan snapped.

"I was," Harry mumbled back.

Oh, the prick had better *not* be focusing on her legs. Ryan shifted his body, and he grabbed for the fluffy material of her skirt again.

She swatted at his hands. "This is entirely too, um, friendly of you. Stop it. Stop!"

His hand came up, holding his prize. The gleaming egg. He'd known Simone had it as soon as he'd heard the telling *clink* moments before. "Just retrieving my property."

Her eyes widened. "Where on earth did that come from?"

His back teeth clenched. "It was in one of the hidden pockets of your dress." No wonder she loved those damn pockets so much.

"That is crazy. It must have fallen into my pocket when you were lifting me over your shoulder."

Why the hell did he have to fight a smile at her words? Slowly, deliberately, Ryan shook his head. "No. It did not *fall* into your pocket. You took it from me." He wasn't exactly sure when. Perhaps when they'd been kissing? Riding the horse? Or, hell, could have been when they'd still been in the stables. He remembered her hands sliding over him before they'd ridden out on the stallion. "You are good."

"Oh, I've got it. The egg must have fallen into my dress when we were on the horse together. Bouncing around and all that." Her eyes were very wide. "Amazing."

Oh, something was amazing, all right. *And it's her.*

"What's happening back there?" Harry asked.

"Keep your eyes on the road and get us to a safe location." Ryan inhaled. He also tried to focus on his job. "Am I going to have to search you?"

Her head tilted. "Search me...for what?"

"For whatever else you're hiding?"

"I'm afraid I have to decline your fun invitation for a search." A bit colder. Harder. Not nearly as semi-amused as she'd been before. "I do have rights, you understand. Also, Mr. CIA Operative, we are not in the US. You threatened me with arrest, but I don't recall doing anything other than saving your life again and again."

"Saving me?"

"Um." She shoved the skirt completely down over her killer legs. "And seeing as how I apparently just retrieved a very important item for you, I would appreciate some gratitude."

"That's the story you're going with now? That you *retrieved* it?" He'd bet a million dollars that Simone had been intent on stealing the egg from him.

"It's kinda what I do." No blinks. No hesitation. "I'm a retrieval specialist, at your service."

"Bullshit," he called. "You're a thief."

A gasp. "That's hurtful."

Dammit, were those tears welling in her eyes? "Don't you dare cry." Because he had a feeling that her tears might break something in him.

I am in trouble.

Her lower lip trembled. "Don't you know that you should never kiss a woman and then insult her? That's extremely poor manners."

"*Shit. Company. Incoming.* Get down, get down!" Harry yelled.

There was no more room on her side of the vehicle, so Ryan immediately yanked Simone down on top of him, completely flattening her against his body as he slammed against the seat. Every single inch of her...against him.

"The windows are tinted," she whispered.

Yes, they were.

"If this is an MI6 vehicle, I would think it would at least be bulletproof, too," she added. Her breath blew lightly against his neck. Her head was nestled between his shoulder and his chin.

His dick could not swell anymore.

"It is bulletproof," Harry assured her from the front. "But I just saw no point in taking chances. Got four blokes in two cars, heading fast for the little cottage."

"Be cool, Harry," Ryan ordered him. "Don't speed. Stay nice and slow."

"They're looking hard at us. Oh, shit. I think I see a gun."

Ryan felt Simone stiffen against him. "Nice and slow," Ryan repeated. He began to carefully shift them so that he was on top of Simone, his body protectively curling against her. "Just keep driving. Hell, give them a friendly wave if you want. Really fuck with them."

"*What?*" Harry seemed to choke.

For hell's sake. What was this? Harry's first mission? "Wave. And *drive*. Slowly. Normally."

He didn't know if Harry waved, but the man kept driving. Slowly. Good. No sense accelerating and looking suspicious.

The moments ticked past. Beat by beat.

Simone poked at him. "I think you can get up now."

His head lifted, but he didn't take his body off hers. "Better safe than sorry."

"You are *crushing* me."

He shifted his weight and rose a little. "Sorry."

"No, I don't think you are. Not even a small bit." An angry retort. "But you will be. You will be very, very sorry if you don't drop this nonsense about me being some kind of—of a thief and you arresting me. As soon as we get to a safe place, you need to let me go."

He brought his mouth next to her ear. "That's just not going to happen."

She shivered beneath him. "Then it will be your funeral."

Oh, he highly doubted that. "Did you just threaten me?"

"No. I'm *warning* you." A swift inhale from Simone. "I am not a safe woman."

Ryan couldn't help it. He laughed because...he still had blood on him. They'd been kidnapped. He'd had to kill for her. "Sweetheart, tell me something I don't already know."

Chapter Nine

So Ryan wanted to know something he didn't already know? Fine. She was friends with criminals. Lots and lots of criminals. She knew killers. She knew scammers. She knew the worst of the worst. Now, granted, the *worst of the worst* were not what she'd call her closest friends...

But her list of associates was incredibly damning. Especially when viewed through the lens of the CIA.

He'd gotten them back to London. Taken them to a hotel that was beyond swanky just along the edge of Hyde Park. The place screamed money in the loudest possible voice, but hotels like this one—if they were screaming money, then they were also screaming security. The elegant building was truly like Fort Knox. Guards positioned at all exterior doors. Cameras throughout. And in order to get up to the exclusive floor where she was currently residing, you had to have a very special key card that would give you access to a private elevator. An elevator that was, of course, guarded.

They were in a corner suite. One where the decorator had chosen to go hard with a dark blue and lots and lots of shimmering chandeliers. Personally, Simone didn't love the décor, but she was obsessed with the safety so...*it works. It all works.*

A knock sounded on the bathroom door. Because, well, she'd been soaking in the giant claw-foot tub in the suite's bathroom for at least the last half hour. Soaking. Hiding. Plotting. The usual.

"Simone?" The doorknob rattled.

Good luck with the rattling. She'd locked the door.

"Simone, are you alive?"

Her eyes narrowed on the door. "Yes." She sank more comfortably into the tub. Her bubbles were dispersing. Probably a sign that she should get out.

"Fabulous. So glad you're still in the land of the living." And the door flew open.

She gasped and whipped down deeper into the lingering bubbles. Her hands covered her breasts, and then, realizing that she'd left a very important part of herself vulnerable, she immediately slapped one hand over her lower, ah, goods, and kept her left arm over her breasts. "*What are you doing?*"

He turned toward her voice, even as one hand kept gripping the door. "You locked the door." His gaze remained on her face. Only on her face.

"Yes. *Because I am naked in here.*"

His gaze stayed on her face. A muscle flexed along his jaw.

"What did you think I was doing?" Simone snapped.

"Hiding. Plotting. Planning how to get away from me."

Okay, it was both eerie and a bit impressive the way Ryan had listed all of her activities. Time to regroup and distract him. "You picked the lock. That's naughty."

Another flex of the muscle along his jaw. And that stare of his did not leave her face.

"It's also impressive," she heard herself say, "the way you haven't looked down."

"You have no idea how impressive." A growl. Then, "I need to clean up, too, Simone."

"There's, um, a shower right there." She would have pointed to the side, but her hands were busy.

He lifted an eyebrow. "You want me to shower...while you are right here?"

Where was the problem? The bathroom had a tub and a separate shower. "You're seeing me naked."

"I am keeping my eyes on your face."

"Yes, you are, and that's fabulous, but you could have been gentlemanly and never come into the bathroom in the first place. Or, once in...and once you saw that I was not up to some wicked deed, you could have left."

His lips thinned. "Feels fucking wicked." A mumble.

"Um. Also, we are on a higher floor. Not like I was going to open the bathroom window and scale down the building." She'd considered it but tossed the idea after looking outside. Just not really feasible. The odds of her breaking a bone had been too high. "But back to you leaving."

He swallowed.

"You have not left the bathroom yet."

"No."

"If you're not leaving, then why not just jump in the shower? Fair is fair."

"Excuse me?" His hands fisted at his sides.

Maybe it was her imagination, but his breathing seemed to have become decidedly more ragged. "Fair is fair," Simone repeated because that seemed to have been the part he missed. "I'm naked. You're getting the full show."

"I am *not* getting the full show."

Again, only because he was making that intense eye-contact. "I should get the same treatment. The same show. Strip. Shower." A slight pause. "I could even promise not to look." She *could* promise. She would not.

"Fair is fair." Gritted.

Ah, now that was the spirit. She nodded.

He turned away from her.

Her breath left her in a fast rush. She did not normally hold full conversations with men while she was naked in a bathtub. In fact, this had been a jarring first for her. She started to grab for a nearby towel.

Except...

He began to strip.

He jerked off his white dress shirt and tossed it to the floor. He'd long since lost his bow tie someplace, and she could not remember where or when he'd ditched that. But when the shirt hit the floor, her gaze locked on the broad, powerful expanse of his back.

He opened the glass shower door. Yanked on the water.

He backed up to kick away his shoes and ditch his socks, and then his hands went to the waist of his pants.

Do not stop now.

Her body had inched toward the right wall of the tub. She turned on her side, a better position to hide herself, and her hand curled around the tub's top as she peeked at him.

Oh, yum.

He had tattoos. He should not have tattoos. Not. Ryan should have been buttoned up and boring, but...

Her spy was not boring.

He was not some silver-spoon-in-his-mouth, rich tycoon.

He did not spend his days behind a desk or yachting around the world. He had muscles and abs for days, and the most badass, gorgeous tattoos imaginable.

Especially that dragon on his arm. Those claws. Those scales.

Simone bit her lower lip. She'd always had a weakness for a man with tats.

"You're not looking at my eyes, Simone," he rasped.

"No, I am not." A click as she swallowed. "Nice tats." There was more ink on his chest. Dark. Twisting. Gorgeous.

"These are actually my real ones."

Her brows rose. "As opposed to the *fake* ones that you have?"

"Sometimes I get fake ones for jobs. When the job is done, they fade away."

Interesting. "I'm glad the dragon is legit. Because if it were to vanish, I'd be so disappointed."

"You got a thing for dragons?"

She had a thing for hot badasses who killed for her. *Stop it, woman. Stop.* "I like it when a person can handle, ah, hot situations."

"Fuck."

Oh, but she was tempted to do just that. Except that fucking Ryan would only lead to more trouble. "You can't shower with your pants on." An obvious point. She was quite curious to see the rest of the show. *Do not stop now.*

"Thought you promised not to look."

She had turned more on her side so that her breasts were pressed against the wall of the tub. From his angle, she thought he could only see the curve of her hip. Her fingers gripped the edge of the tub as she lifted her head up a little more. "I said I *could* promise not to do that. I didn't actually make the promise." But if he wanted to be a party pooper... "Shall I look away?"

"I'm not shy." He unbuttoned his pants. Unzipped.

She *might* have held her breath.

His pants and a pair of black boxers hit the floor.

Wow.

He was...

"Good show," she whispered.

Big. Heavily aroused. A wide, long cock surged toward her. A fantastically muscled, tatted body. An eager dick that promised an incredible ride.

Her nipples ached. Her sex quivered.

And he strode into the shower. Pulled the glass door shut behind him and stood underneath the heavy fall of water.

Good show, indeed. Her heart raced, her body tingled in all the best ways, and Simone realized that fair was truly fair.

She rose from the tub. The water poured from her body. As if sensing the movement, Ryan craned back around. She could have grabbed a towel to cover herself, but what would have been the point in that?

Fair was fair.

"Look anywhere," Simone told him, raising her voice to be sure he could hear her over the thunder of the shower, "but at my eyes."

The water and a few bubbles slid down her body as she climbed from the tub. Her feet touched the ultra-soft, ultra-thick bath rug that waited. Ryan angled his body fully toward her. She felt his gaze like a hot, sensual touch on her skin.

Her feet edged closer to him so that she stood in front of

the closed shower door. No hiding for her. Just standing right there. Offering him the full show.

He moved closer to the glass door, too. Big, strong body. So powerful. Only the thin glass separated them. She really hated that glass because if it wasn't there, then maybe he'd be touching her.

What are you doing, Simone? The last bit of her rational self seemed to scream from somewhere deep inside. *Grab a towel. Put on a robe. Get out of here.*

But...

No one had ever protected her the way he had. No one had ever fought so fiercely for her.

And she'd never wanted someone quite as much.

"It's a shame that door is between us," she whispered. Low words. He probably couldn't make them out. Not with the roar of the water. "Because I'd rather you be touching me." Her right hand rose, skimmed down her chest. Over her stomach.

He tensed behind the door.

Down her hand went. Her thighs parted.

"*Simone.*"

Her fingers slid between her legs. Feathered over her clit. "I bet it would feel so much better if you touched me."

He ripped open the door. Jumped onto the rug right in front of her. Ryan grabbed Simone and hauled her against him. His mouth crashed onto hers. Her mouth was open, eager. Her lips and tongue waiting for him because hunger and lust consumed her.

She felt his hand slide away from her hip. It angled between them. His broad, wet fingers pushed between her legs. Over her clit. Stroked her even as he dipped into—

Something was ringing. No, pealing? Like...

Her mouth tore from his. "What is that sound? Bells?"

His fingers raked over her clit.

She shuddered. Her knees almost gave way. Her body was on the edge, way too tight and needy.

But she was hearing the freaking bells again.

He stroked her, harder, more demanding.

A moan broke from her even as her hands clamped around his shoulders. "There are bells! It's an alarm or—*ah, yes!* It's...something."

His head lifted. His eyes were almost blind with lust. Burning dark.

"Ryan?"

He let her go. Backed away. Nearly hit the edge of the shower. "Bells?" His eyes narrowed. "Fuck!"

If only.

She grabbed a fluffy robe and yanked it around her body. "I'm assuming..." Simone stopped and cleared her throat. "I'm assuming this swanky place has some sort of doorbell for each suite? That's the sound I'm hearing?"

He reached into the shower and turned off the water. "Yes." A hiss.

"Then we have company." Company who had just interrupted before they could cross a very big line. Maybe it was for the best. Sex with Ryan probably would have been a major mistake.

But, oh, she bet it would have felt incredible.

Simone belted the robe with fingers that shook. "Why do we have company? And is it the kind of company that is here to potentially kill us?"

He grabbed a towel and wrapped it around his hips. Water trickled down his chest. That fantastic chest. "Stay here." He anchored the towel against his left hip and strode out.

She watched him go. "Yeah, sure, no problem. I'll just stay in the bathroom and wait to see if we live or die. Cool."

He froze in the doorway. Then Ryan glanced back at her. "I'm damn well not dying before I fuck you."

Her lips parted, but she could not speak. No flippant remark at all because his words had sounded entirely like a vow.

The door clicked closed behind him.

Her hands shoved into the pockets of her robe. "Good to know," she whispered. Very, very good to know.

Chapter Ten

He paused to peer through the peephole on the suite's main door, even though Ryan was pretty sure he knew the identity of the guest who'd just interrupted at the worst possible time ever.

Sure enough, his MI6 contact, Harry Wilson, waited.

Sighing heavily, Ryan yanked open the door.

Harry blinked. His mouth gaped. His stare swept over Ryan's body.

"Yo, eyes here." Ryan pointed toward his eyes.

Harry's gaze jerked back up. "Why are you wearing a towel?"

"Because you interrupted me while I was in the shower." No, actually, it had been way, way worse than that. A thousand times worse. *You interrupted me when I was touching the sweetest heaven ever. I had just dipped my finger into Simone's tight, hot core.*

He should punch the bastard for that sin.

"You...uh, can we talk inside the suite?" Harry asked, craning to look behind him.

Fine. Ryan tossed out a hand and grabbed the MI6

agent by the shirtfront. He hauled Harry inside, slammed the door, and locked it. "Better?" Ryan asked as he stalked away from the guy.

"Uh, yeah. It is better." Harry followed on his heels as Ryan made his way to the small sitting room area. "Look, you need to know, I checked with my supervisors, and they do not like this plan. They think you should be in hiding. Not checking in to the most expensive hotel in London."

"Good thing I don't report to your supervisors, huh?"

"It's a *joint* operation. And MI6 is footing the bill!"

Ryan shrugged as he turned toward Harry. "Then I'll pay. Whatever." He could handle it. Not like he normally talked about his actual finances. He'd chosen the hotel for its security. Finding a safe place for Simone had been a necessity. If MI6 was balking at the bill, he'd just cover the expense.

"My supervisors are also, uh, not sure about the situation with Simone Sailor. They want her brought in for questioning."

Footsteps. Soft, padding footsteps that came from the bathroom. He whirled, and sure enough, looking far too sexy in a white robe, Simone headed for him and Harry. Her wet hair slid over her shoulders. Her beautiful face showed her curiosity, and her gorgeous eyes gleamed. "Brought in...where?" Simone asked with raised eyebrows.

Ryan marched toward her. "You're in a robe."

"And you're in a towel." An amused curl of her lips. "Aren't you giving quite the show to Harry?"

His jaw locked. "You were supposed to stay in the bathroom."

"Whoops." Then she shrugged. "I heard Harry's voice. I knew it was safe to come out. I mean, you are working with him, yes? So he's safe?"

This was his first ever case to work with Harry Wilson. Did he trust him? Somewhat. But not entirely. There were only a handful of people that he did trust completely in this world. Most of those individuals were family.

"Excuse me." Harry cleared his throat. "Were you two in the bathroom, showering, together?"

Ryan looked back at him. A hard look. A don't-piss-me-off-look. "How the hell is that relevant to you?"

Harry backed up.

And then the bell rang again.

Ryan instantly tensed. "Do you have backup who was joining this talk?"

Harry shook his head.

Fuck. And he didn't have a gun in the suite. He reached for Simone. Closed one hand around her shoulder. "Will you *please* go and hide?"

"But what if you need me?"

"Hide."

She stormed away. Her robe fluttered around her legs.

He hurried for the main door.

"Should I hide, too?" Harry asked.

Ryan froze. "Are you fucking kidding me?"

"I was just...you know, ah, considering the element of surprise and all that. I thought if I hid, and then jumped out at any enemies, it would work to our advantage."

Ryan squeezed the bridge of his nose. "Tell me again how many field missions you've worked." His hand fell as his gaze cut to Harry.

Harry straightened his shoulders. "This is my third one."

"Third one. Fantastic. Yeah, know what? Go hide. Do that. Or, even better, go hide *with* Simone. If some asshole actually manages to get past me, then you kill the fucker before he can touch her, got me?"

Harry seemed to pale.

"I am not sure this is the right line of work for you," Ryan muttered. "*Hide.*"

Harry rushed after Simone.

Ryan checked the peephole. Only instead of seeing a threat, he saw one of those wonderful individuals that he actually did trust. Not family, at least not by blood, but still...

Ryan unlocked the door, swung it open, and smiled at his CIA supervisor, Jezebel Jenkins. "Jez, hell of a surprise to see you! I had no idea you were on this side of the pond."

"Ryan, get some clothes on your damn self." She marched past him without even sparing him a second glance. "And tell me what sort of fuckery we're facing."

* * *

SIMONE SNAGGED the broach and the earrings from the spot where she'd frantically stashed them before—under the mattress. Yes, a cliché spot, but time had been of the essence, so she hadn't been given the luxury of finding a better location. Just as it was of the essence now, too. Simone shoved the items into the left pocket of her robe, and she—

The bedroom door shut.

She'd left the door *open.*

Simone grabbed the lamp from the bedside and whirled around, her arm up and ready to throw her weapon.

"No!" Harry crouched. "It's just me! I'm hiding with you!"

"What?"

"Protecting you," he corrected as his cheeks flushed. "Hiding and protecting. That way, if the enemy gets past Ryan, I can save you."

He was going to save her? The man crouching in front of the door? "In this scenario, who saves Ryan?"

"I...am hoping he can save himself."

This was ridiculous. She marched forward and glared at him. "Move."

Harry moved to the side. Then seemed to realize her plan. "Wait, what are you—"

She yanked open the bedroom door. She still had her weapon at the ready. Up and in swinging position. Except when she opened that door, she came face to face with Ryan.

He eyed the lamp. Then smiled at her. "Planning to bash someone in the head?"

If necessary, yes.

"It was a friendly visitor. No worries." His gaze darted to Harry. "By the way, she wants to meet you, too, Harry."

Simone slowly lowered the lamp. "She?"

"Um, yes, my boss." His head cocked to the right. "She wants to meet you, Simone. Meet you, interrogate you. You know, the usual."

Does she want to arrest me? Simone tried to buy some time while she tried to find a way out of this mess. "Any chance I could get some clothing soon? It's not exactly fun to go around meeting new people in a robe." Though he was definitely working that towel of his.

"One moment." He disappeared down the narrow hallway.

The floor creaked behind her.

"Where did he go?" Harry asked.

Glancing over her shoulder, she had to question, "Are you truly MI6? Or is this some joke?"

He straightened. "Why would it be a joke?"

"You just seem...green." The greenest of greens.

"Don't you worry about my capabilities. This is my third mission."

Simone nodded. "That tracks."

He frowned.

But Ryan was back. So her focus returned to him. He was back and edging past her as he carried a very large brown suitcase toward the bed. "Courtesy of Jezebel," he explained as he put down the luggage. "Clothes for you. Toiletries. Makeup. Everything you need. I received a similar delivery of necessary supplies." His hand motioned toward Harry. "Let's give Simone privacy to change." An order. He quirked an eyebrow at Simone. "I'll get dressed, too. Then meet you in the sitting area in five minutes?"

Yes. Fine. Five.

He closed the door. She changed as fast as possible. She also made sure to hide her precious trinkets. Because when she finally slipped away from Ryan—and she would be slipping away, sooner or later—she intended to take her prizes with her. After all, she had a job to complete. Someone very important needed to have those items returned, and there was no world in which Simone planned to disappoint this particular individual.

* * *

"So you're Simone Sailor."

Simone blinked. She'd just walked into the very blue sitting room. Blue sofa. Blue chair. Blue curtains over the window that looked out at Hyde Park and the Wellington

Arch. In contrast to the blue, the walls were a dark brown. Dark brown end tables on either side of the couch. Dark brown desk near the window. Dark brown coffee table. All of the wood gleamed, as if it had been carefully polished, and, overhead, a crystal chandelier caught the light and seemed to sparkle.

But it certainly wasn't the décor that captured Simone's attention. It was the woman who sat, sipping tea, in the blue chair. A woman with short, dark hair. Small, pearl earrings hung from her lobes, and she wore an austere, gray suit that should have swallowed her delicate frame. It didn't, though. Somehow, the suit just made her look extra refined.

The woman took another sip of her tea and then put the fragile cup back on its saucer. She rose, her stare assessing, as she took in Simone.

When the lady rose, Simone realized that the CIA operative barely clocked in at five feet.

"I'm Jezebel Jenkins." She extended a hand toward Simone. No trace of an accent shaded her words.

Simone took the offered hand. "Should I be pleased to meet you or terrified?"

Ryan grunted from his sprawled position on the couch. "You can be both. Most people are."

Good to know.

Harry wasn't seated. He sort of bobbed around nervously near the window.

"He was both," Ryan said, waving toward Harry. "They were introduced moments before you joined the party in here."

Well, Harry was not being threatened with an arrest so what had been his excuse for terror?

"You don't exist," Jezebel announced, still holding

Simone's hand. Her dark gaze flashed with a cunning intelligence.

Simone forced a smile. "Of course, I do. I'm right here." She tugged her hand back.

Jezebel let her go, even as she sent Simone a cold smile. "On paper, you don't exist. In computer databases, you don't exist. There is no Simone Sailor from Asheville, North Carolina."

"Oh, did I say that I was from Asheville? I don't remember doing that." She darted a glance at Ryan. "There must be some confusion."

"There is *some* confusion." Ryan seemed certain. "You caused it. You put Asheville down on your employment paperwork with Frederick. *That's* where we got the idea that you were from Asheville."

"Sorry. Can we back up?" A very polite inquiry, and then, "You accessed my paperwork?"

"Guilty," Ryan murmured.

"Guessing you are *not* from Asheville?" A faint curl of Jezebel's lips.

"I moved around a great deal while growing up." That was completely true and wonderfully vague. "I did visit Asheville for a time, but I wasn't born there."

"Where were you born?" Jezebel asked. "While we're at it, how about you give me your social security number? Your real date of birth? And a couple of people who can vouch for every single thing that you say to me? Because that would be great."

"My, but you do request a lot." Simone's words were cool even as her heart raced. She could play this scene in an assortment of ways. Simone decided it was time to just roll with things. "So I fibbed a bit on my resume. Who hasn't committed that particular crime?" Now her right hand waved casually toward Ryan. "Case in point, our bored billionaire." Time to direct attention his way. Her body shifted as her stare pinned him. "Do you really want to talk about *causing* confusion? You were the one who caused chaos and confusion in the gallery when you *stole* your precious egg. Then I got blamed for the theft and nearly died." A ragged exhale. "Honestly, I should probably get an apology for the entire chain of events." She peeked at a watchful Jezebel. "Will I get a full apology? Perhaps one from the CIA as a whole?"

"I don't think so."

"Unfortunate."

"Yes, well, here's a bit of even more unfortunate news. You're currently on a hit list," Jezebel informed her. Very casually. Very flatly. "As of an hour ago, you've got a bounty on you."

Simone absorbed that tidbit without changing expression. "You're right. That is even more unfortunate to know."

But Ryan erupted off the couch. "Unfortunate? That's all you both have to say?" He closed in on Simone. "Jez tells you that you're got a bounty on your head. By the way, it's *fucking* high from what I was told before you came into the room. And you act like it's nothing?"

What did he expect her to do? Panic? Cry? Not going to happen. She was far too used to masking her emotions in order to do any of those things. "It's certainly not nothing. It's my life."

He growled.

Simone's heart raced frantically in her chest. "I'm assuming that Ryan has informed the CIA of Alexei's death?"

"We are aware," Jezebel replied. "But, FYI, his body seems to have vanished."

"Oh, dear." Her heart raced *faster*. "Vanishing bodies are never good."

"No." Jezebel was definite. "They are not." Jez resumed her seat. She picked up her tea. Eyed the liquid a moment and said, "I only drink this in London. When I'm in the US, I love sweet tea. Ice cold, sweet tea on a warm summer day." She sipped delicately. "But when you are in foggy London, there is just something about warm tea, isn't there?"

Ryan's arm brushed against Simone. He wore black dress pants. A crisp, light blue shirt. Shining black dress shoes. The man looked like money. He also looked dead sexy because that shirt had the top three buttons undone and his hair was tousled and faint stubble lined his hard jaw.

She should stop staring at his jaw and focus on other details. Like the fact that people wanted to kill her. "If you don't mind, may I get a few more details on the hit that has been placed on me?" Excruciatingly polite.

"The hit was launched after you killed a Russian mercenary and escaped into the mist." A shrug from Jezebel. "I believe the order came from Frederick Bradwin, but the techs at MI6 would not tell me for certain." Her gaze cut to Harry. "Perhaps you should tell your associates that cooperation means you actually cooperate." Another sip of her tea.

Simone smoothed her hands over the top of her thighs. She wore brown pants that seemed to have been tailored just for her, a cashmere sweater that might have been the softest thing she'd ever touched, and high, pointed brown heels. The outfit felt expensive, she knew it no doubt was, and her instincts said that the fancy clothes—along with all of the other high-end items in the suitcase—had been provided to her for a very specific reason.

"Get the hit called off," Ryan ordered.

A sigh from Jezebel. "Even I can't just snap my fingers and make something like that happen." Her stare lingered on Simone. "But perhaps protection can be arranged."

Oh, she knew where this was going. "Let me guess, if I cooperate?"

"Cooperation means you actually cooperate," Jezebel murmured. "Oh, is there an echo in here? Those words feel familiar."

"Ryan arrested me." Something that was still a sore spot for Simone.

Jezebel blinked. "And here I thought he *saved* you."

"Same thing," Ryan said. "Just sounds different depending on who is saying the words."

That made zero sense. Simone turned on him. "It is not the same. At all. And, for the record, I'm not the one who killed the Russian mercenary." She shook her head. "But Frederick thinks I am? If that's the case, then what does he think about you?"

"As Sherlock Holmes would say, the game is still afoot," Ryan informed her.

"That is not funny. My life is no game." It was also no answer. "Can we all just say what we mean? *Please?* Because that would help me enormously." She might seem calm, but on the inside, Simone was fighting not to shatter apart.

"I would prefer that." Jezebel pointed toward the couch Ryan had just vacated. "Let's all sit and chat in a civilized fashion."

Simone took a seat on the couch.

Ryan sat right next to her.

Harry just lingered awkwardly near the window. Not in front of the window. Near it.

Simone scooted over, attempting to put some distance between herself and Ryan. But the couch was too small or maybe he was too big because there was no distance, there was just him. His heat. His body. His crisp, tempting scent. Reaching out to her.

Then he was physically reaching out and curling his hand under her chin as he carefully tilted her head so that she stared into his eyes. "You will get twenty-four, seven protection."

That sounded promising.

"There is a very, very large bounty on your head. Jez's intel on that was quite specific."

"Um," Jez said. Agreement? Disagreement?

Ryan did not look away from Simone. "In order to stay alive, you need me."

She leaned toward him. "You're sort of the whole reason I got caught. Do you know that you screwed up a perfect, one hundred percent perfect success rate? If *you* hadn't stolen the egg then—"

"Then no one would have been watching when you came back and committed *your* theft?" Ryan asked, voice silky.

Something like that.

"You have connections, don't you, Simone?" Jezebel asked her. "Criminal connections."

"I have connections to all sorts of interesting individuals. I believe in having a wide net of friends and acquaintances. Why limit yourself?"

Ryan's head cocked. "Am I your friend?"

"No." Very definite.

His eyelashes flickered. "That hurts." His hand slid away from her.

"Know what else hurts? Being threatened with arrest. I am about ninety-five percent sure that friends don't go around threatening to arrest friends." A deliberate pause. "That's something that enemies do."

"*Ahem.*"

Their heads turned toward Jezebel.

She smiled at them. "I fear that we have gotten off topic."

Potentially, they had, yes.

"I am aware that you did not kill Alexei Morozov," Jezebel stated with no emotion in her voice. "Ryan told me exactly what happened in those stables."

Goosebumps rose on Simone's body. It took all of her self-control not to lift her hand and touch the small cut on her neck as she remembered just how close her own death had been.

"However, Frederick is not aware of Ryan's true identity. Frederick has it in his head that you are responsible for Alexei's murder."

"Not murder." Simone had to point out this important distinction. "Ryan was defending himself. Defending me. Alexei intended to torture and kill us both."

Jezebel nodded. In silence, she studied Simone for one beat of time. Two. And... "You are a ghost, Simone," Jezebel accused.

She'd been called worse.

"But I am very good at digging into the pasts of ghosts."

"And here I thought the CIA was powered by spooks. That *is* the term for CIA operatives, isn't it? Spooks?" Simone knew good and well that it was the term.

Jezebel sipped her tea. "I will uncover your past. I will find your sins. You do not want me as an enemy. You want me in that wide net of friends and acquaintances you mentioned before."

"Ah." A nod. She could read the writing on the wall. "You're about to offer me a deal. I thought a deal might be coming, when I was given the fancy new clothes. I figured if I was going to prison, you wouldn't bother with the designer labels."

"Work with us," Jezebel said. Not an offer. More of a statement. "We are after some very dangerous, very bad individuals."

Okay, so...time to drop her act and dispense with the bullshit. "You mean men like the one who supplied Frederick with that amazingly gorgeous Fabergé egg?"

The silence in the sitting room was suddenly very, very thick. Actually, the only sound she heard was Harry's loud swallow. The click cut through the room.

Simone tucked a still wet lock of hair behind her ear. "I'd say the Fabergé was worth at least thirty million. That's a very conservative estimate. And seeing as how it was created for the Russian Imperial family, it really only makes sense that it was passed down through Russian hands." She pursed her lips. "Frederick has such an impressive distribution network left over from the textile business that his family once operated. It would be incredibly easy for the right—or, sorry, in this case the *wrong*—person to use that network. But you have to pay in order to play in this world. Everyone understands that rule."

Surprise and what might have been satisfaction flashed on Jezebel's face. "You've met the man pulling the strings."

The man currently keeping Frederick's business empire up and running? "Our paths might have crossed once or twice."

"Fuck," Ryan breathed. She'd managed to surprise him.

"Frederick liked for me to be in his business meetings. I speak Russian, and he wanted to make sure that no one was trying to trick him."

"You speak Russian?" Harry asked. His first question since she'd come in the room.

She'd literally just said that she did, but Simone replied, "It's on my resume, so, yes, I speak it. I also speak French, German, Italian, Spanish, and a wee bit of Mandarin Chinese. Just so you know, I think the Mandarin is by far the hardest. Tones have so many meanings there, but I'm working on it. Pitch can just be tricky."

"You *met* the man who is controlling Frederick?" Ryan seemed to force the question through clenched teeth.

Why did she keep having to re-answer questions? "Yes. I met Konstantin."

Silence.

"We *are* all talking about Konstantin Volkov, aren't we?" Simone decided that she should add more, in order to really seal the deal. "He's Ryan's height. Has brown hair. Green eyes. A scar under his chin. Another over his right eyebrow."

Ryan's gaze cut to Jezebel, then back to Simone.

It took all of her self-control not to nervously tap her foot. Or to jump off the sofa and make a run for it. But, instead, she opted to put a few more cards on the table. "When I looked at the egg before, I saw the little computer chip inside. I believe Konstantin wanted Frederick to transfer that chip for him, and once the transfer was complete, Frederick could keep the egg. A services-rendered type of situation. Or maybe it was a down payment for future business deals. I'm not entirely sure of the specifics."

"*You saw the chip?*" Real emotion in Jezebel's voice. "You knew it was in the egg all along?"

Why were they having so much trouble with her responses? "I was there for the handoff. I was in the room. I heard Konstantin talk about the chip." Yes, she'd known.

"Damn." A wide and what appeared to be a true smile on Jezebel's face. "You're a witness."

"Yes. That's what I am." A vigorous nod. "And what do we do with witnesses?" Not arrest them, certainly, they did not—

"We're going to use you to draw out Konstantin. We're going to set a trap and you're going to help us," Jezebel told Simone. "And in return for your cooperation, you'll get twenty-four, seven protection. Protection that comes in the form of my very best operative."

"That would be me," Ryan's deep, rumbling voice told her.

A shiver skated down her spine.

"But first tell me, Simone," Jezebel continued, her gaze assessing, "just how good are you at undercover work?"

She thought of all the years that she'd lied to everyone she met. "Oh, I can get by."

"Then welcome to the team."

Her gaze swept the team. Jezebel. Ryan. A nervously sweating Harry.

"You work with us, and we'll keep you alive." Intensity sharpened Jezebel's features. "When the mission is successfully completed, the CIA will give you a new life. You can walk away."

"With...no arrest?" Though had they even really talked about her supposed crime?

"With no arrest. Work with us, and I can make all of your sins disappear," Jezebel promised.

That was cute, but no one held that much power. Some of her sins would haunt her until she died. But now was not the time for that reveal. Now she just needed to pretend that she was playing along. Later, she could stage her escape. After all, as Jezebel had said before, Simone was a ghost.

And ghosts knew how to vanish.

For the moment, Simone summoned a big, bright smile and said, "There is nothing more that I love than teamwork. And, you know, being bait to lure in homicidal Russian crime lords. Love, *love* those two things. So this will be a total dream job for me. Thank you for the opportunity."

Ryan growled once more.

Simone's smile stretched a little more. "When do we start?"

Chapter Eleven

"You should not trust her." Jezebel stood just outside of the suite. Ryan was at her side, but his gaze was on the closed suite door.

Two of Jezebel's guards waited down the hallway, poised near the elevator. He recognized Hans and Mayo because they were the two men who typically accompanied Jez wherever she went. Her personal protection service.

When you'd made as many enemies as Jezebel had over the years, you tended to need your own guards. People you could trust completely.

On more than one occasion, Jezebel had hinted to him that she was ready to get out of the business. It was hard to tell her age for sure. When streaks of gray slid into the darkness of her hair, she tended to take steps to ruthlessly eliminate them. A former ballerina, Jezebel still worked out religiously. Her mind was razor sharp, and her instincts were usually on target.

Which meant...

You should not trust her.

Hell. His gaze slid to Jezebel. Her words had only

carried to him. The guards near the elevator would not have been able to pick up her whisper. "You know something you want to share about Simone?"

"She is a ghost, I told you that already. The fact that she has no history should make you extremely nervous. It makes me nervous."

"You have her prints." He was sure of this. Jezebel had causally offered Simone some tea after they'd come to an agreement about Simone's cooperation. As soon as Simone had headed into the bedroom to rest for a bit, Jezebel had made the little tea cup vanish. Thus, the prints. "I know you're going to run them."

"And *I* know that I probably won't get hits in any system on them. Something tells me that your new friend hasn't been apprehended before." A thread of admiration came and went in Jezebel's voice. "She's good at her job." A little hesitation. "Might even make for a good CIA operative."

He took a step back. "We are not recruiting Simone for future missions." No way.

"You're right. We should see how this one goes first before we make future plans. Good call."

His temples throbbed. "You *just* told me not to trust her." Now she wanted Simone to join the CIA? What?

Jezebel smiled. It was her unsettling smile. "Just because we can't trust the woman, it doesn't mean she can't be exceedingly useful. Use her."

Use her. Those two words did not sit well with him. His hand rose, and his index finger skimmed over the bridge of his nose.

"You're doing it again," she murmured. "Feeling guilty, are we?"

His hand dropped.

"That's one of your tells, and I've warned you about it before." She had. "You rub your nose when guilt slides through you."

He'd broken his nose ages ago. When his sister Agnes had fallen out of a treehouse and he'd caught her. In return for his heroic effort, she'd kicked him in the nose. An accident.

And yet...

Funny thing about that whole incident...he felt guilty as fuck about it. *To this day.* Because he was the one who should have been watching Agnes on that fateful occasion. He'd promised to watch her, but he'd gotten distracted and...

He'd barely made it to the treehouse in time.

I won't get distracted ever again. When someone needs me, I will be there.

"Don't feel guilty for doing your job," Jezebel advised him.

"I'm not going to let Simone get hurt." They needed to be very clear on this particular point. "She will not be put in danger."

"The woman is playing a game with international criminals. She's already put herself in danger." A pause. "What was she trying to steal that was so valuable?"

He stared back at Jezebel.

She grunted. "If you don't know, find out. And if you know and you're covering for her, why the hell are you doing that? Red flag. Blazing red flag."

"Jez..."

"My goal is to apprehend Konstantin. He's my target." An inhale. Her slender shoulders seemed to brace. "My final one, by the way."

Shit. "You're seriously retiring?"

She looked toward the waiting guards. "My father had this charming little villa in France when I was a child. It was surrounded by miles and miles of fields. Beautiful green fields." She sucked in the side of her cheek. "No bad guys. No monsters. No death. I was safe there."

He knew her father had been a French artist. He'd fallen hard for Jezebel's mother when he met her in South Africa.

Jenkins was not her real last name. Then again, Jezebel wasn't her real first name, either.

"Sometimes, I miss safety." Her gaze was still on the two guards. "You get tired of worrying about betrayal everywhere you turn."

"Jezebel."

Her gaze slid back to him.

"I would never betray you." A promise that he meant to the depths of his soul.

"I know." A brief smile. A real one that lit her dark eyes. "But everyone isn't you." She pointed toward the door. "I like her."

Okay, that was surprising as hell. Especially since Jezebel had begun their little corridor chat by saying Ryan should not trust Simone.

"Not many people would still be sarcastic as hell after what she experienced. That tells me a couple of important points about her. She's tough. She knows how to hide fear. And she's highly adaptable to high-stress situations. She is a true chameleon." A little furrow dug between her brows. "That makes her incredibly dangerous."

"Being a chameleon?"

A slight incline of her head. "I'm a chameleon. So are you. We're whatever we need others to believe we are. We blend in order to get our missions accomplished. That woman in there—Simone Sailor or whatever her real name is—she is only showing us what she wants us to see. Stay on alert with her."

"You *just* said you liked her."

"You like her, too. Isn't that the problem you have?"

His lips pressed together.

"She'll either help us and cooperate or she'll set us up. Time will tell. Stay on guard." A rough exhale. "Dammit, I wish your brother Nash was still working with us. I could use more people that I trust on this one."

He wished his brother was with him, too, but he was damn grateful that Nash had finally gotten out of the CIA and that Nash was back to focusing on being a doctor once more. But, in terms of people Jezebel trusted... "Oh, you're saying Harry isn't good enough? Do you not have faith that he'll take out all the bad guys in a single, powerful attack?"

She quirked a brow. "Are we being funny?"

"It's his third mission," Ryan murmured. "He's just hitting his groove."

"Why in the world did MI6 give us a green agent?"

Now that was a great question to ask. Dead serious, Ryan responded, "Perhaps because someone wants us to fail." The only answer.

They shared a long, hard look. Then Jezebel asked, "Did you show Simone the chip that had been hidden inside the egg?"

"No. Didn't show it to her. Didn't mention it at all." Things were *classified* for a reason.

"So she *did* see it when Konstantin originally gave Frederick the egg."

"Maybe. Or maybe she found it when she swiped it from me."

"*Excuse me?*" Real surprise.

Yeah, he hadn't been able to tell her that part before. "Uh. The egg. Uh, she might have swiped it from me at one point, but I got it back. No worries."

She did not blink.

"I got it back." A bit defensive.

The wheels seemed to turn behind her dark eyes. "So we don't know if Simone found the chip when she stole it from you or if she really did see it when Konstantin delivered the egg. She could be lying to us in order to avoid arrest."

"We don't exactly have a lot of reasons to arrest the woman." Ryan had to point out, "She stole from Frederick. He'd have to press charges. I was bullshitting with her about the arrest because I wanted to keep her close." *I want to protect her*.

"Oh, I am sure Simone is aware of any pending charges. The very fact that she has agreed to cooperate in lieu of any charges tells me that your friend has committed all sorts of crimes."

He feared the same thing.

"She can be useful or she can be a wrecking ball to this mission. Watch her. Guard her. Protect her." Jezebel began to walk down the hallway. But, after three steps, she looked back at him. "Just be careful and don't fall for her."

Ryan laughed.

Jezebel didn't.

"Oh, come on." Another rough laugh escaped him. "It's me."

"Yes, and I saw the way you looked at her. Be careful. Even spies can get their hearts broken."

He had the feeling she was speaking from personal experience. But she didn't need to worry about him. "No worries. My heart isn't on the line."

She didn't reply. Jezebel took the egg—she'd tucked it into her pocket—and she climbed onto the elevator with her guards. A few moments later, the elevator doors closed, and she vanished from sight.

His heart was *not* on the line. *Not.* One hundred percent not.

He opened the door to the suite.

Harry rushed toward him. "I, uh, couldn't stop her!"

Fuck. "What did she do?" He closed the door. Secured it. He'd left them for minutes. *Minutes.* And Simone should have been sleeping during that time. Only...

She strolled from the narrow hallway, looking extremely bright-eyed and awake. "Calm yourself. I was starving. I figured you had to be starving, too, so I ordered room service." Simone slanted a glance toward Harry. "Someone nearly fainted. Though why he fussed so much, I have no idea. Room service is not a capital offense."

Ryan squeezed his eyes shut. "You couldn't stop her from ordering food? You couldn't stop her from making a phone call?" What if the call hadn't been to room service? What if she'd called someone else and leaked their location?

"Well, I, um, didn't want to hurt her..."

Ryan's eyes flew open. "Damn straight you didn't want to hurt her. You put your hands on her, you hurt her, and we'll have a major fucking problem."

Silence.

Okay, he'd probably been way too aggressive with all of that.

His breath blew out. Slowly. "We're not eating in here. Simone and I are going downstairs to the hotel's restaurant."

"We are?" Surprise flashed on her face. "But...the hit..."

"The goal isn't to stay hidden. The goal is to bring the bad guys out into the open. We'll have eyes on us at the restaurant." Jezebel had already told him that agents would be located throughout the hotel and restaurant. Just not the agents he knew and trusted well.

"Cancel the order," Ryan told her.

She stared at him a beat longer, then spun on her heel and marched back down the hallway to the bedroom.

"How do you know..." Harry's low voice. "How do you know that she isn't calling some of those associates she mentioned? She could be plotting her escape."

"She's definitely plotting an escape." He'd be a fool to think otherwise. "It's just not going to happen. I won't let her go." His gaze had lingered on the hallway as he watched Simone vanish, but now he glanced at Harry. "Don't ever hurt her."

Harry swallowed. "Understood. I-I wouldn't." Then he grimaced. "Unless I had no choice. Unless...unless she is coming at me with a weapon and I had to stop her..."

Ryan moved to stand toe to toe with Harry. "Can I trust you?"

"I'm MI6!" His cheeks flushed. And his voice cracked.

"That's not a yes and that's not a no." He stared into Harry's eyes. "Let me make certain that I am perfectly clear. *Simone doesn't get hurt.*"

"Th-that's...it's not something I can promise. It's not something you can promise!" Fast words. "If she comes at you with a knife or a gun...you'll fight back, too. Unless you're going to vow that you won't ever hurt her, either? What are you going to do, stand there while the woman kills you?" Harry asked Ryan.

"*Ahem.*" Simone's overly loud throat clearing.

Ryan had already heard the tread of her returning steps. The little tap of her heels.

Harry looked over at her, aghast. But Ryan kept his gaze on his prey. *You will not hurt her*.

"I am not planning to kill anyone," Simone announced. "Not a soul. As the saying goes, I'm a fantastic lover, not a fighter."

What? Ryan's head swung toward her.

She smiled at him. "Hi, there, lover." Simone winked.

He growled.

"I'm about five seconds away from hangry, so how about we head out?" She'd swiped some slick, red lipstick across her mouth. Put a little dark shadow over her eyes. The lipstick made her mouth look all the more tempting. The dark shadow somehow had her eyes appearing even bluer. Simone extended her hand toward him. "Shall we?"

He took her hand. Curled his fingers with hers. "No one is killing you."

"Right. Because you're my protector, and they'd have to go through you in order to get to me. That's the deal, isn't it?" Mocking words.

"Yes." Not mocking. One hundred percent serious. "That is the deal."

But her expression changed. What could have been alarm flared in her eyes. "I promise not to kill..." Her stare darted toward Harry. "I will not kill either of you. But in return, how about you two charming gentlemen promise not to die? Because I truly do not want anyone's blood on my hands."

Oh, he did not intend to die.

And he would make no promises as far as killing was concerned.

"I won't die," Harry swiftly said.

Ryan lifted Simone's hand to his mouth. He just could not help himself. His lips brushed over her knuckles, and he reminded her, "Pretty sure I told you before that there's something I intend to do before I die."

Her brow crinkled in thought. Then her eyes widened as she remembered.

I'm damn well not dying before I fuck you.

"Time for you to get the hell out of this suite, Harry," Ryan ordered. "Keep your eyes open. You pick up intel that I need, then you come to me, right away. Until then..." He lowered Simone's hand. "I'll be staying close to our very important witness."

As close as humanly possible.

Chapter Twelve

"I KIND OF THOUGHT THAT YOU'D STOP THE ELEVATOR. That you'd turn to me as we were halted between floors, and you'd pin me against the elevator wall." Simone took a sip of her wine. "Then you'd come in close, and you'd kiss me as if your life depended on it. My lips would part beneath yours. Your tongue would slide into my mouth." Another sip. "Your hand would dip under my shirt—"

Ryan's growl cut through her words.

She sent him a sunny smile. "But you didn't do any of those things. You just escorted me down here." She lifted her glass to indicate the busy restaurant. "And I realize now that seduction was not your game. Instead, your strategy is to publicly parade me around town so that the people who want me *dead* can find me in a very swift manner." She lowered the wine glass to the table because her fingers were shaking, and she didn't want to send the wine sloshing all about. "How incredibly charming of you."

He reached across the table, seemingly intent on reaching out for her. But the back of his hand hit the salt shaker, sending it falling down and scattering a bit of salt over the dark tablecloth. Ryan's hard jaw locked as he brushed aside the salt. "I am *not* parading you around town." His hand casually waved toward his left shoulder. "I am sitting with you in a restaurant because you were starving. I'm feeding you."

But her eyes had gotten caught on his waving hand. Only, had he been waving? Pursing her lips, Simone leaned forward. She looked at the salt shaker. Then his shoulder. "Excuse me."

That jaw of his appeared extra hard.

"Did you just toss salt over your shoulder?" Simone inquired.

He stared her dead in the eyes. "Why would you think I did that?"

Her mouth curved. "Because the lady in the fancy fur coat just got hit in the eye by salt, and she's wiping it off her face."

"Shit." He turned. Saw the lady. "Sorry." He cleared his throat. "My bad."

The woman frowned at him.

A little bubble of laughter escaped Simone. "What on earth was that about?"

His focus returned to her. "Do you want dessert?"

"Of course. There is never any world where I would not want dessert. Didn't you learn that about me on our previous dates?" But she was not going to be sidetracked. "Ryan Quinn." She savored his name. *Is it even his real name?* "Are you superstitious?"

His nostrils flared. "I simply don't see a point in inviting bad luck. Given our current situation, do you think we should go around tempting fate?"

"You fascinate me." Truly, he did. "Tell me your other superstitions."

"I'm not *superstitious*. I'm...minorly so."

She needed to stop being enchanted by him. He was using her. He'd lied to her.

Fine. She'd used him. She'd lied to him.

And...

Why did it feel so good whenever they were together? Correction, whenever they were together and not being kidnapped? Or terrorized? Then it felt good. Right at that moment, she felt *good* with him. Her fingers were no longer shaking, and she didn't feel as if a vise had clamped around her heart. "Are you afraid of black cats? Do you always avoid walking under ladders? Do you think that you'll have seven years of bad luck if you break a mirror?"

A muscle flexed along his jaw. "Yes. Yes." An exhale. "Yes."

Another laugh slid from her. "Stop being fantastic. I am enjoying you far too much." She really, truly was. A dangerous thing. "Come on. Tell me more. Unlock the mystery that is Ryan Quinn for me."

"Only if you unlock the mystery that is Simone Sailor for me." He took a sip of his wine, too. The first sip he'd taken. He'd mostly just been drinking water during their meal. "Is that even your real name? Because Jez is convinced it isn't."

"Simone is the name I use. It's the name my friends use for me. So it's certainly real enough." The waiter approached, and she stopped talking while he removed their empty plates. Had she eaten delicately? Uh, no. She'd torn through the food like a starving woman because she *had* been starving. "You know, you can bring more bread," she told the waiter in her most encouraging tone. Edward. He'd introduced himself when he first arrived at their table. "Bread is always welcome." Bread was one of her addictions in life.

Bread, books, dessert...she'd always believed you should enjoy the good things. Life was worth living. And there was always time for more bread.

"Does the lady want a dessert? Perhaps a chocolate mousse or our famous white chocolate cheesecake?"

She nearly purred. "Chocolate mousse. You sweet, sweet man."

Simone was pretty sure that she felt Ryan's shoe tap against her leg. She frowned at him.

"And for the gentleman?" The waiter turned toward Ryan.

"No dessert. Just coffee."

The waiter nodded and backed away.

"Well, aren't you the buzz kill?" Her head tilted. "Did you kick me under the table?"

"I *tapped* you." His index finger skimmed over the bridge of his nose. "Because you were flirting unnecessarily with the waiter."

"Ah." A sage nod. "You were jealous."

He...flushed.

She'd meant the words to be teasing, but his response caught her completely off guard. Simone straightened in her seat. "You *were* jealous." Surprise pulsed through her. "Because I called the waiter sweet? Look, anyone who brings me bread and chocolate is sweet, but I'm not interested in Edward. The only man I'm fantasizing about is you. You, the surly, unpredictable, superstitious CIA spy that you are."

He glanced around. "How about we *not* announce my spy status to everyone?" His gaze came back to her. "And are you faking your response to me? Was it all just part of your cover and your lies?"

"That hurts." It did. No flashing smile. No teasing tone. She'd gone dead serious. "I happen to like the way I feel when you and I are together. I don't fuck men for cover stories. Never have. Never will. I went out on dates with you because I liked you. I could easily have gotten into that gallery on my own. In case you need the reminder, going there was *your* idea because you were using me."

"*I like the way I feel when you and I are together, too.*" Rasped. Almost angry.

Also...truthful? She thought those words of his might be true. "Well, then."

"Well, then...what?" His brows had shot up.

Beneath the table, Simone slid her right foot out of her high heel. He sat directly across from her, and, honestly, it was a bit too far, but if she stretched, she could make this work. The table was small, intimate, and the long, dark tablecloth would hide her movements.

She stretched.

He jumped.

Then Ryan's hands immediately clamped around the edge of the table near him. "*Simone.*"

"Um?"

"Are you..." He swallowed. "Is your foot *tapping* me?"

"Is that what you want to call it?" Her foot was not, in fact, tapping. It was gliding. Up his calf. Then higher. Above his knee.

He swallowed again. And his right hand flew beneath the table and locked around her ankle before she could go higher. "*What are you doing?*"

"Why don't you let go and you can find out?"

His eyes blazed at her. A dark fire. Lust. Need.

And his hand let go.

Her foot continued its exploration. "What do we have here?" But she knew. She could tell what that very large item was. She arched her foot, rubbed over his heavy cock, and when a low rumble of need tore from him, her own breath caught.

"Here you are!"

The waiter was back.

Ryan cursed.

Her foot slid off him.

"The dessert." Edward put two plates down with a flourish. "And the extra bread that you requested." The waiter beamed at her. "Is there anything else the lady would like?"

Oh, she could think of a few things. But she just thanked the waiter and watched as he hurried off. He hadn't brought Ryan's coffee. Should she have asked about it? Ryan certainly hadn't. He'd appeared...distracted.

"What. Game. Are. You. Playing?" Each word rumbled hard from Ryan.

"The kind that you like obviously." She dropped her napkin. "Whoops." She slanted a glance Ryan's way.

He shook his head. "You are *not*." He'd clearly anticipated her plan. Good for him.

"Dropped my napkin. Better get it." She dipped down low. Slipped under the table.

"*Simone*."

This was a five-star restaurant. She should not be doing this. She knew she should not be doing this. And yet...

Her hand reached out to him. She'd deliberately slipped close to his side of the table. It was so easy to reach out. To reach up. To skim her fingers over the heavy bulge of his arousal. It would be just as easy to unzip his pants and—

"Check!" Ryan thundered. "Check, now!"

She returned to her seat. "But I haven't had dessert."

"I'm about to have *my* dessert." His expression could only be termed savage. "*Check!*"

* * *

HE PULLED her into the elevator. Ryan used the keycard to access their secure floor, and as soon as those elevator doors closed...

He pulled Simone against him. His lips took hers. His dick was so hard that he hurt, and all he wanted to do was strip her. Lift her up. And plunge into her. Again and again.

Had he ever had sex in an elevator before? No. Did he want to have sex right there, right then? Yes. A thousand times, yes.

She moaned. That little ragged, sweet sound that he loved. Her sweater was soft against him, but her skin was softer. He wanted her naked. He wanted her moaning. He wanted her coming around him.

Simone pulled back. Her breath heaved in and out as she stared up at him. "Tell me that this has nothing to do with your case."

"It has *nothing* to do with my case." In fact, the case was the reason why he should be keeping his hands off her.

But she smiled at him. Her smiles were absolutely bewitching. Every time she flashed one at him, Ryan was convinced that he fell a bit more under her spell.

"Good," Simone told him. Her hands dropped to the top of his pants. Her fingers stroked him through the fabric, just as she'd done in the restaurant. *Fuck, fuck, fuck.*

The elevator chimed. The doors began to open.

His hand clamped around her wrist, and he pulled her from the elevator and tugged her down the hallway. Her musical laughter followed him to their suite. He opened the door in record time, briefly pausing to nod toward the guards who lingered in the corridor near the stairwell. As soon as Ryan got her over the threshold and had her safely back in their suite...

He locked the door. Pinned her against the nearest wall. And feasted on her mouth.

She was playing with fire, and the woman didn't understand. He wasn't the kind of man you could tease. His desire for her was too strong.

His tongue plunged past her lips, and he greedily drank up her sweetness. She was way better than the wine he'd sampled. And he could not wait to taste her everywhere.

"Such a shame about dessert," Simone said, voice husky, when he tore his mouth from hers. "Think you can make it up to me?"

His mouth dropped down to her throat. Pressing. Licking. Kissing.

Make it up to her? Hell, yes, he could. He would.

He scooped her into his arms.

"Ryan!" She held on. Tight. "You know, I think you carry me entirely too much."

Nah. Not possible.

There were two bedrooms in the suite. She'd picked one earlier, when they first arrived. He'd taken the other one. He went into his room now. A room lit only by the small lamp near the bed. Without hesitating, he carried Simone straight for the king-size bed. He lowered her onto the mattress.

Nearly pounced, but caught himself. Instead, Ryan

backed up a step. He sucked in a deep breath. One, then another. He tried to clear his head. But she was all he could smell. Her seductive, tempting scent. She was all he could see. Her gorgeous face. Her beautiful body. She was all he *wanted*.

Naked. Spread on the bed. Taking him in deep.

But...

There were some things that, once done, could never be *undone*. They were going to be one of those things. "Choose now."

She pushed onto her elbows. "Choose what?"

"Fuck me or keep it professional."

Her sexy laughter floated to him. "Do you truly think you and I could ever be *professional*?"

No, maybe. *No*.

"I would really like..." Her tongue swiped over her lower lip.

Every muscle in his body locked.

"I'd like for you to finish what you started when you got out of that shower earlier. You know, before a certain doorbell started ringing."

When he'd left the shower earlier, she'd been naked. His fingers had dipped inside of her. Hot. Tight. Heaven. That damn doorbell would haunt his nightmares.

"Also, I'd really like to lick some of your tattoos."

Sweet fuck.

"And..." Her gaze dropped down his body. She sat up in bed. Moved to the edge of the mattress. "I'd like to lick other parts of you, too."

He nearly ripped all of her clothes right off her. He could *never* remember wanting someone so much. "You are playing with fire."

"Am I?" She reached out and undid his belt. Then the

button on his pants. And eased down the zipper. "Let's see if I get burned."

He was on her. Not like he could hold back any longer. He tumbled her onto the bed. His mouth took hers. His hands flew over her body.

He heard her high heels hit the floor.

When that sexy little foot slid against me in the restaurant...

A growl ripped from him as he lifted up enough so that he could yank off her soft sweater. He sent it flying.

For a moment, he got lost staring at her. He'd seen her naked breasts when they'd been in the bathroom together. Sheer and utter perfection. Now her breasts were encased in a white bra with sexy lace that pushed them up, and really, the bra was gorgeous, but he yanked it off her in five seconds.

Then his lips were on her. Kissing her nipples. Licking. Sucking.

Her nails sank into his arms as she arched against him. "Ryan!"

He kissed his way down her body. Broke the button at the top of her pants and didn't care. He jerked down the zipper, and with one hard tug, he pulled her pants and her panties down her body and sent them both hurtling to the floor, too.

He and Simone were now half on and half off the bed. He eased back, mostly so that he could take her all in. Every single, perfect inch of her. His breath shuddered in and out. His dick thrust straight toward her, and all he wanted was...

A taste. First, a taste.

He caught her legs. Pushed them apart. She grabbed for the bedding.

"And here I thought you got full at the restaurant."

Her husky words had his gaze rising to trap hers.

"Still hungry?" she asked as her head tilted to the left and her hair trailed over her shoulder.

"Starving." A primitive rumble. Then he put his mouth on her.

She gasped. Her thighs trembled.

He went *wild*. Because her taste sent him straight over the edge. Licking. Sucking. Tasting. Thrusting his tongue into her and then raking her clit with his fingers. Strumming her. Ferocious need pounded within him, and, in some distant part of his mind, Ryan realized that he should hold back. He shouldn't be letting the full force of his lust surge through him.

But, fuck it.

Part of him knew that Simone could handle everything. That he didn't have to hold back with her.

Because she was moaning and arching against him and demanding *more* with her breathy little whispers. She wasn't afraid of his passion. She wanted everything that he had to give her.

And he wanted her.

First, he wanted her to come against his mouth so he could taste her pleasure.

Then, he wanted her coming around his dick so that he could *feel* her release.

His tongue lashed her. Licking and stroking her clit in a fast and frantic rhythm.

She stiffened beneath him. Her nails dug deeper into his arms, and then she let out a sharp, startled scream.

Fuck, yes.

He lapped up her pleasure, greedy for every single drop. Even as she was still coming, as her body was still shuddering, he yanked the condom from his back pocket and he shoved down his pants and underwear. With fingers that weren't quite steady because his need was far too overwhelming, he rolled on that condom. Then he was climbing onto the bed with her. Partially on the bed, anyway. Half on, half off again, and her legs were open, and she was wet and ready, and he sank into her.

One long hard thrust.

She gasped.

He fucking *lost it*.

She was tight. So insanely tight. Hot. Wet. Her scent was on him. Her taste on his tongue. Her body soft against him. When she lifted her legs up and locked them around him, Ryan erupted. Fast, hard, desperate thrusts. Braced on the side of the bed, he yanked her as close to him as he could. Over and over, he pounded into her, and Simone met him every single time. Fast. Hard.

There was no stopping. No slowing. No time for gentleness or careful touches. There was only a basic, driving need that consumed him.

His eyes locked with hers.

Her breath heaved out. Pleasure flashed across her face even as he felt the inner contractions of her muscles along his dick. She was squeezing him, holding him so fucking tightly, and nothing in his whole life had ever felt this good.

Even as she was coming for him again, Ryan knew he could not hold back another moment. The lust was too consuming. He drove deep and let go. His hips surged against her. Again. Again.

The bed hit the wall.

He came within her and, as he choked out her name, Ryan realized he might just be in the worst danger of his life.

Because he wanted *more.* Because he feared that he might not ever be able to get enough of her. Not. Ever.

* * *

"You are not going to believe this, boss." Hugo crept toward Frederick.

Frederick sat slumped behind the massive, antique desk, with a bottle of scotch open near him. The scent of scotch was heavy in the air, and Frederick's bleary eyes gazed back at him. Or, tried to gaze back at Hugo. It appeared that Frederick was looking a bit to the side of Hugo's actual body, so Hugo took one step to the right.

Frederick tilted his head. "I believe that I'm fucked," Frederick declared, the words coming out very, very slowly. "I believe that you let Simone Sailor vanish and now I have no money. No backing. I don't have the fucking egg and when the Russian finds out that I lost his precious chip, he is going to flay the skin from my body—"

"She's in London."

Frederick narrowed his eyes.

"Simone Sailor is in London," Hugo repeated in case Frederick had not heard him clearly. He rattled off the name of the high-end hotel where she was currently staying.

Frederick lurched upright in his chair. His hand swung out and hit the bottle of scotch, sending amber liquid flying across his desk. "You—you can't be serious!"

"I'm dead serious. She was recently spotted in the hotel's restaurant."

Frederick slapped his hands down on top of the desk and shoved to his feet. For a moment, he swayed, but his hands just shoved down all the harder on the desktop, and he maintained his balance. "We've been...tearing the...

countryside apart...and she's out for a meal? At the fanciest hotel in London?"

So it would seem. "A waiter there is the one who reported the tip. Edward Reginald is part of the network you've been creating." Careful words. It wasn't really Frederick's network, was it? More like it belonged to the Russian, Konstantin. "Edward waited on her in the restaurant. Her and her date."

"What date?" Frederick's voice had risen several octaves.

"Ryan Quinn."

"What. The. Bloody. Hell?"

Hugo nodded. "They're both in London. I think we can conclude our search in the countryside."

Frederick's breath hissed out. "Oh, you think?"

"What's the order?" Hugo asked. "How do we proceed?"

Frederick's shoulders heaved. Up and down. Up and down. The bastard looked like he was choking down vomit.

Hugo waited, barely keeping his disgust in check. Instead of helping track Simone, Frederick had been drinking his ass off all day long.

Some people...they just could not handle their alcohol. They also could not handle dead bodies. Or the violence that was necessary to succeed in this world.

Frederick's hand swiped over his face. Wiping away a bit of vomit that had slid onto his chin?

"Proceed...How to proceed..." A whisper from Frederick. Then he nodded. "I'm getting my arse to London."

"Excellent idea. Maybe plan to head out at first light tomorrow? After you've had a chance to rest?" *After you've sobered up?*

Frederick swayed.

"What about Simone Sailor?" Hugo really needed an answer on this situation. "What do you want done with her?"

"I want her dead."

Hugo nodded. "Pretty sure we can make that happen. In fact, we can do that right now."

Chapter Thirteen

SHE'D MISCALCULATED. SHE'D ALSO FALLEN ASLEEP.

Simone's eyes flew open, and she jerked upright. She had *not* meant to sleep. She had certainly not meant to fall asleep in Ryan's bed, of all places. But the man had given her the best two orgasms of her life and she'd been all blissed out and sated, so closing her eyes for a moment had not seemed like the worst crime in the universe.

She'd miscalculated.

Sex with him had seemed...harmless enough. *Harmless.* What a ridiculous word to describe anything related to Ryan Quinn. But, at the time, she'd thought, why not? Why not have sex with him and get this mad, driving need out of her system? Why not treat herself to one fabulous time after the nightmare she'd experienced?

Why not find out how good it could be with him, before she vanished from his life without a trace?

Because she would vanish. It was just a matter of time before she had to schedule her big, disappearing act. And it had seemed like such a waste to disappear without finding out just how good she and Ryan could be together.

Spoiler alert, he was very, very good.

So good that she'd come twice. That her whole body had surged and hungrily followed his every command. So good that she could swear she still felt him, inside of her.

But unease trickled through her veins and the afterglow was definitely fading because not only was Ryan not in the bed with her...he wasn't in the bedroom *at all.*

Miscalculated. She'd been blissed out on the fabulous sex and he'd...he'd...

Ryan opened the bedroom door. He walked in, wearing his black dress pants and seemingly nothing else. Appearing sexy and rumpled with his tousled hair and the tattoos that she'd wanted to lick—but had not been given the opportunity to do so—looking so badass on his skin. But then Ryan lifted his right hand, and she saw that he was holding the broach and the earrings. *Her* broach and earrings.

Jaw locking, he stared straight at her. "I think it's time we talked about these, don't you?"

Simone said the first thing that came to mind, even as unexpected betrayal and pain knifed through her. "You bastard."

Ryan blinked.

She glared. She also jumped out of bed, naked, and fought the rage that swelled inside of her. "How dare you go through my things!" Then, because she could not have this conversation—correction, argument, fight, whatever—while she was waving her breasts at him, Simone yanked a sheet from the bed and wrapped it around her body. She secured it between her previously waving breasts and stormed toward him. "How. Dare. *You.*"

He blinked again. "I went in your room in order to get a

change of clothes for you. Thought I was being *kind* because I'd broken the button on your pants."

He'd broken the button? She did not remember that event occurring. Then again, she barely remembered him stripping off her pants. Heat of the moment and all that.

"How was I supposed to know you'd hidden these items inside the pocket of your new black pants? They fell out when I lifted the pants out of the suitcase that Jezebel brought over for you."

Imperiously, she held out one hand. "Well, now that you have found *my* items, how about returning them?" Simone wiggled her fingers.

His gaze shifted to the broach and the earrings. "There were so many items worth more in the gallery."

"Um." As if she was not aware of that fact.

"Yet you took the broach and earrings. Only these two items."

"How incredibly observant of you."

"And you are determined to keep them."

"And you seem determined not to put them in my outstretched hand." Once more, she wiggled her fingers. "I don't know if anyone has told you this before, but it is incredibly rude to fuck a woman and then steal from her immediately afterwards. That's down right villainous behavior, FYI."

He put the broach and earrings in her palm. His fingers lingered against her hand. "I'm not stealing from you." His gaze swept over her face. "I'm not going to be a villain in your world."

"That remains to be seen," she muttered. She pulled her hand away from his and immediately curled her fingers over her prize.

"You were hired to steal those, weren't you?"

What was this? A post-sex interrogation? "I was not *stealing*." Her chin notched up. She'd backed away from him, and the sheet trailed over the floor. "I was retrieving items that Frederick had taken illegally. In case you missed it, Frederick is a bit of an asshole. That whole gallery of his? Plenty of stuff inside was *stolen* art work and jewelry."

"Like the Claudel."

"Right. Yes. Like the Claudel. Sticky Fingers Frederick had that piece taken when a certain Italian businessman refused to back a project of his last year. You refuse Frederick, and he finds a way to get revenge on you. He's rather petty and vindictive like that."

Ryan sucked in the side of his cheek, as if thinking, then said, "Frederick screwed over your real employer. You're retrieving the property that was taken, aren't you? Taken in one of Frederick's 'petty and vindictive' retaliations?"

Close. Though this heist was purely pro bono because she owed the person who would be getting the broach and earrings. "I'm not turning these items over to the CIA. I'm keeping the broach and earrings. Consider it payment for my cooperation with you and your spy friends."

"I have no intention of taking them away from you." His hands went to his hips.

The move made his muscles flex. The dragon on his forearm rippled. The dragon's claws stretched.

Do not look there. He's trying to distract you with his tats.

Her breath whispered out. "Great to know."

"Who is your employer?"

"I have no employer." She turned away from him.

"Dammit, don't lie to me!"

Oh, he did not want to go there with her right now. "I have no employer," Simone repeated as she looked back at him. "Sometimes, I do things out of the goodness of my heart." Call her a giver. "Ready for a shocker? I have a heart. I care about people." Not a lot of people, granted, but certainly some.

"Well, of course, you fucking care. Your soft heart is why you told me to run when you should have been yelling for me to kill your enemies."

Her whole body turned toward him, slowly.

"When you were being shoved toward the van, you told me to run."

"Did I?" Careful words.

"Yeah, you did."

"You didn't run."

"Fuck, no. I will *never* leave you behind." He closed in. His hand lifted and skimmed over her cheek. "Baby..."

His voice had gone extra deep and rough and the endearment just seemed to pierce her.

"You aren't some wicked thief. I get that. You made mistakes with me."

"I have not. I don't make mistakes." Now he was just being insulting. This after-sex experience was not as blissful as she'd hoped. Granted, it had been a while since she'd been in an after-sex situation, but she didn't remember the experience being as fraught with conflict.

Ryan quirked a brow. She tried to keep looking at his face, but her traitorous gaze liked to keep darting down to his tats. Such a shame that she had not gotten to lick them.

Woman. Focus. "Fine," she huffed. It was time to put the blame where it belonged. "I should have checked the gallery more thoroughly on my second visit inside."

"Visit?" Ryan seemed to strangle on the word.

"Uh, yes, *visit.* My first visit was with you. Remember, when you set off the alarm?" she inquired sweetly.

He grunted.

"Anyway, I wasn't quite as mission-oriented as I should have been during my second visit. I should have checked the perimeter more thoroughly. I should have realized Alexei was inside." A visual of his dead body flashed through her mind. Her grip on the broach and earrings tightened. She'd never forget taking them from the dead man. Her shoulders rolled back. "You distracted me. So the mistake rests entirely on your shoulders. Your fault."

Ryan's lips parted, but he didn't speak.

"I don't get caught retrieving targets. You distracted me and...okay, why are you smiling?"

Because he was. His lips had just curled up in the most heart-stoppingly gorgeous grin. The grin lit his dark eyes. Took him to a whole other level of handsomeness. Damn him.

"I'm smiling because..." His deep voice seemed to sink right into her. "You just admitted that you're utterly and completely fascinated by me."

"I did no such thing!" Simone remembered her words. She'd said nothing about being fascinated with him. Zero about that.

"Yeah, you did." A nod. "Never been distracted before, super high success rate—"

"I'd had a one hundred percent success rate until you stalked into my life."

"You were the perfect thief, but I got into your head. Got into your body, too." He winked at her.

She frowned harder at him. "Retrieval specialist," she corrected.

"Be careful, Simone, or I might just sneak my way into your heart." He paused. "Like a thief in the night."

Instantly, she retreated. One step. Two. Three and the back of her leg hit the nightstand.

His brow furrowed. "Are you running from me?"

No. Maybe. "You're not getting into my heart."

His smile was gone. He looked away from her. "Yeah, I get that. Relax. I wasn't looking for some undying declaration of love."

Her heart raced far too fast.

He lifted his right hand and yanked his fingers across his jaw. "Know what? This chat has been derailed."

Why would her heartbeat not slow down? And why did her cheeks feel hot?

"Let's get back to the fact that I know you're not some wicked villainess with an icy heart," Ryan directed.

"*Why do you keep talking about my heart?*"

"Maybe because I want it." He blinked.

"*What?*" She'd heard wrong.

But he looked just as shocked as she felt. And then—

A bell rang. The doorbell to their suite.

"Saved by the bell," he groused. "Uh, I'll be right back."

He'd be back? "Who is at the door?" Before he could exit the bedroom, she bounded toward him and grabbed his arm.

Slither.

That would be her sheet. Fluttering down. Leaving her naked. Right in front of him.

His gaze held hers. A muscle flexed along his jaw. "I think you just lost something," Ryan said.

My heart. That's what I'm afraid I'm losing. He'd come way too close to the truth with his words before. Because...

She didn't get involved when she worked her cases. She'd known that she was walking into dangerous territory on the first date with him. She'd known going out with Ryan Quinn was a mistake and yet...

He'd made her laugh during their first date. He'd been so courteous. She'd felt an undeniable spark when they touched. So she'd taken a risk and gone on a second date with him.

Which had led to a third.

And then he'd saved her life. He'd killed for her. Never, ever had she expected someone in this world to kill in order to protect her.

Which brought her to the incredible sex they'd just had. And to the realization that...

Oh, damn. I am falling for a spy. Something that was awful and terrible because the man lied for a living. Figured that when she finally fell, it would be for a man who was just an illusion.

"Please, allow me." With those low, deep words Ryan bent. He picked up the fallen sheet. Brought it up her body. His fingers skimmed over her stomach. Over the curve of one breast. Back up.

She'd gone statue-still.

His breath seemed labored. His stare blazed. But he carefully wrapped the sheet around her and tucked it between her breasts.

His fingers lingered for just a moment, and then he stepped back. "Room service."

Her whole body ached.

"It's room service ringing the bell." He squared his shoulders. "You didn't get to finish your chocolate mousse at the restaurant because I was in such a hurry to fuck you."

Yes, he had been in a hurry. Only fair, she'd been in a hurry, too.

"So I ordered a delivery for you. Thought you might like to have your dessert."

That was actually sweet.

"I'll handle it." He disappeared.

She stared after him and tried to figure out what in the world she was supposed to do. Not fall in love with him. Certainly not that. This was a mission for him. Nothing more. They were not supposed to fall in love. They were just going to lure out the bad guys and get the job done and go their separate ways in life. No happy ending. No big relationship. No—

A gunshot blasted.

One, then another.

She screamed, searched for a weapon, and grabbed the lamp because it was the only thing she saw. Then Simone went scurrying toward the sound of the gunfire.

Apparently, the bad guys had already found them.

And she was not going to let Ryan fight alone.

Also...

Don't you dare be dead, Ryan! Don't you dare.

She'd never forgive the man if he was dead.

Her steps were soundless. At least, she tried to make them soundless. She hurried down the hallway, keeping her body as close to the wall as possible. Not like she wanted to present a target. She wanted to save the day. Not wind up dead.

And Ryan...

Don't you dare be dead. Do not be.

Simone peeked around the corner. Horror filled her as she took in the scene, and, with a sharp cry on her lips, she rushed toward Ryan.

Chapter Fourteen

Three minutes before...

When Ryan glanced through the suite door's peephole, he recognized the waiter who'd served him and Simone during dinner. Ryan frowned because he certainly hadn't expected the same man to be bringing Simone's dessert up to them.

The waiter glanced behind him, peering down the corridor.

Edward. That had been the man's name. He'd introduced himself as soon as he approached their dining table.

Edward looked back at the suite's door. He smiled, a little nervously.

Ryan flipped the lock. Opened the door.

Edward's smile stretched a bit more. "Decided to, uh, finish that chocolate mousse, did you?"

"It's for my girlfriend." Flat words. "Didn't expect you to bring it up personally."

Edward's hands curled around the delivery cart. A square cart covered by a white table cloth. The dishes on the cart were hidden by elaborate, silver cloches. The dome-shaped cloches completely covered the desserts that Ryan had ordered. Two chocolate mousses. And bread. Because Simone liked her bread.

A bottle of champagne chilled in an ice bucket right in the middle of the cart. Two upside down champagne flutes waited near the bucket.

"Our delivery staff was running behind, so I stepped in," Edward told him in a warm, breezy tone. "Shall I wheel this inside for you?"

"I think I can manage to wheel it in."

"Oh, sir." Now Edward looked horrified. "That is not the type of service that we deliver here."

Then why did you ask the question if you intended to wheel in the cart all along?

Edward began to push the cart forward. "I will get these items ready for you. I can even uncork the champagne, if you prefer." The wheels of the cart squeaked.

Ryan stepped back, allowing the other man to enter. He shut the door behind Edward, automatically flipping the extra lock. He caught the faint stiffening of Edward's shoulders, and he knew the waiter had heard that sound.

The cart's wheels stopped rolling. Edward reached for one of the dome-shaped silver cloches that covered one of the plates. "This should be the lady's chocolate mousse..."

It *should* have been the lady's mousse, but as the silver lid rose, Ryan saw the gun that had been waiting on the previously covered plate. A gun placed right on top of the damn chocolate mousse.

Dammit, Simone is not going to get her mousse again.

Ryan didn't yell. Didn't bark at the bastard to drop the

gun that Edward was already grabbing. Instead, Ryan attacked. He launched straight at the waiter.

Gunfire exploded when Ryan slammed Edward into the cart. A wild shot that didn't come close to anyone but did blast toward the wall near the heavy sofa on the right. Edward tried to whirl toward him, but Ryan was not in the mood for that shit. With his left hand, he grabbed the back of Edward's head, and he slammed the guy down, hard, right into the mousse, but that certainly hadn't been a hard enough hit to subdue the waiter.

Another blast of gunfire sounded.

The sonofabitch was pissing Ryan off.

So he slammed Edward's head into the silver cover, the freaking cloche, and then into the champagne bucket.

"Ryan!" Simone's desperate cry.

The gun fell from Edward's slack fingers. Ryan spun him around, and when he did, well, that tricky bastard swiped out with his hand, and Edward grabbed a knife from the table.

Aren't you the determined one?

Ryan leapt back.

Edward surged at him.

And Simone threw a lamp at the waiter. The lamp slammed into the side of his head, a loud, cracking impact, and Edward went down without even a whimper. Knocked out cold, he crashed to the floor as the knife slipped from his fingers.

Simone scampered forward, but Ryan threw out a hand. "Don't!"

"Are you okay?"

No, he was pissed. "Fucking ruined the chocolate mousse."

"What?" She inched forward.

"Simone, stay the hell where you are. He's here to kill you, and I don't want him to get within touching distance of you, understand?" Ryan grabbed the gun that the waiter had been intent on using and tucked it in the back waistband of his pants. Then he reached for the knife. A freaking steak knife.

"It looked to me like he was trying to kill *you*."

No, the bastard hadn't actually shot *at* Ryan once.

"Um, is that our *waiter*?"

A glance at Simone showed her trying to crane her head and get a better view of the man on the floor.

Her lips pursed. "It looks like our waiter." A pause. "To confirm, our waiter just tried to kill you?"

"I don't think he was interested in me." He had to unclench his teeth. He'd just taken in her full attire. Or, rather, her lack of attire. "You're still just wearing the damn sheet!" And looking sexy as fuck while doing so.

"Oh, pardon me!" Her eyes rolled. "So sorry that I rushed to the rescue and didn't stop to put on underwear and clothes first. My bad. The next time I hear gunfire blasting, I'll just bide my sweet little time and let you get shot in the head, will that work better for you?"

Angry fists pounded into the suite's door.

Her eyes went saucer wide. "Reinforcements," she whispered.

"Yeah, but for us, not for him. Simone, *please*, go put on clothes." Because he couldn't think well with her just in a sheet. "Those will be the guards who were stationed in the hallway." People under Jezebel's command. "I'm sure they heard the gunfire."

"I don't know." Her head tilted. Her hair trailed over one bare shoulder. "These fancy rooms are pretty well insulated. Not too sure how far sound traveled."

"*Simone.* Clothes."

"*Ryan.* Potential bad guys."

He frowned at her.

More pounding came from the front door.

And the jerk on the floor let out a groan.

"I have this under control," Ryan assured her as he took a step toward the door.

"I saved you. I came rushing in with the lamp. As far as I'm concerned, this now makes us even."

"Okay, we are even." Fine. Whatever. "But I'm wearing clothes and you're not so...dress? Now?"

She huffed. Started to turn. Stopped. "Will you make sure those are actually your reinforcements before I leave you?" Soft. "Because I don't want to leave you if you're just going to get hurt without me."

"Aw, Simone, you keep talking like that, and I'll think you care." He spared a glance through the peephole and nodded. "My team."

"Ryan." Just as soft as before. "For the record, I do care. Why do you think I ran to the rescue?"

His head whipped toward her, but Simone had already disappeared down the hallway. All he saw was the edge of her sheet, slipping away. He forced himself to take a deep breath. One, then another. Then he opened the suite's door.

Two agents rushed inside. Both CIA. Not agents he knew particularly well, but he was familiar with their work.

"What in the hell happened?" Jamar Miller demanded. "I heard *gunshots.*" His gaze darted around the suite, only to land on the man still sprawled on the floor. "Is that the room service guy? Because I swear, we checked him when he got off the elevator. There were no weapons on the guy's body."

"Right. They weren't on his body. He'd hidden the gun

beneath one of the silver covers, and he had a steak knife wrapped up in a napkin."

"Ohmygosh." From Jamar's partner, Charlotte Webb. True story, that was her name. Her actual, legal name. Her mother had apparently been a huge fan of the book. And the spider. "This should not have happened! I am so sorry!" She bounded toward the fallen man, drawing out her weapon.

Edward's eyes fluttered open. He groaned and came face to face with Charlotte's gun.

"Do you want us to kill him?" Charlotte asked, voice both loud and pleasant at the same time. Her dark hair skimmed her shoulders. "Because we can eliminate him right now. I can shoot him between the eyes, and then my partner can stuff his body beneath this serving cart and we can wheel him out of this place without anyone ever knowing what happened to him."

Edward tried to scramble back. Only there was no place for him to go because Jamar had stepped in behind him. With his weapon. "Hi, there," Jamar said, his voice not nearly as pleasant as Charlotte's had been. "Remember me?"

Ryan picked up the steak knife. "You just fired two bullets in my suite." A shake of his head. "Do you know how much I'll have to pay for damages now?" He closed in on his prey.

"No, please!" Edward's hands flew up. Then he stopped and winced. He also brushed his right hand over his face, sliding away some of the chocolate mousse that still clung to him before touching his temple. "What hit me?"

"Lots of things," Ryan informed him. "But it was the lamp that knocked you out." He pointed the tip of the knife at the SOB. "You recognized her, didn't you?"

Edward's gaze jumped around the sitting room.

"Hello!" Simone's voice. "He's talking about me. And here I am, on cue."

She strode into the sitting room with a smile on her face and, thankfully, clothing on her body. Black dress pants. A sexy, silky little white top that dipped off one shoulder. Black heels. And...

Fuck me. She had the stolen earrings in her lobes and the broach pinned on her blouse.

"So we meet again." She dipped her head toward Edward, but then her stare got caught on the knife that Ryan held. Her eyes widened before she licked her lips. "That's a very big knife you have."

"Yeah, it is," Ryan agreed as his grip tightened on the knife. "Pretty sure he was planning to use it on you." Something that pissed the ever-loving hell out of him.

"Don't worry." Charlotte edged closer to Edward. "He won't hurt you, ma'am. My partner and I are going to kill him, stuff him on the bottom of the cart here, and roll him right out."

"Oh." That was all Simone said. No outrage. No shock. Zero horror. After a beat, Simone nodded. "Good plan." She waved to the terrified man. "Goodbye!"

"No!" Edward screamed. He lunged up to his feet.

Jamar immediately clamped a hand around his shoulder.

"I'm sorry! *I'm sorry!*" Edward cried out. A clump of chocolate mousse fell from his cheek. "I had gotten the hit order on her—everyone knows about it!"

"Everyone?" Simone grimaced. "I sincerely hope not. I hope that not every single person I pass on the street wants me dead." A purse of her lips. "Perhaps you mean everyone in your particular criminal association? In your circle?

People who are working for Frederick Bradwin or for his dangerous associates? All of *those* individuals know?"

Quick nods. "He's offering twenty-five thousand pounds for you."

She gasped. Put her hand to her heart. Even took a step back. "Twenty-five thousand pounds?" Then she frowned. "Wait, that translates to like, what, in American dollars? What is the current exchange rate? Because, honestly, I feel like I should be worth more."

"Don't worry, baby," Ryan assured her as he kept the knife pointed at his target. "You're worth one hell of a lot more than that to me."

"Thank you." She padded closer to him. Her fingers brushed over his shoulder. "I like to be appreciated."

Jamar sent Ryan a quizzical glance, as if he could not figure out what in the hell was happening. Meanwhile, Charlotte just kept rolling with things. That was her style. Jamar tended to be the more by-the-book agent in their partnership.

Not that there was always a book for spies to follow. Sometimes, they all had to wing it.

"How did you know to look for her?" Ryan demanded.

"G-got a text. Her picture went everywhere." A fast exhale from Edward. "When I saw her in the restaurant, I thought...my f-fuckin' lucky day."

Ryan shook his head. "No, it is not, in fact, your lucky day."

Edward's Adam's apple bobbed. "I'm getting that."

"Did you report that she was here?" Ryan pushed. "Did you tell Frederick that she was at this hotel?"

That sonofabitch Frederick. "And he ordered you to kill her? Frederick specifically gave the order?"

Simone's fingers fluttered over Ryan's back again. "That

is just so incredibly rude. One day, you work for a man, and the next, he puts a bounty on your head." She stepped to Ryan's side and pointed toward Edward. "This is a valuable lesson for you to learn. You think you can trust Frederick? You can't. He'll turn on you just like he did on me. Then you'll be the one with killers shooting up your lovely hotel suite."

"I've never killed anyone before," Edward confessed, looking as if he might cry.

"You don't say." Ryan shook his head. "Never would have guessed." The jackass had been firing *wildly* in the suite. "So you thought you'd move up the totem pole by offing Simone? Sorry, but that is just not going to happen."

"What's a totem pole?" Edward scrunched his face.

Fuck. The prick was not staying on task. Ryan stepped closer to him. With the knife.

From the corner of his eye, he saw Simone tense. Dammit, was she remembering her own recent incident with a knife? Or maybe remembering how he'd slashed Alexei's throat and left a knife lodged in his chest?

His head turned toward her. Sure enough, there was fear streaking across her lovely face. "Don't," Ryan bit out.

"Don't what?"

Don't be afraid of me. Don't look at me that way.

But...

She was just staring at him as if she knew that he was a killer. He was. He would always be.

"Aren't you supposed to be some super rich American?" Edward asked, his words tumbling out in a rush. "Heard the check-in staff talking about you." He cleared his throat. "Have to say, you look, uh, really comfortable with that knife."

Ryan turned back to the matter at hand. The dumbass.

"I am comfortable with the knife." He motioned toward Charlotte and Jamar. "And so are my guards."

"Figured you'd have bodyguards close by." A mumble from Edward. "Almost changed my plans when I saw them waiting outside of the elevator."

"But you *didn't* change your plans," Ryan noted. Obviously. "You kept your weapons hidden, and you came into my suite, intending to kill *my* Simone."

"Oh, I'm yours now?" Simone brushed against him once more.

He growled.

"Right." A quick agreement from her. "I'm yours. You're mine. Together forever."

Edward tried to creep away.

Jamar's grip tightened on Edward's shoulder as he yanked him right back to Edward's previous position. "We are about to make you vanish," Jamar told him.

"But I don't want to vanish! *Please!*"

"Yes, well, I don't want my girlfriend being *murdered*, either," Ryan snarled. Which brought them to his new plan. "Take out your phone," he ordered the waiter. "Slowly."

Fumbling, Edward yanked out his phone. Not slowly. Awkwardly. With panic-stricken movements.

"You're going to make a phone call right now. You're going to call the man who sent you the orders for Simone's hit."

Edward nearly dropped his phone.

"You'll tell him that you failed. You'll tell him that I am incredibly pissed off. And you will tell him that if Frederick wants to save his business—and his own damn life—he will come to this hotel, personally, and he will talk to me." Low, angry words. Rage swirled in Ryan's gut. *This prick wanted to kill Simone. Shoot her or stab her. Take her from me.*

Edward had not called anyone on his phone. Fear flashed on his face. "H-he's not gonna want to—"

Ryan was on him. He pressed the tip of the knife to Edward's throat. "You wanted to kill her." His rage flared hotter. Harder. A rage that he'd tried to keep banked.

He saw Edward's eyes go wide.

Even Charlotte tensed.

"She belongs to me, and you wanted to take her." A slow, negative shake of Ryan's head. "That will not happen. You tell your boss that *no one* will be taking her. If something happens to Simone, I will burn down the world. Frederick will beg for mercy. Tell him that. He will beg. And then I'll destroy everything that Frederick values. *Everything*."

Edward's jaw dropped.

"Make the fucking call," Ryan barked.

"Y-you sure you don't want to tell him yourself?"

"Dial. Now."

Edward's shaking fingers flew across the face of his phone.

Charlotte and Jamar shared a very telling look.

Yeah, so he sounded a bit unhinged. That was the way he was playing the scene. The unhinged, super protective lover. And maybe the role felt way too real when he thought of anyone hurting Simone. Maybe *he* felt unhinged. Super protective.

"Hot," Simone whispered.

His head jerked her way.

"Seriously, I don't care what anyone else tells you, but it is seriously hot when you threaten to destroy a person's world for me. That's the kind of sweet talk that a woman loves to hear. Or, at least, it's the kind I like to hear. Full disclosure, I'll burn down the world for you, too. Would not even hesitate."

He could not get a handle on her. He was also pretty sure that Simone might drive him to the very edge of his sanity. Then beyond.

But the phone was ringing and he had a job to do.

"Hello?" A British voice. Male. Familiar. Not Frederick, though.

"It's...ah...it's Edward..."

"I fucking know. I have called ID." The voice turned sharper. "Is the job done already?"

Edward had put the call on speaker. "N-not exactly, Hugo, ah, sir."

Right. Ryan had already recognized Hugo's voice.

"How hard is it to put a bullet in a woman's brain?" Hugo demanded.

Simone cleared her throat. "A lot harder than one might imagine. Also, it's a super dick move."

"*Simone.*"

"Hugo, Hugo, Hugo." She tut-tutted. "I thought we were on the way to being friends, and now I know you are just a serious dick who will forever be on my list of lifelong enemies."

The plan had *not* been for Simone to talk with the bad guy. Time to take control of the situation before it was screwed beyond repair. "Hugo," he growled.

Silence. Then, "Just who is it that I'm speaking with?"

"You're fucking speaking to Ryan Quinn. Remember me? I'm the sonofabitch who was supposed to bankroll your boss."

A bit of heavy breathing, followed by, "Ryan! Uh, how are you?"

"I'm still living, and that's a win. Even better, my fiancée is living, too."

Simone tried to sidle away. Holding the knife with one hand, he caught her wrist with the other. Ryan's head turned toward her. "You are going nowhere."

"Uh, no, no, I'm not leaving," Hugo assured him. He coughed. "I think I might have missed something. Just who is your fiancée?"

"The woman you are currently trying to kill."

"Hi, Hugo," Simone said again. "Remember me?"

"Fuck," Hugo choked.

"Exactly," Ryan assured him, no small amount of satisfaction in his voice. "You are fucked. Your boss is fucked. His entire world is about to be fucked. *Because no one touches what is mine.* Tell your boss if he wants to salvage any part of this deal, he will haul his ass to London. He knows where I am. Obviously. Because I am right beside Simone. I will stay beside her. I will be between her and any threat. *Every* threat."

"Hot," Simone mouthed to him.

He meant the words. This wasn't for show. Someone came after her? He would be guarding her. Always. "Frederick will come to see me, alone, or else..." He let the threat trail away.

But Edward craned his head toward him. Wide-eyed, the waiter-slash-would-be-killer asked, "Or else what?"

Hell. "Or else I start lighting matches and I burn down Frederick's world, one match at a time. One light at a time. One fiery hell at a time. That good for you? Are we clear now?"

Frantic head bobs from Edward.

But Ryan didn't care about being clear with that idiot. It was Hugo who needed to understand. Actually, not just

Hugo… "I know you are there, Frederick," Ryan said, taking a gamble. "And I know you understand me. Call off the bounty on Simone's head. Do it now. Come face me, man to man. We'll either work out a deal, or I'll send you to hell."

Silence.

Ryan let that silence tick a little bit longer and then knew he had to push. "Any deal is off the table in five, four, three, two—"

"I'll be there," Frederick Bradwin said, voice cracking. A very distinct voice. Ryan would have recognized the prick's pompous tone anywhere. "I'll meet you in London. I was, ah, already planning to travel there in the morning."

And that's how you draw your prey right to you. "Good. I'll be waiting. Plan to get your ass here by eight. You *know* where I am, so I'll meet you in the hotel's restaurant." Ryan rattled off a specific meeting time because he wanted to be very clear. Then Ryan motioned to the waiter. "Hang up the phone, Edward."

"Right, right—"

"*Did you kill Alexei?*" Frederick demanded before Edward could end the call. "Or was it Simone? Who did it? Who—"

"Me," Simone said. "I'm the guilty one. Don't screw with me again, or you'll meet the same fate. A knife in the heart."

Ryan's back teeth ground together. He let go of Simone's wrist and snatched the phone from Edward. He ended the call. Tossed the phone aside. Slapped the knife down on a nearby table.

"I think that went really, really well," Edward told him, all big eyes, sweaty forehead, and desperate expression. "Now, will you please not kill me? *Please?*"

"I make no promises," Ryan snapped. "Especially considering you came to kill what is *mine*."

"I have a name," Simone pointed out. "Not just 'mine' but an actual name. It's Simone."

He was not dealing with her, not then. Not after the woman had just announced that she'd killed Alexei. He knew she'd done that deliberately, to put a bigger target on herself when he should have been the one receiving Frederick's fury. Ryan's breath heaved. "Get him out of here," he ordered Charlotte and Jamar. "And make sure you smooth over any issues with the hotel's management."

Charlotte nodded. "Consider them smoothed."

His nostrils flared. "Put every agent on alert. We will have a visitor incoming. VIP."

"Very important person." A murmur from Simone.

"No." A hard shake of Ryan's head. "Very important prey."

Jamar shoved Edward toward the door. But Charlotte hesitated and pointed to the cart. "Are we sure that we don't want to stuff him under there?"

Ryan studied the shaking waiter. "Edward is going to cooperate fully with us. I think he is going to tell us everything he knows about this criminal organization that he finds himself all tangled up with. If Edward plays his cards just right, he'll get to live to see another day."

"I would really like that," Edward whispered. "I want to see another day. More than anything."

"Get the hell out of here," Ryan snapped. Because that fool had come to kill Simone.

"Give us his gun?" Charlotte prompted. "We can check it, see if it was used in any other crimes."

"It wasn't!" Edward swallowed three times. "This was my first—uh, my first—"

"Murder for hire?" Simone chimed in to say. "Go big or go home, as the saying goes."

Jaw clenched far too hard, Ryan reached the gun he'd tucked into the back waistband of his pants. He gave the weapon to Charlotte.

The two agents took Edward to the suite's door.

"Nice to meet you," Charlotte called back to Simone. She sent Simone a friendly wave. "Maybe we can go out for drinks sometime soon. You know, to toast your new engagement and all that."

"Yes." One of Simone's eyebrows crooked up. "I can't wait to celebrate my engagement. I'm over the moon with joy."

"Yeah, I could see that." Charlotte fought a smile.

Then she was gone. So was Jamar. And their would-be killer.

Ryan locked the door. Flipped the extra bolt. He tried to get his rage under control, but, nope, it kept right on surging within him. What had happened to him? He'd once been able to control his emotions so easily.

"Oh, look." Simone's voice. All but purring with delight. "There is another chocolate mousse under this silvery thing. An untouched one. Want to share?"

He whipped around to look at her.

She'd just dipped a bit of the mousse into her mouth. The spoon was still between her lips. Her eyes were gorgeous and so blue they almost hurt to see. She stood there, calm, poised, eating the chocolate mousse as if a man hadn't just come in that suite intending to end her life.

"Does this happen a lot?" Ryan asked as he stalked toward her. "Because I am thinking it must. You are way too cool for this to be a one-time occurrence."

She slowly pulled the spoon from her mouth. Pausing,

she licked the edge, swiping away a bit of leftover chocolate. "Does what happen? Me, finding a perfectly good chocolate mousse? I wish."

How could she just stand there calmly—and sexily—eating the mousse? "Did you consider that it could be poisoned?"

Horror briefly flashed across her delicate features before she rallied. "It would take a true bastard to poison a chocolate mousse this good."

Where was her fear? Where was her fury? How could she be so controlled and cool while his skin seemed to be burning from the inside out?

"If poison was his game..." Simone picked up a little more of the mousse on the edge of her spoon and brought it to her lips. She savored the bite, moaning slightly.

That moan. His cock went rock hard.

Simone put the spoon down. "If poison was his game, I don't think he would have bothered with the gun, do you?"

Probably not.

"Or with the steak knife as his back-up attack option," she added.

Again, probably not.

Their gazes held. "So...is it going to happen now?" Simone finally asked him after too many moments crawled past.

His hands had clenched into fists at his sides. "Is what going to happen?" He'd never been as confused by a person in his life as he was by her. He just could not predict her actions. When she'd come out of that hallway, throwing the lamp...

"Are you about to get down on one knee and propose to me?" Simone fluttered her lashes. "Because I'm waiting." she told him with more than a hint of relish.

Fuck.

Chapter Fifteen

"You're not going to just...waltz into the man's hotel. Seriously, promise me that you're not."

Frederick's body swayed. How many glasses of scotch had he actually downed? Things were sort of hazy after glass number four.

"It's a trap," Hugo told him.

Frederick slapped his hands down on his desk. Yes, the move looked dramatic and intense, but it was mostly so he would stay upright and not fall on his face. "It's...not." He'd intended to go to bed earlier, but he'd waited, wanting to hear about Edward's attack. He'd hoped to discover that Simone had been eliminated.

But the woman had survived. Survived and was now... engaged to Ryan Quinn?

Hugo marched toward him. He'd shoved his phone back into the pocket of his coat. "It is. One hundred percent, it is a trap. Look, I know you ran a background check on Ryan Quinn..."

Well, Frederick hadn't done it personally. He had people who did that sort of thing. Someone in HR? "He's rich. And he's pissed." Frederick glared at Hugo. "You shouldn't have told that waiter to attack Simone."

"*You* gave that order," Hugo gritted.

"Things are blurry." The words sounded slurred to his own ears. He should sit down. Maybe eat something?

No. Sleep. Sleep would be best. Not like he wanted to storm Ryan Quinn's hotel room right then and there. "Tomorrow." That was the plan. "Tomorrow morning, I will meet Ryan for breakfast. We'll settle this...unpleasantness. Put it behind us."

Hugo sucked in a breath. "I get that you're drunk off your arse."

He was *not*.

"By the way, boss, murder isn't 'unpleasantness' to most people. It's a crime. And the fact that Ryan Quinn has casually committed murder should alarm you."

Frederick shook his head. The whole room seemed to swirl around him. "He didn't do it. It was her."

"I disagree. I think it was *him*."

Hugo could disagree all he damn well wanted. But Frederick knew what was happening. "You just have a soft spot for her." A nod. "I get it. I wanted to fuck her, too."

Hugo's round face didn't look quite so friendly.

"Women are dangerous. Traitorous." Oh, how he knew that to be true. "She's pulling the strings. Somehow, she's got Ryan thinking they are going to get married." That bombshell had blindsided him. "I can fix this."

"It's a trap," Hugo repeated. "He's setting you up. You would be an absolute fool to just walk into his hotel."

Even drunk, Frederick did not like the man's tone. "Watch it," he snapped. "You forget who pays your salary." He raised his hands off the desk. Slowly. Then he pulled out his own phone. He thought about calling Konstantin, to give the man a head's up, but...

No, that would just be more problematic. Better to resolve this issue himself. Frederick tossed the phone onto his desk. "I'm getting some sleep." Maybe the room would stop spinning once he'd slept for a few hours. "And tomorrow, I'll meet with Ryan." Good. Done. Excellent. "I'll fix things."

"I doubt that," Hugo muttered.

He'd started to weave his way to the door, but at Hugo's mutter, Frederick paused. "What did you say?" He hadn't fully caught Hugo's response.

"I said..." Louder, "I don't doubt that."

Good. Excellent. "It's too hot in here." His fumbling hands yanked at his collar even as Frederick kept heading for the door. When had he put *two* doors in his study? His hand reached out, and he missed the doorknob. Oh. Maybe only one door was actually there. His hand slid to the side. Fumbled. And found the doorknob.

"What about the hit on Simone?"

Why would Hugo not stop talking? He was making Frederick's head hurt.

"Do you want me to call off the hit on her?"

Now that was a weird question. "Why would I want you to do that? She's a thief and a killer. She needs to be eliminated." Simone was a problem.

"But—"

"*Eliminated.*" He yanked open the door and stumbled out.

* * *

"You're a dumb bastard," Hugo groused as he watched Frederick weave out of the study. The man nearly crashed to the floor and had to grab the doorframe for support.

Hugo propped a hip against the desk and watched the drunken idiot stumble away. Ryan Quinn had given a very clear order. No one was to harm Simone Sailor in any way, shape, or form.

Or there would be hell to pay.

Apparently, Frederick was too drunk to be afraid.

Major mistake.

He was also too drunk to listen to reason. Hugo had warned him that the morning meeting at the hotel would be a trap, but Frederick refused to listen to reason. His funeral.

And, as far as who paid his salary, Hugo certainly could not forget that important detail. His hand reached out, and he scooped up the phone that Frederick had left behind. His fingers swiped over the screen. He knew Frederick's passcode. He'd watched the bastard type it in earlier that night. It had taken three fumbling attempts before Frederick had done it properly.

So unlocking the phone was easy. Scrolling to check through the recent call log was easy, too. And hitting the screen to dial one of those numbers again...

So easy.

Hugo smiled as he put the phone to his ear. It rang twice before it was answered.

A gravelly voice demanded, "What now?" A voice with the hard hit of a Russian accent.

"Hello, Konstantin," Hugo greeted him.

"Who is this? You are not Frederick!"

"Don't hang up! Don't! I have news that you want to hear."

"You have Frederick's phone."

Indeed, he did. "Frederick is currently passed out drunk." If he wasn't dead to the world yet, he would be soon. "And I really felt you needed to know about some of his plans for tomorrow morning."

Konstantin didn't hang up.

He did listen.

"A trap is about to be sprung," Hugo began.

Chapter Sixteen

He did not drop to one knee. He did not look soulfully into her eyes. And Ryan did *not* ask for her hand in marriage.

Simone sighed. "Disappointing."

He stalked toward her. A slow, intense stalk that made her feel very hunted. Not that she'd let him know a tremor of fear had just darted down her spine. She'd learned to stop showing her fear a very long time ago. At the third foster home she'd lived in. So, instead of letting the fear appear, Simone summoned her brightest smile. "Guessing you did not mean it when you said you'd fallen hopelessly in love with me and you could not live another day without me by your side?"

Ryan stopped. Right in front of her. His expression was all dangerous and dark. Stubble lined his hard jaw, and his eyes glittered. "I never said that I had fallen in love with you."

Hello, knife to the heart. Oh, such a bad thing to be thinking, especially considering all that had happened recently. "You didn't?"

"Simone." A long growl of her name. "I am trying to keep you alive."

"And I am trying to keep *you* alive." Her hand rose and pressed to his chest. Right over his heart. Bare skin. Hot. Tempting. He should really have put on a shirt. But, then again, she liked the view, so she wasn't going to complain. "Didn't you see me rush to the rescue? Me and my lamp?"

"I did not need rescuing!"

"Of course, you did." Now she was just pissed. "You were living a life of absolute solitude and sadness, and then I walked into your world and things have never been the same since."

"What?" Ryan shook his head.

She kept her hand over his heart. She liked touching him.

"There is no solitude in my life!" Ryan huffed out. "I've got a wonderful family that's always in my business. My sister Agnes can drive me crazy, but I'd do anything for that woman, and she knows it. My brother Nash always has my back, just like I have his. We're pretty damn inseparable, and don't even get me started on holidays with them..."

Her hand snatched back. "Good for you." Was that jealousy biting at her? Sure felt that way. She would never know what it was like to have a wonderful family around her. She'd never know what it was like to have a big holiday with happy laughs and silly gifts being exchanged and...*Why did I ever think he was a loner like me?* Why on earth had she come to that conclusion? Why had she thought that she'd found a man who was her match?

Maybe I wanted him to be. Maybe I wanted him to be just for me.

"My life isn't sad." Rough, hard words from Ryan. "I

work cases that make the world safer. I ride adrenaline, I stop bad guys, and I get shit done."

"Even better for you." Did she make the world safer? Uh, no. A resounding no. Did she stop bad guys? Again, no. But Simone did like to think that she got shit done. She helped, in her way. Just as she'd helped when she threw the lamp. "He was attacking you. I threw the lamp to stop him. It was a good deed."

A little furrow appeared between Ryan's eyes. "I told you to stay in the bedroom."

"Oh, no." She pulled a dramatic face. "Shocking twist. I didn't do what I was told. Horrors!"

His lips thinned. "If I'm keeping you alive, you have to follow orders."

"Orders are boring. Don't be boring, darling. Be the adrenaline-crazed badass that I want you to be." She turned away.

His hand swept out to curl around her wrist. "Keeping you alive is my priority."

Her gaze dropped. Fell to his strong fingers. A hot surge had gone through her body when those fingers of his wrapped around her. But, then again, she'd felt the same surge when she touched his chest. Touching him ignited her. Problematic, but manageable. "And here I thought your priority was capturing Frederick and Konstantin. My mistake."

Using his hold, he pulled her back toward him. "Something has made you sad."

"What?" Her voice rose. "Don't be ridiculous."

"Don't lie to me."

Why not? She didn't matter to him. Not like he'd sworn undying love to her. Not like she wanted him to do that. *Oh, wait, I kinda do.*

"What upset you?" Ryan asked. His thumb stroked along her inner wrist, right over her pulse point. He had to feel the frantic racing of her pulse.

"I don't know," she murmured. "Maybe it was the waiter who came to kill me. The gunshots that blasted." Shouldn't other guests on the floor have been disturbed? The guards in the hallway had heard the gunfire and come running, but there had not been a peep from any other guests on the floor. And shouldn't the hotel management have rushed in with their own security team? Something? "Maybe it was seeing you face off with the jerk as you gripped a knife in your hand." The same hand that circled her wrist. "Flashbacks and all that."

He let her go. "You're afraid of me?"

She prepared to lie and deny any fear. But when Simone opened her mouth..."Yes." Wait, what? Why had that response just whispered out? Simone swallowed. She was not physically afraid of Ryan. Perhaps she should have been physically afraid. She had seen him kill, but he'd done it to protect her. Just as he'd fought in that very hotel suite for her.

He kept being brave and bold and proving that he'd take any risk for her, and each time he did that, her heart softened toward him even more. So what scared her? What really scared her about the whole situation? It was the idea that she might be falling hopelessly in love with someone who was never meant to truly be hers.

"I will not hurt you," Ryan vowed. "I would sooner cut out my own heart than do that."

"Not necessary." Her hand rose once again to touch his chest. "I like your heart right where it is." They were standing too close. The longing inside of her was rising too strongly again. She needed to back away. To regroup.

Simone pulled in a breath. "Why didn't more guests come running?"

"Because I made sure that we are the only ones on this floor. There are no other guests close by."

All right, that explained some things. "And what about hotel security? Management?"

"Jamar and Charlotte will handle them."

"They'll also handle our killer waiter, Edward?" Curious, she pushed, "Just what will happen to him?"

"He'll go to a black site."

"That sounds incredibly spy-like."

"It is. He'll be held at an isolated location, questioned at length, and, depending on the intel he is able to give us, he'll either cut a deal or face hell." His gaze was far too sharp. "Why are you sad?"

"Why do you keep focusing on that?" Didn't he see her bright smile? She was flashing it deliberately.

"Gorgeous smile," he noted. "But fake." He studied her. The kind of too in-depth assessment that made her feel like she was under a microscope. Ryan's mouth tightened. "You don't have to fake a smile with me. If you're sad, you tell me why. If you're mad, you tell me. I can't fix things if I don't know what's broken."

"I'm not asking to be fixed. I don't particularly see myself as broken."

"You're not. You're beautiful. You're strong. And you risk yourself far too much." His head dipped toward her. "Stop trying to save me."

"But what if you need saving?" she whispered. His mouth was so close to hers.

"My brother typically rushes in at that point. Like I said, he watches my back, and I watch his."

"I hate to tell you." Her hand inched up. Curled around his shoulder. "But I don't see your brother here."

"Nash is always close when I need him."

"Must be nice, to have family like that." She pushed up onto her toes. The better to get closer to his mouth.

"Aren't you close to your family?" His lips nearly brushed hers.

"My family died when I was six years old." Horror filled her as she seemed to hear the words echoing around them. Simone sucked in a breath, and instead of pulling him toward her, her grip on his shoulder suddenly pushed Ryan away even as she tried to surge back.

But his hands curled around her waist, holding her in place. "What's wrong?"

"You are a sneaky bastard." And what was up with her? How had she allowed her guard to be lowered? She never talked about her family. Never. "Luring me in, just so you could ask me personal questions when all I was thinking about was the way your mouth would feel against mine. Talk about a hardcore interrogation technique. Do they train all CIA spies to use desire as a weapon?"

"Uh, no. That would be a hard negative." His grip tightened on her.

"Let *go*."

Slowly, his hands lifted.

She put three steps between them.

"I'm sorry," he said, voice gruff. "About your family."

She blinked rapidly. Holy crap, were those *tears* trying to fill her eyes? Not happening. She blinked twice more. "You need to be sorry for manipulating me. Dammit, I knew the way I felt about you was going to get me in trouble!" Why had she told him about her family? *Why*?

"What happened to your parents?"

She spun away from him. Her racing heart seemed to shake her chest. "Shouldn't we focus on the bad guys? The killers who might be coming for me? The end boss Russian guy that the CIA wants to take down?"

"I want to focus on you."

Too bad. "I don't normally pull up my pain and introduce it to strangers, but thanks for the invitation. Sadly, I'll be declining that request." The suite that had once felt massive now seemed incredibly small. "I need to get out of here." She stormed for the suite's main door. Simone flipped the deadbolt and yanked on the golden door handle. The door began to open.

But his hand flew down and pushed the door closed almost immediately. She felt his body, his heat, surrounding her even as Ryan warned, "It's not safe out there. You can't go out alone."

"Fine. Then you come with me. My big, bad bodyguard." Simone stared dead ahead. There was a warning sign pasted to the back of the door. A little map that showed the room's occupant where to go in the event of a fire. The hotel's staircases and exits were clearly marked.

She made a mental note of that handy little map.

"There's a bounty on your head," Ryan rumbled.

"It's night." The last of the daylight had long since faded. "No one will be able to see me clearly out there. I need air. I need to breathe. I need *out*." Because the walls were closing in on her. Dammit, just mentioning her parents had stirred up the old fears.

Can't breathe. Too tight. Closing in. Everything is closing in. I am drowning.

"Why are you so afraid?" His breath blew against the shell of her ear.

"I need to get out of this suite. Now." She'd shown him

too many weaknesses. It was getting harder and harder to hold her shiny mask in place. If the mask fell, he'd see what she was really like. He'd find all the darkness that she tried to bottle inside.

"I wish you'd turn to me when you're afraid," Ryan rasped.

The words seemed to pierce right through her. Her body trembled.

"Because I would slay any fucking dragon for you."

Her gaze fell to his forearm. To the twisting, scaled tattoo of a dragon that had been etched into his skin. "What if you are the dragon?" Simone asked.

A swift inhale. "*I will never hurt you.*"

"I need to get out of here, Ryan. Now. Out. Take me out of here." Did a plea enter her voice? Maybe. Definitely.

He swore. "Let me finish dressing and get my gun."

Yes, he was just still wearing his pants. Awkward. Sexy but awkward.

His breath blew against her ear once more. "Do not dare leave this room without me. There are guards stationed throughout this hotel."

Guards or CIA spies? Maybe MI6? Where had Harry gone?

"If you try to run, they will just bring you right back. Then I'll probably have to handcuff you to me because you will *not* get away from me."

Yes, she would get away. Soon. "I'll stay here while you dress." She could certainly hold it together for that long. "And while you get your gun. Guessing the gun was in the bag Jezebel brought to you?" She pushed hard for a breezy, flippant tone. "How unfair. She only brought me makeup."

He choked out a sound that could have been a laugh or a curse. Then he was gone. She eased out one breath. Then another. She began to count in her mind as she tried to slow her racing heart.

One.

Two.

Three.

Counting did not help. Memories crashed through her mind.

"*Mom! Dad! Please, please, wake up! Wake up!*" Water rushed up her body. So cold. So icy. It was swallowing her whole, and she could not *breathe*.

Her hand flew out for the door.

"Let's go," Ryan said from behind her. He yanked open the door. Simone immediately tried to bound out, only to have him clamp his hands around her waist and lift her up. He put her down behind him. "Sweetheart..." A sigh. "In case there is another jackass waiting to collect the bounty on your head, let me go first, okay? That way, I can either take a bullet for you..."

She didn't want that to happen. "Don't!"

"Or kill the bastard so he doesn't hurt you," Ryan finished. "Either way, I protect you. Consider me your human shield from this moment forward."

Chapter Seventeen

SOMETHING WAS WRONG.

Simone's breath seemed too fast. Her skin too pale. And her frantic gaze had locked on the elevator doors. Her body was way too tense, and he did not like this shit.

"Simone?"

She jumped.

And the elevator...stilled.

"Ohmygod." Her body swayed. "I cannot get stuck in this elevator. That can't happen. Not *now*."

"Are you claustrophobic?" Simone sure as hell seemed to be acting that way.

She surged toward the panel on the right. Her hand flew down, and she started hitting buttons, just as the elevator had begun to move again.

Unfortunately, when her hands frantically flew over the buttons, the elevator jerked to a halt. A hard halt.

"No!" Simone tried to punch the buttons again.

He caught her hands. "It's okay. Give the system a second." Actually, he thought she might have accidentally shoved the stop button. An alarm was sounding nearby, and that was not good. "Simone? Look at me."

Her gaze crashed toward him. Her pupils were too small. Her body trembled.

Static crackled from the elevator's speaker. A female voice inquired, "Is everything okay in there?"

"We've stopped!" Simone cried out. "Get us moving, please."

"Of course. Please stay away from the doors. Movement will resume shortly."

Ryan pulled Simone away from the control panel and the doors. "You're terrified."

She didn't deny the charge.

She'd laughed in the face of torture, but the elevator ride made her nervous? She'd seemed *fine* in the elevator earlier. When he'd been kissing her, she'd certainly seemed, um, more than fine.

Something had changed. Something had set her off.

Her family? Had his questions about her past stirred up old fears? "How did your family die, Simone?"

A shudder worked her delicate frame. "Not now. I can't talk about them now. *Not while I am in here.*" Panic underscored the words. "*I can't breathe.*"

He'd done this to her. He knew it. He'd brought up pain for her, and now she was hurting when he'd sworn that he would not hurt her. Ryan's hand flew to cup her jaw.

"Ryan?" Confusion. Pain. Fear.

He needed to distract her from her terror. Needed to give Simone another focus.

He took her mouth. Took that precious, gorgeous mouth and kissed her with all of the passion and hunger surging through him. As soon as their lips touched, a long shudder raked over her body. She grabbed for his shoulders, holding on tightly, as if he were a lifeline when he wasn't. He was the problem.

Her nails bit into his shirt and coat. Her body pressed hard to his. His touch on her jaw remained light, but his mouth kissed her with undeniable intent. Driving passion. Burning lust. His tongue thrust past her lips. He tasted her, and she met him with a greedy, desperate lust.

The elevator began to move again, but he wasn't sure she realized what was happening. She'd pushed her body even closer to his. Her mouth was wild against his.

Ding.

He forced his head to lift.

"Thank you," Simone whispered. "I really, truly needed that."

He'd needed it, too. Ryan had a feeling that he might always need her. A sobering thought especially since he was using her.

His hand lowered, but Simone immediately caught it in her grip. She threaded her fingers with his. "My fiancé should at least hold my hand," she explained with a cheeky grin as they turned for those open doors.

Her fear seemed to have passed as quickly as it appeared, but Ryan wasn't about to let the matter drop.

Simone is too good at wearing a mask. At showing the world a bright and shiny surface while pain lurks inside.

They exited the elevator, and, because he was watching her so closely, he saw the slight exhale that she gave, as if sighing in relief.

They'd arrived in the hotel's lobby. A quick glance around showed him the MI6 agents and the CIA operatives who were lounging around. Appearing casual, but, after the recent attack upstairs, Ryan knew they would all be on high alert.

"Oh, look, there's Harry." Soft words from Simone. "I guess I'm not supposed to wave at him, am I?"

No, she was not. "Act like you don't know anyone here."

"That's easy enough to do." She strolled along the marble floor. Her head tipped back as she peered up at a massive crystal chandelier. "I really only know you. And we're still just surface-level, aren't we?"

"Sweetheart." He brought her hand to his lips. Kissed her knuckles. "I fucked you less than an hour ago."

Red flashed in her cheeks as her head turned toward him.

"I'd certainly call that more than surface." From the corner of his eye, he saw Harry put down the book he'd been reading. Harry would follow them when Ryan and Simone left the hotel. When he'd gone to collect his gun and to finish dressing, Ryan had paused to text his team and let them know that he would be taking Simone on a short stroll.

Considering the attack that had just happened in the suite, Jezebel had been less than pleased with his plans. But...

Simone needs air. She'd been having a panic attack or close to one. She needed to get out, desperately, so he'd get her out. He'd keep her safe outside. And the other agents knew to keep watch over them.

Besides, a cleanup crew needed to get the suite back in shape. Those bullets had to be removed from the wall. All signs of a struggle should vanish. The crew could do their work faster and better without him and Simone present.

"Stay close to me," Ryan told her, as they passed the doorman and walked into the night.

"No," she murmured back as her gaze darted to the left,

then to the right. "I plan to flee from you at the very first opportunity. Do not trust me for a moment."

Her words held a teasing edge, but his whole body tensed. He stopped just holding her hand. Ryan wrapped an arm around her shoulders and pulled her against him. Both to protect her and to keep the woman from fleeing because he feared she had been all too serious with her words. "It's safer for you to stay with me."

Her hand brushed against the side of her body as they moved away from the hotel's entrance. "Because you're the big, bad spy?" A gust of wind slid against them.

"Because plenty of people want you dead, but I happen to want you to stay in the land of the living." He very much wanted that. With all of his being.

She turned to the right, and he realized that Simone had a destination in mind. This wasn't just some mad dash into the darkness in order to escape her anxiety. As he turned with her—and kept her tucked against his body—Ryan was fully aware of the fact that Simone could be leading him straight into an ambush.

What had she said before? That they were only surface level? "What's your real name?"

Her heels tapped as they walked into the night. London at night was always a special sight for him. Fog had started to roll in, as it so often did. A little spooky, a little sinister. He liked that sinister edge.

Simone appeared to be heading toward the nearby Wellington Arch. It was hard to miss the massive structure, and he'd always been fond of the bronze sculpture that rested atop of the Arch. The Angel of Peace, surging on to the Chariot of War.

Ryan knew way too much about war, and, some days, far too little about peace.

Lights illuminated the Arch, and, despite the fact that tourists normally flocked to the place, he didn't see anyone at all near the structure. Maybe it was the deepening fog. Or the light rain that he could feel beginning to fall...maybe that was why they had the place to themselves.

A black cat suddenly rushed right in front of them.

His arm tightened around Simone's shoulders. "I don't like this." *Hello, bad omen.*

Soft laughter. *Real* laughter spilled from her. Damn but he enjoyed the sound of her laughter. The look of her smiles. Her scent. Her taste. Fuck, he enjoyed everything about her.

Like that doesn't spell trouble for me.

"Oh, come now, Ryan," Simone chided. "Dark-and-dangerous you can't be afraid of a little kitty."

It wasn't that he was afraid. He was simply cautious. "Black cats are bad luck." Didn't everyone know that?

"In France, they are actually viewed as good luck." She crouched. "Here, kitty, kitty."

No, she was not *calling* a black cat to her. Was the woman just trying to invite bad luck? After the danger she'd already faced?

"Kitty!"

With a soft *meow,* the cat bounded back toward Simone. The thinnest, roughest looking cat he'd ever seen. One complete with a scraggly ear that looked as if a bigger animal might have tried to claw it off at one point.

She offered her hand to the cat, and Ryan could have sworn the black cat nodded before it allowed Simone to stroke its head. "Aren't you beautiful?" Simone cooed to the harbinger of darkness.

All right, fine, the cat was probably not the actual

harbinger of darkness but... "Do you need to pet it? Now?" *Ever?*

"Yes, I do. Because my mother was French and, as I told you, in France, black cats are good luck. There is nothing bad about this beautiful darling."

The cat was purring.

Ryan glanced around, searching for threats. As far as he was concerned, the cat was just a sign that this side trip out into the night was about to take an unfortunate turn.

As if the attack in the suite had not been bad enough.

"Good luck, good fortune, and maybe even a bit of good magic for you in life." Another careful pat on the cat's back before Simone rose to her full height. "I had a black cat when I was a child. When I was with my parents. His name was Lucky."

Unlucky would have been more fitting. Now that she was talking about her past, he found that he could not move. He wanted to hear every detail, though he feared the story was going to be painful. Dark.

The rain began to fall a bit harder.

The cat ran away.

"Wait!" Simone called out, but the cat was already gone. Her head tipped back. "I don't really like the rain," she said. A shiver skated over her body. "When we were at Frederick's country estate, I wasn't lying about the fact that I can't stand storms." Raindrops sprinkled over her face, and she shuddered. "Reminds me too much..." Her words trailed away as another shiver rocked her.

"Let's go back to the hotel." Where he could better control the environment and where she wouldn't be shivering from the cold and the rain.

But Simone shook her head. "I need to be outside. I need to *breathe*."

She could breathe in the hotel—

"The Arch," she decided. "Let's go there. If we're under the Arch, we'll be sheltered from the rain."

The sky seemed to open up around them as they rushed toward the Arch. The rain wasn't a trickle any longer. It hit far harder. More of a downpour and would it have killed Jezebel to mention the weather forecast to him when he'd updated her and said they were going out? Hell. Talk about getting drenched.

He yanked off his coat and tried to cover Simone with it as they raced toward the waiting Arch. She darted forward, and he was right with her. Moving fast, faster...

Until they were under the massive Arch. Until the stone walls were on either side of them, and they were protected from the downpour.

He realized that he still had his coat raised over her head.

She stood on the edge of the Arch, watching the rainfall. There was no sign of the cat she'd been so enamored with moments before. No sign of anything but the rain. They appeared to be the only people out, but he knew other agents had to be watching them in the darkness. Jezebel had promised more eyes would be monitoring them.

"I hate the rain." Simone's shoulders sagged. "It wouldn't stop that night. The car was in the ditch. I was trapped, and the water was just rising and rising."

He lowered the coat. Tossed it to the stone floor. "Simone?"

She backed away, moving toward the nearby wall. The lights around the Arch let him see that he hadn't protected her from the rain fast enough. Her white blouse was soaked and clung to her. It had also gone far too transparent.

His gaze jumped back to her face. "Simone..."

She motioned toward him. "You're wet. A man in a wet, white shirt is sexy as hell, just so you know. I can see all those bulging muscles of yours. That fabric clings so tightly in all of the best ways."

He swallowed. "Same, sweetheart...*same*."

"I don't have bulging muscles to—oh." She'd looked down at herself. "Right." A delicate clearing of her throat as her head tilted back and she met his stare. "Guess we both got soaked, huh?"

He didn't give a shit about the rain except for what it was doing to her. *Bringing up her past. Hurting her*. "You're trying to distract me by talking about my wet shirt and muscles."

Her back pressed to the wall near her. In that location, she was quite protected from prying eyes. All eyes but his, that was.

"Would it be hard to distract you?" she asked. "You distracted me when I was afraid in the elevator. I quite liked the distraction."

He'd quite liked kissing her.

"What if I told you that I wanted your mouth?" Simone asked. "What if I said that I'd like for you to kiss me, right here? Right now? Would that distract you?"

He glanced around the Arch. A ladder had been left out. Appeared someone had been doing repairs, and a ladder had been placed against the wall opposite of Simone. Shoddy work, that. Someone could get hurt with a ladder left hanging around.

"Don't you want to kiss me?" Simone pushed him.

"Baby..." His gaze returned to her. "I want to devour you." Just so they were clear. "I want to kiss you. I want to taste you. I want to fuck you until you scream for me. Those items are always on my to-do list where you are concerned."

"Then what are you waiting for?" Such very tempting words. "I'm right here."

He closed in on her. His hands lifted, then moved to press against the stone behind her, caging her between his body and the wall. "Stop playing games with me." When would she learn that she couldn't play with him?

"I'm not playing games. I'm offering to fuck you right here. Unless you're afraid of fucking in public?"

Not like it was something he'd ever done before. And, also, they were not quite *in* public. In this particular spot, he had them hidden from sight. His head lowered toward hers. "There is nothing I want more than to fuck you."

Her head tipped back. "Then do it."

"You're scared. You don't want to face your pain." Gritted words. His control held. Barely.

"What is the point in facing your pain?" Simone seemed truly confused. "It's better to just bury it and walk away. Facing it does nothing but make the ache worse."

He wanted to make all of her pain vanish, forever. "I upset you in the hotel suite." He could see past her mask. Did she realize that? "When I talked about my family. As soon as I mentioned them, I noticed a difference with you."

Her gaze darted away from his.

Ryan didn't think she was going to respond.

The rain kept falling, so hard and heavy now.

"I was jealous." Simone's soft response. "I won't ever know what it means to belong with a family like yours. To grow up in that kind of home." Her stare slowly drifted back to him. "I can be jealous and also be happy that you have them. I can feel both things at the same time. I'm a multitasker that way."

His chest ached. "Tell me about your past."

"My past? Why? Isn't it just better to focus on the

present?" One delicate hand rose between them. She unhooked the top three buttons on his shirt. The fourth button.

"*Simone.*" This was important–she was important. "You were in the ditch. The water was rising. Why didn't your parents help you?"

Her fingers had slipped inside of his open shirt to press against his skin. "Because the dead can't help you."

Fuck.

"I was trapped in the car. We all were. It had gone off the road. Into the ditch. I called for my parents, but they were dead in the front seat. I didn't realize that, you see. Six year olds don't understand that their parents can be laughing and talking with them one moment and then just *gone* in the next instant. They also don't understand that creeks can overflow far too fast and the water can rush into ditches and that it can destroy everything. *Everything.*"

"Simone..."

"So I just kept crying and screaming for them as the water rose. I couldn't get out. It was on my ankles. Then my calves." A shudder shook her body. "Then my knees. It was dark and thunder boomed constantly. The water rose higher, going for my waist. My chest. My..." Another shudder. "Will you just kiss me?"

"*You got out of the fucking car.*" She was there with him. Alive. Safe. Yet a dark, yawning fear lived and breathed inside of him because...

She could have died.

Years ago.

Long before their paths had ever crossed and she'd flashed him that fantastic grin of hers.

"I got out of the fucking car." Brittle words. "They didn't. After that night, there was no more family for me.

No more Lucky the cat. No more happy endings. Just rain and endless storms to chase me forever."

This was real. She was being real with him, and he desperately wanted to protect her. To promise her that he'd be her shelter in any storm. That he would give her *anything*. Everything. That he could be her family.

He was sinking, drowning, in her, and Ryan did not care.

"Now either kiss me or let me go," Simone told him.

He'd never let go.

His mouth took hers. A savage need pounded through his veins, but the kiss was careful. Soft. Gentle. Soothing because he knew she needed soothing. He wanted to show her how precious she was. He wanted to show her that he could handle precious things. That he could be—

"What in the hell is this?" she whispered. "Kiss me with your passion. Kiss me like you can't wait to strip this wet blouse off me. *Don't kiss me like you pity me.* Please don't ever do that."

His head lifted. "I do not pity you."

Her chin notched up.

"I do not." She needed to understand this. "I hate that you lost your parents. I am so damn sorry for what you had to endure. I feel grief for you, with you. I *hurt* with you." He did. "You're strong. You're determined. You're also kinda scary, in a way that I like. I admire the hell out of you. I will never pity you."

"That is the sexiest thing a man has ever told me." A quick inhale. "You think I'm scary? Truly?"

"Sweetheart, I think you're hell on wheels, and I love that about you." *Love.*

Fuck.

What. The...

Fuck?

It had just been an expression. Something people said. *Hell on wheels* was an expression. *I love that about you...* another expression. Casual expressions did not equal undying declarations.

Except the words felt like more. *I love that about you* almost felt like...*I love you.*

She was smiling at him again. Her big, beautiful smile. The one that made his heart race faster and made his whole world seem to realign so that she was his axis.

He kissed her again, unable to help himself. Ryan kissed Simone the way she'd wanted to be kissed. With passion. With the primitive need that surged through his veins. Like he couldn't wait to strip that wet blouse off her. Like he couldn't wait to claim her.

Her mouth opened wide beneath his. Her tongue met his. She moaned. He growled. He moved closer to her, pressing his body against hers. Feeling every single inch of Simone against him, but it wasn't enough.

He wanted her naked. He wanted in her. But he was not taking her there. Not where agents and guards and tourists and who the hell else could pop out at any moment. He was not—

Something blasted past the side of his right arm. He felt it rip across him like a hot burn a moment before...

Wet. Why the hell does my arm suddenly feel even wetter than before?

And his mind processed too slowly. Too slowly because he'd gotten lost kissing Simone.

But then he realized...

Blood. My arm is bleeding. That was a freaking bullet that just tore past me.

Only he'd heard no gunshot. He'd thought they were

inside the Arch far enough, tucked against the left wall enough that they'd be safe. He'd thought wrong.

He spun around, making sure to put Simone behind him.

"What are you doing?" Simone cried out. "This is seriously confusing behavior. You can't kiss me one moment and then—"

"Gun," he snarled.

"What? Ryan, I don't—*gun!"* she screamed.

Yes, yes, dammit, he saw the shooter. The bastard had just come from the nearby doorway that led up to the balcony beneath the Arch's bronze sculpture. The prick had his gun raised, a gun with a long silencer on the end of it, so, yeah, that explained why there had been no loud gun blast when the weapon fired.

The man was cloaked in shadows, but once he advanced...

"That's the hotel uniform!" Simone sucked in a sharp breath. "I saw some of the bellhops with the same outfits when we were on our way out."

Yeah, he'd seen them, too. "Let me guess," Ryan said to the shooter, "you and Edward the waiter happen to run in the same circles, huh?"

"You're not supposed to die," the shooter told him in a voice that rose a bit too high with nerves. "Get away from her. She's the one I'm after. You *live*."

"Cute." Ryan did not move. "You think you get to snap out orders? To me?"

"I'm the man with the gun!" A gun that was shaking in his grasp. "She's not worth your life, is she? Walk away. Now. Get out of here. Walk into the rain and don't look back!"

Simone's fingers brushed over Ryan's back. "You should

listen to him." Quiet words. "It's okay. I promise, I'll survive."

What in the actual hell was that response about?

"No, lady," the man told her in his cracking voice. "You will not. It's not personal, I swear. But you will not survive because I have to put a bullet in your brain."

"Over my dead body," Ryan swore.

The shooter sighed. "Okay." A wince. "If that's the way you want it. Really sorry about this, sorry to you both..."

And Ryan knew the jerk was about to fire again.

Chapter Eighteen

"No!" Simone screamed. Then she darted to the side. "Stop it!" She waved her hands, frantic. "Don't shoot him!"

"*Simone*," Ryan roared her name with true fury.

Whatever. He could be furious, and he could also be alive.

The shooter's attention was on her. His gaze on her. His weapon—yep, on her, too. Simone licked her lips. "I'm the target, right? No sense wasting bullets on him. You literally said you weren't even here for him."

"Don't want to shoot him." A nod from the shooter. "This isn't personal, lady. Promise." A nod. "Maybe close your eyes? And it will be over quickly."

The gun was shaking. The shooter was drawing in a deep breath. And Ryan was—

Shooting. At the jerk with the gun.

She didn't even know where Ryan had gotten his gun. One minute, his hands were empty, and in the next—*bam*. The echo of gunfire reverberated around her. The man in the hotel uniform staggered back when the bullet Ryan had fired tore into him. Ryan rushed at their wounded attacker. The two men collided, slammed back, and, oh, no. *No, no, no.*

They went beneath the ladder.

Ryan would not be a happy man.

They'd gone beneath the ladder, ensuring that Ryan would have a significant amount of bad luck, and the ladder crashed down on top of the struggling figures.

Ryan shoved the ladder away and somehow managed to kick the creep's gun out of the guy's reach at the same time. Simone used that moment to surge forward herself. She grabbed the discarded weapon and held it tightly, aware that her heart was about to jump out of her chest. "That was fabulous!" she praised Ryan. "Where in the world did you get your gun?" She hadn't seen one on him, but in a blink, it had been in his hand, and he'd been firing.

Ryan currently had his weapon pointed at the forehead of the fallen attacker. "*It was strapped to my fucking ankle.*"

Her gaze flew over him. "Oh." Well, he'd certainly moved quickly. She hadn't even seen him grab it. Her stare returned to Ryan's face. "Good thing I created a distraction, huh? I gave you the chance to draw your weapon. Talk about some phenomenal teamwork."

A savage growl. "Do *not.*" Ryan's head turned toward her even as he kept his gun muzzle pointed on the downed man. "Do *not* talk to me about teamwork. I warned you about taking risks."

"Someone is ungrateful." Extremely so. "I saved your life! You know what...I get it." A jerking nod. "You're upset about the ladder and the incoming back luck that you'll have. It's all right. We'll deal with it."

"You *are* my bad luck," Ryan snapped.

She sucked in a breath. Those snapped words of his

hurt. "You try to save someone. You try to help..." *And you're called bad luck.* He might as well have said she was trouble.

Then again, she was trouble. Trouble and a CIA operative were not meant to be together. She surveyed the scene. Ryan was safe. He had things under control. The gunman was practically sobbing as his shoulder bled profusely, and Ryan's gun remained shoved toward the jerk's head. Time for her to get back to her real life. The perfect opportunity was right in front of her. "Forget this. I'm done."

She was done because...this was her chance.

"See you around, Ryan."

Still clutching the gun she'd snagged, Simone bounded to the right, intent on rushing out of the Arch and into the rain and into the safety of the night.

Except...

Harry appeared.

Damn Harry. Why did the MI6 agent have to show up at that exact moment?

He bolted out of the rain, soaking wet, and he appeared straight in her path. She did have a gun. She could shoot him. An option. But not really one she wanted to take. Truth be told, she didn't exactly love shooting the good guys. Or, anyone for that matter.

"Going somewhere?" Harry asked her, and he didn't look quite as green and fresh faced as he'd seemed before.

She sent him her most innocent smile. "Hurray!" Which sounded a lot like *Harry*. "Help has arrived!" Simone darted a glance over her shoulder and found Ryan glaring at her and still holding his gun on the moaning-in-pain man. "Look, Ryan, the cavalry is here to help."

"Simone..." Ryan's gritted rumble. "Your ass is mine."

Oh, that sounded both very promising and a little bit frightening. And, unable to help herself, she threw back, "Good luck with that." Because by the time dawn arrived, she intended to be far, far away from the spy who was breaking her heart bit by bit.

* * *

THE WATCHER COUNTED at least five individuals who swarmed from the darkness and rushed toward the Arch. He'd been preparing to storm forward, but the others had beaten him.

Now he waited in the shadows, the rain falling steadily, as he tried to see his target. Time ticked past far too slowly. *Come on. Come on...*

And there she was. Stumbling out in a wet blouse, with a hulking figure by her side. A figure who had a coat positioned over her head. How very chivalrous.

His eyes narrowed. He could partially make out the man's face. A face that was familiar to him. He'd expected to encounter strangers but...surely...not...

He backed up.

Fucking hell. I know that face. I know that dangerous sonofabitch.

Simone's chivalrous protector was a lying, killing *spy*.

What have you gotten yourself into this time, Simone? And how was he going to reach her?

Simone was being rushed back to the hotel by the spy. Another man was trailing behind her. The watcher was very, very curious about the scene that might have been left in the Arch. He was pretty sure a slumped figure had been shot. Killed or just injured? Did it even matter?

Simone had not been the victim. Simone still lived.

Now if he could just get her away from the spy and make her disappear completely...

* * *

"Oh, yes, fabulous idea," Simone huffed. "Let's go back to the hotel where not one but *two* staff members have clearly demonstrated their wish to have me dead. I one hundred percent feel like we are returning to the safest place in the world for me."

Ryan stopped in front of the hotel. Two doormen froze nearby. "I'm getting you back in the suite."

She leaned toward him. For the moment, she ignored Harry. Sneaky Harry. He'd trailed behind them every step as they returned to the hotel. And the way he'd just burst out of the rain to block her path...*I did not expect that.* She'd have to remember he liked to lurk about. For the record, Simone had to declare, "I think we should check in to another hotel. Clearly, this one is not working for us. I may have to leave a one star review due to the fact that staff members keep making attempts on my life."

Ryan wrapped his wet coat around her shoulders. "We're going inside now."

But one of the doormen moved forward to block their path. "Sir, sir, is that a gun?"

Yes, it was. A gun tucked in the front waistband of his pants.

"Deal with him," Ryan barked at Harry.

"Guns are not allowed!" The doorman appeared scared but still determined. "I will be phoning the authorities!"

Harry pulled the doorman close. "About that..."

Ryan hustled her into the hotel. He was double-timing it toward the elevator bank, and her stomach twisted in anticipation of that tight ride, but then Ryan stopped, right in the middle of the lobby. "Stairs," he snapped. "We'll take the fucking stairs."

Aw, that was sweet. She knew he'd made the change for her. "It's all right. I'm better now. I can handle the..." Her words trailed away. The light in the lobby seemed incredibly bright. And, under that bright light, she could see the redness on his wet, white shirt. The right sleeve. "Ryan, I think you got some of that man's blood on you."

"It's not his blood. It's mine. From when the bastard shot me."

"But he..." She had to pick her mouth up off the floor as she surged toward him. "He shot you? When?" She did not remember that. She distinctly remembered only hearing *one* blast of gunfire. That had been when Ryan fired.

"When I had you pinned against the wall and all I wanted was to fuck you into oblivion." Snarled words. "I let my guard down and you almost got hurt. Bastard had a silencer on his weapon."

What, what, *what*? "You got shot and you didn't tell me?"

"Was kinda busy taking down the shooter. And trying to stop you from offering yourself up as a willing victim—stop doing that shit, by the way. *Stop.*"

He'd been shot. In the arm, yes, but his arm was inches away from his *heart*. "You got hurt!" She tried to grab for his shirt so she could check out the injury.

Only to find herself tossed over his shoulder. The shoulder connected to his non-injured arm. The arm that did not have a *gunshot wound*.

"What is happening?" Simone cried out.

"You said you could handle the elevator. I'm not risking it. I'm not having you stressed and scared, so I'll just carry you up the stairs." He was hurrying with her across the lobby. Moving past a stunned Charlotte.

"Hi," Charlotte mumbled. "Having a good night?"

No, they were not. "He's *shot!*" Simone didn't want to struggle too hard because she was trying not to hurt the man any worse than he'd already been injured, but...seriously, he couldn't carry her when he was suffering from a gunshot wound!

"A graze," Ryan tossed back as if the wound didn't matter at all. "Is the stairwell clear?"

"Uh, yeah." Charlotte shoved open the stairwell door. "You know that your suite is like four flights up from here, right?"

"I can climb those flights in my sleep."

"Good for you." Charlotte craned her head and waved to Simone. "Have fun."

Fun?

The stairwell door clanged shut. Simone grabbed the back of Ryan's wet shirt and pulled hard. "Let me down *now*. Or I will be kicking you in the dick." She was pretty sure that she could make the kick from this position.

"Don't make me spank you."

Her breath caught. "Okay, save the kink for later, and we'll talk about spanking options."

"*Simone.*"

"Down! Now! Dammit, you're hurt!" Tears stung her eyes. "And I'm about to cry! Shit! This night sucks—and, *ah!*"

He'd put her down. Instantly. "You will *not* cry."

A threat of a kick to the dick had not done the trick, but he listened when she mentioned crying? Good point to know for future reference.

She also found herself immediately pinned between

him and a wall. Simone glared up at Ryan. "You do this a lot."

"Do what? Nearly go insane because of you? Yeah, that does seem to occur, granted. I swear, I never lost control before you came rolling into my life. My sanity was never in question. Never. Not once."

"Your insanity is your own business. What I meant was you *use your body to intimidate me.* You do that a lot, and it is not cool!"

"Uh, again, wrong wording. Did you mean I use my body to *protect* you? Is that what you meant to say? Because I'm surrounding you so that you'll be safe if any threats appear. You know, threats like the one we just faced. I tried to shield you *with my body* at the Arch. Only, instead of staying behind me, you moved to the side! You made yourself a target. Why in the hell would you do that?"

So he could keep living. Obviously. "You're not my human shield." Her gaze zeroed in on his arm. His blood-covered arm. Even though she blinked repeatedly, two tear drops raced down her right cheek. "I don't like for you to get hurt. And I specifically *hate* for you to get shot."

"It's a graze." His thumb slid under her chin and tipped her head up. "It is only a graze, and I am fine. I swear it." His mouth brushed over hers.

The kiss steadied her. It quieted the terrible fear that had been blooming inside of her ever since she'd realized it was his blood and not the other jerk's.

Ryan eased back.

Her breath whispered out.

"We're going up to our suite," he said.

"I really think we should get out of this hotel. Who is going to come after me next, one of the cleaning staff? A cook? The concierge?"

His stare held hers. "I need you to trust me."

The problem was that she did trust him. When she rarely trusted anyone. "I need you...to let me go."

"It's just not going to happen." Then his mouth brushed against hers again. "Now do I get to carry you up the stairs?"

"No, I can get up the stairs just fine on my own."

And she did. He went first, determined to keep up his human shield act, and at every new floor they reached, they encountered another guard. Guard, spy—same thing? She realized that his people were stationed at every level of the hotel.

So much for her plan to sneak away via the stairs. If these guards were going to stay in position for the rest of the night, she'd barely get down one flight before being intercepted. Maybe if she couldn't go down...then she could go up. Escape via the roof?

Simone filed that option away for later. For the moment, she had a bleeding Ryan to handle.

Jamar was waiting when they reached the top floor. He held open the stairwell door for them. "Enjoyed the fresh air, huh? Was it as invigorating as you hoped?" He waved toward Ryan. Specifically, Ryan's arm. "Got to tell you, you have a little something on you."

"I want that bastard interrogated. Thoroughly," Ryan ordered.

"Jezebel is on the case. You know she always gets her answers. Guess the plan to use Simone as bait worked." An approving nod. "Nice job. You are taking down bad guys left and right."

Bait.

Is that all she was? A juicy lure to pull out more and more bad guys? No wonder Ryan didn't want to switch hotels. He was accomplishing his mission there.

Ryan opened the door to their suite. He went in first. She lingered in the hallway and perhaps she shot a sullen glare Jamar's way. The term *bait* had truly rubbed her the wrong way.

Ryan closed a hand around her wrist and tugged her inside. When the door shut, the sound seemed incredibly final.

"Oh, look," she murmured, aware that she was dripping water onto the floor. "We're back where we started." Her shoulders hunched in his coat. "I'll go change, get into something dry, and when I come back, I'll get you bandaged up." She tried to walk away from him.

Only Ryan did not let go of her wrist.

He stood before her, all big and strong and dripping, too. His shirt clung to him like a second skin, and the man appeared way too sexy and dangerous.

"You were leaving me," he accused.

"I'm attempting to leave you *now,*" she clarified, tugging on her wrist.

But he just tightened his grip. Not hurting her. Physically, he'd never hurt her. But his hold seemed unbreakable.

"I'm talking about at the Arch, Simone. You were going to run away from me. You knew I had to stay with the perp. You were trying to take that opportunity and *run.* If Harry hadn't been there, would you have vanished into the night?"

That had been her plan, yes. *Now you see me, now you don't.*

"What. The. Hell?" Each word from Ryan was bitten off. "You were leaving me? Is that your MO? You have sex then vanish?"

Her stomach twisted. "Release my wrist. Now."

He did. "Look, dammit, I'm sorry, I—"

"I'm not your bad luck."

His dark brows shot up. "What?"

"Frankly, I'm the best thing that ever could have happened to you." She squared her shoulders. "But you are too much of a jackass to realize that fact. All too focused on being a super spy and not seeing what is right in front of you." Anger vibrated in her voice. Anger shook her body. But so did pain. "And I don't fuck randomly. I am very, very particular when it comes to my lovers. I thought you were someone special." He'd saved her life. He'd fought for her. He'd...

Dammit, he'd made her *care.*

"I am no one's bad luck," she said once more.

His eyes had widened. "Baby..."

"Don't you dare 'baby' me right now." She put some needed space between them and hurried for the hallway that led to her room. "You should have let me go."

"I don't want you to go."

There was a ragged edge in his voice that had her pausing. Glancing back.

"I didn't mean it," he told her.

Her heart *hurt.*

"I don't even remember saying that bit about bad luck. Hell, I was fucking terrified and furious, and I just wanted to destroy the bastard who'd come to kill you."

"You were terrified?" Mocking laughter as she glanced back at him. "I don't think so."

"I do." And he stalked toward her.

Chapter Nineteen

SIMONE WHIRLED TO FULLY FACE RYAN.

"I was terrified because, what if I'm not there?" His expression became even harder as he closed in on her. "The next time an attacker strikes, *what if I am not there?*"

"Ryan..."

"There's a bounty on your head, and two would-be killers have come for you in one night."

"Amateurs." A lump rose in her throat. She choked it down.

"What if the next one isn't an amateur?" He stopped right in front of her. "What if you run from me, you disappear into the night, and the next attacker who finds you—when I'm not there—isn't an amateur? What the hell happens then?"

"Watch yourself," she chided. "Or I'll begin to think you care about the woman you fucked."

His hands flew up to curl around her shoulders. "I should never have fucked you."

He was a master at delivering heartbreak.

"Do you know how many rules I shattered doing that?

But I wanted you too much to stop. I've *never* crossed lines like this on other cases. I don't fuck randomly, either. I'm particular with my lovers, and I will tell you with one hundred percent honesty, I have never wanted anyone the way I want you."

Simone had no ready response.

"I do care," he added, voice ragged, "and that's the problem because I am not used to—" Ryan broke off abruptly. He shook his head, and then his right hand rose from her shoulder. He pushed back her hair.

"Ryan?"

"You're missing an earring."

Oh, no.

His other hand lifted so he could brush back the hair on the opposite side of her head. "Two earrings. You're missing them both."

"They must have fallen off during the struggle. Excuse me, I need to go change. I'm freezing in these wet clothes." She spun abruptly, intending to hurry to her room.

But when she spun, his hands caught the coat she'd been wearing. His coat. He pulled it away from her.

"*Simone, stop.*"

She didn't want to stop, but it was not like she could escape right then. He'd just follow her to her room. Sucking in a deep breath, she paused. "Was there something else? Some big, heart-felt confession you wanted to make?"

"Turn toward me."

She whirled toward him, making sure to have her innocent expression in place. "Yes?"

His sharp gaze swept over her. A muscle flexed along his now clenched jaw. "You aren't wearing the broach."

Simone gasped. Her hand flew up, and she touched the blouse, in the spot where the broach had been attached earlier. "Oh, no." A sad shake of her head. "Again, it must have fallen off during the struggle at the Arch."

"I don't remember you *struggling* at the Arch. You were behind me, then beside me, and when I launched at the prick, he and I slammed into the ladder." His gaze had lifted to hold hers. "You grabbed the gun he'd dropped."

"Yes, I was rushing around, lunging up and down." A nod. "Totally understandable that I would lose the broach and earrings in all the confusion and drama."

"You grabbed the gun, then you tried to run away. You didn't get far."

Because of Harry.

"You were running to *him,* weren't you?" Ryan demanded.

"Him?" Her brows climbed. "To Harry? Hardly. I didn't even know he was lurking in the dark." Until she'd nearly slammed right into him.

"You were running to the man who hired you to steal the broach and the earrings."

"I didn't *steal.* I *retrieved.*" A shiver skated over her. The wet clothing really was quite cold. "Pretty sure we have covered my whole retrieval process before."

"You were running to him." Certainly. "He's here, isn't he?"

Not like he was in the suite with them. But...

At the hotel? Yes. Not an employer, though. A friend. No, more like...part of her very, very small family.

"You left the broach and the earrings somewhere outside for him, didn't you, Simone?"

Guilty as charged. She'd actually dropped the broach and the earrings when they'd been at the front of the hotel. And they'd been picked up instantly. She'd seen their rightful owner and had known he'd realize what she was doing.

He'd always understood her so well. He had, since they'd been children. Growing up together in Vegas.

"He's here," Ryan said again. "*Who the hell is he?*"

Her best friend. The one person who'd been there with her during her desperate years as she grew up. The port for most of her storms. They'd met in foster care. Had wound up in the same place at the right time. Only his grandmother had eventually taken custody of him, so he'd been pulled from the system.

A year later, he and his grandmother had pulled Simone, too. Just in time...

I owe them everything. I will repay them until my last breath. "I don't know what you mean."

But Ryan just appeared all the more determined. "He is not going to take you from me. He won't be able to protect you."

You should not underestimate him. Without another word, she turned on her heel and headed down the hallway. She entered her bedroom and closed the door with a soft click.

Then she wiped away the teardrop that had slid down her cheek. Why couldn't life ever be easy? But nothing had been easy, not since she was six years old. She'd lost everything that horrible night.

She was about to lose again. And this time, she'd be losing her spy.

* * *

SHE LEFT him holding the dripping coat. Snarling, Ryan

wadded up the coat and tossed it to the side. He yanked out his phone and called Jezebel.

Jezebel answered on the second ring. "I haven't even started my interrogation," she announced. "I am good, but not a miracle worker. Give me time, Ryan."

"We need to review every guest in this hotel. I want video footage to show me every single person who was in the lobby when Simone and I left earlier." His arm throbbed where the bullet had grazed him. He ignored the throb as he began to pace the suite. "I also want footage of the exterior of the hotel."

"What's happening?" Jezebel's voice had sharpened.

"Simone."

"Uh, yes, Give me more. What about her?"

"Her employer is here. She gave him back the broach and the earrings."

Silence. Then, "She did this right in front of you?"

He actually didn't know exactly when she'd done it. "She's good, all right?"

"Yes, she is." Jezebel whistled, clearly impressed. "Right in front of you...my, my. Bet that makes you feel like an ass, doesn't it?"

He growled. *I was distracted.* As he so often was, when Simone was close. "I need that footage."

"We'll get it. I'll have it sent to your phone and laptop ASAP."

She'd brought his laptop in the bags she'd delivered earlier.

"I don't think this man is a threat to her," she continued, tone musing. "We can determine his identity, but it sounds like she was just completing a job. The focus of this mission is on Frederick Bradwin and Konstantin Volkov. They are the targets. They are the end goals."

She tried to run to him. She was going to leave me.

But...

Only after he'd called her bad luck.

He'd hurt her. Ryan had seen the pain in her eyes, and it gutted him. "I want to know who he is. How the hell he knew she was here. Any unknown is a threat."

"Um, Ryan." A pause. "Sorry, but I have to ask, are you being properly detached on this mission?"

Uh, no, he was not. "I want to know who he is."

"Your meeting with Frederick is scheduled to occur in the morning. If it goes well, we can shut this case down very soon. You and Simone could potentially be going your separate ways within twenty-four to forty-eight hours."

Screw that. He didn't want to go separate ways. He wanted her. "She's not bad luck."

"Excuse me?"

His right hand rose, and his fingers skimmed over the crooked bridge of his nose. "When she was six years old, her parents were killed in an auto accident. She was trapped in some sort of ditch, the water was rising, and Simone thought that she would die."

"That's...quite tragic. I'm very sorry for her loss." A careful clearing of Jezebel's throat. "Is this case becoming personal for you?"

The case had been personal from the moment Simone had been threatened. "She grew up in foster care. I'm telling you this story so you can help narrow things down and find out who she really is."

"Sounds to me like you know who she really is."

He didn't. She still confused and maddened him and... she made him want to put the world at her feet. The story about her family had gutted him, and all he'd wanted to do was make sure she never knew pain again.

"She's a survivor," Jezebel added. "She came from pain. She learned to adapt quickly. That's the chameleon aspect showing through."

Her bright smiles. The charming laughter. Masks that she wore to hide the truth. To hide her pain.

"She's strong. Intelligent. Determined. Very resourceful." There was no missing Jezebel's admiration. "It's really no wonder that you find yourself falling for her."

"I'm not falling for her!"

Laughter. "Say that to someone who can't tell when you lie."

His heart slammed into his chest.

"I'll use the background information you gave me to hunt for more intel on her past. I'll also get the security footage sent to you. But, right now, I have an idiot to interrogate. And you have a meeting to prepare for. Do not let this case go off the rails. The end is in sight. Eyes on the prize and all that." She hung up.

He gripped the phone and then he turned and glanced back down the hallway. He should not have been surprised to see Simone standing there, but he was.

She'd changed. Put on a silky, black pajama set. Her feet were bare and that would be why he hadn't heard her approaching steps. But, from the look on her face, Simone had heard plenty of his conversation.

I'm not falling for her!

What the hell should he say?

"I came back to clean and bandage your wound." She tucked a lock of hair behind her ear. "But then I heard you telling all my secrets to the person on the other end of the phone."

"Jezebel. I was talking to Jezebel."

"Yes, I figured it was her." One delicate hand pressed to

her heart. "Do you know, before you, there is only one other person in the world that I told about my parents and what it was like to be in that car with them?"

Fuck. *Betrayal.* He saw it on her face. He'd betrayed her. He'd shared her secrets. He'd *done this.* All because he was obsessed with unwrapping the mystery that was Simone.

"No, I guess there is no way for you to know that, is there? Because we're still surface. Surface that fucks, but surface." A slow exhale. "Here's the thing, though. Surface isn't supposed to hurt this badly. At least, I don't think it should. I always believed casual hookups were supposed to be fun and exciting. No complications."

There was nothing casual about them. "Simone—"

"You're not falling for me. I won't fall for you." She turned away. "If you need help with your wound, you know where I am. Otherwise, though, do me a favor, will you?"

"Anything." He stumbled after her, helpless.

Simone glanced back at him. Tears glittered in her eyes. "Fuck off, spy."

Chapter Twenty

A SOFT KNOCK RAPPED AGAINST HER BEDROOM DOOR. Simone stared up at the ceiling as she sprawled on the bed. Not sleeping. Not even close to sleeping.

Not crying anymore, either, so that was good.

But glaring. She was hardcore glaring at the ceiling.

The soft knock came again.

"Go away!" Simone called. Then...hell. *He was shot. He might need me.* She tossed aside the covers and marched for the door. With an angry hand she wrenched the door open. "Do you need my help with your wound?"

And, no, one swift glance told her that he did not.

Because he had a white bandage around his upper arm. His bare upper arm. Ryan had ditched the soaking, white shirt. He'd ditched his black dress pants. His shoes and socks. He wore a pair of gray jogging pants that clung to his hips, and his insane abs were on full display. He looked big, foreboding, and far too sexy.

Damn him. Was it just too much for him to occasionally look rumpled and unkempt?

He propped his non-injured forearm against the doorframe and leaned toward her. "I'm a liar."

"Tell me something I don't know. You've been lying to me from day one." Granted, she'd been doing the same thing but...

At some point, the lies got old. Was it so wrong to wish that she could be honest with him? That he could be honest with her?

"Lying is part of my job, but I was always good at pretending. Long before I joined the CIA, I was good at lying. I was good at fighting. I was good at killing."

Goosebumps rose onto her body.

"I started in the Marines," he revealed. "*Semper Fi.*"

She shook her head, not understanding where this was going.

"Always faithful," Ryan explained. "*Semper Fidelis.* That's the motto of the Marines. I protected. I defended. I served my country, and I made a difference. Never even thought about becoming a spy back in those days. Didn't even appear on my radar, not until my brother Nash had a sudden career change and became a spook."

Why was he telling her all of this? "Was he a Marine, too?"

"Nah. Nash was supposed to be a doctor. That is what he *is* going to be. Now. But life—fate—was twisted back then, and he had to make hard choices. I didn't even know why he was changing everything. He didn't tell me. When, normally, Nash told me everything. All I knew was that something was wrong, he was walking into danger, and I couldn't let him walk that path alone." A twisted smile came and went on his lips. "So I followed him into the CIA, and I discovered that I am a very good liar. I am very good at manipulation. I'm good at compartmentalizing my life. At not letting emotions get in the way of a mission. I'm good at becoming someone new every few months or every other year."

She curled her arms around her stomach. "Is Ryan Quinn even your real name?"

"Funnily enough, it is. The CIA built me a very solid background using that name. I don't employ it on most missions, but I did on this one." His gaze held hers. "Is Simone Sailor your real name?"

"Simone is my real name."

"But not Sailor?"

"My father was a sailor." Memories whispered through her. Of a time when the feeling of water on her skin hadn't been terrifying. Her father had taken her out on the water again and again. She'd been sailing her own small Sunfish sailboat by the time she was four, but he'd been beside her. Always beside her.

Until he wasn't.

Ryan's arm slid away from the doorframe. "You chose it for him."

She shrugged. But, yes, she had. She used the last name of Sailor because it was part of a happier time.

"I'm a liar," Ryan told her again.

"I think we've covered that part pretty thoroughly. No need to rehash."

"I didn't intend to fall for you, but I did."

She'd misheard. Simone shook her head. "Quite sure you told Jezebel that you were *not* falling for me."

"*That* part was the lie. And she called me on it."

Her body tensed.

"I met you, I knew you'd be useful to me, so I asked you out that first day. It was never supposed to go past being a purely platonic, casual experience between us. But

I went out with you, and I...liked you." Gruff. A little awkward.

She'd liked him, too.

"Sometimes, you meet someone, and you realize that they know you. More than that, they *get* you. The more I learn about you, the more secrets that are revealed, I realize that you get me, Simone. You don't flinch away from who I am or what I've done. You saw me kill a man, and you barely batted an eyelash."

"You killed to protect me." She'd been grateful to be alive. Besides, she only batted her lashes when she was trying to play innocent and throw someone off balance.

"I'd kill to protect you a million times over."

Her gaze cut away from his. "That would be a lot of dead bodies. Totally unnecessary. Overkill, some would say."

He eliminated even more of the distance between them. His hand slid under her chin, and, slowly, carefully, he turned her head so that she looked at him once more. "I lied when I said that I wasn't falling for you. I lied to Jezebel, and, like I told you, she immediately called me on it. Jez always does that. Calls me out on my BS."

Her heart raced far too fast. "You're telling me what you think I want to hear. You're trying to manipulate me. You want my help, so you're attempting to smooth things over. Unnecessary. I already promised to cooperate with the CIA."

"No, I'm not interested in manipulating you. I'm telling you what I need to say. Because I don't want to be a liar with you. I want you to know me. All of me. Not just surface level."

Her gaze drifted over him. "Your surface has some interesting tattoos."

He'd mentioned that he'd gotten both real and fake tattoos. Kinda like the man himself. Real and fake. Real hero. Fake asshole billionaire?

But as she studied him, her gaze became caught on the dragon tattoo. Such an impressive beast. Every scale seemed to be alive with energy and dangerous intent.

"I got that one for my sister. Agnes...she lost someone very special to her a long time ago. His murder changed her life. She became someone different, and all she wanted was for the killer to be brought to justice. I was helping to hunt him. But when you hunt monsters for too long, you can become one, far too easily. You can become something that other people fear."

Her arms stopped hugging her body. They fell to her sides. "I am not afraid of you."

"I know. Maybe you should be, though, because where you are concerned, I can't compartmentalize. I can't shut down my emotions. I *can't* keep my control, no matter how hard I try."

They were hours from dawn. From the promised meeting with Frederick. For an end to the mission.

When they parted ways, she'd never again get to do the things she wanted to do with Ryan. With him. To him. "Did you help your sister? Did you stop the monster?"

"Her monster is gone."

"That's good." She rocked forward onto the balls of her feet. "Why are you sharing so much with me?"

"Because I never told anyone else all of this. Because I want you to be the one who carries my secrets. Because I will not betray you again."

Her lower lip trembled. "It's easy to make promises. Not so easy to keep them."

"I want you."

I want you, too.

"I'm not just talking about right now, right here, though, hell, yes, I do." His stare was so focused. So hot. Scorching. "I'm talking about forever."

Shock had her stepping back. "You—you can't."

"Why not?"

"Because liars don't get forever. That's not what happens to people like us." They weren't made for happy endings. A happy ending would not be in the cards for her, she understood that. They didn't have a bright, shiny future just waiting in the wings once the mission was over. They only had the dangerous here and now.

"Who says we can't have forever?" Ryan wanted to know.

But she shook her head. "What are we going to do? Get a house with a picket fence in a small town? Take the kids trick-or-treating and hold Easter egg hunts in our front yard?" Mocking words but...

The image...

The idea...

The temptation...

I want that life. A secret whisper in her mind. She wanted a home. She didn't care if the town was big or small. She wanted a family. Trick-or-treating. Oh, but she could design an amazing haunted house and she could scare everyone and she'd dress up as a witch and laugh as her own little demons rushed home. Maybe a son with dark eyes like Ryan's. Or a daughter with her smile.

No. That life is not for me.

She couldn't have fantasies like that. Fantasies like that hurt too much. They reminded her of when she'd been a kid and she'd used to dream and wish that her parents would come back. That it had all just been some terrible mistake.

They weren't really dead. They were going to show up, at any moment. With her cat. And they were going to go back home. And she'd ride in her Sunfish with her dad. And she'd go trick-or-treating. Finally get to wear the dragon costume that her mother had so carefully made for her that last year. A costume she'd never gotten to wear because the car accident had occurred three weeks before Halloween.

I can't have fantasies. I can't have dreams.

"We could do all that," Ryan said, speaking thoughtfully. "The house with the picket fence. I happen to know a really great city on the bay, and the sheriff there is top-notch, though I am a bit biased when it comes to Agnes."

What?

"Or, we could let you run through Europe. Jezebel happens to think that you have all the makings for a fabulous spy."

A spy. A life with more lies. No, thanks. She was full up on lies.

"Exciting places," Ryan murmured. "Big cities. A new background story every few months."

"And danger." She swallowed to choke down the lump in her throat. "Not too sure I'm big on the constant danger. It can get a little tiring after a while."

"So you're saying you're a small-town girl at heart?"

No, she was saying... "Some people are afraid to dream, so they're not really sure what they want."

A nod. "You're being honest with me."

"And you're being honest with me." Talk about a completely new experience.

He crept toward her. "Little scary, isn't it?"

It was. "Not quite as scary as being kidnapped and

waking up to a guy saying he'll cut off your fingers but, yes, it's intense."

Ryan studied her a moment longer, then nodded. "I'll be down the hall. You know where my room is." He turned away.

Hold up. That was it? "You're leaving?"

He glanced back at her. "I'm sorry. I've never fallen in love before, so I'm pretty sure that I've been screwing things up with you from the beginning."

What. The. Hell? Had he just said *love?*

"But I wanted you to know how I felt. I *didn't* want to lie to you about my feelings. I wanted to be able to stare you in the eyes and just tell you the truth. Confession is supposed to be good for the soul, isn't it?" The faint lines around his mouth deepened.

"You...you are not falling in love with me."

He simply stared back at her.

"Ryan?" A fist seemed to squeeze her heart.

"I lied to Jezebel. I am not lying to you. I *am* falling in love with you." He reached for the door. He walked away. He left her there when her emotions were all over the place. When she was thrilled and terrified and completely lost as to what she should do next.

Ryan Quinn was falling for her.

Ryan was...

Gone.

He pulled the door closed behind him. She stood in the hotel bedroom, trying to decide what she should do and then...

She knew.

She yanked open that hotel room door and raced after him.

***

He heard the door open behind him. Ryan turned around. Dammit, he'd been trying to do the right thing. Even as it gutted him. All he'd wanted was to pull Simone into his arms. To kiss every inch of her. To show her how much he truly did *love* her.

She ran to him. She threw her body against his. His arms opened automatically, then closed around her. He pulled her up, and his mouth crashed onto hers. They kissed with desperate need and ferocious hunger, and she was everything that he had ever wanted in his entire life.

His match.

His fantasy.

His heart.

Her tongue licked against his. Her breasts pushed against his chest. Her body rubbed against his, and his eager dick could not get harder. He wanted to strip her. He wanted to take her. Over and over again.

Hold her while you can.

Take her before you lose her.

That was his greatest fear—losing her.

His mouth tore from hers. "Want you." Speech was a major struggle. He mostly just wanted to growl and devour her.

"Good. Because I am planning to lick you all over."

Wait, what? *What* had Simone just said? And could she say it again?

But she pulled back from him. Her lips were red and full. Her bright eyes gleaming. "You cannot walk around with tats like that and not expect to get licked."

Every muscle in his body tightened. "That's a...bad idea." A guttural warning.

But her hands were fluttering over his chest. Dipping down to his stomach. And her mouth was following the path. Kissing him lightly. Licking...

My control will not last. Then again, as he'd told her, his control never lasted where she was concerned.

"Oh, I disagree." A purr from Simone. "I think it's a fabulous idea. Let's follow the beautiful ink and see where this low one on your abdomen goes..."

And she was following it. Dropping to her knees. Caressing his skin with those luscious lips of hers. Feathering over him and tormenting him. Ryan's hands clenched into fists at his sides because if he touched her, it would be over.

He'd fuck her in the narrow hallway.

Against the wall.

When there was a perfectly good bed not far away.

Technically there were *two* good beds near them and...

She'd just shoved down his jogging pants. Ryan sucked in a hard breath. "There is *no* tattoo there." As if he'd let a tattoo needle near his dick.

"Are you sure?" Her breath blew over the dick that surged toward her. "I really need to check. Have to be thorough and all of that."

He looked down at her. One of her delicate hands curled around the base of his dick. She guided him toward her mouth. Her lips parted, and she took the head of his cock inside.

Fuck.

Fuck.

She sucked him. Her tongue swirled around the head of his cock, licking him, and then she was pulling him in ever deeper.

They weren't making it to either of the beds near them. Nope.

His control shattered. Ryan yanked her up. Ripped away her silky, black pajama bottoms. Distantly, he heard the sound of fabric tearing. He thought it might have been her panties because he'd managed to get her pajama pants off just fine. He left her button-up pajama top on, no time to get rid of it. He heaved her up against him, and she smiled. Pure temptation.

"You are so lickable, Ryan Quinn."

"And you are incredibly fuckable, Simone Sailor."

Her legs curled around his hips. He drove into her. Right there. Standing up in the hallway. Because there was no waiting. No holding back. He spun and pressed her back to the wall. Her heels dug into his ass as she arched toward him. Their mouths collided. Their bodies heaved. Her nails bit into his shoulders as she surged against him, and lust exploded.

Kisses were frantic.

His thrusts were deep, hard, and unrelenting.

She arched toward him again and again. Her soft whispers urged him on. Her head tipped back against the wall. His mouth flew to her neck. He licked and sucked, and he drove into her even as he worked one hand between their bodies. He strummed her clit. Rubbed it fast and hard. Again. Again.

She jerked against him. Shoved her tight core against him *hard*, and then he felt the contractions of her inner muscles around him. He looked at her face and saw the flash of pleasure sweep across her features.

He kissed her while she came, and then his own climax was on him. No way to stop, not with her hot, clenching paradise around him. He spilled into her, erupting endlessly even as the drumbeat of his heart echoed in his ears.

And with each beat he thought...

Need her.

Love her.

Always.

* * *

That had been...

Simone opened her eyes. She found Ryan staring at her. Face all hard and tight and, typical for Ryan, dangerous. Her breath still panted out, and her legs maintained a death grip around his waist.

Lowering her legs would probably be appropriate at this point in time. Except...

Ryan just eased both of his hands around her hips. He held her in place, and, with her curled against him and still experiencing truly lovely aftershocks in her core, he carried her down the hallway and into his room. Still in her. Actually, getting *bigger* in her as he carried her.

This was new. This was fun.

She tightened her inner muscles around him, and they both moaned.

He stopped in the doorway of his bedroom. The man's strength was quite impressive. So was his stamina. Her hands lingered on his shoulders. She just had to press her sex against him, rub hard, and...oh, no.

Horror flashed through her. Her head whipped up "Ryan!"

"I know," he growled back. "I didn't use protection."

Wait...uh, right. He had not. But that hadn't been why she was experiencing horror. "I'm on birth control. And you don't have anything to worry about with me. Told you before, I'm very particular about my lovers." She'd *always* had a lover use a condom in the past.

Why had she been so far gone with Ryan?

He stared at her with an unblinking gaze.

"Ryan?"

"I would love to have a baby with you."

Okay, whoa. "That's...a lot."

He swallowed. "You don't have anything to worry about with me. The CIA gets us checked out regularly, and you're the only woman I've ever gone bare with in my life."

Their gazes held. "I..." An exhale. "I was worried I'd hurt your wound." When she'd been grabbing him so hard.

He smiled at her. With his thick dick inside of her—and with it growing bigger by the moment—Ryan said, "Fuck the wound."

Simone grimaced. "No, that's super unhygienic. I'd rather fuck you."

He laughed. The sound was deep and rumbling and sexy. He kissed her and carried her to the bed.

And he fucked her.

She fucked him.

No...no...

It didn't *feel* like fucking.

The kisses were slower. Their touches more careful. The strokes lingered. Their bodies came together with arches and shudders, and their gazes held and it felt like...

It felt like making love.

Even as the next orgasm hit her, so did a deep, earth-shattering understanding. *I've fallen in love with my spy.*

Chapter Twenty-One

"What's the endgame?" Simone asked softly.

She was beside him in bed, her body curled against his, while his hand stroked along the graceful line of her back.

The endgame. "Catch the bad guys. Lock them away." *Marry you. Spend the rest of my life watching your smile and falling in love with you again every single time that it flashes.*

"What's Konstantin done that made him get so much focus from the CIA and MI6?"

His head turned toward her. It was dark in his bedroom, but his eyes had adjusted to the darkness. "Terrorism. Human trafficking. Worldwide weapons distribution. Right now, he's getting involved in drugs. That's why he's working with Frederick. He wants to use the old textile business and distribution sites as a cover. There is no new surveillance company in the works—that was a lie. The whole setup is designed to get Konstantin's drug shipped to as many locations as possible." Konstantin's new drug had raised plenty of alarms. "His drug is a real nasty new addiction that will either kill you on the first hit or have you hooked for the rest of your days." Hooked and willing to do anything in order to get the next rush.

He heard her sharp inhale. "Sounds like a real charmer."

"He's normally insulated. The chip was his mistake. Years ago, he stole the Fabergé egg from a museum because he wanted to send a fuck-you to certain individuals in Russia."

"Konstantin does seem like a fuck-you type of guy. But I have to say, hiding the chip in the Fabergé egg feels over the top."

"Who would ever think to look inside for it?" Ryan asked. "Most people would only focus on the egg itself. The chip contains all kinds of details about Konstantin's criminal enterprises and his international ties. The egg and the chip weren't going to be in Frederick's gallery for long. He was supposed to transfer the chip, and after the transfer was complete, he could keep the egg."

"Services rendered. Down payment. Whatever you want to call it," Simone concluded.

"Yes. But I made the interception in time to stop the big delivery from happening."

"With some fantastic assistance from me," she murmured.

His fingers pressed to the warmth of her skin. "I never intended for you to get hurt. Having a bounty put on your head was not on my agenda."

"Having you jump in on my kidnapping was not on my agenda, either," she returned softly. "But then again, getting kidnapped in the first place was not on my to-do list. So much for those best-laid plans, huh?"

He had so many questions about her. Ryan had discovered that when it came to Simone, he wanted to know everything. "Why do you do it?" he asked her. "Why...retrieve?" That was the word she liked. *Retrieve.* Not...*steal.*

"Because people shouldn't lose the things that matter to them."

I don't want to lose you.

"I lost everything when I was a kid."

He *hated* her pain.

"Not just my parents, my family, but the life I'd had. The house. Even the damn cat."

Yeah, okay, at the first opportunity, he was finding the black cat that she'd liked in London. The cat would be going home with her.

"My toys. My clothes. Everything that was me, everything that was *mine,* it was all gone in an instant. Guess you could just call what I do now some serious overcompensation. I return things to others because I lost everything myself." A yawn. "Or maybe I've just got some seriously sticky fingers, who knows? Not gonna lie and say there is no thrill involved. I get a rush."

"Adrenaline." Oh, yes, he could certainly understand that.

"I was afraid to feel anything for years. Afraid of more pain coming. So the adrenaline surges I got from my retrieval missions made me feel alive again."

"What's the first thing you retrieved?"

A sliver of laughter. "My buddy Logan lost a baseball card when we were kids."

Logan. The name slid through his mind and an alarm bell rang. A loud one.

"We were both in foster care back in those days." Slightly slurred, as sleep pulled at her.

He shouldn't be questioning her when she was so tired.

She was revealing things that she might not normally say. "You don't have to tell me more," Ryan heard himself say.

"I want to tell you everything."

His heart ached.

"You get little bags when you're in foster care." Not so tired. Not so slurred. "Your whole life fits in those bags. My bag was mostly donated clothes. A scarf. A photo of my parents." Her hand slid over his chest. "Logan had this old baseball card. It wasn't valuable. Not like it was from some famous player. It was a card he'd gotten at a minor league game. He'd gone with his dad before his whole world imploded, too. The thing was dog-eared to hell and back. Wrinkled and bent from the times he'd carried it everywhere with him."

He knew where this story was going. "Someone took the card. It wasn't lost. It was stolen, wasn't it?"

"Logan was sad. Couldn't have that." Her fingers began to make small circles on his chest. "So I got it back for him. Don't know what was better at the time, the rush I got from actually snagging the card and slipping away unnoticed or the way I felt when Logan smiled."

Logan. Another piece of her puzzle. A piece that could prove highly dangerous to the mission. "You and this Logan sound like you were close." Sure, yes, jealousy *would* claw at him. But he held it back.

"I guess he's the only family I have. Don't worry..." A sigh. "We never fucked."

His hold on her tightened. "Fantastic to know."

"Like I said, he's family so that would have just been... gross."

A smile tugged at his lips. "Logan is gross. Got it."

Sleepy laughter. "Family isn't just blood."

Her words pierced through him. Ryan found that he

had to swallow—twice—before he could speak. "I know. Couldn't agree more." His lips brushed against her temple. "My brother Nash is adopted, and I don't care what anyone else says—he *is* family. To his core. I'd kill for that guy in a heartbeat."

"Knew you'd understand." Simone snuggled closer. "You understand a lot about me, don't you?"

He did. Just as she understood him. "You're not nearly as bad as you'd have the world think."

"Don't give me too much credit. I get a finder's fee for most of my work. Not like I always do things out of the goodness of my heart."

"But you are on *this* case." Careful words. "You retrieved the broach and earrings for free."

"Yes. This case is personal."

Very personal. Because he'd just realized this case was about family to her. Before he'd gone to Simone's room, he'd gotten the security footage from Jezebel. He'd been damn surprised to see a face that he recognized.

Not from this mission.

From another time.

A case in the US.

A case that had nearly ended with Nash being killed.

A case that had occurred beneath the bright lights of Vegas and had brought Ryan and his team into contact with a very dangerous individual who happened to be named Logan Sterling. A shifty sonofabitch with extremely suspect criminal ties.

Logan Sterling should have been an ocean away. He wasn't. He was in London. More specifically, Logan was in their hotel. Because he'd come for Simone. A dangerous addition to a powder keg situation that could blow at any moment.

"My first retrieval was for Logan. And this case—my most recent retrieval—it's for him, too."

I know, baby. But what he didn't know was *why* the broach and earrings were so important. Why she was risking her life for them. "Logan shouldn't send you off on such a dangerous retrieval."

"The broach and the earrings actually belong to his grandmother. The woman who pulled us in. Who brought me into her home when I needed her the most." Emotion strained through her voice. "She...forgets things these days. Logan and I first started noticing the spells about five years ago. We took her to so many doctors, but the progression couldn't be stopped." Her sadness pulsed in the air. "Frederick found out about Nana. He learned where she'd been living, and he thought it would be so easy to strike at her. She's vulnerable. Easy pickings. He took the broach and the earrings that her husband had given to her so long ago. Maybe he thought no one would notice. But when I went to see her, *I* noticed. Many of her memories were stolen from her, but she loved to look at her broach. She'd look at the broach and the earrings, and she'd smile." A pause. "Frederick took her smile away. I couldn't let that happen. She deserves to smile as much as she can. We all deserve to smile, don't we?"

Frederick was a sonofabitch. "He targeted your *friend's* grandmother because—"

"Because Logan told Frederick to fuck off. He didn't want to get into business with Frederick. My friend has hotels and casinos all over the world. His ties might sometimes be a little shady, but he's not one of the monsters out there." Absolute certainty. "He's not. No matter what stories your CIA buddies may dig up on him in the future."

Oh, Logan Sterling was definitely on the CIA's radar.

And they already had plenty of stories about the man. "He sent you to retrieve the stolen jewelry." *The bastard should have come and gotten it his own damn self.*

"No. He had no idea what I was doing. He would have been pissed as hell if he'd figured it out. He doesn't exactly approve of my jobs."

Something we have in common.

"He's here," Ryan said. No point in dancing around this particular truth.

She didn't speak.

"He needs to stand the hell back," Ryan added. "Things are going to be extremely volatile in the morning." Actually, it was already far too close to morning.

"Oh, just in the morning? Considering the two hits so far, I'm pretty sure things are already volatile." A yawn. "Unfortunately, Logan is not good at standing back."

Neither am I. "I'll protect you."

"I'll protect you, too," she vowed.

He realized that she had been doing that, all along. Protecting him. Again and again, and, honestly, he needed that shit to stop. He needed her removed from the equation. Jezebel thought that Simone's presence was necessary at the upcoming meeting with Frederick.

As for Ryan...

He wanted her safely out of harm's way.

And he thought he knew just how to accomplish that goal. With the hand that was not currently stroking her back, he reached for his phone and fired out a quick text. Then he shifted a bit in the bed, he stared up at the ceiling, and he waited for the attack that he knew was coming.

* * *

It was the faint rustle in the hallway that alerted him. Two hours had passed. Two hours of holding Simone, enjoying the feel of her body against his, of trying to memorize everything about her.

The softness of her skin.

The sweet scent that clung to her.

Even the gentle sound of her breathing.

He'd wanted to remember everything because he knew that he'd be losing her.

Ryan's hand slid under the pillow that rested beneath his head.

He'd shut the bedroom door earlier and made sure that the heavy curtains covered the windows. He waited, body deliberately at ease, one leg shoved from beneath the covers, his right hand still around Simone, as the door slowly opened. No sound. His gaze pierced through the darkness, and he saw the figure coming into the room.

A shadow that moved swiftly, that edged toward the bed and...

Put a gun to Ryan's head.

So expected. "Hello, Logan," Ryan said softly. "It took you longer to make an appearance in here than I anticipated. Even after I told the guards to be sure and let you pass by with minimal fuss..."

"*What the hell...?*" Logan Sterling began. He eased the weapon back.

"Ryan?" Simone's sleepy voice. "What's happening?"

Ryan yanked his gun from beneath the pillow and aimed it at their intruder. "I believe your *family* decided to stop by for a little visit, sweetheart."

She started to roll away from Ryan, but he stopped her with a soft, "You're naked."

"*Shit.*" Simone yanked the covers around herself. *Then*

she rolled away from Ryan, hit the button on the nearby lamp, and then let out a hard shriek. "*Logan!* Logan, *you're pointing a gun at Ryan!*" Then, in the next heartbeat, "*Ryan, you're pointing a gun at Logan!*"

Indeed, they were pointing weapons at one another. "Ready to start firing?" Ryan asked, keeping his tone polite with an extreme effort. "Or do you want to talk?"

Chapter Twenty-Two

THERE WERE LOTS OF NICE, SOOTHING WAYS TO WAKE up. You could wake up to the smell of freshly brewed coffee. You could wake up to the amazing sight of someone actually bringing you breakfast in bed. The soft, sweet sound of birds chirping could bring you to wakefulness.

Or you could open your eyes and find the two men that you cared about most in this world...aiming guns at each other. That was *not* a nice, soothing way to wake up, FYI. It was horrifying. Thus, her scream.

"Put the guns down!" Simone blasted as she clutched the sheet to her chest with both hands. "*Now!*"

They did not.

Ryan sat up in bed. Part of the comforter had pooled at his waist, so his dick was covered, a good thing. Meanwhile, Logan was dressed like a true cat burglar. All in black, from his head to his feet, and his intent gaze was locked on Ryan with icy determination. And more than a bit of rage.

There was also—as crazy as it seemed to her—what appeared to be recognition in Logan's stare. Something that unsettled her far more than the rage ever could. "You two..."

Her head turned between them. "Have you two *met* before?"

A jerky nod from Logan.

A slow, scary smile from Ryan. "Our paths have crossed."

Oh, no. She jumped out of the bed, and Simone yanked the sheet with her. She kept it wrapped around her body as she glared at Ryan. "If you knew who he was all along, if you knew I was connected to him and if I find out that you were just stringing me along in some sort of elaborate manipulation scheme with your CIA buddies in order to trap or hurt Logan in some way..." Pain stabbed through her. "I will *not* forgive you!" Ever.

"What?" Ryan gaped at her. And, ignoring the gun that Logan had pointed at him, Ryan leapt from the bed. "Hell, no, I didn't know who he was all along. You didn't *tell* me who you were retrieving the broach and earrings for until about two hours ago! You were protecting him as if your life depended on concealing his identity—"

"Aw, thanks, Simone, that's touching," Logan drawled.

"And you told me his identity only *after* I'd already viewed security footage from the lobby that showed me the guy's image as he lurked about. One look, and I recognized him from a case in Vegas that exploded in my face."

Security footage? A case in Vegas?

"You seemed to have healed nicely from that gunshot wound in Vegas," Logan allowed. "Glad to see you up and about, but hey, how about you put some clothes on, asshole?"

Growling, Ryan slapped down his gun and hauled on a pair of sweatpants. Then he picked up the weapon again and aimed it at Logan.

But she stepped right between him and Logan. "You

were shot in Vegas?" Simone asked Ryan. When she'd been, um, exploring and following his tats with her mouth, she had noticed a few scars. She just hadn't realized that she was licking *bullet wounds*.

"Simone? I hate to point out the obvious, but the man was shot here in London, too," Logan chimed in to say. "I was watching the Arch drama from a distance. Plus, I can see the fresh bandage on his arm. He gets shot a lot. That would be a hazard in his line of work. Or, maybe he's just careless, who knows? And, damn, but that is one hell of a shiner near his eye. The man obviously attracts far too many enemies."

Another growl came from Ryan.

"He has to be careless," Logan decided, "considering that he's allowed not one but *two* attacks on your life, and I was able to just sneak right inside the suite here. Hey, quick question...*why the hell haven't you taken Simone far away from here and put her in a new, safer location?*"

"Because I'm bait." Simone shifted from her left foot to her right.

Logan's face darkened. "The fuck you are."

"*Because you're taking her away,*" Ryan fired back at the same moment. "That's why I rolled out the welcome mat and was patiently waiting for you to arrive."

"Rolled out the welcome mat?" Logan laughed. "Dumbass, I crawled through the air ducts and tight tunnels in this place for damn near an hour. I bypassed every bit of security you have and—"

Ryan laughed.

She was just *thrilled* they were having themselves a good time. Meanwhile, she'd gotten stuck on Ryan's words. *Because you are taking her away*. What had that BS line from Ryan been about?

"You didn't need to crawl through air ducts," Ryan informed Logan. "As soon as I realized who Simone's *friend* was, I understood that you weren't a threat. The guards in the hallway were told to let you pass. To put up a minimum amount of effort, of course, but you could have slipped in...without crawling around the walls of the hotel."

"Oh, I will show you a threat." Logan surged forward.

So did Ryan.

"*Enough.*" Simone slapped a hand on each of their chests.

And her sheet slithered to the floor.

"*Do not look down,*" Ryan ordered in a tone gone coldly lethal. "I will break every bone in your body if you look down right now, Logan."

"*She's like my sister.* Relax, man. *Relax.* I'm not looking down."

She grabbed the sheet and yanked it around her body. "You two are idiots, and I have no idea why I love you both." Oh, wait, *no.* She had not just said those words. They had not come out of her mouth.

"Simone?" Ryan pounced. "Simone, did you just say what I *think* you said?"

"I do *not* function well when I am woken up after so little actual sleep time!" A huff. "Dammit, Logan, you were not supposed to break in! I planned on meeting up with you, *after* the mission is complete."

"What mission?" Low. Hard. Demanding.

Typical Logan.

She turned her head toward him. The fireworks were about to start, she could feel them igniting. "The one where I'm bait, and I pull in an international killer."

"*Fuck, no.*" He dodged around her and flew at Ryan.

Sighing, Simone hooked her ankle under his leg and sent him tumbling to the floor.

"Marry me," Ryan urged her. "Really, let's do it. Marry. *Me.*"

Ignoring the pain in her heart, she glared at him. "Oh, fine, now, you make the proposal." With a shake of her head, she focused on Logan. It was easier to focus on him than to look at Ryan. "I appreciate you rushing to the rescue for me and all, but I'm afraid I must insist you climb back into the air ducts and get the hell out of here."

Still holding his gun, Logan hoisted himself up. "Not happening."

She smiled at him. "We'll see about that."

* * *

"Fate's funny, isn't she?" Logan Sterling asked as he sprawled in the suite's sitting room. "By the way, this is too freaking much blue décor. You will *never* find this much in one of my hotels."

"Your hotels are in Vegas. Reno. Monte Carlo. And I've noticed that you tend to focus on a whole lot of red in them." Ryan sat in the blue chair. Logan was on the blue sofa. They both still had their guns.

Simone was dressing. Ryan had already changed into fresh clothing, and he was currently being on his best behavior and not attacking the only family that Simone had in the world. Her family...Logan. Logan's grandmother.

Though, that really wasn't the case, was it? They weren't her *only* family. Because...

She feels like family to me.

She felt like the woman he wanted to marry. She felt

like...everything. He'd been dead serious when he asked her to marry him.

Or maybe he'd *told* her to marry him. Mentally, he winced. That had not been his best moment. He'd have to ask. Do an elaborate proposal.

After they locked up all the bad guys.

"Blue colors are supposed to make people feel calm. Peaceful." Logan's lips twisted. "I'm not exactly going for peaceful in *my* places. I want people on the edge of their seats."

"You want them gambling their asses off in your casinos."

A soft chuckle from Logan. "That, too." He rolled back his shoulders. "Red makes you feel alive. It increases your excitement level. Makes your heart race."

"What are you?" Ryan asked as he surveyed the man who could either be an ally or an enemy. "A color expert?"

"Simone is. She's the one who helped me decorate most of my properties."

Why had he tensed when Logan mentioned Simone's name? There was nothing romantic happening between Simone and Logan. Simone had told Ryan that fact. He trusted her. He...

I don't trust Logan.

The CIA had been watching Logan Sterling since he'd leapt onto their radar in a very big way in a recent case. Logan had actually assisted the CIA at the time. A shock, considering some of his darker ties. The CIA had dug into Logan's past. Had found out that he was an only child, that he'd been raised by his maternal grandmother after his parents had been killed.

The CIA background check had clearly been missing a few pertinent details. Like the fact that he'd done a stint in foster care before his grandmother had taken custody of him. And, of course, there was Simone.

The CIA was just looking for blood kin. A mistake. Some ties went way deeper than blood.

"I didn't send Simone after the broach and earrings," Logan suddenly announced. "I've been trying to get her to give up her retrieval business for years." The fingers of his left hand tapped against his thigh. "I would never *willingly* send her into danger." A subtle emphasis on *willingly* even as his gaze sure seemed to say…*Unlike you, prick.*

Ryan forced his jaw to relax. "Things are not as they seem."

"No?" Logan leaned forward. "You are not keeping my Simone captive in this fancy suite? Stopping her from fleeing—as she clearly wanted to do at the Arch? You are not using her to lure in some, ah, how did she term it?"

"International killer," Simone supplied as she entered the sitting room. She'd changed into a blue dress that matched her eyes. Black sandals that tied around her ankles and had small, dainty heels. "Using me as a lure for an international killer."

Ryan inhaled. "I am *protecting* her from killers."

Logan swept his stare to Simone. "That what he's doing? You agree with his words?"

Simone came toward Ryan. She perched on the edge of his chair. He tensed because he'd expected her to go and sit beside Logan. The fact that she seemed to be physically signaling that her allegiance was with Ryan…

Hell, yes.

"Why don't you put down the gun and take my hand?" Simone whispered.

Ryan kept the gun. And took her fingers with his free hand.

Her soft laughter rolled over him. Then she told Logan, "He has managed to save my life...I believe on at least two separate occasions."

"Do tell me more." Logan kept leaning forward, his expression intent.

"Well, the first instance occurred when I was kidnapped. I did tell him to run but..."

Ryan turned his head and found her gaze on him.

"He didn't," she concluded. "He got taken with me. That would be when he got this lovely shiner, by the way. Trying to help me." A soft sigh. "I may have gotten knocked out during an unfortunate van ride."

There was no *may* about it.

"When I woke," Simone continued her tale, "Ryan and I were both tied up, and we had a mercenary intent on torture parading around with his knife." Her gaze darted toward Logan. "Spoiler, he wanted to slice off my fingers. You know how attached I am to my fingers."

"Sticky fingers," he groused, but his expression had sharpened with rage. "The mercenary is dead." A promise.

Ryan nodded. "Yes. He is. I took care of the situation."

He caught Logan's flash of surprise.

"Then there was the waiter..." Simone picked up her story. "You expect a delivery of a delectable chocolate mousse, and instead, you get a guy with a gun hidden underneath a shiny, silver dish. So disappointing." Her head tilted as she seemed to consider the matter. "Know what, though? I think I saved *you* then, Ryan. I'm the one who threw the lamp."

"A save for a save." As if he'd ever forget her rushing in with that lamp.

She sent him one of her slow smiles.

"Fuck." From Logan.

They both looked his way.

"I knew it would happen eventually," Logan lamented. "Not like guys could ever help themselves from falling at your feet. But to see *you* fall, Simone? And for a spy? What kind of life is that going to be for you? I wanted you to stop retrieving so you'd be safe. I didn't want you jumping right into the fire over and over again!"

"I haven't fallen anywhere." She sniffed.

"Bullshit." A hard return from Logan. "Tell me you don't love him. Go on, do it. I dare you. Look me straight in the eyes and tell me that you have not given your heart to the spy right beside you."

She tried to pull her hand away from Ryan's hold.

He didn't let go. Instead, his head turned right back to her. "Go ahead," he forced out the words. "You can tell him. You can let him know that everything going on between us is just a cover."

"A cover doesn't involve you two actually getting naked together," Logan pointed out. "And that is how I found you. Naked. Cuddled together. A vision that will scar me for life."

Ryan ignored him and held Simone's gaze. "Tell him," he said. "Better yet, tell *me*. Tell me how you feel." He held his breath.

Her stare seemed to search his.

Say something, Simone. Tell me—

She glanced back at Logan. "You can climb back through the air duct at any point. I'm not going with you. I have a meeting to keep." She pointed toward a metal grate near the ceiling. "Has to be a tight fit. I am most impressed with your skills in shimmying in and out of tight situations. Personally, I'd be horrified to find myself stuffed in a place like that. Talk about a nightmare come true."

Ryan took his gaze off her and discovered that Logan was watching her with the intensity of a snake ready to strike. "You actually love the damn spy, don't you?" Logan asked.

Ryan was still holding his damn breath. Good thing he could hold his breath for an incredibly long time.

Simone let out a long suffering sigh. "I do."

Fuck. Yes. *Fuck.*

A smile tugged at her lips as her focus shifted to Ryan. "I'm also pretty sure that I've slipped up and *told* you that I love you before so no need for you to look so incredibly shocked. Like, I literally slipped up and said it just a few minutes ago."

His heart slammed into his chest. Hard. Then the drumming, too fast racing echoed in his ears. Ryan shook his head.

She pulled her hand from his.

But...

Then she was cupping his chin. Simone leaned in close to him. "It's actually quite a novel and invigorating experience, if you want the truth. I wasn't even sure I *could* fall in love with someone, not until you." Her thumb brushed across his jaw. "I know I can love, sure. I love Logan. I've loved him since we were kids." An easy, unhesitating statement. "But loving someone like family and falling *in* love are two different things, aren't they? Thank you for letting me experience that difference."

Shock held him immobile. Her hand slowly slid away from him. She rose, standing beside his chair.

"I appreciate you coming to check on me," she said to Logan.

Uh, how had Logan even known where to come? He would ask that question. Once he stopped being deliriously thrilled. *Simone loves me. She has fallen in love with me.* Not a lie. Not a cover. The real deal.

"But I'm good, truly." She pointed to the vent. "You can go on your way at any time."

Yeah, um, about that. Ryan tried to shake himself from his stupor. "When Logan leaves, he's taking you with him." Ryan shot to his feet. He needed to say something about her confession. Something like...*Holy hell, you have just made me the happiest bastard in the world.*

"Uh, no, I'm not going with him. I don't do tight spaces, remember? Consider elevators my limit from now on. Nothing beyond that."

No way would he make her face a tight space nightmare. "Then he'll just waltz with you right out of the hotel suite and down the corridor and to whatever ride he has waiting. You're *done.*" He paced away from her. He had to get away from her. Because he wanted to pounce far too badly.

But she grabbed him. "Excuse me?" What could have been pain broke beneath her words. "I say that I love you and you say we are done? *That* is your response?"

No, his response was...*Marry me. Spend forever with me. Let's make fantasies and dreams come true.*

"How is that an even exchange?" Simone exclaimed. "That is a sucky exchange!"

"It does suck, man," Logan told him. "You need to tell me to fuck off. You need to beat the hell out of me and whisk Simone away. Seriously, *do it.*"

But Ryan ignored him and went toe to toe with Simone. "What do you want me to say? That you just made me the fucking happiest man in the world?"

"That would be a start."

"That I can't *breathe* because I'm so damn thrilled that you love me?"

"Yes, that is better."

"That I want you to marry me, and I'm standing here, trying to figure out how the hell to propose to you in the right way, but I can't do that yet because we have freaking asshole criminals to stop?"

She wet her lips. "All of that...that is a way better exchange."

He could not look away. "I love you so fucking much."

"Yo. Other people are in the room." Logan's annoyed voice. "I would be the *other*. How about we save this love chat for later? Got more pressing priorities, you know?"

Fine. Dammit. Ryan glanced his way. He pointed at Logan. "How did you know she was here? Did she call you? Signal you in some way?"

"I did *not*," Simone fired.

"I knew she was here because there is a bounty on her head. One that was doubled recently."

It had been doubled?

"Let's just say that I keep my ear to the ground about details that concern her. When her pic popped up on some sites that I might, shall we say, frequent—"

"Dark web hit sites?" Ryan wasn't going to dance around. Time to get straight to the real deal.

Logan nodded. "When I saw her pic, I knew that I needed to step in. I was already in London, dealing with other business, so it was easy to reach this hotel. Before making my appearance tonight, I let it be known that anyone touching her would meet with a swift and brutal end." Logan smiled. The smile didn't reach his eyes. "I'm protective like that."

"Great. Then when you take her out of here, you can

keep right on protecting her." Because Ryan would not be there to do it. "She needs to be long gone before—"

"*Stop!*" Simone erupted. "I am not leaving you. You need me!"

In so many ways. For so many things. But mostly...

He needed her *alive.*

The plan to use her as bait had seemed fine before two different hitmen had come for her. The waiter and the prick at the Arch. Ryan wasn't about to let jerk number three close in for the kill. "The CIA can handle this without you, Simone."

"But I'm the one who ties Konstantin to Frederick!"

No. "Frederick is the tie. He'll roll at our meeting." A meeting that was fast approaching. "I can count on him to serve the Russian up to me." An inhale. "Your services are no longer needed."

"What?" She gaped at him.

"You were going to run away at the Arch."

"I was..." Her words trailed away.

His head cocked. "When did you realize that Logan was here?" He replayed things in his mind. "You had the broach and earrings on you right before we went out for that walk to the Arch."

She wet her lips. "When we first walked out of the hotel suite, I didn't know Logan was here. I took the broach and earrings because if the chance to disappear presented itself, I-I wanted to be ready to take it."

He nodded even as his heart squeezed. "And you couldn't disappear without your prizes."

"I spotted Logan when we were downstairs. I knew he'd recognize the broach and the earrings. I decided to make a quick drop of the jewels as we left the hotel. Logan knows me. He would be watching carefully, and he'd collect the items as soon as I left them behind." She swallowed. "You did collect them, right, Logan?"

"I've got them," he replied, voice hard. "After I secured them, I tailed Simone to the Arch. When I heard the gunfire, I was going to step in, and then all the spies started swarming. I realized then that getting to Simone was going to be tricky."

So the guy had climbed through the ducts.

"And here we all are..." Logan drawled.

Here they were. But they were about to go in different directions.

"I didn't want to leave you," Simone suddenly said. "Not at the Arch. And I don't want to leave you now. I don't have to be bad luck. We can be good together, I know it."

He shook his head. "Not good. Great." Life with her would be great. She'd be everything he wanted. A lifetime of her smiles...*I want a life with Simone.*

But first, he had a case to close, and he would not risk her. There were too many uncertainties. Her safety was the priority. So he had to say, "I want you to go, Simone." He'd been trying to figure out how to protect her, and then Logan had slid into place perfectly. Someone Simone trusted. Someone who would keep her safe.

"What does your boss Jezebel want?" Simone snapped out. "Is this cool with her? Because I'm pretty sure she said I would only stay out of prison if I cooperated with your team."

"Oh, that's some bullshit." Now Logan was on his feet, too. Though he'd put down his gun. "You blackmailed Simone into helping you? Threatened her with jail? That totally deserves a punch in the face."

Ryan put down his gun, too. "I can handle Jezebel." And, no, Jez did not know that he was removing Simone from the equation. Because maybe Ryan had learned a valuable lesson on his last mission in Vegas. Maybe he'd realized that you couldn't always trust everyone on your team. He trusted Jez, but the others around her? No. No, he couldn't risk betrayal.

Two hitmen have gained access to Simone while she should have been protected by CIA operatives and MI6 agents. Two...

Bullshit that he didn't like. So he needed to remove her from the grip of the CIA and of MI6. Logan Sterling had no allegiance to either organization. As far as Ryan could tell, Logan's only allegiance was to Simone. So Logan was her pass to freedom.

Ryan's lips curled in a sad smile as he studied Simone. "You are the love of my life," he told her, and he meant those words. He'd gone years drifting from mission to mission. Then he'd found her. No, she'd found him. That was her thing, wasn't it? She found what was lost. "That's why I am telling you this with absolute conviction..."

"Ryan?" Her eyes were very, very wide.

"I want you to get the hell away from me."

Chapter Twenty-Three

Frederick's head fucking hurt. A loud groan broke from him as his eyes slit open. Just a fraction because the light suddenly shining down on him was far too bloody bright. "Turn it off!" he snarled.

"Can't do that, boss," a flat voice told him. "You've got a very big day ahead of you, remember?"

He rolled over on the bed. Frederick was a bit surprised to realize that he was on top of the covers, not beneath them. He was also still fully dressed. A horrible, grimy taste seemed to fill his mouth, and his temples throbbed so hard that nausea rolled through his whole body. "I'm going to be sick."

"Not unexpected, considering how much you drank last night."

Memories flooded through him. He'd drank so much because everything was screwed to hell and back. He closed his eyes and let his head sag back against the pillow. "That bitch Simone..." It was all her fault. "She's fucked me over." He tried to remember. "Is she dead yet?" He *had* put a hit on her. Had he doubled it? Or canceled it? Things were blurry. But he *did* remember being on the laptop near his bed. He remembered tapping out something before the whole world got super hazy.

"Simone is not dead. Which is a good thing because she's going to be an important player in the game."

"Not a game." He needed something to drink. Water this time. Because his throat was parched. "This is my life!" His voice had risen, but a raised voice just made his head ache more, so he lowered it, fast. "My life," he rasped. "She's wrecking it. All because of those jewels she stole."

"About those..." The wooden floor creaked as Hugo walked toward the bed. "I did some digging on the pieces she took. Alexei had texted you, saying he'd recovered a broach and matching earrings from her. Those items were not in the stables, so we can assume that Simone swiped them before she made her exit."

"Before she *killed* Alexei and made her exit." Should he try opening his eyes again? No. Too much nausea still filled him. Frederick concentrated on taking slow, shallow breaths. Those small breaths helped steady him.

"You had those particular pieces taken in order to get revenge against Logan Sterling, didn't you? Logan...I believe he's the hotel and casino owner from the States?"

So, fine, color him impressed. Hugo was a thug. Sure, a thug with some serious fighting skills, but not exactly someone Frederick had thought was overly high on the intelligence scale. Yes, the pieces had belonged to Logan Sterling. Or, rather, to someone in Logan's family. "Bastard thought he was too good to do business with me. He owns those gaudy hotels and casinos but wouldn't invest in *me*. *Me*. I'm related to royalty!"

"How fantastic for you," Hugo murmured.

"I showed him. He's not better than me. No one is

better!" The nausea might be fading. Good. Because he did have work to do.

The meeting with Ryan Quinn had to be a success. He had to convince Ryan that Simone was trouble. "Turn out those lights, would you? They're too freaking bright." Before he opened his eyes again, he needed those overhead lights off.

"You're a petty man, Frederick. When someone makes you angry, you immediately strike out. So much of that fancy stuff in your gallery was stolen. Trophies you'd taken to get back at your enemies. You'd go in there, all smug, and you'd stare at your prizes, and you would think you were so much better, so much *smarter* than everyone else."

His eyes cracked open. "You didn't turn off the lights." He'd given an order. How hard was it to follow a basic order?

"Then Simone Sailor came along. She tricked you. Played you for a fool, and she took those prizes right out of your precious gallery. You lost the broach, the earrings, and, let's not forget, the egg. The egg and the ever-so-important chip that was inside of it."

"Don't really need a recap." He swallowed down a bit of bile as he sat up and swung his legs to the side of the bed. "I need the lights turned *off*."

But Hugo made no move to kill the lights. He just kept standing near the bed and...what was in the guy's hand?

"You promised Konstantin that you would take care of the chip. You were supposed to make sure it was delivered to the proper individuals."

Yes, well... "I'll work on getting the chip back today from Ryan. I'll let him know that Simone is a thief and that she took it from me. I'm sure we can come to some sort of an agreement. As long as Konstantin doesn't know what's happening, I can salvage this situation." There was still time to turn everything around. He could do it. He knew that he could.

"You can't salvage shit."

Frederick leapt to his feet. He immediately weaved but was able to maintain his balance. "How dare you talk to me that way? I am your boss! I give the orders, and you can't—"

"You're not really my boss. You're dead broke. The person who pays the bills—the person who makes sure I get the money that I am owed—that would be Konstantin."

He'd just realized what item Hugo held in his hand. A shiver of fear slid down Frederick's spine. Hugo's right hand was curled around the brass handle of a knife. A long blade, double-sided, pointed straight at Frederick. "Wh-why do you have that?"

"This knife is a favorite among British Special Forces. Has been, since WWII."

Did he look like he wanted a history lesson? "Get it away from me, you bloody fool!" He needed to shower. To change. To get in his car and have his driver take him to the meeting in London. What time had Ryan said? Eight?

But Hugo didn't move the knife. "Seven-inch blade," he explained. Unnecessarily. "Sharp on both sides. A lethal tip. It's great for fighting in close quarters with an enemy. The blade is narrow enough in design that it can easily go right through a person and dive into, say, a ribcage. Here, let me show you."

"What? No! You—*ah!*"

The knife had just slid into him.

Into him.

For an instant, Frederick was stunned. So certain that this could not be happening. Then he was horrified.

Terrified. In pain. "Stop!" His hands clamped around Hugo's shoulders.

Hugo pulled the blade out of him. "And here I thought you wanted me around because of my bloodthirsty skills. Wasn't that why you hired me in the first place? So that I'd take care of the dirty work—the bloody work—that you didn't have the stomach to do yourself?"

Hugo...he had such a friendly face. Round, almost babyish. And his eyes would shine when he smiled. He hadn't been the scary one. That had been Alexei. Alexei had been the one to do the dirty work.

Hugo and Alexei both began working for me at the same time. But Alexei had been sent by Konstantin and Hugo had been...Hugo had been...

"Want to know a secret?" Hugo asked him. "Alexei let me know early on that if I ever had important news, then that news should go to Konstantin. He told me that Konstantin would always pay well for loyalty." Hugo glanced down at the bloody knife he held. "It's made for up close killing. Killing that can be fast."

No, no, no.

"I made a phone call to Konstantin after you passed out last night. Didn't take long for Konstantin and I to connect the dots regarding the broach and the earrings. Logan Sterling was the key. Once we had him, we could understand Simone. She is actually a woman with skills that we need."

His fingers gripped Hugo's shoulders too hard. "You... *stabbed me.*"

"You can't get the egg and the chip back, but Konstantin believes Simone can. Simone and Logan are the two people who interest him the most right now. I regret to inform you that your services are no longer needed."

Frederick shook his head. He could feel blood soaking his shirt. "I...get...ambulance..."

"Why?"

"Doctor—"

"A doctor can't help a dead man." The blade hit him again. Fast. Hard. Vicious strikes over and over.

They hurt...

Or, at least, they hurt at first. After the fourth, no, fifth one? After that one, Frederick stopped feeling the stabs. He could just hear sloshing sounds when the blade slid out of him. Again and again and...

"There. See, it's done. Wasn't so bad, was it?" Hugo lowered him onto the bed. Frowned down at him. "You can close your eyes and go back to sleep now. I'll be heading out for that meeting in London." He grabbed some covers and tossed them over Frederick's body. "I'll make sure that the egg and chip are retrieved." His footsteps began to pad away.

Frederick was glad that Hugo had tossed the covers over him. He'd been feeling cold. His eyes fluttered as he stared straight up. "The...light..."

Hugo turned off the light right before he left the room. Or at least, Frederick thought he'd turned out the light.

Everything just went—dark.

* * *

"It's done," Hugo said, speaking into Frederick's phone. Not like Frederick would be using it again. He walked out of the country estate and headed straight toward the Rolls Royce Phantom that waited. "I'm on my way to London now. I'll go to the meeting with Ryan Quinn."

"You know what to do with him?" Konstantin asked.

"The same thing I just did with Frederick, got it. That's my skill set." Up close kills had always been a specialty of his. "And you have Simone covered?"

"Simone and Logan are handled." Flat. "I will get back what belongs to me."

Right. That was what Hugo wanted. A happy Konstantin. A happy Konstantin paid well. A pissed Konstantin? Well, he just delivered death.

Then again, that was what Hugo did, too. He thought this new employment arrangement would work out far better for him. He'd never liked that stuffy prick, Frederick. But Konstantin? The Russian seemed a far better fit for him.

"Your intel has proved invaluable," Konstantin praised. "I'll make certain you are appropriately compensated."

"I certainly appreciate that." He was nearly at the Rolls Royce. The driver waited, wearing a black uniform with gold buttons and a shiny hat. Frederick had always insisted the guy wear that dumb outfit. "See you in London."

Konstantin hung up. Hugo tucked the phone into his coat pocket.

"Where is Mr. Bradwin?" the driver asked, a frown pulling at his features. The man had to be eighty if he was a day. Hugo knew the driver had been with Frederick's family for decades.

No sense ruining the man's morning by letting him know that his boss was dead. "Frederick decided to sleep in. He really doesn't want to be disturbed."

The driver looked toward the windows on the second story of the manor. "Another bender." Disapproval underscored his words.

"I'll be handling the meeting today. Let's head out, shall we?" He climbed into the back of the vehicle. The driver shut the door behind him, and, in moments, they were on the road.

A private driver. A luxury car. He could sure get used to living like this.

Hugo pulled out his bloody knife. Then he took his handkerchief and carefully wiped the blood away.

He could live easily like this, but one more person needed to die first. Ryan Quinn.

You're not a billionaire. You're not some rich prick. You're a spy.

News that had come through Konstantin.

Hugo found he was looking forward to killing Ryan. He did enjoy a challenge.

Chapter Twenty-Four

"So strange," Simone murmured as a faint tremble shook her body. "In my most vivid nightmares, I could never imagine that a man would say that I was the love of his life in one breath, and, then, in the next, he'd tell me to get the hell away from him." She let out a long sigh. "You know how to make a woman feel incredibly special."

He'd changed before going to the little chat with Logan in the sitting room. Expensive dress pants. Crisp, fresh, white button-down. Not a wet one that clung lovingly to his muscles. So disappointing. He'd even put on a suit coat. Gray, to match his pants. She strongly suspected he had a gun holster—and a gun—hidden beneath that coat.

Logan's jaw hardened. His dark eyes glittered. "You are special."

"Thanks. Just beautiful words. Really."

"You are special to me. That's why I need you safe. I need you away from me. *I can't trust the team here.* I told you before, I trust my brother, one hundred percent, but Nash isn't with me. I don't know Harry. I barely know Jamar and Charlotte."

"Surface level," she heard herself say.

He nodded. "If I can't count on the people near me, then I have to count on the person *you* trust."

Her head turned toward Logan.

"I am not trustworthy," Logan fired back in an instant as his hands fisted. "Ask anyone."

She rolled her eyes. "You know I trust you with my life."

"Don't," Logan bit out.

"We don't have time for this!" Ryan snapped. "Look, I need you to take her away." He took a phone from his pocket and pressed it into Simone's hands. "I'll call you when things are safe. Until then, I need you to go with him."

Her fingers curled around the phone. "You expect me to just leave you to face the danger on your own?"

"Oh, baby." His hand rose to caress her cheek. "This is what I do. It's what I've done for years. I will close this mission. Count on it."

"You need me."

"More than you will ever realize. More than I thought could be possible." His head lowered. His lips brushed against hers. "There have been too many attacks on your life." Another careful kiss. "I can't trust the people near me. That means I can't keep you safe. *Please.*" Rough. Gruff. "Go with Logan. I swear, this phone will ring as soon as the case is over."

She didn't want to leave him.

"Yeah, okay, before you two start making out again..." Logan cleared his throat. "I happen to have a few questions of my own. Question one, just how the hell did you two even hook up? How do a spy and a, uh, retrieval specialist get together?"

"We were in the same gallery, taking different prizes." Ryan's hand lingered against her cheek.

"We got together before that. The gallery incident was during date number three, remember?" Her head turned. Her lips pressed against his palm. "I expect date number four to be killer. Know that my expectations are high."

"Yeah..." Logan sidled closer. "I get what you were retrieving Simone, but, Ryan, what were you there to take?"

"An egg," Simone supplied. "Fabergé. Worth a cool thirty million."

Logan whistled. "I could go for an egg like that."

"It had secrets inside of it." Simone squared her shoulders. "The kind of secrets that spies need."

"So..." Logan was right beside them. "Where might the egg and the secrets be right now?" He glanced around the suite. "Guessing they aren't just stashed in the suite's safe, huh?"

"No." Ryan pulled away from Simone. "Jezebel has them."

"Oh, shit." Logan rocked back on his heels. "She's here, too? Look, that lady came to see me a time or two after the big dust up in Vegas. Got to tell you, I think she was threatening me. Maybe even blackmailing me." His voice went flat. "Really fucking hate it when I'm blackmailed."

Ryan just nodded. "Sounds like Jezebel." He looked at his wrist. At the big, silver watch that circled his wrist. "Time to get moving. I need Simone *out* of here before the meeting. Out of the suite. Out of the hotel. Hell, out of the city would be good."

Logan grimaced. "Sure, I'll just fly her back to Vegas. No big deal."

"It is a big deal." Simone remained rooted to the spot. "I don't want to leave you, Ryan."

"People are going to die, baby. It's going to get worse before it gets better."

That terrified her. She did not want *him* dying. In fact, that was going to have to be something that was completely forbidden. No dying for Ryan. Ever.

"I'm trained for this." His voice was low. Soothing. "You aren't. If you are here, I will be focused on you. My attention will be split. That split attention could jeopardize the mission."

"You're just saying that, so I'll feel guilty and agree to leave." He hadn't been talking about any split attention when he and Jezebel had been pulling her into the big mission in the first place. Now, two *tiny* attempts on her life later, and he was singing a new tune.

Ryan's lips kicked into a half-smile. "I'm saying it because it's true *and* because I need you to feel guilty and leave with Logan."

Tears stung her eyes. "This phone had better ring the instant you are done. And you do not get shot. You do not die, understand?"

"Say you love me. One more time." He swallowed. "I want to hear it."

"I love you." Easy. So why did emotion nearly choke her as she spoke those precious words? "I love you."

"Good, then—"

"But I am not crawling through an air duct vent for you. That is just not happening." She actually would do it if necessary. She was just pissed that he was sidelining her.

"You don't have to do that," Ryan assured her. "I'll get the guards to move position. I'll clear the hall long enough for you and Logan to make an exit via the stairwell. I strongly suspect you already plotted a way out that would have you hidden from pretty much everyone's line of sight anyway, didn't you?"

Yes, she had. "The guards in the stairwell will need to take a break." It wasn't enough to just clear the hall outside of the suite.

He nodded.

"And you will absolutely have to *stay alive*." How many times should she press that particular point?

Logan began to pace. "I really don't like this plan. It's shit."

They both looked at him. "You got a better option?"

"I'm not the damn spy!"

No and neither was she. She was just a thief who had fallen completely and totally for the spy who swore that he loved her.

* * *

MEETING TIME.

Eight a.m. Ryan sat at a table in the back of the restaurant, one that would allow him a perfect line of sight to study every person who entered the establishment. He'd already ordered the full English breakfast—eggs, hash browns, black pudding, toast, and sausage. The waitress brought him freshly blended coffee along with the meal. The waitress—Charlotte. She sent him a covert wink before disappearing into the kitchen.

And he waited.

Time ticked past ever so slowly. He kept a napkin in his lap. A gun beneath the napkin.

He didn't need to check his watch to know that Simone should have left the hotel by now. She'd left, and she would be safe.

Her safety was what mattered most to him.

"Excuse me..." A voice said into his ear. Directly into the earpiece that he'd put in place during his elevator ride down to the restaurant. The female voice belonged to Jezebel. "I can't help but notice that you seem to be missing a companion."

He brought the coffee mug to his lips and blew softly over the rim. "Did Charlotte just tell you that news? Or do you have a little camera in here?" He used the mug to cover the movements of his mouth. His words had been nearly soundless. That was the thing about CIA tech. Sophisticated as hell. And nearly microscopic.

He'd always enjoyed the toys that he was given from the CIA.

"Both," Jezebel responded. "Simone was supposed to be there with you for this meeting."

"Um. Change of plans." He sipped the coffee. Then he caught sight of a familiar figure striding into the restaurant. Ryan tensed. "It looks like I may not be the only one experiencing a change of plans." He put down the coffee. His hand drifted toward the napkin in his lap and to the gun that waited beneath the napkin. Tension poured through him as he watched Hugo Thomas approach the table.

Hugo eased into the chair right across from him.

Beneath the napkin, Ryan's hand curled around the gun. He pointed the weapon at Hugo. He'd had the chair Hugo now occupied positioned in that exact spot deliberately. *To give me the perfect shot.* "Pretty sure I was supposed to meet with your boss. Not you."

"He's otherwise occupied. So you get me."

Charlotte began to approach the table.

"I don't want you." Ryan was not interested in

underlings. "My deal was with Frederick. Clearly, that deal is over."

Charlotte was mere steps away.

Hugo reached out and snagged a piece of sausage from Ryan's plate. "I am starving. Killing someone does that. Always gives me an appetite. Maybe it's the adrenaline." He munched on the sausage. "I don't know." His head tilted. "What happens to you when you kill a man? What happened when you killed Alexei Morozov?"

Charlotte arrived. "Good morning, sir." She beamed at Hugo. "What can I get you?"

"Same thing he's got." Hugo flashed her a grin. "And he'll be picking up the tab. Why don't you bill it to his suite?"

He knows about my suite. He knows far too much, I can see the truth in his cocky grin.

Charlotte backed away.

Hugo kept his asshole grin in place.

Ryan kept his hold on his gun.

"Oh, come on," Hugo chided. "Please don't be boring. I know who you are. What you are." He snatched another sausage from Ryan's plate. "You're no billionaire. You're a spy. You think you're going to take down Konstantin, but that isn't going to happen. He's miles ahead of you."

"I want to see Frederick."

"I can make that happen." A nod. "Let's get out of here. The Rolls Royce is waiting."

"I don't need to go anywhere. Frederick can drag his ass in here."

Laughter. "Doubtful." Hugo's fingers tapped on the table. "Okay, let's try it this way..." His smile vanished. "If you don't leave this restaurant with me right now and get your ass into the Rolls Royce, then I'll tell Logan to kill Simone."

What. The. Fuck?

"Good for you? Bad for you?" Hugo's boyish face twisted. Flashed with evil intent. Then he pulled out his phone. Held it up. "One phone call is all it takes. So you tell me, super spy, do you want Simone to live or die?"

This isn't happening. "You are bluffing."

"Nope. Not at all. See, Konstantin heard every word of your conversation with Logan earlier. Easy to do...because Konstantin has access to listening devices, too." He touched his ear then motioned to Ryan. "You got one in right now, don't you? Konstantin said you'd be monitored by your boss. A lady named Jezebel."

Wasn't Konstantin a bastard who knew far too much? Ryan was so over that prick. But he really wanted to get back to the part of the conversation about how Konstantin and Hugo had heard *"every word of your conversation with Logan earlier."*

"You gave Simone up to Logan, thinking she was safe." Mocking laughter from Hugo. "What a fucking dumbass move that was."

He knows that Simone left with Logan. The sonofabitch knows.

"Here you go," Charlotte announced brightly as she appeared at the table and put the fresh food down near Hugo. "Let me know if there is anything else you'd like. Coffee, tea or—"

Hugo grabbed her. Yanked her down in front of him. Shoved his gun into her side.

Ryan did not look away from Hugo's scowling face. "I think you're scaring our waitress."

"Get on your feet, spy! Walk the fuck out of here with me. And I won't put a hole in the pretty lady."

He saw Charlotte's jaw lock.

"Better plan," Ryan counter offered. "You let her go, and I don't shoot your dick off. Because, see, I'm aiming at it right now beneath the table."

"What?" Automatically, Hugo glanced down.

And Charlotte slammed her fist into his face. First her fist, then she yanked up the plate she'd just delivered and rammed it into his forehead. The plate shattered, sending chunks of porcelain and chunks of eggs to the floor.

In a flash, Ryan was on his feet, around the table, and yanking Hugo against him. He put his gun to Hugo's chest. "*What in the hell is happening with Simone?*"

"Uh, Ryan..." Charlotte began.

Hugo started laughing.

Ryan nearly killed him. Right then and there. But he was supposed to be the *good fucking guy*. Wasn't he?

But...*Simone. No one hurts Simone.*

Then Hugo yanked out a hidden knife and drove it toward Ryan's chest.

Chapter Twenty-Five

They exited via the back of the hotel. Through the door marked STAFF ONLY. She'd shoved her hair beneath a broad, white summer hat that Logan had grabbed from the hotel's gift shop and given to her. A pair of oversized sunglasses shielded her eyes, and Simone double-timed her steps to match Logan's as they hurried down a side street.

They were going to do this. Get away clean. And—

"Simone?"

Dammit, *Harry*. How could she have forgotten how much that man liked to lurk?

A swift glance behind her shoulder showed her that Harry was rushing toward her.

"Simone!" he yelled. "You're not supposed to be out here!"

"Fuck." Logan grabbed her hand. "Hurry!"

She *was* hurrying. Harry was just oddly fast, and he did not really seem like such a green agent any longer. She and Logan rounded a corner. An engine revved. She jerked at the sound, right before a black Bentley Mulsanne shot forward. It raced past her. It—

A choked scream.

A thud.

And...Simone whipped around.

Harry. "Harry!" She began running toward him because the black luxury car had just slammed into Harry. The MI6 agent sprawled on the side of the narrow road, and she could see blood all around him.

"No!" Logan locked his arms around her and hauled her up against his chest. "No, Simone!"

The Bentley Mulsanne braked. She saw the flash of its taillights as it backed up. Surely the driver was coming back to help? Simone struggled against Logan's hold because she needed to help Harry, too. There was no way that she was just going to leave the man to bleed out in the street!

"I'm so sorry," Logan whispered in her ear as his grip tightened even more. "I tried to tell you...over and over again in the suite. I said...*don't trust me.* Literally said those exact words. But did you listen? No."

"Logan, stop this! He is *bleeding*! That's an MI6 agent!" He probably didn't understand exactly who Harry—

"I know." Low. Rough. "And the man getting out of the car and aiming a gun at his head? That's Konstantin."

She stopped struggling. Just went dead still in his arms. Because the left, rear door of that sleek, black Bentley had opened, and Logan was right about the identity of the man who'd climbed out and who now pointed a gun at an unmoving Harry.

Konstantin. Dressed in a black overcoat. Hair cropped close to his head. Face intent and deadly with purpose. They were on a back street near the hotel, and no one else was around. There was no one to see what Konstantin was doing. No one to stop him.

Screw that. There is me.

Even though she loved Logan like a brother, she drove her elbow back into his ribs as hard as she could. His grip eased, and she shot forward like a rocket, screaming, "Stop! No! Don't do it! *Do not kill him!*"

Just like that, the gun stopped being aimed at Harry's prone form, and it pointed at Simone. She stumbled to a stop. Nearly wound up falling into Konstantin but she caught herself just in time.

"We meet again." His native Russia drifted beneath the words. "Hello, Simone."

"Hi, Konstantin." Her heart nearly burst right out of her chest. "Fancy seeing you on this deserted street with a horribly injured man at your feet."

He smiled at her.

Ice filled her veins. He was tall like Ryan, his shoulders broad. Fit. His brown hair was shorter than it had been when they'd met before, and sunglasses covered his green eyes. When he smiled, the scar under his chin stretched a bit. And when he raised his brows at her, the long, thin, white scar over his right eyebrow seemed to thicken. If she had to guess, she'd wager that both of those scars had come from the slice of a knife.

"Such a coincidence, isn't it?" he murmured. "Almost as if...I knew where you'd be."

Logan raced up behind her. His hands clamped around her shoulders, and he immediately jerked her back, putting her behind his body. "You aren't shooting Simone! There is no world where you shoot her. That is not happening!"

"Fine, then I'll just shoot you and the MI6 agent."

"No!" Simone screamed.

Cars honked in the distance. She also could have sworn that she heard the sound of approaching voices.

Konstantin cursed in Russian, a guttural curse that basically translated to *fucking tourists*. Then he was motioning toward his car. When she looked toward the Bentley—surprise, surprise—Simone saw that his driver stood next to the front of the vehicle, and that driver had a gun clutched in his hand.

"Get in the vehicle," Konstantin ordered. "Now."

She locked her legs. "See, I have this rule about not going to secondary locations. The last time I went to a secondary location, I woke up and there was this seriously angry Russian who wanted to cut off my fingers and—"

He'd just slammed his gun into the side of Logan's head. Logan went down, hard, and Konstantin lunged at her. His left hand fisted in her hair even as he pressed the gun into her left cheek. Simone refused to let tears fall from the pain of his grip. "I know there are plenty of wonderful, amazing Russian people in this world. A few of them are my friends. One was even my college roommate." His grip tightened even more and she almost yelped. "Lovely people who make the most mouth-watering *medovik* that you've ever tasted." She tried for a hopeful tone as she asked, "Any chance you could stop being so scary and dangerous and become like those fabulous individuals?"

He leaned in closer to her. His hot breath blew over her face. "Alexei was my cousin."

"That tracks." Simone cleared her throat. She was pretty sure that she'd just seen Harry's hand move. The right one. The left appeared broken. No way that twisted angle of his wrist could be anything *but* broken. "I totally see the resemblance." She also realized that the driver bore a strong resemblance to Konstantin, too. *Probably another cousin.*

Logan jumped to his feet. But he didn't attack Konstantin. Probably because Konstantin had a gun shoved hard into her cheekbone.

"You are useful to me alive," Konstantin told her. "That is the only reason I allow you to continue breathing."

"I've always found it great to keep breathing."

He hauled her toward the car. Shoved her into the back seat. Climbed in with her and kept his gun pointed at her. Logan tried to follow, but...

"Kill the MI6 agent," Konstantin barked at him. "Now."

"No!" How many times would Simone need to scream that word? "Logan, don't!"

"*Logan...*" Mocking from Konstantin. "*Do.* Or else I tell the associates who have dear, sweet Nana that *she's* the one who will get the bullet to the brain."

When Konstantin said those words, Simone could have sworn her heart stopped. Her whole chest iced, and a faint squeak slid from her because that was all that she could manage.

Logan leaned halfway into the back of the vehicle. His gaze slid to her. "I'm sorry," he said.

No, no, no.

He eased back. Turned around. But as he turned, she saw him pull out a gun. The same gun he'd had aimed at Ryan when she woke in the suite's bedroom. She tried to grab for Logan, but Konstantin's hold was unbreakable. Actually, he *did* nearly shatter her wrist. She felt the bones rub together even as—

Boom.

Logan jumped into the front, passenger seat of the car. The driver climbed inside, too, slamming his door.

"Toss the gun out, Logan, now," Konstantin thundered.

Logan tossed the gun.

It will have his prints on it. He'll be tied to Harry's murder. He'll be hunted. Caught—

"Get us the hell out of here," Konstantin snarled.

The Bentley lurched forward even as she strained to see Harry through the back window. Not dead, please. But...*no, no, no, no, no...*

"I hear that when it comes to retrieving precious items that have been stolen..." Konstantin's musing voice. "There is no one better than you for the job."

She had tears on her cheeks. She could feel them. Her head turned, and she found Konstantin staring straight at her. "There are quite a few people who have been looking for you." Hoarse words.

He shrugged. "Here I am. Interesting, isn't it? That the British and the Americans wanted me so badly, and they did not know I was watching them all along. Watching so closely."

"I'm sorry, Simone," Logan said from the front seat. "His asshole goons got to Nana sometime last night."

When she'd been with Ryan?

"They had her before you went to the Arch," he revealed. "I...shit, he first contacted me when you were heading out into the rain. They knew about you, about me. About our past. They knew you had gotten the broach and the earrings."

"Alexei mentioned them to me." Konstantin let go of her wrist, but then he stroked the back of his hand against her cheek. "Alexei always knew to report good intel directly to me. He informed me of the broach and the earrings before you killed him."

There was no way she'd ever reveal to Konstantin that

Ryan had been the one to end Alexei's life. It would only make him determined to destroy Ryan. "In my defense, Alexei was going to cut off my fingers."

"I'll cut them, off, too, unless you give me what I want."

She could not look away from him.

"I'm sorry, Simone." Logan's miserable voice.

Right. He'd said that before. She was sorry, too.

"I would have fucking shot him in the street if I could," Logan added, voice tight with fury. "But only he can call off the men who have my grandmother."

"Yes, sweet, confused Nana. I'll cut off her fingers, too," Konstantin added, as if giving the matter thought. "I have two men with her now. They said she lived in a beautiful facility. Terrible security, but pretty place."

"H-how did you even have men in Vegas?" Simone asked as she tried to figure a way out of this nightmare. Maybe he was lying. Maybe Nana was safe. Maybe—

He laughed. A chilling sound. "I have people *everywhere.* And they are ready to do my bidding at a moment's notice."

Logan had craned around in his seat. "I've seen the videos. They aren't faked. They are real. They have her. Dammit, they sent me a live feed right before I crawled through the hotel's duct tunnels. Called it 'extra fucking motivation' for me."

"She's quite terrified," Konstantin continued in his mock sympathetic tone. "Poor woman doesn't know why she's tied to a chair and men with knives keep taunting her."

Simone's whole body shuddered. "You bastard."

He shrugged and glanced toward Logan. "You didn't kill Ryan Quinn."

"No." Gritted from between Logan's clenched teeth.

"I sent you in to kill him."

"Yes, well, you thought the only way to get Simone away from the guy was to kill him. I got her without killing him, so there. Job done."

She did not like Konstantin's slow smile. Actually, there was nothing she liked about him. A true monster.

"Don't worry." Konstantin lounged against the seat as the car zipped through the city. "I have a new employee who will be completing the job. Fun detail, he made the connection with the broach and earrings, too. The man could not wait to tell me all about Logan Sterling. Of course, I'd already made the connection, thanks to Alexei." He glanced at his watch. "Still, my new employee is promising. He should be taking care of the situation with Ryan Quinn at any moment."

Someone was about to kill Ryan? Oh, hell, no! "Call him off!" The words exploded from her. "If you've got someone going after Ryan, *call him off*!"

Konstantin's attention shifted back to her. "You aren't the one giving orders, *lisichka*."

Little fox.

"I'll do whatever you want," she promised, meaning those words. "Just do not hurt Ryan. Call off any attacker. Keep Ryan safe. Keep Nana safe."

"Oh, you'll do what I want. You're the best at the job, after all."

Her eyes narrowed.

"You retrieve things that have been taken. My egg was taken, along with something very special inside the egg."

"I know all about the damn chip! I was in the room when you gave the freaking thing to Frederick in the first place!" Simone huffed. Did he not remember this?

"Good." A shrug of his shoulders. "Then you know where it is now."

Jezebel had it. "It's with the CIA."

He brought his face in close to her. "You will retrieve it. You will get it away from them, or I will cut off your fingers. I will cut off Nana's fingers. I will make you watch while she dies."

Simone swallowed. "You don't have to keep adding threats. Just one is enough, thanks." A slow exhale. "Ryan stays alive. That's a condition for me."

He shook his head. "You have no conditions." Then, "And your spy is dying as we speak."

No!

"Hugo was going to shoot him at their restaurant meeting. Hugo wanted to impress me, so I'm sure that he made no mistakes."

Your spy is dying as we speak.

"He's not dead." Her whole body hurt. "He's not. You're wrong. There is no way that Ryan is dead!"

A phone rang. A loud, shrill cry that had her jumping. The ringing sound came from Konstantin's suit coat. A fancy coat to hide the monster he was. Taking his time, Konstantin put his gun back into the holster beneath his left arm. Tucked beneath that coat...

The phone kept ringing.

Slowly, Konstantin pulled out the phone. He swiped his finger over the screen and put the call on speaker. "Hello, Hugo," Konstantin greeted. "Is it done?"

"Ryan Quinn is a dead man," Hugo fired back. "Mission accomplished."

A scream tore from her throat. She launched at Konstantin, going straight for his eyes. She would claw out the fucking bastard's eyes. Her fingers curled, and she went in hard for him. She made contact. She clawed and she fought, and he threw her back against the rear door near her. She grabbed for the door handle, intent on jumping out because she could do it. She'd get away. She'd go find Ryan because he was not dead.

"*Don't, Simone, please!*" Logan begged.

The car slammed to a stop. She flew forward, and her head slammed into the back seat. Even as she was pushing back, Simone saw the driver aim his gun at Logan.

And Konstantin—a bleeding Konstantin, blood dripped down his cheek and some pooled in his right eye—yanked his gun out again and pointed it at her. "Let's make sure you understand the situation."

Mission accomplished.

Mission accomplished.

"You're going to retrieve my missing prizes, and if you don't, I will kill everyone you care about in this world. Starting with Nana. Moving on to Logan. Then I will make you beg for death before I finally grant you that ever-so-painful release." The blood dripped onto his coat. Blood from where she'd clawed the hell out of his face. "Do we understand each other, *lisichka?* Do we have a deal?"

Oh, they had a deal, all right. The deal was...she was going to kill him at the first opportunity.

Chapter Twenty-Six

"Happy now?" Hugo bit out as blood poured from his broken nose and busted lip. He glared at Ryan.

No, Ryan was not happy. "She screamed." That had been Simone's scream, right before the line went dead. "She was supposed to be *safe.* Logan was supposed to keep her *safe.*" He'd sent Simone away with Logan because the prick should only have allegiance to her. She was Logan's family, after all. *Family first.* But Logan—he'd betrayed her?

I sent her off to die.

Rage and fear nearly splintered him apart.

Hugo spat blood at him.

Ryan punched the jerk again. Hard. Right in the face. After that prick had come at him with a blade, Ryan had unleashed on the fool.

He'd pummeled the bastard into the floor, only to be hauled back by Jamar and Charlotte.

And, even as Ryan's fist connected with Hugo's face again...

Jamar hauled him back once more. "*Focus!*" Jamar blasted.

Oh, he had focus. The focus of his fist hitting Hugo's face.

"*Control,*" Jamar snapped as his grip tightened on Ryan's shoulders. "Get your control back so we can deal with this clusterfuck."

It was a major clusterfuck. They'd forced all of the customers and staff out of the restaurant. Now it was just filled with CIA and MI6 operatives. Even Jezebel was on her way over.

Everyone was there but...

Where the hell is Harry? He hadn't seen that green agent anywhere. What was Harry off doing? Shoveling more updates to the pencil pushers back at MI6's main office? Ryan shook free of Jamar's hold.

"Told him what you wanted...me to say..." Blood dripped down Hugo's chin. "Happy?" Hugo sat in a chair right in front of Ryan.

Ryan leaned forward so that he could be on eye level with the bastard. "You came to kill me."

Hugo's mouth curled into a half-smile.

"You are working for Konstantin." Obviously. "Were you doing that shit all along? Were you running behind Frederick's back the whole time?" Where the hell was Frederick?

Unfortunately, Ryan had a bad suspicion about Frederick's location. What had Hugo told him...that he could be *seeing* Frederick soon? Considering that Hugo had come to the restaurant intending to kill Ryan, then he must have meant...what, exactly, about Frederick's location?

That I'd see him in hell?

Hugo hadn't answered Ryan's questions. So he pushed, "He's dead, isn't he? You killed Frederick?"

Not a half-smile any longer. A full smile stretched

across Hugo's face. Dammit. Ryan's head whipped toward a watchful Charlotte. "Get a crew out to Frederick's country estate. Search the place. Top to bottom."

She whirled away, already pulling out her phone.

And, speaking of phones, Ryan tossed the one he still held at Jamar. The phone that Hugo had brought into the restaurant. Hopefully, he hadn't damaged it too much when he'd closed his fist around the damn thing. "We just called Konstantin. Try getting the bastard again. Triangulate signals. Track the prick. *Find him.*"

Jamar closed his hand around the phone. "On it."

But Ryan knew it wouldn't be easy. Hell, if *he'd* been Konstantin, he would have immediately trashed the phone after that call.

"We need to trace Konstantin." Ryan's mind was racing. "We need to trace Simone." *Simone.* "I gave her a phone." Excitement surged within him. "We can track her that way." He rattled off instructions and details about Simone's phone to the agents around him, and they sprang into action.

Have to find Simone. Konstantin took Simone. She screamed. I have to find her. Ryan's breath shuddered in and out. In and out. "You know where he took her." Ryan glared at Hugo.

"Sounds like you think you can find her." Mocking laughter rolled from Hugo. "Good luck with all that. You don't need me."

Ryan turned back to the table and he swiped the knife there—the knife that he'd taken from Hugo. He recognized the particular weapon. He'd seen it before with the British Special Forces teams. Now he studied the knife with narrowed eyes. Ryan was pretty sure he could see traces of dried blood near the tip.

Oh, yeah, Frederick is dead. The poor, dumb sonofabitch.

"You think I'm scared of you?" Hugo suddenly challenged. "I can handle a fool like you in my sleep. You are not going to get me to break down in some interrogation. You won't get me to—"

In a blink, Ryan had the tip of the blade pressed against his enemy. "It's good for slipping between the ribs, isn't it?" His voice was low, carrying only to Hugo.

Hugo had gone dead still.

"You think you're the only one who knows that trick? I can slide it between your ribs. I can kill you before you can even draw the breath to scream. But, I won't." It was his turn to smile. "Because your death does not benefit me. Not yet. Instead, I will torture you. Moment by moment. Piece by piece. Bit by bit. Believe me when I say that Alexei had nothing on me."

"Y-you're bluffing. I was Special Forces, I won't—"

"Cry me a fucking river. I don't care what you were. *You* need to be more concerned with what I am." Ryan pressed the tip of that blade into him. Other agents had already zip-tied Hugo's hands behind his back. "I'm the man who will destroy anyone who is between me and my goal."

Hugo tried to ease away from the blade.

There was nowhere for him to go.

"You know what my goal is?" Ryan demanded, voice still low.

"K-Konstantin?"

"*Konstantin has someone important to me.* My goal is Simone. If anything happens to her before I get her back..." The blade pierced Hugo's skin.

Hugo sucked in a breath.

"You'll be begging for death before I'm done with you," Ryan swore.

"*Ryan!*" Jamar's booming voice.

He left the blade in Hugo.

"Dammit, Ryan, stop!" Jamar tried to haul him back.

"Oh, my bad." Ryan stepped away from Hugo. For the moment. "Didn't realize I was so close to him."

Jamar glared at him, nostrils flaring and gaze hard. Aw, Jamar. One of the truly *good* guys. A guy who was lucky enough to have a wife and twin boys at home. A family that loved him. But even good guys could break, and Ryan knew that if anyone ever touched Jamar's family...

There will be hell to pay.

Because you did not fuck with family.

Family.

The word whispered through his head. He'd trusted Logan because the guy should have been Simone's family. Yet Logan had still betrayed her. Why? Why would Logan do that to Simone?

Family.

"We've got her!" Another agent suddenly called out. "Found her phone! We've got Simone!"

Hell, yes.

* * *

BUT THEY DIDN'T FIND Simone. They found Harry. Or rather, the bleeding, tangled mess that was the MI6 agent.

Simone's phone *had* been discovered near the agent. Stomped. Shattered. And as for Harry...

Ryan watched as the guy was loaded into the back of an ambulance. The authorities had closed off the street, making the entire area a crime scene. The pounding of Ryan's heart echoed in his ears.

Jezebel had joined them on the scene. She was in the

back of the ambulance right then, leaning over Harry's form. Barking out orders to the EMTs. Ryan stood about five feet from the ambulance, his hands clenched into fists at his sides as he tried to keep from stumbling straight into the pool of rage that wanted to suck him under.

Harry left for dead.

Simone gone...gone...

In his mind, he could hear the endless echo of her scream.

"*Ryan!* Ryan, dammit, get your ass in here! He's talking!" Jezebel shouted.

He bounded into the ambulance. Not like there was a ton of room in there, and, oh, no, but Harry looked like hell. Face swollen. So much blood. Broken bones.

"Simone was here," Jezebel said.

Well, yes, he got that. Her phone had been found at the scene. The phone Ryan had given her. *I was supposed to call her when it was safe. Supposed to meet up with her again and then we were going to—*

"Tried..." A strained whisper from Harry. "H-help me..."

"We are getting you help," Jezebel assured him as she squeezed his right shoulder. One of the few parts of his body that did not seem injured.

"No..." Harry's eyes cracked open. "She...help..."

Simone had tried to help him? Was that what Harry was attempting to say? "Who did this to you?"

Harry's eyes opened a bit more. "K-Konstantin."

Jezebel stiffened. "You *think* it was him or you know?"

"S-saw him...right in f-front..."

Jezebel's gaze cut to Ryan. "The bastard is too confident and far too sloppy. We've got an agent who can testify that

Konstantin tried to kill him. That means we have the man, dead to fucking rights."

Dead was the operative word. Konstantin had clearly thought Harry would not survive and live to tell anyone about the attack. As brutal as it was to think, Ryan was surprised that Konstantin hadn't finished off the job and ended Harry then and there.

"Sh-shot..."

What? Ryan and Jezebel both leaned closer to Harry because the word had been so low.

"K-Konstantin...told the guy to shoot me..."

"What guy?" Jezebel demanded. "And you're shot?" She grabbed the arm of the nearby EMT, a woman who'd been working on Harry's left leg. "Are you treating a bullet wound? Why is this vehicle not flying to a hospital? *Get us going!*"

Harry shook his head. "H-he missed...deliberately..." A gasp. "Konstantin...he thinks...I'm...dead."

The siren wailed. The ambulance seemed to vibrate around them. "Who missed?" But Ryan had a suspicion.

"Was...with S-Simone." Harry's lashes fell. "He...pulled her..."

"We're leaving, now," the ambulance driver barked from the front.

"I'm staying with him." Jezebel pushed Ryan. "You go find Simone. You find Konstantin. You take that bastard down, you understand me?"

He was already leaping from the ambulance. He cleared it right before another attendant slammed the rear doors shut.

Charlotte rushed toward him, with her phone held near her ear.

The ambulance roared away.

"We have a body!" Charlotte cried.

Not Simone. Not—

"Frederick Bradwin was just found in his bed. Stabbed multiple times. Someone tossed covers over him and left the guy there." She shook her head in disgust.

"That someone is Hugo Thomas." He was sure of it. "Get the ME to compare the wounds Frederick has to the knife we retrieved from Hugo." Ryan whirled and stared hard at the bloody scene.

Harry's injuries told him that the poor guy had been hit by a car. There were no skid marks in the area, so the vehicle hadn't slowed. The hit had been intentional. No cameras on this street. No witnesses left behind.

Why had Harry been out there? Had he perhaps seen Simone and Logan? And he'd been chasing after them? Only to get hit by Konstantin's vehicle when the prick came to collect Simone and Logan?

Ryan kept replaying the scene from the suite in his head, and certain things that Logan had said took on all new meaning now for him.

Like when Logan had told him... *"You need to tell me to fuck off. You need to beat the hell out of me and whisk Simone away. Seriously, do it."*

Oh, but Ryan wished he'd beaten the hell out of Logan Sterling when he'd had the chance. But he'd truly believed Logan cared for Simone. Logan and Simone had known each other since they were children. They'd grown up together, with Logan's grandmother taking care of them both.

Yet in the suite, Logan had told Ryan and Simone, *"I am not trustworthy. Ask anyone."*

He remembered that Simone had just rolled her eyes in response. *"You know I trust you with my life."*

And Logan, he'd just said—

"Ryan, what are the orders?" Charlotte asked. Jamar wasn't with her. He'd taken Hugo to a secure holding.

"Don't," he whispered.

"What?" She lowered her phone. "Don't what?"

When Simone had said that she trusted Logan with her life, he'd told her... "*Don't.*" The man had been telling them that he was working with Konstantin. The truth had been right there. "He was trying to make us understand." Ryan rubbed his forehead. "He asked about the egg. Wanted to know if it was stashed in the suite's safe."

"I am really lost," Charlotte informed him. "Trying to keep up, truly trying, but you're going to have to tell me more."

His gaze collided with hers.

"The body at the country estate is being transported." She nodded. "Crime scene techs will document everything, but we are back to having no clue where Konstantin took Simone. His phone has gone dark, as in, just utterly vanished. Tracing them that way isn't going to be possible. And her phone is a dead end."

Konstantin would have known to ditch his phone so he could not be traced.

As for Simone's phone, had it deliberately been crushed? Or had she accidentally dropped it when she'd been trying to help Harry?

How could Logan do this to her?

Family.

Family.

Family. Ryan sucked in a breath. "We need to find Logan's grandmother."

"I'm sorry." She shook her head, hard. "I seem to say this a lot but...what? We're hunting for a grandmother now? I thought we were looking for Simone and Konstantin."

"We are. Simone retrieved the broach and the earrings for Nana."

"Again...*what?*"

"Logan Sterling's grandmother," he gritted between clenched teeth. He could not hear the wail of the ambulance any longer. But he did hear a faint...

Meow.

He whirled and searched the street.

"Why is Logan's grandmother important right now?" Charlotte asked as she darted around him. "Ryan, seriously, focus."

He was focusing. "Where's the damn cat? I need to get it for her."

"Uh, okay." She reached out a hand to touch his shoulder. "I get a lot is happening. If you need to step back, I can take lead on this one. Sometimes, when things are too personal, we need a break."

"*I am not stepping back.*" He'd just seen the cat. The black cat with the scraggly ear. The same one he and Simone had seen during their trip to the Arch. He bounded forward and grabbed the cat, clutching it to his chest when he straightened.

"I do not know what is happening right now." Charlotte eyed him with no small amount of worry. "I am concerned."

"It's Simone's cat," he snapped. Or, it would be. When he got her back, he'd have the cat for her.

"That's a stray, Ryan. The thing looks half-starved and seriously in need of a vet trip."

It would get a vet trip. It would get plenty of food. It would get a lifetime of love.

"And I hate to break this to you, but black cats are bad

luck. We don't need any more bad luck considering the way this case is going." She still gripped her phone.

"The cat is good luck. In France, they are good luck."

"We are not in France."

The cat rubbed his head beneath Ryan's chin. "Find Logan Sterling's grandmother. She should be in Vegas. She has dementia issues." *The broach and earrings had made her smile.* Simone had been willing to travel across an ocean, get a job working for Frederick, and then lift those items right out of the guy's heavily guarded gallery. She'd done all of that because she loved the woman she called Nana.

There was no doubt that Logan would love the woman just as much. So what would he be willing to do for her?

But Logan didn't kill Harry. Harry had said Konstantin thought he was dead but...

"Got a bullet here!" An agent was pointing to a crack in the road. A space near where Harry had been sprawled in a pool of blood.

"Damn." The agent whistled. "Looks like it was about an inch or two away from Harry's head."

A deliberate miss on Logan's part.

"Weapon!" Another agent shouted. "Discarded gun. It was half-hidden in a bush over here. Getting it bagged and tagged."

Ryan's gaze darted to the weapon that the agent was, indeed, bagging and tagging. He'd seen a gun exactly like that one earlier, when Logan had pointed it straight at his face.

Logan, what are you doing? Leaving his gun behind would tie him directly to the crime. But maybe that was exactly what Konstantin wanted. Konstantin had thought Logan shot and killed Harry. Konstantin wanted Logan to be hunted by the CIA and MI6. He wanted Logan going down...

While Konstantin had the chance to slip away.

You're not getting away, you bastard. It will not happen.

"Find the grandmother," he told Charlotte. "In Vegas. I want operatives to close in. I want them beside her."

"Why? Is this woman some kind of threat?"

"No, I think she *is* being threatened." He had to go. He clutched the cat and rushed toward the line of waiting cars.

"Wait!" Charlotte caught his arm. "We have to find Simone!"

He nodded. "I found her."

"No, you found a cat. One that may have fleas so don't let him rub on you like that." She grimaced. "We have no idea where Simone is."

"Simone is a retrieval specialist."

"Ah...okay?"

"If Konstantin wanted her dead, she'd be dead. We would have found her next to Harry." But they hadn't. "You'll do anything for family."

Charlotte's golden eyes narrowed on him. "Where is Simone?"

"She's going after the egg. Konstantin wants her to retrieve the egg and the chip."

"*Explain slowly. For me.*"

"Jezebel has both items. Jezebel has an off-the-books location she was using here in London. Jezebel isn't there now because she just rushed to the hospital with Harry. That means this is the perfect time for Simone to slip inside. The place will barely be guarded. All the agents are swarming out here." He had to haul ass.

"How would Simone even know about the location?"

Charlotte chased after him as he rushed toward the waiting vehicles.

"She wouldn't know. But Konstantin can get all sorts of intel. We know his reach extends nearly everywhere." It would be easy enough for him to learn about the CIA's hidden site, a place that technically was shared with MI6. All it would have taken to get the location was the wrong agent speaking at the wrong time.

Ryan yanked open the door to the car he'd used earlier.

"Most of the agents *are* here," she mused, glancing around. "There will only be a skeleton crew at the site Jezebel used. It *would* be the perfect time for an attack."

An attack or...a theft.

Ryan put the cat in the back seat. "Gonna need you to be a really good kitty and not shred the seat to pieces, got me? A new home and lots of food will be in your future if you can follow orders."

"I'm coming with you!" Charlotte raced around to jump in the passenger seat.

As he revved the engine and shot away from the scene, she was already on her phone, rushing out instructions about Logan Sterling. Demanding a search in Vegas for his grandmother.

Meanwhile, Ryan's hands had clenched tightly around the steering wheel. Every breath, every heartbeat, was focused on Simone.

Be alive.

Be safe.

Need you.

Love you.

He sucked in a breath. Let it out slowly. *Be alive. Be safe. Need you. Love you.*

Be alive.
Be safe...

Chapter Twenty-Seven

"It's really quite simple." Konstantin smiled at Simone. "You do your job, and everyone lives to see another day."

She was still in the back of the damn car. Her right cheek throbbed because he'd hit her, hard. But Simone had left her mark on him, too. Konstantin currently sported jagged claw marks going down his cheeks and his right eye was still bloody.

He'd done something to his phone earlier. Even tossed part of it from the moving vehicle. They'd driven and driven, seemingly going in circles through the city before they'd stopped.

"You are supposed to be incredible at your job. That's certainly what Logan swears."

"I'm fucking sorry," Logan bit out. He sounded miserable. He'd been miserable during every single one of his apologies.

But she understood what was happening. Nana's life was on the line, and Logan had needed to choose...*Me or her*.

"It's the perfect time for you to break inside. This is a CIA black site. I've had eyes on the location for the last twelve hours."

He had?

"Oh, come on," he scoffed. "You think I didn't know that Ryan Quinn and the CIA were trying to take me down? They are always trying. Always failing. All I have to do is pay the right people for the right intel, and I stay steps ahead of them all."

Fine, if his money could do so much then..."Can't you just pay those same people to get your chip back?"

"No."

Understanding dawned. "That means you tried, huh?" Simone flashed a teasing smile that made her throbbing cheek ache a bit more. "No dice? Too bad." She cleared her throat. "Have you considered that the CIA already got all the info off your precious chip and that retrieving it does nothing at this point? Kinda like shutting the doors of a stable after a big stallion has already raced out to freedom with you clinging wildly to his back."

"They have only begun their work with the chip. It has advanced hardware security and encryption. Retrieving it is key for me. And I also just want the fucking egg back. The CIA doesn't get to have what is *mine*."

"Of course not. Not like you'd want to share your toys with others." Another big smile. "Here's a thought. Maybe if you wanted to keep the egg, then you shouldn't have given it to Frederick in the first place?"

He smiled in return. "You won't be so pretty when you have slices going across your face."

"You already have slices going across yours," she threw back even as fear raced through her.

"You fucking sonofabitch." Logan tried to heave into the

back seat. He'd heaved before, when she got punched, and he'd been hauled back by the driver.

The driver grabbed for him again, and, this time, he sliced a blade across Logan's cheek.

"*No!*" Simone screamed.

"Doesn't fucking matter." Logan ignored the blood that poured from his cheek. "Cut me all you want. I never gave a shit about being pretty." And his laughter was cold. Hard.

Konstantin pointed his gun at Logan.

"This will turn around on you," Logan promised. "You think I'll ever let you just walk away after what you've done to the two women I care about most in this world?"

"I *think* I'll kill you now." A nod from Konstantin. "You're really not useful to me any longer."

"*No!*" Simone screamed because she was terrified he'd shoot Logan right in front of her. She couldn't handle that. Simone knew she'd shatter apart. "I'll go in. I'll get your prizes back, but Logan does not die, understand me? You don't shoot him. Your goon in the front does not slice him. You keep your hands off him, and I'll do what you want."

Konstantin angled his head toward her. "Was that so hard? A little cooperation can go a long way."

Her heart slammed over and over into her chest. A rhythm that hurt. "Cooperation." She'd come to despise that word. "Everyone seems to be asking me about that lately. Know what? There's this lady who is super into cooperation. The two of you need to meet. Soon. Bet you'd have one hell of a fun time together." *I bet Jezebel Jenkins will toss your ass into a deep, dark hole, and you will never be seen again.*

"Get in the building. Do not set off any alarms. Retrieve my possessions."

"I need blueprints. Schematics that will show me where

the alarms are. I need locations of any guards." Getting into a CIA site was going to be incredibly difficult. "It will take a few days to prep—"

"You're going in now. Only a small staff should be inside."

Should be?

"Most of the agents would have rushed out recently. Probably because of that dead MI6 agent we left behind."

"You...you knew that Harry was an MI6 agent?"

"I know lots of things."

How fantastic for him.

"The dead MI6 agent and your dead CIA friend...they were great distractions."

Ryan could not be dead.

"This the best time to infiltrate the facility and acquire my items." Konstantin was so confident.

Ryan could not be dead. "Blueprints," Simone said again, her voice tight with pain. "And I-I need tools. I will need—"

He put down his gun. Reached under the seat and pulled out a small, black bag. "Here you go." He slapped a flashlight into her palm. And what turned out to be a tiny lock picking set.

She stared at the items. Hysterical laughter wanted to bubble from her. "You can't be serious. You expect me to infiltrate a CIA site and steal two super valuable items with only a flashlight and a lock picking set?" Talk about an impossible task.

"That's exactly what I expect. If you don't, if you alert anyone, if you try to reach out for help from *anyone,* then when you come back to this car, you'll find Logan's dead body. In Vegas, that sweet, precious Nana will also be dead. And you'll follow them to hell soon enough after that."

"So I get in with a flashlight." She inhaled. "And the tiniest lock picking set in the world. Sure, why not?" Simone looked toward the front seat. Blood drenched the side of Logan's face.

"Piece of cake," he told her. "You got this."

She did not. Not in any way, shape, or form. "We could really use some good luck right about now..."

Chapter Twenty-Eight

SHE'D HAD TO CRAWL THROUGH AIR DUCT TUNNELS. Her shoulders had barely fit. They'd scraped against the edges of the duct's long and winding tunnel system. She'd wedged herself and twisted and pushed forward with the flashlight between her teeth as she accessed the black ops building. Sweat utterly drenched her body. Fear pounded through her. Fear because she was afraid that Konstantin would kill Logan. That he'd hurt all the people she cared about.

And fear because the tunnel was too tight. Closing in on her. Her breath shuddered in and out, and her chest squeezed with every slow crawl and creep of her body. The journey seemed to take forever. She had no schematics, so she was truly going blindly through the building. Hoping like hell that she would wind up in the right place. She'd passed multiple rooms already and peered down through the vents in those rooms, looking for her prizes. Looking for a room, also, without a guard inside.

No luck, so far. The first two rooms had contained guards. Or agents. Or whatever they were. But she was approaching another vent. Light spilled into the duct tunnel through that vent. Good luck *had* shined down on her because a lot of the old buildings in the area didn't have air conditioning tunnels. Unlike in the US, air conditioning wasn't commonplace in England. And though the exterior of this particular building made it look as if it had been there for over a hundred years, she'd discovered that looks were deceiving.

Konstantin had informed her that the CIA had overhauled the building. From top to bottom, it was completely renovated, on the inside. That renovation included a state-of-the-art air conditioning and ventilation system. To keep the agents comfortable? To keep rare objects that might be brought in at some sort of climate-controlled level? She had no clue as to the *whys*. Instead, Simone was just grateful for the gift. For the good luck. Because without the vent access that she'd discovered after scaling the side of the building, she would have been truly fucked.

She'd gotten the idea of using the ventilation system from Logan. He'd done the same thing at her hotel. And, again, the hotel had only had the system because it was so freaking fancy. Over the years, she'd crashed at plenty of London hotels without AC.

I'm lucky this time. Maybe I need to listen to Ryan more when he talks about good luck. Good luck is a valuable thing and...

Ryan.

Ryan could not be dead. If he was dead, if he was gone...

He is not dead.

Ryan was strong. He was smart. He was so much tougher than Hugo. *He is not dead.*

Because if he was...

If he was...

Her breath shuddered out. She needed to get out of the tunnel! It was closing in on her. Bit by bit. Breath by breath.

Konstantin should have retrieved the stupid chip and egg himself. But, oh, no, even though only a small staff remained in the building, he'd worried that he might be walking into a trap. That anyone inside the clandestine location might shoot first.

He didn't want to get shot.

He didn't care if she died.

She'd reached the end of the current tunnel. A peek through the metal grate showed what appeared to be an empty office. Lots of filing cabinets. This was as good of a place as any to exit her tunnel of torture. Simone shoved hard against the metal grate, and it popped forward. It didn't fall to the floor, just sort of dangled on one side.

A map of the building would have been so incredibly useful. But maybe she'd find a map or *something* to help her in one of those filing cabinets. Konstantin had been all proud of just finding the building's location. Right before she'd started her retrieval mission, he'd boasted to her that just discovering the building's location had cost him one hundred thousand American dollars.

Now she was his tool. She was supposed to get in. Get the prizes he wanted. And get out. All without being shot by any CIA operatives or MI6 agents who might happen to be around. Oh, and for an extra challenge, she had *no* weapon. She'd begged to be given something to defend herself, but he'd said she would just turn any weapon on him. And, yes, fine, guilty. She totally would. So that left her with the flashlight and the lock picking set.

Konstantin clearly expected her to work miracles.

What an idiot.

She was good, but not that good. No one was that good. So...

She had to think fast. She had to strategize like hell. She had to—oh, look. What fun. A man in a black coat and black pants was pointing a gun at her. He'd just walked into the room, and the door was still wide open behind him as he gaped up at her as she sort of balanced half in and half out of the air vent.

Fantastic.

Simone let the flashlight fall from her mouth. It tumbled out and onto the floor. Floor that was a greater distance away than she'd realized at first glance. "Hi," Simone said, forcing a smile.

"Get the bloody fuck out of there!"

"I would love to do that," she assured him. "Love it. Crawling through what amounted to a very long and tight hole was a nightmare for me. Every moment was hell. But sometimes, we have to do things we really do not want to do." *For example, I really do not want to hurt you. I'm pretty sure you're one of the good guys.*

"Put your arms up!"

They were up. Mostly. "Not a lot of room to do that, given my current position. How about I jump out, you catch me because it looks like I'm higher up than I intended, and then I can show you that I'm not armed, okay? Good plan for you?"

"Lady, I will shoot you between the eyes." A sharp British accent.

"Let me guess. MI6?"

"*Out, now.*"

Fine. Her hands slapped on the walls near the vent, and Simone heaved herself forward. She was preparing to tumble hard and fast for the floor, but, as she'd anticipated—

fine, more like *hoped*—the MI6 agent surged forward to catch her. Her body slammed into him, and they both crashed to the floor. When they crashed, she made extra sure to clip his nose with her elbow. To drive her fist into his stomach. And to rip the gun from his hand. So once they slammed into the floor, she was on top of him. She had the weapon. "Hi, again."

He stared at her with absolute shock in his pale blue eyes.

"I get that a lot," she told him, nodding. "Now, I am seriously going to need some help from you. *Cooperation.* Everyone keeps going on and on about how that is key. So, tell me, is a lady named Jezebel here?"

He blinked.

"Is that a yes or a no?" Her hand shook around the gun. "Look, I am barely holding my shit together. I need to know —Ryan Quinn isn't dead, is he?" Tears trickled down her cheeks. "I need you to go and get Jezebel to find Ryan. You get up, you run out of here, and you get Jezebel to find Ryan." Had she just said that twice? Yes, panic had made her do that. Konstantin had told her to alert no one, but the agent had been right there, so he'd been *alerted* already. "You make sure that he's not dead because I really, really need Ryan to not be dead and—"

Footsteps pounded as another agent raced into the room. Her head whipped up. Her eyes locked on the figure in the doorway, and Simone's jaw dropped.

Ryan filled the doorway.

Ryan...Her Ryan.

"Not dead," Simone whispered.

The man beneath her locked his hands around her hips. He tossed her off him, and she slammed into the side of a desk. Her head hit the desk's edge, and she saw stars for a minute and then she felt his hand curl around her own as he fought to rip the gun from Simone's fingers.

"*Stand down!*" Ryan shouted. "*Now!*"

The MI6 agent did not. He drew back his fist to punch Simone.

Ryan didn't let that fist touch her. He grabbed the agent around the shoulders and ripped him away from Simone. "*No! I said stand the fuck down!*" Ryan placed himself between Simone and the agent. "You don't touch her. You don't hurt her. *You try to hit her again, and I will break every part of you.*"

That was Ryan. Ryan's snarling words. His furious, *alive* form in front of her. Without hesitation, Simone leapt at him. She jumped onto his back, wrapping her arms and legs around him, and hugged him as tightly as she could with her entire body. "I am so happy that you are not dead!"

"Same, baby, *same.*" His body was rock hard as she hung on for dear life. "You *know* who I am," Ryan snarled at the other agent. "Holster your weapon and go get backup! Now!"

"But—" the man began, eyes wide.

"Backup isn't really going to help." Yes, she was still on Ryan's back and holding him for all she was worth. "Konstantin was outside, waiting down the road, but I'm afraid if he saw you enter the building, Ryan, then he's already long gone." Her throat threatened to close. "He had Logan with him. Konstantin told me that if I didn't bring back the egg and the chip, Logan would be dead." Not just Logan, though, as she'd learned in the back of that stupid Bentley...*Logan and Nana.*

"*Get. Out.*" Ryan's arctic order to the blond agent. "Stand guard beside the door."

"You're really giving some conflicting orders here, mate," the man snapped.

"*Out. Stand guard at the door.*"

Jaw locking, the MI6 agent went out. She assumed he was heading to stand guard at the door.

She should let go of Ryan. Stop clinging to his back. But everything was about to get horrible because, if Konstantin had seen Ryan come in...

Logan...oh, God, Logan...

Her legs unhooked from Ryan. Her arms. She slid down his body. Her knees felt incredibly weak, and Simone was sure she could fall to the floor in a puddle.

But Ryan whirled and caught her. His hands locked around her waist. "Baby." His gaze swept over her. "You are soaked in sweat. What in the hell happened to you?"

"A whole lot of fear." He was *alive*. "Had to crawl through some seriously tight places." She shuddered even as she pointed back toward the open air vent.

His gaze darted to the vent. His curse was extremely inventive.

"I am so happy that you're alive," Simone told him, and she *meant* those words. "But if you're here, and Konstantin saw you, then that means...it means *Logan is dead.* Konstantin was going to kill Logan if anything went wrong on this *retrieval mission*."

"No one outside the building saw me enter. I came in via the secret corridor."

"Secret corridor?" *And this is why schematics and blueprints are so important when doing a job.*

"It starts at an old museum four buildings over. Snakes under the street. Comes out in the basement."

Her breath shuddered. "Would have been great if I

knew that beforehand. Wasn't exactly given adequate time to prepare for this mission."

His hand slid under her chin. He tilted her head toward the light. "Why the fuck is your cheek so red?"

"Because a fist hit it? A fist belonging to Konstantin."

"*He's dead.*"

"He needs to be," she agreed. "But it's rather tricky because he has his goons holding Logan's grandmother, and they are going to kill her and—do not *smile* at me when I tell you that people are threatening Nana! I happen to love that woman!"

He leaned forward. His lips brushed hers. "I've got her."

"You do not have her. You have me. You are holding *me*." So much panic and fear filled her. "I have to get the egg and that damn chip and get back to him. You have to help me, Ryan, *please*. Please help me."

Another careful kiss. "There is nothing in this world I will not do for you."

"I am so glad that you are alive." Had she told him that already? "I was scared to death. When Hugo said that 'mission accomplished' crap, I could feel something breaking inside of me. I do not *ever* want to feel that way again. I get that you're a spy and you're all about danger but, Ryan, it *gutted me*."

"I'm not all about danger. I'm all about you. I want a life with you. Any kind of life that you want to live."

She wanted that, so badly. But...

International criminal.

Logan's life on the line.

Nana...

"Nana is safe. Operatives recovered her two minutes before I walked in the door to this room."

A sob tore from her. "Don't you *dare* be lying to me."

Ryan hauled her against him, holding her tightly. "She's safe, and we're going to get Logan. Then we're going to lock Konstantin away. I have a plan."

Her eyes squeezed tightly shut. She held onto him with all of her strength. She loved this man. So much.

A throat cleared. Not Ryan's. Not hers...

Simone's eyes flew open. She craned her head around Ryan and saw the figure in the doorway. It was not the agent Ryan had kicked out moments before.

Instead, Jezebel inclined her head toward Simone. "Ryan meant to say that *we* have a plan. Our plan will require your cooperation."

Ah, that word again. "Can I get a weapon in return for my cooperation? Because that would be outstanding."

Jezebel quirked one brow. "I have just the thing for you."

Chapter Twenty-Nine

Simone rushed back to the waiting black Bentley. The driver stood at attention near the vehicle, and when he saw her approaching, he immediately opened the rear door for her. She dove into the vehicle.

"Did you get it?" Konstantin demanded eagerly.

She lifted up the egg and tossed it toward him. Not the real egg, of course. Turned out that the CIA had a very close look-alike in their secret site. Ryan had told her that the CIA had prepared several fakes before he'd done his swap at Frederick's country estate. Spies did like to plan ahead.

"What are you doing?" Frantic, he grabbed it. Caught it in desperate fingers. "Do you know how much this egg is worth?"

"I have a really good idea." *Not nearly close to thirty million.* The CIA had not let her get near the original. What had they thought? That her sticky fingers might take it for good?

"Where is the chip?" Konstantin demanded. "Did anyone see you?"

She sucked in her right cheek. It still ached. "I figure I'm dead now. My usefulness to you is at an end. You're going to shoot me and probably Logan." The driver was making his way around the vehicle. But he wasn't inside, not just yet. And that was why... "Act fast, Logan," she yelled to the silent figure in the front passenger seat. "They don't have Nana any longer!"

Logan *erupted.* He shoved open his door even as she was thrusting open the back passenger door, too. The driver rushed back toward Logan, but Logan was ready. And furious. Logan began pounding his fist into the driver's face. Over and over again. Logan took him down to the pavement and pummeled him.

Konstantin's hands grabbed for Simone's back. She twisted and heaved away from him, hearing the material of her dress tear, and then Simone yanked her weapon from the pocket of her dress. She truly adored a dress with pockets. The weapon that she pulled out? A flashbang. The perfect weapon that Jezebel had given to Simone. All Simone had needed was to get close enough to Konstantin, to preferably have him trapped in the vehicle when she deployed her weapon. He'd never even realized she had it, not with the device tucked into her pocket and resembling the size and shape of the flashlight she'd had before.

She *loved* pockets.

"Choke on it, asshole!" Simone activated and threw the small flashbang into the Bentley. She slammed the passenger door shut and ran.

A huge part of her had been *terrified* to carry the flashbang. It was a freaking *grenade,* after all. But Jezebel had emphasized that it was a *stun* grenade. No shrapnel. Non-lethal, because Jezebel wanted Konstantin brought in alive. Simone didn't particularly care about him being brought in *alive.* She just wanted him stopped. Jezebel had promised that the stun grenade would stop him.

"Simone!" Logan's voice. "What are you—

The flashbang erupted. The loud blast reverberated behind her, and Simone found herself falling to her knees. The hard road tore through her dress and scraped off her skin. Dazed, she looked back. She'd been promised a boom, big flashes, and disorientation so that the agents could swarm and take down Konstantin.

Konstantin hung half-in, half-out of the rear passenger door. His hands had slapped down against the pavement. His head sagged in front of him.

"*You fucking sonofabitch!*" Ryan tore past Simone. He grabbed Konstantin...and started pounding the hell out of him. "*You hit her! You took her!*"

Konstantin didn't fight back. He seemed too dazed.

Simone pushed to her feet. She thought she might have just seen a few of Konstantin's teeth hitting the road. Yes, yes, that definitely looked like two bloody teeth not too far away from her. "Uh, Ryan?"

"You kidnapped Simone! You were going to kill Simone? *My Simone?*"

Weaving a bit, Logan headed toward Ryan and Konstantin. Had Logan been too close to the blast? She'd told him to run, hadn't she? Maybe not.

Logan took a swing at Konstantin. Only it was a wild swing that missed the Russian by a mile. Oops. Yes. He might have been too close to the blast. He definitely seemed disoriented, too.

Her ears were throbbing. She kept hearing a *whoosh.* Huh. Maybe she was disoriented, too.

As she watched and tried to get her body back under her control, Ryan whirled toward Logan. He drove his fist into Logan's face. "That's for betraying Simone, you dick!"

Logan nodded. Didn't even try to punch back. "Deserved..."

Ryan hit him again, then spun back for Konstantin but...

The other agents had closed in. MI6. CIA. Jezebel. Simone had to crane her head and stand on tiptoes in order to see what was happening. She definitely heard, "Under arrest" and the phrase, "Never seeing the light of day again..."

But Ryan didn't stay in that swarm around Konstantin. He left the agents and the Russian and stalked toward her.

Her hands twisted. "Flash," Simone heard herself say.

He stopped right in front of her.

"Bang," she whispered. It had gone just as Jezebel predicted. The plan that Ryan and Jezebel had hatched. Simone had just needed to get close to the car. To let Logan know that his grandmother was safe. To distract Konstantin and to *throw* the flash grenade inside the car and haul ass away. That was all she'd needed to do...

And she'd been promised that the agents would finish everything else.

So she'd run back to the waiting vehicle, trembling and acting afraid as she frantically glanced over her shoulder, as if looking back to see if she was being followed. Acting like the perfect prey who was just doing as she'd been ordered by the big, bad international criminal...

And then, when Konstantin's guard had been lowered, when he'd been frantically clutching that prized egg...

She'd made his world explode.

Ryan hauled her into his arms. Or maybe she hauled him into her arms. His mouth took hers, and he kissed her with wild, utterly uncontrolled passion, and she kissed him back just as frantically. Joy, adrenaline, leftover terror—her whole body shook, and he was her anchor. She held tightly to him and knew that she never, ever wanted to let this man go.

Not dead.

Very much alive.

Kissing her. Holding her. And...

His mouth tore from hers. "I love you."

Loving her.

A soft *meow* sounded near her feet. Shocked and delighted, she glanced down. A familiar black cat with a ragged ear stared up at her. "What...?"

"Good luck," Ryan told her. "We're taking the cat home with us. He's gonna be our good luck charm and we are going to have the best life together." A promise.

"Did you...bring the cat here?" She was trying to follow along. It had been one hell of a day.

"I might have."

"You...you don't like black cats."

"Hell, yes, I do." Ryan scooped Simone into his arms. "They're lucky. You're lucky. *I'm* a lucky bastard because I am going to spend the rest of my life with you."

The joy she felt buried her terror. "Again, I don't think that is a real marriage proposal. You seem to have issues with that concept. A *real* proposal."

Agents were running everywhere, but Ryan was walking away from the chaos and heading back toward the lurking off-the-books building with her cradled in his arms... and with a black cat dodging his feet.

"You're going to have the best proposal in the world," Ryan assured her. "Just wait and see."

Simone curled one arm around his neck. Truth be told, she didn't give a damn about the proposal. All she cared about was the man holding her. "I'm so glad you're not dead."

"Told you once before, I'd kill for you a million times over, but there is no way I'm dying. I've got too much to live for." His gaze held hers. "I have a life with you waiting."

* * *

"I'M...SORRY." Logan stared at the floor, broad shoulders sagging. "I betrayed you, Simone. I put your life on the line, and I know that you fucking hate me. I fucking hate myself."

She gave her new *lucky* cat a long stroke and then let her sweet baby bound off through the hotel suite. *Not* the same hotel, thank goodness. They'd switched to a new location once the insane scene with Konstantin had finally ended. At the new place, they were on the top floor. She had a killer view. And while the last hotel had gone heavy on the blues, this place was all about white and gold and she loved it.

What she didn't love? The way Logan couldn't seem to look her in the eyes. "I understand."

"Understanding doesn't make shit right," he rasped. A bandage covered his cheek. He'd gotten seven stitches in that cheek. She knew because Jezebel had told her. Jezebel had taken a very strong interest in Logan.

Something that couldn't be good.

"I love you both," he said, voice gruff. "You and my grandmother are more important to me than anything else. *I love you both,*" he repeated. "Always have, always will. I was planning to kill Konstantin. I just was waiting for the best moment."

She shook her head. "You couldn't kill him when his goons were with Nana."

"I'm flying back to see her. As soon as Jezebel and your CIA boyfriend give me the all clear. She has to be scared to death." A ragged sigh. His hands fisted in front of him. "I'm so fucking sorry."

She paced toward him. Her hand rose and cupped his cheek. The one that wasn't currently sporting seven stitches. "Logan."

His jaw clenched.

"Logan, look at me."

Slowly, his gaze found hers.

"Hi, there," she whispered to him. "Remember me? The girl you saved when she was a kid? The one who didn't have a real home, not until you came along?"

"You had a home. They were taken from you."

"Just like your parents were taken from you." Two lonely kids. They'd become a family. "You think I don't know you, deep inside? You think I don't *forgive* you? Screw it. I do. I love you, Logan."

The suite's door opened. Her gaze automatically darted that way even as she kept her hand on Logan's cheek.

Ryan frowned as he stood on the threshold, clutching a white bag. "I know I shouldn't be jealous..." he began.

Logan stepped away from her.

Her hand slid to her side. Her gaze had slipped down and just gotten fixated on the bag. A bakery?

"I know she loves you like a brother. I'm just an asshole, that's all." Ryan exhaled on a rough sigh. "I will work on the jealousy. It's on my to-do list."

"You want to take another swing at me, don't you?" Logan asked.

Her attention shifted away from the bag and back to

Ryan's face. His slow smile was the answer to Logan's question.

"Do it," Logan invited.

"Trying to make that guilt you feel go away, huh? Me beating the hell out of you won't make you feel better. But, just so we are clear." Ryan's smile fled. "You ever fucking put Simone in danger that way again, and you won't need to worry about me taking a *swing* at you. I'll bury your ass. No one will ever find you. When I want to make someone vanish, they vanish. It's a fun CIA trick." His stare swept toward Simone. "Hello, sweetheart."

"Hi," she whispered.

"Konstantin has been handled," he said, and she could imagine what sort of "handling" the CIA had done with the criminal mastermind. Probably the kind that meant he would vanish into a black site for the rest of his days.

A shiver skated down her spine.

"And I brought you a present." Ryan walked right past Logan. He lifted the bag toward Simone.

She could *smell* the goodness teasing her. "Tell me there is some wonderful, freshly baked bread in that bag."

"There is some wonderful, freshly baked bread in this bag."

She snatched it from him. "I love you so much."

"I know." His dark eyes gleamed at her.

And Logan slipped quietly away.

* * *

But Logan didn't get to slip far. Because as soon as he stepped into the hallway beyond the suite...

"Hello, there." Jezebel leaned causally against the wall

that was mere steps away from Simone's new suite. "Fancy meeting you here."

He tensed. He and Jezebel had crossed paths a few times, and none of those instances had ever been what he'd call positive experiences.

"Someone looks guilty as hell." She whistled. "Hate that for you."

He looked guilty as hell because he *was* guilty. "I put Simone in danger. I nearly got her killed." How could he ever atone for that? Simone had trusted him, and he'd let her down. *Betrayed her.*

"Um, but you *didn't* get her killed, did you? She's safe, and, unless I miss my guess, she's about to convince my best agent that they should run away together and start some amazing new life." She pointed toward the closed suite door.

He glanced back. He'd seen the way Simone looked at Ryan. As for how Ryan looked at Simone...

Yeah, Jezebel was not wrong. He hoped like hell that Simone got the most amazing life ever.

"Hate to lose a good agent," Jezebel mused. "Especially with such a big case coming up. Good thing I have you. You're going to be such a perfect secret weapon for me."

Wait—what? He shook his head. Maybe he was still feeling a bit dazed from the flashbang stun grenade. Disoriented. Because surely this woman with the fancy pearl earrings and the deadly gaze had not just called him a secret weapon. Nah. No way.

"I *do* have you," she emphasized. "Granted, I'm also planning on getting out of the biz soon, but I want to go out with a bang, if you know what I mean."

"I one hundred percent do not."

Jezebel merely smiled. "Walk with me."

He'd prefer not to do that. "I am planning to leave the country. I have someone important that I need to see back in the States." Nana's dementia had gotten so much worse over the last few years. Sometimes, she knew who he was. Sometimes, she thought he was his father. Sometimes, she did not know him at all.

But he always knew her. The woman who'd loved him. Who'd saved him. And he had to make sure she was safe. He would be getting new guards for her. Making damn sure she had far, far better security. He would never let her be jeopardized again.

"You know that CIA operatives saved your grandmother, don't you?"

Fuck. He began to walk with Jezebel. After all...*I owe her*.

"I believe in a reciprocal relationship. I help you, you help me." Jezebel stopped in front of the elevator. "You want to help me, don't you, Logan?"

"Hell."

"Excellent choice." She pushed the button on the small panel near the elevator. "And if you're really feeling guilty, do consider this your way to atone. You can assist in making the world a better place. A safer place. You can get rid of some seriously bad guys and help shield a member of my team at the same time."

A member of her team?

The elevator doors opened. He stepped inside with her. A moment later, they were descending.

"The CIA operative you are shielding will be undercover. The operative will need complete access to all areas of your life. You'll need to stay close to the agent, twenty-four, seven."

Sounded like a total and complete pain in his ass.

But Jezebel was not done. "It's going to be dangerous. The mission will be intense. You could die." Jezebel slanted a glance his way. "You understand the risks?"

"You are really selling this thing, aren't you?" The CIA had saved his grandmother. Fuck, yes, he would pay them back.

"I'm sort of required to do that. Don't want you coming to me later, riddled with bullets, and being all...'*Oh, I had no idea I could potentially die.*'"

He stared at her.

She did not blink.

But he was pretty sure she'd just made a joke. Or maybe not. Maybe it had been a threat. "What do I have to do?"

The elevator stopped. They'd only gone down two floors. The doors opened.

A gorgeous brunette stepped onto the elevator. Her hair skimmed her shoulders. And when her head turned a little and the overhead light slid over her, Logan caught the hint of red buried in the darkness of her hair.

She sent him a considering stare. Her golden gaze lingered on the bandage that covered his cheek. Then she quirked a brow, as if waiting.

Waiting for what?

The elevator doors closed once more.

"Logan Sterling," Jezebel murmured. "This is Charlotte Webb. She's going to be your new personal assistant. At least, that's the job title you'll give her. Really, though, she'll be your shadow, your bodyguard, your twenty-four, seven companion."

"*What?*" The elevator descended.

Face serious, Charlotte told him, "I will do my best to ensure that you survive the mission."

Hell.

Epilogue - One

THEY WERE BACK AT THE WELLINGTON ARCH. THERE was no rain. No bad guys chased them. No danger waited.

Konstantin had been taken away. His empire was being dismantled by MI6 and the CIA. The doctors expected Harry to make a full recovery. Jezebel, well, she was already at work on another mission.

And Ryan was hoping to close the most important case of his life.

He dropped to one knee.

"Uh, Ryan, what are you doing?" Simone asked him.

He pulled a small, blue box from his pocket. "If you don't like it, we can get something different." He'd gone to the jewelry shop on Old Bond Street, desperate to find the right ring for her. He hoped that she loved the sapphire and diamond engagement ring that he'd picked out. The square-cut sapphire was pretty damn close to the color of her eyes. Swallowing, he opened the box. "I love you."

"*Ryan.*" She seemed to have frozen.

"And I would like nothing more than to spend the rest of my life with you." Every day with her would be an adventure, and he could not wait. "Simone Sailor, will you please marry me?"

"*Ryan! Yes!*" She snatched the ring from him. Put it on her finger and held it up to the sky. "Better than any star. OhmyGod, I love it! I love *you*!" She hauled him to his feet and dragged him in for a kiss. "I love you, I love you, *I love you.*"

Relief had him feeling nearly lightheaded. His arms closed around her. He would never, ever forget the stark terror he'd felt after hearing her scream on that horrible phone call. He'd been terrified every second until he saw her again.

His Simone.

But the fear was gone now. He was the happiest that he could ever remember feeling and it was because...*She loves me.*

And she was going to marry him.

Hell, yes.

He couldn't wait for her to meet his family. Ryan knew they'd love her as much as he did.

Epilogue - Two

TWO WEEKS LATER...

"I HOPE THEY LIKE ME." Her knees were knocking together.

"They aren't going to like you," Ryan informed her flatly. "They are going to *love* you."

She was not so sure. The twisting, churning in her gut told her this whole scene could be a disaster. "What happens if they don't like me?" A question that would not stop running through her mind.

"Uh, I tell them to fuck off? That they're idiots?"

Horror filled her. "You *cannot* tell your brother and sister to fuck off!" Oh, no. This was bad. So bad. They'd arrived along the shores of a super cute, little southern town earlier that day, and now they were supposed to walk through the doors of a dive bar that was situated right on the gleaming, blue waters of the bay. She'd already spied a few sailboats out on that water, and they'd made her happy and optimistic but...

"What if they don't like me?" she whispered. If his family hated her, then maybe Ryan would change his mind about her. His family was so important to him and she—

"They will *love you.* And, who the hell cares if they don't? They aren't marrying you. I am." He pressed a kiss to her temple. "Now, are we standing in the parking lot all evening or do you want to go inside?"

"Ryan..." A swift inhale. "You said that your sister is the sheriff here." Actually, he'd revealed that his sister was a former FBI agent who was now the sheriff. "I'm...I'm a thief."

"Who in the hell said you were that?"

Uh, she'd just said it.

"You are a retrieval specialist. You find the things that are lost." He stood in her path. "You found me. I was lost until you came into my life." His hand reached up, and he tucked a lock of hair behind her ear. "I'd still be lost without you."

Oh, that was sweet. He could say some of the sweetest things. He could *do* some of the sweetest things. After they'd left London, he'd taken her to Vegas so that she could see Nana. So that Simone could hug her over and over again, and Nana had been having such a *good* day. She'd recognized Simone. She'd retold stories from Simone's teenage years and she'd...

Nana smiled her sweet, beautiful smile when she put on her broach and earrings.

"I don't care if my brother and sister love you or not," Ryan added, voice rough and hard. "They can fuck off. I love you. You love me. That's all that matters."

A light peal of laughter drifted on the wind. A female voice ordered, "Oh, Ryan, stop being so charming!"

Ryan jerked in surprise, and then he whirled around.

He whirled around just as a small woman with red hair, a very pregnant belly, and a big sheriff's badge on her hip rushed toward him.

"Agnes!" Ryan called out in delight.

The sister.

He picked Agnes up into his arms and held her very, very carefully.

But Agnes had not been alone. A tall, broad-shouldered man with dark hair stood on the threshold of the dive bar. His eyes were locked on Simone. One brown eye. One blue. They glittered with hard curiosity. This guy was just... intimidating. Intense. He studied her with sharp focus and Simone found herself shifting nervously from foot to foot. This guy did not look welcoming. He did not look as if he'd *love* her. He—

He smiled at her. "I'm Nash. Welcome to the family."

Ryan had put Agnes back down on her feet.

The big, dangerous guy with the unusual eyes walked toward Simone. He had a hand extended toward her. Had he...had he really said welcome to the family?

"Forget shaking her hand," Agnes called out. "Hug the woman, Nash! She's marrying our brother!" Then she let out a cry that could only be described as delight. "*She's marrying our brother!*"

Then there were a lot of hugs. There was laughter and raised voices and more people spilled out of the bar to join their little group.

A man with lots of tattoos, hard eyes, and an expression that would melt with love whenever he looked at his wife, Agnes.

A woman who rushed to hold Nash's hand and who stared up at him as if he hung the very moon.

They greeted Simone with open arms. They rushed her

into the bar. Music played and everyone celebrated and laughed and...

Simone might have cried. But she tried really, really hard not to let anyone see her tears. She swiped them away whenever they tried to trickle out. It was just...

Welcome to the family.

Her breath shuddered out.

Ryan pulled her onto the dance floor. A small dance floor in a small-town bar with people who accepted her without question.

"I love you," he whispered into her ear. "I meant what I said, I'd be lost without you."

Her hands curled around his shoulders, and she held him tight. She'd been afraid to dream, afraid to fantasize, for far too long. But everything she wanted was right there.

Found. *Finally*. The man she loved. The life she'd longed for...it was all right there. She'd found it. She'd fought for it. And she would never, ever let it go.

THE END

Looking for chills, thrills, steam...and romance? Then be sure and check out my romantic suspense, TEMPTATION.

Desire can be born in darkness.

Buried alive. He wakes in darkness to find her on top of him. Preston Byron has been buried alive, but he's not alone in the dark. Sloane Armstrong is with him. On top of him. Kissing him to hold their panic at bay, promising that they will survive the nightmare around them. That help is coming...And they do survive. They are rescued. They return to reality...

But she haunts him.

Preston isn't going to let his attacker escape. He plans to hunt the killer who targeted him. A man who made Preston relive a nightmare from his past. But there was an angel in the dark with him, a woman who captivates Preston. Preston isn't about to let Sloane slip from his life. She saved him, she charmed him, and she made the critical mistake of fascinating him. Now, he will do whatever it takes to unlock all of her secrets.

Killers are her specialty. The darker the monster, the more savage the crime...

Sloane studies killers. Or, actually, she is currently studying the adult children of serial killers. Her work brought her into billionaire real estate mogul Preston Byron's life. Fine—she was semi-stalking him. Learning every detail about the gorgeous and sexy Preston that she could. Preston was kidnapped as a teen. Buried alive. Preston believed that he was just another victim of the Last Breath Killer—the only victim to survive—but Sloane has learned the shocking truth...Preston was the serial killer's biological son. Preston doesn't know about his serial killer parent. He certainly doesn't know that his father was trying to push his son into following in his own sick, murderous footsteps.

Because the darkness calls...and it tempts...

Something unlocked inside of Preston in the darkness. A beast that he'd kept chained for a long time is pressing close to the surface, demanding that he find his abductor, that he eliminate the threat. The only one who can soothe the beast is the same woman who comforted him, who kissed him, in the dark. Sloane is the key to his control...and also the one person who may be able to shatter it into a million pieces.

She's keeping secrets from him, and when the truth comes out, it will upend Preston's world.

Better take a deep breath. It just might be your last.

A predator is hunting—a copycat who is enacting the Last Breath Killer's crimes, and his next target...is Sloane.

Author's Note: Preston wants her before he even sees her face. Desire sinks into his very bones, and she's his lifeline, his link to sanity when the dark presses in. There is no rule that he will not break for her, no risk that he will not take, and when the danger starts to grow around Sloane, Preston will let his beast off its careful leash, and he will eliminate every threat to her. Because she saved him when he was in the dark. And he will never, ever allow anyone to take her from him.

Author's Note

Thank you so very much for reading WHEN HE LIES. I hope that you enjoyed Ryan's tale as he finally met his match with Simone...and don't worry, I will be giving Logan a happy ending of his own, too!! Coming soon!!!

I love writing the "Protector and Defender Romance" books. They are just such a joy for me to create. I love having fun with the characters, being able to add humor to the stories—and still including lots of danger and action. Thanks for journeying into the world of these protectors with me!

If you have time, please consider leaving a review for WHEN HE LIES. Reviews help readers to discover new books—and authors are definitely grateful for them!

If you'd like to stay updated on my releases and sales, please join my newsletter list. Did I mention that when you sign up, you get a FREE Cynthia Eden book? Because you do!

By the way, I'm also active on social media. You can find me chatting away on Instagram and Facebook.

Happy reading!

Best,

Cynthia Eden

cynthiaeden.com

More Books By Cynthia Eden

Poison In My Veins

- Compulsion

Protector & Defender Romance

- When He Protects (Book 1)
- When He Hunts (Book 2)
- When He Fights (Book 3)
- When He Defends (Book 4)
- When He Guards (Book 5)
- When He Loves (Book 6)

Ice Breaker Cold Case Romance

- Frozen In Ice (Book 1)
- Falling For The Ice Queen (Book 2)
- Ice Cold Saint (Book 3)
- Touched By Ice (Book 4)
- Trapped In Ice (Book 5)
- Forged From Ice (Book 6)
- Buried Under Ice (Book 7)
- Ice Cold Kiss (Book 8)

- Locked In Ice (Book 9)
- Savage Ice (Book 10)
- Brutal Ice (Book 11)
- Cruel Ice (Book 12)
- Forbidden Ice (Book 13)
- Ice Cold Liar (Book 14)
- Ice Cold Christmas (Book 15)

Wilde Ways

- Protecting Piper (Book 1)
- Guarding Gwen (Book 2)
- Before Ben (Book 3)
- The Heart You Break (Book 4)
- Fighting For Her (Book 5)
- Ghost Of A Chance (Book 6)
- Crossing The Line (Book 7)
- Counting On Cole (Book 8)
- Chase After Me (Book 9)
- Say I Do (Book 10)
- Roman Will Fall (Book 11)
- The One Who Got Away (Book 12)
- Pretend You Want Me (Book 13)
- Cross My Heart (Book 14)
- The Bodyguard Next Door (Book 15)
- Ex Marks The Perfect Spot (Book 16)
- The Thief Who Loved Me (Book 17)

The Fallen Series

- Angel Of Darkness (Book 1)
- Angel Betrayed (Book 2)
- Angel In Chains (Book 3)
- Avenging Angel (Book 4)

Wilde Ways: Gone Rogue

- How To Protect A Princess (Book 1)
- How To Heal A Heartbreak (Book 2)
- How To Con A Crime Boss (Book 3)

Night Watch Paranormal Romance

- Hunt Me Down (Book 1)
- Slay My Name (Book 2)
- Face Your Demon (Book 3)

Trouble For Hire

- No Escape From War (Book 1)
- Don't Play With Odin (Book 2)
- Jinx, You're It (Book 3)
- Remember Ramsey (Book 4)

Death and Moonlight Mystery

- Step Into My Web (Book 1)
- Save Me From The Dark (Book 2)

Phoenix Fury

- Hot Enough To Burn (Book 1)
- Slow Burn (Book 2)
- Burn It Down (Book 3)

Dark Sins

- Don't Trust A Killer (Book 1)
- Don't Love A Liar (Book 2)

Lazarus Rising

- Never Let Go (Book One)
- Keep Me Close (Book Two)
- Stay With Me (Book Three)

- Run To Me (Book Four)
- Lie Close To Me (Book Five)
- Hold On Tight (Book Six)

Bad Things

- The Devil In Disguise (Book 1)
- On The Prowl (Book 2)
- Undead Or Alive (Book 3)
- Broken Angel (Book 4)
- Heart Of Stone (Book 5)
- Tempted By Fate (Book 6)
- Wicked And Wild (Book 7)
- Saint Or Sinner (Book 8)

Bite Series

- Forbidden Bite (Bite Book 1)
- Mating Bite (Bite Book 2)

Blood and Moonlight Series

- Bite The Dust (Book 1)
- Better Off Undead (Book 2)
- Bitter Blood (Book 3)

Mine Series

- Mine To Take (Book 1)
- Mine To Keep (Book 2)
- Mine To Hold (Book 3)
- Mine To Crave (Book 4)
- Mine To Have (Book 5)
- Mine To Protect (Book 6)

Dark Obsession Series

- Watch Me (Book 1)

- Want Me (Book 2)
- Need Me (Book 3)
- Beware Of Me (Book 4)

Purgatory Series

- The Wolf Within (Book 1)
- Marked By The Vampire (Book 2)
- Charming The Beast (Book 3)
- Deal with the Devil (Book 4)

Bound Series

- Bound By Blood (Book 1)
- Bound In Darkness (Book 2)
- Bound In Sin (Book 3)
- Bound By The Night (Book 4)
- Bound in Death (Book 5)

Stand-Alone

- Waiting For Christmas
- Monster Without Mercy
- Kiss Me This Christmas
- It's A Wonderful Werewolf
- Never Cry Werewolf
- Immortal Danger
- Deck The Halls
- Come Back To Me
- Put A Spell On Me
- Never Gonna Happen
- One Hot Holiday
- Slay All Day
- Midnight Bite
- Secret Admirer
- Christmas With A Spy

- Femme Fatale
- Until Death
- Sinful Secrets
- First Taste of Darkness
- A Vampire's Christmas Carol

About the Author

Cynthia Eden loves romance books, chocolate, and going on semi-lazy adventures. She is a *New York Times*, *USA Today*, *Digital Book World*, and *IndieReader* best-seller. She writes romantic suspense, paranormal romance, and fun contemporary novels. You can find out more about her work at www.cynthiaeden.com.

If you want to stay updated on her new releases and books deals, be sure to join her newsletter group: cynthiaeden.com/newsletter.

www.ingramcontent.com/pod-product-compliance
Lightning Source LLC
Chambersburg PA
CBHW010953260526
45652CB00013B/317